SHARPE'S EAGLE

BERNARD CORNWELL was born in London and raised in Essex, and now lives mainly in the USA, with his wife. In addition to the hugely successful Sharpe novels, Bernard Cornwell is the author of the highly praised Starbuck Chronicles, the acclaimed Warlord trilogy, and the recent bestsellers *Harlequin* and *Gallows Thief*.

For more information, visit:
www.bernardcornwell.net

D0318092

BERNARD CORNWELL

Sharpe's Eagle

Richard Sharpe and
the Talavera Campaign,
July 1809

HarperCollins*Publishers*

This edition produced for The Book People Ltd,
Hall Wood Avenue, Haydock, St Helens. WA11 9UL

HarperCollins*Publishers*
77–85 Fulham Palace Road,
Hammersmith, London W6 8JB

www.harpercollins.co.uk

This paperback edition 1994
1

Previously printed in paperback by Fontana 1981
Reprinted twelve times

First published in Great Britain by
Collins 1981

Copyright © Rifleman Productions Ltd 1981

ISBN-13 978-0-00-787076-9

Typeset in Baskerville by
Palimpsest Book Production Limited,
Polmont Stirlingshire

Printed and bound in Great Britain by
Clays Ltd, St Ives plc

For Judy

'Every man thinks meanly of himself
for not having been a soldier'

SAMUEL JOHNSON

FOREWORD

This was the first book I wrote, and it is the only book of mine that I have never dared go back and re-read. I still do not dare, for I am sure I would be horrified by the crudity of its writing, but I am constantly told by readers that it is one of their favourites.

It tells the story of the battle of Talavera, which occurred towards the beginning of the Peninsular War. It was not where I wanted to start the Sharpe series. I really wanted to begin with the tale of Badajoz (which turns up in *Sharpe's Company*), because Badajoz is such an extraordinary and dramatic event, but I decided it would be a good idea to write a book or two before Badajoz, rather like a bowler warming up before he takes on the opening batsman. I had never written a novel before, never tried to write a novel before, and so *Sharpe's Eagle* is where I was going to make all a beginner's mistakes, and where, if I was successful in my ambition to write a series of tales about the adventures of a British rifleman in the Napoleonic Wars, I was going to learn some of the tricks of the trade. One of the first things I learned was that Sharpe's enemies, by and large, had to be British. I had thought, before I began writing, that the French would provide him with enemies enough, but the circumstances of war meant that Sharpe spent much more time with the British than with the enemy French, and if he was to be unendingly challenged, irritated, obstructed and angered then the provocations had to come from people with whom he was constantly associated.

In time Sharpe is to meet many foul enemies, but few, I think, are as nauseating as Sir Henry Simmerson who, I seem to remember, becomes a tax inspector in his later career.

I said Sharpe's enemies were British. In fact most of them, like me, are English, while his friends are often Irish. This arose from the happy fact that I had been living in Belfast in the years immediately prior to writing Sharpe and had acquired a fondness for Ireland which has never abated. It also reflected a truth that Wellington's army was heavily recruited from the Irish, and indeed the Duke (as he was to become) had been born there. That was not a fact of which he was proud. 'Being born in a stable,' he once remarked, 'does not make a man a horse.' The Duke was a difficult, cold and snobbish man who was also one of the greatest soldiers ever to take the field. Like Sharpe I admire him, but would not particularly wish to dine with him. His story, though, is intimately linked with Sharpe's, which is to Sharpe's good fortune. But Sharpe, if he is to make his reputation, must do it with action, rather than by his distant connection with the Duke, and there was no act more admired on a battlefield than the capture of an enemy's standard. In Napoleon's army those standards took the form of small statuettes of eagles – thus the book's title. I decided that if I was not to launch Sharpe against the great walls of Badajoz in his first adventure, then he should face another task just as impossible, and so I set him to capture an eagle. Poor Sharpe.

But there were much greater events resting on his shoulders than the seizing of an eagle. I had fallen in love with Judy, an American to whom the book is dedicated and who, for family reasons, could not live in Britain, which meant I had to earn a crust in the United States if the course of true love was ever to flow smooth. The American Government, in its Simmerson-like wisdom, refused me a work permit so I airily told Judy that I would support us by writing books. Sharpe had to succeed if that irresponsible promise was to be kept. That was twenty-one years ago, and we are still married, so in truth *Sharpe's Eagle* is a dazzling romance. And one day I shall read it again.

PREFACE

In 1809 the British army was divided into Regiments, as today, but most Regiments were described by numbers not by names; thus, for instance, the Bedfordshire Regiment was properly called the 14th, the Connaught Rangers the 88th and so on. The soldiers themselves preferred the names but had to wait until 1881 for their official adoption. I have deliberately not given the South Essex, a fictional Regiment, any number.

A Regiment was an administrative unit; the basic fighting unit was the Battalion. Most Regiments consisted of at least two Battalions but a few, like the imaginary South Essex, were small single-Battalion Regiments. That is why, in *Sharpe's Eagle*, the two words are used interchangeably of the South Essex. On paper a Battalion was supposed to have about a thousand men but disease and casualties, plus the shortage of recruits, meant that Battalions often went into battle with only five or six hundred troops.

All Battalions were divided into ten companies. Two of these, the Light Company and the Grenadier Company, were the elite of the Battalion and the Light Companies, in particular, were so useful that whole Regiments of Light troops, like the 95th Rifles, were being raised or expanded.

1

A Battalion was usually commanded by a Lieutenant Colonel, with two Majors, ten Captains, and below them the Lieutenants and Ensigns. None of these officers would have received any formal training; that was reserved for officers of the Engineers and the Artillery. About one officer in twenty was promoted from the ranks. Normal promotion was by seniority rather than merit but a rich man, as long as he had served a minimum period in his rank, could buy his next promotion and thus jump the queue. This system of purchase could lead to very unfair promotions but it is worth remembering that without it Britain's most successful soldier, Sir Arthur Wellesley, later the Duke of Wellington, would never have risen to high rank early enough in his career to form the most brilliant army Britain has ever possessed; the army in which Richard Sharpe fought the French through Portugal, Spain, and into France between 1808 and 1814.

CHAPTER 1

The guns could be heard long before they came into sight. Children clung to their mothers' skirts and wondered what dreadful thing made such noises. The hooves of the great horses mixed with the jangling of traces and chains, the hollow rumbling of the blurring wheels, and above it all the crashes as tons of brass, iron and timber bounced on the town's broken paving. Then they were in view; guns, limbers, horses and outriders, and the gunners looked as tough as the squat, blackened barrels that spoke of the fighting up north where the artillery had dragged their massive weapons through swollen rivers and up rain-soaked slopes to pound the enemy into oblivion and defeat. Now they would do it again. Mothers held their smallest children and pointed at the guns, boasted that these British would make Napoleon wish he had stayed in Corsica and suckled pigs which was all he was fit for.

And the cavalry! The Portuguese civilians applauded the trotting ranks of gorgeous uniforms, the curved, polished sabres unsheathed for display in Abrantes' streets and squares, and the fine dust from the horses' hooves was a small price to pay for the sight of the splendid Regiments who, the townspeople said, would chase the French clean over the Pyrenees and back into the sewers of Paris itself. Who could resist this army? From north and south, from the ports on the western coast, they were coming together and marching east on the road that led to the Spanish frontier and to the enemy. Portugal will be free, Spain's pride restored, France humbled, and these British soldiers can go back to their own wine-shops and inns leaving Abrantes and Lisbon, Coimbra and Oporto in peace. The soldiers themselves were not so confident. True they had beaten Soult's northern army but, marching into their lengthening shadows, they wondered what lay beyond Castelo Branco, the next town and the last before the frontier. Soon they would face again the blue-coated veterans of Jena and Austerlitz, the masters of Europe's battlefields, the French Regiments that had turned the finest armies of the world into so much mincemeat. The townspeople were impressed, at least by the cavalry and artillery, but to experienced eyes the troops gathering round Abrantes were pitifully few and the French armies to the east threateningly big. The British army that awed the children of Abrantes would not frighten the French Marshals.

Lieutenant Richard Sharpe, waiting for orders in his billet on the outskirts of town, watched the cavalry sheath their sabres as the last spectators were left behind and then he turned back to the job of unwinding the dirty bandage from his thigh.

As the last few inches peeled stickily away some maggots dropped to the floor and Sergeant Harper knelt to pick them up before looking at the wound.

'Healed, sir. Beautiful.'

Sharpe grunted. The sabre cut had become nine inches of puckered scar tissue, clean and pink against

4

the darker skin. He picked off a last fat maggot and gave it to Harper to put safely away.

'There, my beauty, well fed you are.' Sergeant Harper closed the tin and looked up at Sharpe. 'You were lucky, sir.'

That was true, thought Sharpe. The French Hussar had nearly ended him, the man's blade half way through a massive down-stroke when Harper's rifle bullet had lifted him from the saddle and the Frenchman's grimace, framed by the weird pigtails, had turned to sudden agony. Sharpe had twisted desperately away and the sabre, aimed at his neck, had sliced into his thigh to leave another scar as a memento of sixteen years in the British army. It had not been a deep wound but Sharpe had watched too many men die from smaller cuts, the blood poisoned, the flesh discoloured and stinking, and the doctors helpless to do anything but let the man sweat and rot to his death in the charnel houses they called hospitals. A handful of maggots did more than any army doctor, eating away the diseased tissue to let the healthy flesh close naturally. He stood up and tested the leg. 'Thank you, Sergeant. Good as new.'

'Pleasure's all mine, sir.'

Sharpe pulled on the cavalry overalls he wore instead of the regulation green trousers of the 95th Rifles. He was proud of the green overalls with their black leather reinforcement panels, stripped from the corpse of a Chasseur Colonel of Napoleon's Imperial Guard last winter. The outside of each leg had been decorated with more than twenty silver buttons and the metal had paid for food and drink as his small band of refugee Riflemen had escaped south through the Galician snows. The Colonel had been a lucky kill; there were not many men in either army as tall as Sharpe but the overalls fitted him perfectly and the Frenchman's soft, rich, black leather boots could have been made for the English Lieutenant. Patrick Harper had not been so fortunate. The Sergeant topped Sharpe by a full four inches and the huge Irishman had yet to find any trousers to replace his faded, patched and tattered pair that were scarcely fit to scare crows in a turnip field. The whole company was like that, reflected Sharpe, their uniforms threadbare, their boots literally tied together with strips of hide, and as long as their parent Battalion was home in England Sharpe's small company could find no Commissary Officer willing to complicate his account books by issuing them with new trousers or shoes. Sergeant Harper handed Sharpe his uniform jacket. 'Do you want a Hungarian bath, sir?'

Sharpe shook his head. 'It's bearable.' There were not too many lice in the jacket, not enough to justify steeping it in the smoke from a grass fire and to smell like a charcoal burner for the next two days. The jacket was as worn as those of the rest of his company but nothing, not the best tailored corpse in Portugal or Spain, would have persuaded Sharpe to throw it away. It was green, the dark green jacket of the 95th Rifles, and it was the badge of an elite Regiment. British Infantry wore red, but the best British Infantry wore green, and even after three years in the 95th Sharpe took pleasure in the distinction of the green uniform. It was all he had, his uniform and what he could carry on his back. Richard Sharpe knew no home other than the Regiment, no family except for his company, and no belongings except what fitted into his pack and pouches. He knew no other way to live and expected that it would be the way he would die. Round his waist he tied the red officer's sash and covered it with the black leather belt with its silver snake buckle. After a year in the Peninsula only the sash and his sword denoted his officer's rank and even his sword, like the overalls, broke regulations. Officers of the Rifles, like all Light Infantry officers, were supposed to carry a curved cavalry sabre but Sharpe hated the weapon. In its place he wore the long, straight sword of the Heavy Cavalry; a brute of a weapon, ill balanced and crude, but Sharpe liked the feel of a savage blade that could beat down the slim swords of French officers and crush aside a musket and bayonet.

The sword was not his only weapon. For ten years Richard Sharpe had marched in the red-coated ranks, first as a private, then a Sergeant, carrying a smooth-bore musket across the plains of India. He had stood in the line with the heavy flintlock, gone terrified into broken breaches with a bayonet, and he still carried a longarm into battle. The Baker rifle was his mark, it set him aside from other officers, and sixteen-year-old Ensigns, fresh in their bright new uniforms, looked warily at the tall, black-haired Lieutenant with the slung rifle and the scar which, except when he smiled, gave his face a look of grim amusement. Some wondered if the stories were true, stories of Seringapatam and Assaye, of Vimeiro and Lugo, but one glance from the apparently mocking eyes, or a sight of the worn grips on his weapons, stopped the wondering. Few new officers stopped to think of what the rifle really represented, of the fiercest struggle Sharpe had ever fought, the climb from the ranks into the officers' mess. Sergeant Harper looked out of the window into the square soaked in afternoon sunlight.

'Here comes Happy, sir.'

'Captain Hogan.'

Harper ignored the reproof. He and Sharpe had been

together too long, shared too many dangers, and the Sergeant knew precisely what liberties he could take with his taciturn officer. 'He's looking more cheerful than ever, sir. He must have another job for us.'

'I wish to God they'd send us home.'

Harper, his huge hands gently stripping the lock of his rifle, pretended not to hear the remark. He knew what it meant but the subject was a dangerous one. Sharpe commanded the remnants of a company of Riflemen who had been cut off from the rearguard of Sir John Moore's army during its retreat to Corunna the winter before. It had been a terrible campaign in weather that was like the travellers' tales of Russia rather than northern Spain. Men had died in their sleep, their hair frozen to the ground, while others dropped exhausted from the march and let death overtake them. The discipline of the army had crumbled and the drunken stragglers were easy meat for the French cavalry who flogged their exhausted mounts at the heel of the British army. The rabble was saved from disaster only by the few Regiments, like the 95th, which kept their discipline and fought on. 1808 turned into 1809 and still the nightmarish battle went on, a battle fought with damp powder by freezing men peering through the snow for a glimpse of the cloaked French Dragoons. Then, on a day when the blizzard bellied in the wind like a malevolent monster, the company had been cut off by the horsemen. The Captain was killed, the other Lieutenant, the rifles wouldn't fire and the enemy sabres rose and fell and the damp snow muffled all sounds except for the grunts of the Dragoons and the terrible chopping of the blades cutting into wounds that steamed in the freezing air. Lieutenant Sharpe and a few survivors fought clear and scrambled into high rocks where horsemen could not follow but when the storm blew out, and the last desperately wounded man died, there was no hope of rejoining the army. The second Battalion of the 95th Rifles had sailed home while Sharpe and his thirty men, lost and forgotten, had headed south, away from the French, to join the small British garrison in Lisbon.

Since then Sharpe had asked a dozen times to be sent home but Riflemen were too scarce, too valuable, and the army's new commander, Sir Arthur Wellesley, was unwilling to lose even thirty-one. So they had stayed and fought for whichever Battalion needed its Light Company strengthening and had marched north again, retracing their steps, and been with Wellesley when he avenged Sir John Moore by tumbling Marshal Soult and his veterans out of North Portugal. Harper knew his Lieutenant harboured a sullen anger at his predicament. Richard Sharpe was poor, dog poor, and he would never have the money to purchase his next promotion. To become a Captain, even in an ordinary Battalion of the line, would cost Sharpe fifteen hundred pounds and he might as well hope to be made King of France as raise that money. He had only one hope of promotion and that was by seniority in his own Regiment; to step into the shoes of men who died or were promoted and whose own commissions had not been purchased. But as long as Sharpe was in Portugal and the Regiment was home in England he was being forgotten and passed over, time and again, and the unfairness soured Sharpe's resentment. He watched men younger than himself purchase their Captaincies, their Majorities, while he, a better soldier, was left on the heap because he was poor and because he was fighting instead of being safe home in England.

The door of the cottage banged open and Captain Hogan stepped into the room. He looked, in his blue coat and white trousers, like a naval officer and he claimed his uniform had been mistaken for a Frenchman's so often that he had been fired on more by his own side than by the enemy. He was an Engineer, one of the tiny number of Military Engineers in Portugal, and he grinned as he took off his cocked hat and nodded at Sharpe's leg. 'The warrior restored? How's the leg?'

'Perfect, sir.'

'Sergeant Harper's maggots, eh? Well, we Irish are clever devils. God knows where you English would be without us.' Hogan took out his snuff box and inhaled a vast pinch. As Sharpe waited for the inevitable sneeze he eyed the small, middle-aged Captain fondly. For a month his Riflemen had been Hogan's escort as the Engineer had mapped the roads across the high passes that led to Spain. It was no secret that any day now Wellesley would take the army into Spain, to follow the River Tagus that was aimed like a spear at the capital, Madrid, and Hogan, as well as sketching endless maps, had strengthened the culverts and bridges which would have to take the tons of brass and wood as the field artillery rolled towards the enemy. It had been a job well done in agreeable company, until it rained and the rifles wouldn't fire and the crazy-eyed French Hussar had nearly made a name for himself by his mad solo charge at the Riflemen. Somehow Sergeant Harper had kept the damp out of his firing pan and Sharpe still shivered when he thought of what might have happened if the rifle had not fired.

The Sergeant collected the pieces of his rifle lock as if he was about to leave but Hogan held up his hand. 'Stay on, Patrick. I have a treat for you; one that even a heathen from Donegal might like.' He took a dark bottle out of his haversack and raised an eyebrow to Sharpe. 'You don't mind?'

Sharpe shook his head. Harper was a good man, good at everything he did, and in their three years' acquaintanceship Sharpe and Harper had become friends, or at least as friendly as an officer and a Sergeant could be. Sharpe could not imagine fighting without the huge Irishman beside him, the Irishman dreaded fighting without Sharpe, and together they were as formidable a pair as Hogan had ever seen on a battlefield. The Captain set the bottle on the table and pulled the cork. 'Brandy. French brandy from Marshal Soult's own cellars and captured at Oporto. With the compliments of the General.'

'From Wellesley?' Sharpe asked.

'The man himself. He asked after you, Sharpe, and I said you were being doctored or would have been with me.'

Sharpe said nothing. Hogan paused in his careful pouring of the liquid. 'Don't be unfair, Sharpe! He's fond of you. Do you think he's forgotten Assaye?'

Assaye. Sharpe remembered all right. The field of dead outside the Indian village where he had been commissioned on the battlefield. Hogan pushed a tin cup of brandy across the table to him. 'You know he can't make you into a Captain of the 95th. He doesn't have the power!'

'I know.' Sharpe smiled and raised the cup to his lips. But Wellesley did have the power to send him home where promotion might be had. He pushed the thought away, knowing the nagging insult of his rank would soon come back, and was envious of Hogan who, being an Engineer, could only gain promotion by seniority. It meant that Hogan was still only a Captain, even in his fifties, but at least there was no jealousy and injustice because no man could buy his way up the ladder of promotion. He leaned forward. 'So? Any news? Are we still with you?'

'You are. And we have a job.' Hogan's eyes twinkled. 'And a wonderful job it is, too.'

Patrick Harper grinned. 'That means a powerful big bang.'

Hogan nodded. 'You are right, Sergeant. A big bridge to be blown into the next world.' He took a map out of his pocket and unfolded it on to the table. Sharpe watched a calloused finger trace the River Tagus from the sea at Lisbon, past Abrantes where they now sat, and on into Spain to stop where the river made a huge southwards loop. 'Valdelacasa,' Hogan said. 'There's an old bridge there, a Roman one. The General doesn't like it.'

Sharpe could see why. The army would march on the north bank of the Tagus towards Madrid and the river would guard their right flank. There were few bridges where the French might cross and harass their supply lines and those bridges were in towns, like Alcantara, where the Spanish kept garrisons to protect the crossings. Valdelacasa was not even marked. If there was no town there would be no garrison and a French force could cross and play havoc in the British rear. Harper leaned over and looked at the map.

'Why isn't it marked, sir?'

Hogan made a contemptuous noise. 'I'm surprised the map even marks Madrid, let alone Valdelacasa.' He was right. The Tomas Lopez map, the only one available to the armies in Spain, was a wondrous work of the Spanish imagination. Hogan stabbed his finger down on to the map. 'The bridge is hardly used, it's in bad repair. We're told you can hardly put a cart across, let alone a gun, but it could be repaired and we could have "old trousers" up our backsides in no time.' Sharpe smiled. 'Old trousers' was the Rifles' strange nickname for the French and Hogan had adopted the phrase with relish. The Engineer lowered his voice conspiratorially. 'It's a strange place, I'm told, just a ruined convent and the bridge. They call it El Puente de los Malditos.' He nodded as if he had made his point.

Sharpe waited a few seconds and sighed. 'All right. What does it mean?'

Hogan smiled triumphantly. 'I'm surprised you need to ask! It means "The Bridge of the Accursed". It seems that, years ago, all the nuns were taken out of the convent and massacred by the Moors. It's haunted, Sharpe, stalked by the spirits of the dead!'

Sharpe leaned forward to peer more closely at the map. Give or take the width of Hogan's finger the bridge must be sixty miles beyond the border and they were that far from Spain already. 'When do we leave?'

'Now there's a problem.' Hogan folded the map carefully. 'We can leave for the frontier tomorrow but we can't cross until we're formally invited by the Spanish.' He leaned back with his cup of brandy. 'And we have to wait for our escort.'

'Escort!' Sharpe bridled. 'We're your escort.'

Hogan shook his head. 'Oh, no. This is politics. The Spanish will let us blow up their bridge but only if a Spanish Regiment goes along with us. It's a question of pride, apparently.'

'Pride!' Sharpe's anger was obvious. 'If you have a whole Regiment of Spaniards then why the hell do you need us?'

Hogan smiled placatingly. 'Oh, I need you. There's more, you see.' He was interrupted by Harper. The Sergeant was standing at the window, oblivious of their conversation, and staring into the small square.

'That is nice. Oh, sir, that can clean my rifle any day of the week.'

Sharpe looked through the small window. Outside, on a black mare, sat a girl dressed in black; black breeches, black jacket, and a wide-brimmed hat that shadowed her face but in no way obscured a beauty that was startling. Sharpe saw a wide mouth, dark eyes, coiled hair the colour of fine powder and then she became aware of their scrutiny. She half smiled at them and turned away, snapped an order at a servant holding the halter of a mule, and stared at the road leading from the plaza towards the centre of Abrantes. Hogan made a small, contented noise. 'That is special. They don't come out like that very often. I wonder who she is?'

'Officer's wife?' Sharpe suggested.

Harper shook his head. 'No ring, sir. But she's waiting for someone, lucky bastard.'

And a rich bastard, thought Sharpe. The army was collecting its customary tail of women and children who followed the Regiments to war. Each Battalion was allowed to take sixty soldiers' wives to an overseas war but no one could stop other women joining the 'official' wives; local girls, prostitutes, seamstresses and washerwomen, all making their living from the army. This girl looked different. There was the smell of money and privilege about her as if she had run away from a rich Lisbon home. Sharpe presumed she was the lover of a rich officer, as much a part of his equipment as his thoroughbred horses, his Manton pistols, his silver dinnerware for camp meals, and the hounds that would trot obediently at his horse's tail. There were plenty of girls like her, Sharpe knew, girls who cost a lot of money, and he felt the old envy rise in him.

'My God.' Harper, still staring out of the window, had spoken again.

'What is it?' Sharpe leaned forward and, like his Sergeant, he could hardly believe his eyes. A Battalion of British Infantry was marching steadily into the square but a Battalion the like of which Sharpe had not seen for more than twelve months. A year in Portugal had turned the army into a Drill-Sergeant's nightmare, the soldiers' uniforms had faded and been patched with the ubiquitous brown cloth of the Portuguese peasants, their hair had grown long, the polish had long disappeared from buttons and badges. Sir Arthur Wellesley did not mind; he only cared that a soldier had sixty rounds of ammunition and a clear head and if his trousers were brown instead of white then it made no difference to the outcome of a fight. But this Battalion was fresh from England. Their coats were a brilliant scarlet, their crossbelts pipeclayed white, their boots a mirror-surfaced black. Each man wore tightly-buttoned gaiters and, even more surprising, they still wore the infamous stocks; four inches of stiffly varnished black leather that constricted the neck and was supposed to keep a man's chin high and back straight. Sharpe could not remember when he had last seen a stock; once on campaign the men 'lost' them, and with them went the running sores where the rigid leather dug into the soft flesh beneath the jawbone.

'They've taken the wrong turning for Windsor Castle,' Harper said.

Sharpe shook his head. 'They're unbelievable!' Whoever commanded this Battalion must have made the men's lives hell to keep them looking so immaculate despite the voyage from England in cramped and foul ships and the long march from Lisbon in the summer heat. Their weapons shone, their equipment was pristine and regular while their faces bulged red from the constricting stocks and the unaccustomed sun. At the head of each company rode the officers, all, Sharpe noted, mounted superbly. The colours were cased in polished leather and guarded by Sergeants whose halberd blades had been burnished to a brilliant, glittering sheen. The men marched in perfect step, looking neither right nor left, for all the world, as Harper had said, as if they were marching for the Royal duty at Windsor.

'Who are they?' Sharpe was trying to think of the Regiments who had yellow facings on their uniforms but this looked like none of the Regiments he knew.

'The South Essex,' Hogan said.

'The who?'

'The South Essex. They're new, very new. Just raised by Lieutenant Colonel Sir Henry Simmerson, a cousin of General Sir Banestre Tarleton.'

Sharpe whistled softly. Tarleton had fought in the American war and now sat in Parliament as Wellesley's bitterest military opponent. Sharpe had heard said that Tarleton wanted the command of the army in Portugal for himself and bitterly resented the younger man's preferment. Tarleton was a man of influence, a dangerous enemy for Wellesley, and Sharpe knew enough about the politics of high command to realise that the presence of Tarleton's cousin in the army would not be welcomed by Wellesley.

'Is that him?' He pointed to a portly man riding a grey horse in the centre of the Battalion.

Hogan nodded. 'That is Sir Henry Simmerson, whom God preserve or preferably not.'

Lieutenant Colonel Sir Henry Simmerson had a red face lined with purple veins and pendulous with jowls. His eyes, at the distance Sharpe was seeing them, seemed small and red, and on either side of the suspicious, questing face there sprung prominent ears that looked like the protruding trunnions either side of a cannon barrel. He looked, Sharpe thought, like a pig on horseback. 'I've not heard of the man.'

'That's not surprising. He's done nothing.' Hogan was scornful. 'Landed money, in Parliament for Paglesham, justice of the peace and, God help us, a Militia Colonel.' Hogan seemed surprised by his own lack of charity. 'He means well. He won't be content till those lads are the best damned Battalion in the army but I think the man has a terrible shock coming when he finds the difference between us and the Militia.'

Like other Regular officers Hogan had little time for the Militia, Britain's second army. It was used exclusively within Britain itself, never had to fight, never went hungry, never slept in an open field beneath a cloudburst, yet it paraded with a glorious pomp and self-importance. Hogan laughed. 'Mustn't complain. We're lucky to have Sir Henry.'

'Lucky?' Sharpe looked at the greying Engineer.

'Oh, yes. Sir Henry only arrived in Abrantes yesterday but he tells us he's a great expert on war. The man's not yet seen a Frenchman but he's lectured the General on how to beat them!' Hogan laughed and shook his head. 'Maybe he'll learn. One battle could take the starch out of him.'

Sharpe looked at the companies marching steadily through the square like automatons. The brass badges on their shakoes reflected the sun but the faces beneath the brilliance were expressionless. Sharpe loved the army, it was his home, the refuge that an orphan had needed sixteen years before, but he liked it most of all because it gave him, in a clumsy way, the opportunity to prove again and again that he was valued. He could chafe against the rich and the privileged but he acknowledged that the army had taken him from the gutter and put an officer's sash round his waist and Sharpe could think of no other job that would offer a low-born bastard on the run from the law the chance of rank and responsibility. But Sharpe had also been lucky. In sixteen years he had rarely stopped fighting and it had been his fortune that the battles in Flanders, India and Portugal had called for men like himself who reacted to danger the way a gambler reacted to a deck of cards. Sharpe suspected he would hate the peacetime army, with its church parades and pointless drills, its petty jealousies and endless polish, and in the South Essex he saw the peacetime army he did not want. 'I suppose he's a flogger?'

Hogan grimaced. 'Floggings, punishment parades, extra drills. You name it and Sir Henry uses it. He will have, he says, only the best. And they are. What do you think of them?'

Sharpe laughed grimly. 'God keep me from the South Essex. That's not too much to ask, is it?'

Hogan smiled. 'I'm afraid it is.'

Sharpe looked at him, a sinking feeling in his stomach. Hogan shrugged. 'I told you there was more. If a Spanish Regiment marches to Valdelacasa then Sir Arthur feels, for the sake of diplomacy, that a British one should go as well. Show the flag; that kind of thing.' He glanced at the polished ranks and back to

Sharpe. 'Sir Henry Simmerson and his fine men are going with us.'

Sharpe groaned. 'You mean we have to take orders from him?'

Hogan pursed his lips. 'Not exactly. Strictly speaking you will take your orders from me.' He had spoken primly, like a lawyer, and Sharpe glanced at him curiously. There could be only one reason why Wellesley had subordinated Sharpe and his Riflemen to Hogan, instead of to Simmerson, and that was because the General did not trust Sir Henry. Sharpe still wondered why he was needed; after all Hogan could expect the protection of two whole Battalions, at least fifteen hundred men. 'Does the General expect there to be a fight?'

Hogan shrugged. 'He doesn't know. The Spanish say that the French have a whole Regiment of cavalry on the south bank, with horse artillery, who've been chasing Guerilleros up and down the river since spring. Who knows? He thinks they may try to stop us blowing the bridge.'

'I still don't understand why you need us.'

Hogan smiled. 'Perhaps I don't. But there won't be any action for a month; the French will let us go deep into Spain before they fight, so Valdelacasa will at least be the chance of a scramble. And I want someone with me I can trust. Perhaps I just want you along as a favour?'

Sharpe smiled. Some favour, wet-nursing a Militia Colonel who thought he knew it all, but he hid his feelings. 'For you, sir, it will be a pleasure.'

Hogan smiled back. 'Who knows? It might be. She's going along.' Sharpe followed Hogan's gaze out of the window and saw the black-dressed girl raise a hand to an officer of the South Essex. Sharpe had an impression of a blond man, immaculately uniformed, mounted on a horse that had probably cost more than the rider's commission. The girl spurred her mare forward and, followed by the servant and his mule, joined the rear of the Battalion that was marching down the road that led to Castelo Branco. The square became empty again, the dust settling in the fierce heat, and Sharpe leaned back and began to laugh.

'What's so funny?' Hogan asked.

Sharpe pointed with his cup of brandy at Harper's tattered jacket and gaping trousers. 'Sir Henry's not exactly going to be fond of his new allies.'

The Sergeant's face stayed gloomy. 'God save Ireland.'

Hogan raised his cup. 'Amen to that.'

CHAPTER 2

The drumbeats were distant and muffled, sometimes blending with the other sounds of the city, but insistent and sinister and Sharpe was glad when the sound stopped. He was also glad they had reached Castelo Branco, twenty-four hours after the South Essex, after a tiresome journey that had consisted of forcing Hogan's mules along a road cut with deep, jagged ruts showing where the field artillery had gone before them. Now the mules, laden with powder kegs, oilskin packets of match-fuse, picks, crowbars, spades, all the equipment Hogan needed for Valdelacasa, followed patiently behind the Riflemen and Hogan's artificers as they pushed their way through the crowded streets towards the main square. As they spilled into the bright sunlight Sharpe's suspicions about the drumbeats were confirmed.

Someone had been flogged. It was over now. The victim had gone and Sharpe, watching the hollow square formation of the South Essex, remembered his own flogging, years before, and the struggle to keep the agony shut up, not to show to the officers that the lash hurt. Sharpe would carry the scars of his flogging to his grave but he doubted whether Simmerson knew how savage was the punishment he had just meted to his Battalion.

Hogan reined in his horse in the shade of the Bishop's palace. 'This doesn't seem to be the best moment to talk to the good Colonel.' Soldiers were taking down four wooden triangles that were propped against the far wall of the square. Four men flogged. Dear God, thought Sharpe, four men. Hogan turned his horse so that his back was to the Battalion. 'I must lock up the powder, Richard. Otherwise every bloody grain will be stolen. I'll meet you back here.'

Sharpe nodded. 'I need water anyway. Ten minutes?'

Sharpe's men collapsed at the foot of the wall, their packs and rifles discarded, their mood soured by the reminder before them of a discipline the Rifle Regiments had virtually discarded. Sir Henry rode his horse delicately to the centre of the square and his voice carried clearly to Sharpe and his men.

'I have flogged four men because four men deserted.' Sharpe looked up, startled. Deserters already? He looked at the Battalion, their faces expressionless, and wondered how many others were tempted to escape from Simmerson's ranks. The Colonel was half standing in his saddle. 'Some of you know how those men planned their crime. Some of you helped them. But you preferred silence so I have flogged four men to remind you of your duty.' His voice was curiously high pitched; it would have been funny if the man's presence was not so big. He had been speaking in a controlled manner, almost conversationally, but suddenly Sir Henry turned left and right and waved an arm as if to point at every man in his command. 'You will be the best!' The loudness was so sudden that pigeons burst startled from the ledges of the convent. Sharpe waited for more, but there was none, and the Colonel turned his horse and rode away leaving the battle cry lingering behind like a menace.

Sharpe caught Harper's eye and the Sergeant shrugged. There was nothing to be said, the faces of the South Essex proclaimed Simmerson's failure; they simply did not know how to be the best. Sharpe watched as the companies marched from the plaza and saw only sullenness and resentment in their expressions. Sharpe believed in discipline. Desertion to the enemy deserved death, some offences deserved a flogging, and if a man was hung for blatant looting then it was his fault because the rules were simple. And for Sharpe, that was the key; keep the rules simple. He asked three things of his men. That they fought, as he did, with a ruthless professionalism. That they stole only from the enemy and the dead unless they were starving. And that they never got drunk without his permission. It was a simple code, understandable by men who had mostly joined the army because they had failed elsewhere, and it worked. It was backed by punishment and Sharpe knew, for all that his men liked him and followed him willingly, that they feared his anger when they broke his trust. Sharpe was a soldier.

He crossed the square towards an alleyway, looking for a water fountain, and noticed a Lieutenant of the South Essex's Light Company riding his horse towards the same dark-shadowed gap between the buildings.

It was the man who had waved to the black-dressed girl and Sharpe felt a stab of irritation as he entered the alley first. It was an irrational jealousy. The Lieutenant's uniform was elegantly tailored, the Light Infantry curved sabre was expensive, and the black horse he rode was probably worth a Lieutenant's commission by itself. Sharpe resented the man's wealth, his privilege, the easy superiority of a man born to the landed gentry, and it annoyed Sharpe because he knew that

23

resentment was based on envy. He squeezed into the side of the alley to let the horseman pass, looked up and nodded affably, and had an impression of a thin, handsome face fringed with blond hair. He hoped the Lieutenant would ignore him; Sharpe was bad at small talk and he had no wish to make stilted conversation in a foetid alley when he would doubtless be introduced to the Battalion's officers later in the day.

Sharpe was disappointed. The Lieutenant stopped and stared down at the Rifleman. 'Don't they teach you to salute in the Rifles?' The Lieutenant's voice was as smooth and rich as his uniform. Sharpe said nothing. His epaulette was missing, torn off in the winter's fighting, and he realised that the blond Lieutenant had mistaken him for a private. It was hardly surprising. The alleyway was deeply shadowed, Sharpe's profile, with slung rifle, all helped to explain the Lieutenant's mistake. Sharpe glanced up to the thin, blue-eyed face and was about to explain when the Lieutenant flicked his whip so that it slapped Sharpe's face.

'Damn you, man, answer me!'

Sharpe felt the anger rise in him, but stayed still and waited for his moment. The Lieutenant drew the whip back.

'What Battalion? What company?'

'Second Battalion, Fourth Company.' Sharpe spoke with deliberate insolence and remembered the days when he had no protection against officers like this. The Lieutenant smiled again, no more pleasantly.

'You will call me "sir" you know. I shall make you. Who's your officer?'

'Lieutenant Sharpe.'

'Ah!' The Lieutenant kept his whip raised. 'Lieutenant Sharpe who we've all been told about. Came up from the ranks, didn't he?'

Sharpe nodded and the Lieutenant drew the whip back further.

'Is that why you don't say "sir"? Has Mr Sharpe strange ideas on discipline? Well, I will have to see Lieutenant Sharpe, won't I, and arrange to have you punished for insolence.' He brought the whip slashing down towards Sharpe's head. There was no room for Sharpe to step back, but there was no need, instead he put both hands under the man's stirrup and heaved upwards with all his strength. The whip stopped somewhere in mid stroke, the man started to cry out, and the next instant he was flat on his back on the far side of his horse where another horse had dunged earlier.

'You're going to have to wash your uniform, Lieutenant.' Sharpe smiled.

The man's horse had whinnied and gone forward a few paces and the furious Lieutenant struggled to his feet and put his hand to the hilt of his sabre.

'Hello there!' Hogan was peering into the alley. 'I thought I'd lost you!' The Engineer rode his horse up to the two men and stared cheerfully down on the Rifleman. 'Mules all stabled, powders locked up.' He turned to the strange Lieutenant and raised his hat. 'Afternoon. Don't think we've met. My name's Hogan.'

The Lieutenant let go of his sword. 'Gibbons, sir. Lieutenant Christian Gibbons.'

Hogan grinned. 'I see you've already met Sharpe. Lieutenant Richard Sharpe of the 95th Rifles.'

Gibbons looked at Sharpe and his eyes widened as he noticed, for the first time, that the sword hanging by

Sharpe's side was not the usual sword-bayonet carried by Riflemen but was a full-length blade. He raised his eyes to look nervously at Sharpe's. Hogan went cheerfully on. 'You've heard of Sharpe, of course; everyone has. He's the laddie who killed the Sultan Tippoo. Then, let me see, there was that ghastly affair at Assaye. No one knows how many Sharpe killed there. Do you know, Sharpe?' Hogan ignored any possible answer and ground on remorselessly. 'Terrible fellow, our Lieutenant Sharpe, equally fatal with a sword or gun.'

Gibbons could hardly mistake Hogan's message. The Captain had seen the scuffle and was warning Gibbons about the likely consequence of a formal duel. The Lieutenant took the proffered escape. He bent down and picked up his Light Company shako then nodded to Sharpe.

'My mistake, Sharpe.'

'My pleasure, Lieutenant.'

Hogan watched Gibbons retrieve his horse and disappear from the alleyway. 'You're not very gracious at receiving an apology.'

'It wasn't very graciously given.' Sharpe rubbed his cheek. 'Anyway, the bastard hit me.'

Hogan laughed incredulously. 'He what?'

'Hit me, with his whip. Why do you think I dumped him in the manure?'

Hogan shook his head. 'There's nothing so satisfying as a friendly and professional relationship with your fellow officers, my dear Sharpe. I can see this job will be a pleasure. What did he want?'

'Wanted me to salute him. Thought I was a private.'

Hogan laughed again. 'God knows what Simmerson will think of you. Let's go and find out.'

They were ushered into Simmerson's room to find the

Colonel of the South Essex sitting on his bed wearing nothing but a pair of trousers. A doctor knelt beside him who looked up nervously as the two officers came into the room; the movement prompted an impatient flap of Simmerson's hand. 'Come on, man, I haven't all day!'

In his hand the doctor was holding what appeared to be a metal box with a trigger mounted on the top. He hovered it over Sir Henry's arm and Sharpe saw he was trying to find a patch of skin that was not already scarred with strangely regular marks.

'Scarification!' Sir Henry barked to Hogan. 'Do you bleed, Captain?'

'No, sir.'

'You should. Keeps a man healthy. All soldiers should bleed.' He turned back to the doctor who was still hesitating over the scarred forearm. 'Come on, you idiot!'

In his nervousness the doctor pressed the trigger by mistake and there was a sharp click. From the bottom of the box Sharpe saw a group of wicked little blades leap out like steel tongues. The doctor flinched back. 'I'm sorry, Sir Henry. A moment.'

The doctor forced the blades back into the box and Sharpe suddenly realised that it was a bleeding machine. Instead of the old-fashioned lancet in the vein Sir Henry preferred the modern scarifier that was supposed to be faster and more effective. The doctor placed the box on the Colonel's arm, glanced nervously at his patient, then pressed the trigger.

'Ah! That's better!' Sir Henry closed his eyes and smiled momentarily. A trickle of blood ran down his arm and escaped the towel that the doctor was dabbing at the flow.

'Again, Parton, again!'

The doctor shook his head. 'But, Sir Henry . . .'

Simmerson cuffed the doctor with his free hand. 'Don't argue with me! Damn it, man, bleed me!' He looked at Hogan. 'Always too much spleen after a flogging, Captain.'

'That's very understandable, sir,' Hogan said in his Irish brogue and Simmerson looked at him suspiciously. The box clicked again, the blades gouged into the plump arm, and more blood trickled on to the sheets. Hogan caught Sharpe's eye and there was the glimmer of a smile that could too easily turn into laughter. Sharpe looked back to Sir Henry Simmerson who was pulling on his shirt.

'You must be Captain Hogan?'

'Yes, sir.' Hogan nodded amiably.

Simmerson turned to Sharpe. 'And who the devil are you?'

'Lieutenant Sharpe, sir. 95th Rifles.'

'No, you're not. You're a damned disgrace, that's what you are!'

Sharpe said nothing. He stared over the Colonel's shoulder, through the window, at the far blue hills where the French were gathering their strength.

'Forrest!' Simmerson had stood up. 'Forrest!'

The door opened and the Major, who must have been waiting for the summons, came in. He smiled timorously at Sharpe and Hogan and then turned to Simmerson. 'Colonel?'

'This officer will need a new uniform. Provide it, please, and arrange to have the money deducted from his pay.'

'No.' Sharpe spoke flatly. Simmerson and Forrest turned to stare at him. For a moment Sir Henry said nothing, he was not used to being contradicted, and

Sharpe kept going. 'I am an officer of the 95th Rifles and I will wear their uniform so long as I have that honour.'

Simmerson began to go red and his fingers fluttered at his side. 'Damn you, Sharpe! You're a disgrace! You're not a soldier, you're a crossing sweeper! You're under my orders now and I'm ordering you to be back here in fifteen minutes . . .'

'No, sir.' This time Hogan had spoken. His words checked Simmerson in full flow but the Captain gave the Colonel no time to recover. He unleashed all his Irish charm, starting with a smile of such sweet reasonableness that it would have charmed a fish out of the water. 'You see, Sir Henry, Sharpe is under my orders. The General is quite specific. As I understand it, Sir Henry, we accompany each other to Valdelacasa but Sharpe is with me.'

'But . . .' Hogan raised a hand to Simmerson's protest.

'You are right, sir, so right. But of course you would understand that conditions in the field may not be all that we would want and it may be as well, sir, I need hardly tell you, that I should have the dispositions of the Riflemen.'

Simmerson stared at Hogan. The Colonel had not understood a word of Hogan's nonsense but it had all been stated in such a matter-of-fact way, and in such a soldier-to-soldier way, that Simmerson was desperately trying to find an answer that did not make him sound foolish. He looked at Hogan for a moment. 'But that would be my decision!'

'How right you are, sir, how true!' Hogan spoke emphatically and warmly. 'Normally, that is. But I think the General had it in his mind, sir, that you would be so burdened with the problems of our Spanish allies and then, sir, there are the exigencies of engineering that Lieutenant Sharpe understands.' He leaned forward conspiratorially. 'I need men to fetch and carry, sir. You understand.'

Simmerson smiled, then gave a bray of a laugh. Hogan had taken him off the hook. He pointed at Sharpe. 'He dresses like a common labourer, eh, Forrest? A labourer!' He was delighted with his joke and repeated it to himself as he pulled on his vast scarlet and yellow jacket. 'A labourer! Eh, Forrest?' The Major smiled dutifully. He resembled a long-suffering vicar continually assailed by the sins of an unrepentant flock and when Simmerson's back was turned he gave Sharpe an apologetic look. Simmerson buckled his belt and turned back to Sharpe. 'Done much soldiering then, Sharpe? Apart from fetching and carrying?'

'A little, sir.'

Simmerson chuckled. 'How old are you?'

'Thirty-two, sir.' Sharpe stared rigidly ahead.

'Thirty-two, eh? And still only a Lieutenant? What's the matter, Sharpe? Incompetence?'

Sharpe saw Forrest signalling to the Colonel but he ignored the movements. 'I joined in the ranks, sir.'

Forrest dropped his hand. The Colonel dropped his mouth. There were not many men who made the jump from Sergeant to Ensign and those who did could rarely be accused of incompetence. There were only three qualifications that a common soldier needed to be given a commission. First he must be able to read and write and Sharpe had learned his letters in the Sultan Tippoo's prison to the accompaniment of the screams of other British prisoners being tortured. Secondly the man had to perform some act of suicidal bravery and

Sharpe knew that Simmerson was wondering what he had done. The third qualification was extraordinary luck and Sharpe sometimes wondered whether that was not a two-edged sword. Simmerson snorted.

'You're not a gentleman then, Sharpe?'

'No, sir.'

'Well you could try to dress like one, eh? Just because you grew up in a pigsty that doesn't mean you have to dress like a pig?'

'No, sir.' There was nothing else to say.

Simmerson slung his sword over his vast belly. 'Who commissioned you, Sharpe?'

'Sir Arthur Wellesley, sir.'

Sir Henry gave a bray of triumph. 'I knew it! No standards, no standards at all! I've seen this army, its appearance is a disgrace! You can't say that of my men, eh? You cannot fight without discipline!' He looked at Sharpe. 'What makes a good soldier, Sharpe?'

'The ability to fire three rounds a minute in wet weather, sir.' Sharpe invested his answer with a tinge of insolence. He knew the reply would annoy Simmerson. The South Essex was a new Battalion and he doubted whether its musketry was up to the standard of other, older Battalions. Of all the European armies only the British practised with live ammunition but it took weeks, sometimes months, for a soldier to learn the complicated drill of loading and firing a musket fast, ignoring the panic, just concentrating on out-shooting the enemy.

Sir Henry had not expected the answer and he stared thoughtfully at the scarred Rifleman. To be honest, and Sir Henry did not enjoy being honest with himself, he was afraid of the army he had encountered in Portugal. Until now Sir Henry had thought soldiering was a glorious affair of obedient men in drill-straight lines, their scarlet coats shining in the sun, and instead he had been met by casual, unkempt officers who mocked his Militia training. Sir Henry had dreamed of leading his Battalion into battle, mounted on his charger, sword aloft, gaining undying glory. But staring at Sharpe, typical of so many officers he had met in his brief time in Portugal, he found himself wondering whether there were any French officers who looked like Sharpe. He had imagined Napoleon's army as a herd of ignorant soldiers shepherded by foppish officers and he shuddered inside at the thought that they might turn out to be lean, hardened men like Sharpe who might chop him out of his saddle before he had the chance to be painted in oils as a conquering hero. Sir Henry was already afraid and he had yet to see a single enemy, but first he had to get a subtle revenge on this Rifleman who had baffled him.

'Three rounds a minute?'

'Yes, sir.'

'And how do you teach men to fire three rounds a minute?'

Sharpe shrugged. 'Patience, sir. Practice. One battle does a world of good.'

Simmerson scoffed at him. 'Patience! Practice! They aren't children, Sharpe. They're drunkards and thieves! Gutter scourings!' His voice was rising again. 'Flog it into them, Sharpe, flog! It's the only way! Give them a lesson they won't forget. Isn't that right?'

There was silence. Simmerson turned to Forrest. 'Isn't that right, Major?'

'Yes, sir.' Forrest's answer lacked conviction. Simmerson turned to Sharpe. 'Sharpe?'

'It's the last resort, sir.'

'The last resort, sir.' Simmerson mimicked Sharpe but secretly he was pleased. It was the answer he had wanted. 'You're soft, Sharpe! Could you teach men to fire three rounds a minute?'

Sharpe could feel the challenge in the air but there was no going back. 'Yes, sir.'

'Right!' Simmerson rubbed his hands together. 'This afternoon. Forrest?'

'Sir?'

'Give Mr Sharpe a company. The Light will do. Mr Sharpe will improve their shooting!' Simmerson turned and bowed to Hogan with a heavy irony. 'That is if Captain Hogan agrees to lend us Lieutenant Sharpe's services.'

Hogan shrugged and looked at Sharpe. 'Of course, sir.'

Simmerson smiled. 'Excellent! So, Mr Sharpe, you'll teach my Light Company to fire three shots a minute?'

Sharpe looked out of the window. It was a hot, dry day and there was no reason why a good man should not fire five shots a minute in this weather. It depended, of course, how bad the Light Company were at the moment. If they could only manage two shots a minute now then it was next to impossible to make them experts in one afternoon but trying would do no harm. He looked back to Simmerson. 'I'll try, sir.'

'Oh you will, Mr Sharpe, you will. And you can tell them from me that if they fail then I'll flog one out of every ten of them. Do you understand, Mr Sharpe? One out of every ten.'

Sharpe understood well enough. He had been tricked by Simmerson into what was probably an impossible job and the outcome would be that the Colonel would have his orgy of flogging and he, Sharpe, would be blamed.

And if he succeeded? Then Simmerson could claim it was the threat of the flogging that had done the trick. He saw triumph in Simmerson's small red eyes and he smiled at the Colonel. 'I won't tell them about the flogging, Colonel. You wouldn't want them distracted, would you?'

Simmerson smiled back. 'You use your own methods, Mr Sharpe. But I'll leave the triangle where it is; I think I'm going to need it.'

Sharpe clapped his misshapen shako on to his head and gave the Colonel a salute of bone-cracking precision. 'Don't bother, sir. You won't need a triangle. Good day, sir.'

Now make it happen, he thought.

CHAPTER 3

'I don't bloody believe it, sir. Tell me it's not true.'
Sergeant Patrick Harper shook his head as he stood with
Sharpe and watched the South Essex Light Company
fire two volleys to the orders of a Lieutenant. 'Send this
Battalion to Ireland, sir. We'd be a free country in two
weeks! They couldn't fight off a church choir!'

Sharpe gloomily agreed. It was not that the men
did not know how to load and fire their muskets; it
was simply that they did it with a painful slowness
and a dedication to the drill book that was rigorously
imposed by the Sergeants. There were officially twenty
drill movements for the loading and firing of a musket,
five of them alone applied to how the steel ramrod
should be used to thrust ball and charge down the
barrel and the Battalion's insistence on doing it by
the book meant that Sharpe had timed their two
demonstration shots at more than thirty seconds each.
He had three hours, at the most, to speed them up
to twenty seconds a shot and he could understand
Harper's reaction to the task. The Sergeant was openly
scornful.

'God help us if we ever have to skirmish alongside
this lot! The French will eat them for breakfast!' He was
right. The company was not even trained well enough

to stand in the battle-line, let alone skirmish with the Light troops out in front of the enemy. Sharpe hushed Harper as a mounted Captain trotted across to them. It was Lennox, Captain of the Light Company, and he grinned down on Sharpe.

'Terrifying, isn't it?'

Sharpe was not sure how to reply. To agree might seem to be criticising the grizzled Scot who seemed friendly enough. Sharpe gave a non-committal answer and Lennox swung himself out of the saddle to stand beside him.

'Don't worry, Sharpe. I know how bad they are, but his Eminence insists on doing it this way. If he left it to me I'd have the bastards doing it properly but if we break one little regulation then it's three hours' drill with full packs.' He looked quizzically at Sharpe. 'You were at Assaye?' Sharpe nodded and Lennox grinned again. 'Aye, I remember you. You made a name for yourself that day. I was with the 78th.'

'They made a name for themselves too.'

Lennox was pleased with the compliment. Sharpe remembered the Indian field and sight of the Highland Regiment marching in perfect order to assault the Mahratta lines. Great gaps were blown in the kilted ranks as they calmly marched into the artillery storm but the Scotsmen had done their job, slaughtered the gunners, and daringly reloaded in the face of a huge mass of enemy infantry that did not have the courage to counter-attack the seemingly invincible Regiment. Lennox shook his head.

'I know what you're thinking, Sharpe. What the devil am I doing here with this lot?' He did not wait for an answer. 'I'm an old man, I was retired, but the wife died, the half pay wasn't stretching and they needed officers

36

for Sir Henry bloody Simmerson. So here I am. Do you know Leroy?'

'Leroy?'

'Thomas Leroy. He's a Captain here, too. He's good. Forrest is a decent fellow. But the rest! Just because they put on a fancy uniform they think they're warriors. Look at that one!'

He pointed to Christian Gibbons who was riding his black horse on to the field. 'Lieutenant Gibbons?' Sharpe asked.

'You've met then?' Lennox laughed. 'I'll say nothing about Mr Gibbons, then, except that he's Simmerson's nephew, he's interested in nothing but women, and he's an arrogant little bastard. Bloody English! Begging your pardon, Sharpe.'

Sharpe laughed. 'We're not all that bad.' He watched as Gibbons walked his horse delicately to within a dozen paces and stopped. The Lieutenant stared superciliously at the two officers. So this, Sharpe thought, is Simmerson's nephew? 'Are we needed here, sir?'

Lennox shook his head. 'No, Mr Gibbons, we are not. I'll leave Knowles and Denny with Lieutenant Sharpe while he works his miracles.' Gibbons touched his hat and spurred his horse away. Lennox watched him go. 'Can't do any wrong, that one. Apple of the Colonel's bloodshot eye.' He turned and waved at the company. 'I'll leave you Lieutenant Knowles and Ensign Denny, they're both good lads but they've learned wrong from Simmerson. You've got a sprinkling of old soldiers, that'll help, and good luck to you, Sharpe, you'll need it!' He grunted as he heaved himself into the saddle. 'Welcome to the madhouse, Sharpe!'

Sharpe was left with the company, its junior officers, and the ranks of dumb faces that stared at him as though fearful of some new torment devised by their Colonel. He walked to the front of the company, watching the red faces that bulged over the constricting stocks and glistened with sweat in the relentless heat, and faced them. His own jacket was unbuttoned, shirt open, and he wore no hat. To the men of the South Essex he was like a visitor from another continent. 'You're in a war now. When you meet the French a lot of you are going to die. Most of you.' They were appalled by his words. 'I'll tell you why.'

He pointed over the eastern horizon. 'The French are over there, waiting for you.' Some of the men looked that way as though they expected to see Bonaparte himself coming through the olive trees on the outskirts of Castelo Branco. 'They've got muskets and they can all fire three or four shots a minute. Aimed at you. And they're going to kill you because you're so damned slow. If you don't kill them first then they will kill you, it is as simple as that. You.' He pointed to a man in the front rank. 'Bring me your musket!'

At least he had their attention and some of them would understand the simple fact that the side which pumped out the most bullets stood the best chance of winning. He took the man's musket, a handful of ammunition, and discarded his rifle. He held the musket over his head and went right back to the beginnings.

'Look at it! One India Pattern musket. Fifty-five and a quarter inches long with a thirty-nine-inch barrel. It fires a ball three-quarters of an inch wide, nearly as wide as your thumb, and it kills Frenchmen!' There was a nervous laugh but they were listening. 'But you won't kill any Frenchmen with it. You're too slow! In the time it takes you to fire two shots the enemy will probably manage three. And, believe me, the French are slow. So, this afternoon, you will learn to fire three shots in a minute. In time you'll fire four shots every minute and if you're really good you should manage five!'

The company watched as he loaded the musket. It had been years since he had fired a smooth-bore musket but compared to the Baker rifle it was ridiculously easy. There were no grooves in the barrel to grip the bullet and no need to force the ramrod with brute force or even hammer it down. A musket was fast to load which was why most of the army used it instead of the slower, but much more accurate, rifle. He checked the flint, it was new and well seated in its jaws, so he primed and cocked the gun. 'Lieutenant Knowles?'

A young Lieutenant snapped to attention. 'Sir!'

'Do you have a watch?'

'Yes, sir.'

'Can it time one minute?'

Knowles dragged out a huge gold hunter and snapped open the lid. 'Yes, sir.'

'When I fire you will keep an eye on that watch and tell me when one minute has passed. Understand?'

'Yes, sir.'

He turned away from the company and pointed the musket down the field towards a stone wall. Oh God, he prayed, let it not misfire, and pulled the trigger. The swan neck with its gripped flint snapped forward, the powder in the pan flashed, and a fraction later the main charge exploded and he felt the heavy kick as the lead ball was punched out of the barrel in a gout of thick, white smoke.

Now it was all instinct; the never-forgotten motions. Right hand away from the trigger, let the gun fall in the left hand and as the butt hits the ground the right hand already has the next cartridge. Bite off the bullet. Pour the powder down the barrel but remember to keep a pinch for the priming. Spit in the ball. Ramrod out, up, and down the barrel. A quick push and then it's out again, the gun is up, the cock back, priming in the pan, and fire into the lingering smoke of the first shot.

And again and again and again and memories of standing in the line with sweating, mad-eyed comrades and going through the motions as if in a nightmare. Ignoring the billows of smoke, the screams, edging left and right to fill up the gaps left by the dead, just loading and firing, loading and firing, letting the flames spit out into the fog of powder smoke, the lead balls to smash into the unseen enemy and hope they are falling back. Then the command to cease fire and you stop. Your face is black and stinging from the explosions of the powder in the pan just inches from your right cheek, your eyes smarting from the smoke and the powder grains, and the cloud drifts away leaving the dead and wounded in front and you lean on the musket and pray that the next time the gun would not hang-fire, snap a flint, or simply refuse to fire at all.

He pulled the trigger for the fifth time, the ball hammered away down the field, and the musket was down and the powder in the barrel before Knowles called 'Time's up!'

The men cheered, laughed and clapped because an officer had broken the rules and showed them he could do it. Harper was grinning broadly. He at least knew how difficult it was to make five shots in a minute and Sharpe knew that the Sergeant had noticed how he had cunningly loaded the first shot before the timed minute began. Sharpe stopped the noise. 'That is how you will use a musket. Fast! Now you're going to do it.'

There was silence. Sharpe felt the devilment in him;

had not Simmerson told him to use his own method? 'Take off your stocks!' For a moment no one moved. The men stared at him. 'Come on! Hurry! Take your stocks off!'

Knowles, Denny, and the Sergeants watched, puzzled, as the men gripped their muskets between their knees and used both hands to wrench apart the stiff leather collars.

'Sergeants! Collect the stocks. Bring them here.'

The Battalion had been brutalised too much. There was no way he could teach them to be fast-shooting soldiers unless he offered them an opportunity to take their revenge on the system that had condemned them to a flogger's Battalion. The Sergeants came to him, their faces dubious, their arms piled high with the hated stocks.

'Put them down there.' Sharpe made them heap the seventy-odd stocks about forty paces in front of the company. He pointed to the glistening heap. 'That is your target! Each of you will be given just three rounds. Just three. And you will have one minute in which to fire them! Those who succeed, twice in a row, will drop out and have a lazy afternoon. The rest will go on trying and go on trying until they do succeed.'

He let the two officers organise the drill. The men were grinning broadly and there was a buzz of conversation in the ranks that he did not try to check. The Sergeants looked at him as though he were committing treason but none dared cross the tall, dark Rifleman with the long sword. When all was ready Sharpe gave the word and the bullets began smashing their way into the pile of leather. The men forgot their old drill and concentrated on shooting their hatred into the leather collars that had given them sore necks

41

and which represented Simmerson and all his tyranny. At the end of the first two sessions only twenty men had succeeded, nearly all of them old soldiers who had re-enlisted in the new Battalion, but an hour and three-quarters later, as the sun reddened behind him, the last man fired his last shot into the fragments of stiff leather that littered the grass.

Sharpe lined the whole company in two ranks and watched, satisfied, as they shot three volleys to Harper's commands. He looked through the white smoke that lingered in the still air towards the eastern horizon. Over there, in the Estramadura, the French were waiting, their Eagles gathering for the battle that had to come while behind him, in the lane that led from the town, Sir Henry Simmerson was in sight coming to claim his victory and his victims for the triangle.

'For what we are about to receive,' Harper said softly.

'Quiet! Make them load. We'll give the man a demonstration.' Sharpe watched Simmerson's eyes as the slow dawning of his men's unbuttoned collars and the significance of the leather shreds on the grass occurred in his brain. Sharpe watched the Colonel take a deep breath. 'Now!'

'Fire!' Harper's command unleashed a full volley that echoed like thunder in the valley. If Simmerson shouted then his words were lost in the noise and the Colonel could only watch as his men worked their muskets like veterans to the orders of a Sergeant of the Rifles, even bigger than Sharpe, whose broad, confident face was of the kind that had always infuriated Sir Henry, provoking his most savage sentences from the uncushioned magistrates' bench in Chelmsford.

The last volley rattled on to the stone wall and Forrest

tucked his watch back into a pocket. 'Two seconds under a minute, Sir Henry, and four shots.'

'I can count, Forrest.' Four shots? Simmerson was impressed because secretly he had despaired of teaching his men to fire fast instead of fumbling nervously. But a whole company's stocks? At two and threepence a piece? And on a day when his nephew had come in smelling like a stable hand? 'God damn your eyes, Sharpe!'

'Yes, sir.'

The acrid powder smoke made Sir Henry's horse twitch its head and the Colonel reached forward to quiet it. Sharpe watched the gesture and knew that he had made a fool of the Colonel in front of his own men and he knew, too, that it had been a mistake. Sharpe had won a small victory but in doing so he had made an enemy who had both power and influence. The Colonel edged his horse closer to Sharpe and his voice was surprisingly quiet. 'This is my Battalion, Mr Sharpe. My Battalion. Remember that.' He looked for a moment as if his anger would erupt but he controlled it and shouted at Forrest to follow him instead. Sharpe turned away. Harper was grinning at him, the men looked pleased, and only Sharpe felt a foreboding of menace like an unseen but encircling enemy. He shook it off. There were muskets to clean, rations to issue, and, beyond the border hills, enemies enough for anyone.

CHAPTER 4

Patrick Harper marched with a long easy stride, happy to feel the road beneath his feet, happy they had at last crossed the unmarked frontier and were going somewhere, anywhere. They had left in the small, dark hours so that the bulk of the march would be done before the sun was at its hottest and he looked forward to an afternoon of inactivity and hoped that the bivouac Major Forrest had ridden ahead to find would be near a stream where he could drift a line down the water with one of his maggots impaled on the hook. The South Essex were somewhere behind them; Sharpe had started the day's march at the Rifle Regiment's fast pace, three steps walking, three running, and Harper was glad that they were free of the suspicious atmosphere of the Battalion. He grinned as he remembered the stocks. There was a sobering rumour that the Colonel had ordered Sharpe to pay for every one of the seventy-nine ruined collars and that, to Harper's mind, was a terrible price to pay. He had not asked Sharpe the truth of the rumour; if he had he would have been told to mind his own business, though, for Patrick Harper, Sharpe was his business. The Lieutenant might be moody, irritable, and liable to snap at the Sergeant as a means of venting frustration, but Harper, if pressed, would have described

44

Sharpe as a friend. It was not a word that a Sergeant could use of an officer, but Harper could have thought of no other. Sharpe was the best soldier the Irishman had seen on a battlefield, with a countryman's eye for ground and a hunter's instinct for using it, but Sharpe looked for advice to only one man in a battle, Sergeant Harper. It was an easy relationship, of trust and respect, and Patrick Harper saw his business as keeping Richard Sharpe alive and amused.

He enjoyed being a soldier, even in the army of the nation that had taken his family's land and trampled on their religion. He had been reared on the tales of the great Irish heroes, he could recite by heart the story of Cuchulain single-handedly defeating the forces of Connaught and who did the English have to put beside that great hero? But Ireland was Ireland and hunger drove men to strange places. If Harper had followed his heart he would be fighting against the English, not for them, but like so many of his countrymen he had found a refuge from poverty and persecution in the ranks of the enemy. He never forgot home. He carried in his head a picture of Donegal, a county of twisted rock and thin soil, of mountains, lakes, wide bogs and the smallholdings where families scratched a thin living. And what families! Harper was the fourth of his mother's eleven children who survived infancy and she always said that she never knew how she had come to bear such 'a big wee one'. 'To feed Patrick is like feeding three of the others' she would say and he would more often go hungry. Then came the day when he left to seek his own fortune. He had walked from the Blue Stack mountains to the walled streets of Derry and there got drunk, and found himself enlisted. Now, eight years later and twenty-four years old, he was a Sergeant. They would never believe that in Tangaveane!

It was hard now to think of the English as enemies. Familiarity had bred too many friendships. The army was one place where strong men could do well and Patrick Harper liked the responsibility he had earned and enjoyed the respect of other tough men, like Sharpe. He remembered the stories of his countrymen who had fought the redcoats in the hills and fields of Ireland and sometimes he wondered what his future would be if he were to go back and live in Donegal again. That problem of loyalty was too difficult and he kept it in the back of his mind, hidden away with the vestiges of his religion. Perhaps the war would go on for ever, or perhaps St Patrick would return and convert the English to the true faith? Who could tell? But for the moment he was content to be a soldier and took his pleasure where it could be found. Yesterday he had seen a peregrine falcon, high over the road, and Patrick Harper's soul had soared to meet it. He knew every bird in Ulster, loved them, and as he walked he searched the land and sky for new birds because the Sergeant never tired of watching them. In the hills north of Oporto he had caught a quick glimpse of a strange magpie with a long blue tail, unlike anything he had seen before, and he wanted to see another. The expectation and the waiting were part of his content and his pleasure.

A hare started up in a field next to the road. A voice shouted 'Mine' and they all paused while the man knelt, took quick aim, and fired. He missed and Riflemen jeered as the hare twisted and disappeared in the rocks. Daniel Hagman did not miss often, he had learned to shoot from his poacher father, and all the Riflemen were secretly proud of the Cheshire man's ability with the rifle. As he reloaded he shook his head sorrowfully. 'Sorry, sir. Getting too old.'

Sharpe laughed. Hagman was forty but he could still outshoot the rest of the company. The hare had been running at two hundred yards and it would have been a miracle if it had ended up in the evening's cooking pots.

'We'll take a rest,' Sharpe said. 'Ten minutes.' He set two men as sentries. The French were miles away, there were British cavalry ahead of them on the road, but soldiers stayed alive by taking precautions and this was strange country so Sharpe kept a watch and the men marched with loaded weapons. He took off his pack and pouches, glad to be rid of the eighty pounds of weight, and sat beside Harper who was leaning back and staring into the clear sky. 'A hot day for a march, Sergeant.'

'It will be, sir, so it will. But better than that damned cold last winter.'

Sharpe grinned. 'You managed to keep warm enough.'

'We did what we could, sir, we did what we could. You remember the Holy Father in the Friary?' Sharpe nodded but there was no way to stop Patrick Harper once he was launched into a good story. 'He told us there was no drink in the place! No drink, and we were as cold as the sea in winter! It was a terrible thing to hear a man of God lie so.'

'You taught him a lesson, Sarge!' Pendleton, the baby of the company, just seventeen and a thief from the streets of Bristol, grinned over the road at the Irishman. Harper nodded. 'We did, lad. You remember? No priest runs out of drink and we found it. My God, a barrel big enough to drown an army's thirst and it did us that night. And we tipped the Holy Father head first into the wine to teach him that lying is a mortal sin.' He laughed at the memory. 'I could do with a drop right now.' He looked innocently round the men resting on the verges. 'Would anyone have a drop?'

There was silence. Sharpe leaned back and hid his smile. He knew what Harper was doing and he could guess what would happen next. The Rifles were one of the few Regiments that could pick and choose its recruits, rejecting all but the best, but even so it suffered from the besetting sin of the whole army; drunkenness. Sharpe guessed there were at least half a dozen bottles of wine within a few paces and Harper was going to find them. He heard the Sergeant get to his feet. 'Right! Inspection.'

'Sergeant!' That was Gataker, too fly for his own good. 'You inspected the water bottles this morning! You know we haven't got any.'

'I know you haven't any in your water bottles but that's not the same thing, is it?' There was still no response. 'Lay your ammunition out! Now!'

There were groans. Both the Portuguese and the Spanish would gladly sell wine to a man in exchange for a handful of cartridges made with British gunpowder, the finest in the world, and it was a fair bet that if any man had less than his eighty rounds then Harper would find a bottle hid deep in that man's pack. Sharpe heard the sound of rummaging and scuffling. He opened his eyes to see seven bottles had magically appeared. Harper stood over them triumphantly. 'We share these out tonight. Well done, lads, I knew you wouldn't let me down.' He turned to Sharpe. 'Do you want a cartridge count, sir?'

'No, we'll get on.' He knew the men could be trusted not to sell more than a handful of cartridges. He looked at the huge Irishman. 'How many cartridges would you have, Sergeant?'

Harper's face was sublimely honest. 'Eighty, sir.'

'Show me your powder horn.'

Harper smiled. 'I thought you might like a drop of something tonight, sir?'

'Let's get on, then.' Sharpe grinned at Harper's discomfiture. In addition to the eighty rounds, twenty more than the rest of the army carried, Riflemen also carried a horn of fine powder that made for better shooting when there was time to use it. 'All right, Sergeant. Ten minutes fast, then we'll march easy.'

At midday they found Major Forrest with his small, mounted advance party waving to them from a stand of trees that grew between the road and the stream Harper had been hoping for. The Major led the Riflemen to the spot he had chosen for them. 'I thought, Sharpe, that it might be best if you were some way from the Colonel?'

'Don't worry, sir.' Sharpe grinned at the nervous Major. 'I think that's an excellent idea.'

Forrest was still worried. He looked at Sharpe's men who were already hacking at the branches. 'Sir Henry insists on fires being built in straight lines, Sharpe.'

Sharpe held up his hands. 'Not a flame out of place, sir, I promise you.'

An hour later the Battalion arrived and the men threw themselves on to the ground and rested their heads on their packs. Some went to the stream and sat with blistered, swollen feet in the cool water. Sentries were posted, weapons stacked, the smell of tobacco drifted through the trees, and a desultory game of football started far away from the pile of baggage that marked the temporary officers' mess. Last to arrive were the wives and children mixed with the Portuguese muleteers and their animals, Hogan and his mules, and the herd of cattle, driven by hired labour, that would provide the evening meals until the last beast was killed.

In the somnolent afternoon Sharpe felt restless. He had no family to write to and no desire to join Harper vainly tempting non-existent fish with his maggots. Hogan was sleeping, snoring gently in a patch of shade, so Sharpe got up from the grass, took his rifle, and strolled towards the picquet line and beyond. It was a beautiful day. No cloud disturbed the sky, the water in the stream flowed clear, a whisper of a breeze stirred the grass and flickered the pale leaves of the olive trees. He walked between the stream and a field of growing corn, jumped a crude, wicker dam that stopped an irrigation channel, and into a rock-strewn field of stunted olives. Nothing moved. Insects buzzed and clicked, a horse whinnied from the camp site, the sound of the water faded behind him. Someone had told him it was July. Perhaps it was his birthday. He did not know on which day he had been born but before his mother died he remembered her calling him a July-baby, or was it June? He remembered little else of her. Dark hair and a voice in the darkness. She had died when he was an infant and there was no other family.

The landscape crouched beneath the heat, still and silent, the Battalion swallowed up in the countryside as though it did not exist. He looked back down the road the Battalion had marched and far away, too far to see properly, there was a dust cloud where the main army was still on the road. He sat beside a gnarled tree trunk, rifle across his knees, and stared into the heat haze. A lizard darted across the ground, paused, looked at him, then ran up a tree trunk and froze as if he would lose sight of it because of its stillness. A speck of movement in the sky made him look up and high in the blue a hawk slid silently, its wings motionless, its head searching the ground for prey. Patrick would have known instantly what it was but to Sharpe the bird was just another hunter and today, he thought, there is nothing for us hunters and, as if in agreement, the bird stirred its wings and in a moment had gone out of view. He felt comfortable and lazy, at peace with the world, glad to be a Rifleman in Spain. He looked at the stunted olives with their promise of a thin harvest and wondered what family would shake the branches in the autumn, whose lives were bounded by the stream, the shallow fields, and the high, climbing road he would probably never see again.

Then there was a noise. Too hesitant and far off to sound an alarm in his head, but strange and persistent enough to make him alert and send his right hand to curl unconsciously round the narrow part of the rifle's stock. There were horses on the road, only two from the sound of their hooves, but they were moving slowly and uncertainly and the sound suggested that something was wrong. He doubted that the French would have cavalry patrols in this part of Spain but he still got to his feet and moved silently through the grove, instinctively choosing a path that kept his green uniform hidden and shadowed until he stood in the bright sunlight and surprised the traveller.

It was the girl. She was still dressed like a man, in the black trousers and boots, with the same wide-brimmed hat that shadowed her beauty. She was walking, or rather limping like her horse, and at the sight of Sharpe she stopped and looked at him angrily as if she was annoyed at being seen unexpectedly. The servant, a slight, dark man leading the heavily loaded mule, stopped ten paces behind and stared mutely at the tall, scarred Rifleman. The mare also looked at Sharpe, swished its tail at the flies, and stood patiently with one hind leg lifted off the ground. The shoe was hanging loose, held by a single nail, and the animal must have suffered agonies on the heat of the stony road. Sharpe nodded at the hind foot. 'Why didn't you take the shoe off?'

Her voice was surprisingly soft. 'Can you do it?' She smiled at him, the anger going from her face, and for a second Sharpe said nothing. He guessed she was in her early twenties but she carried her looks with the assurance of someone who knew that beauty could be a better inheritance than money or land. She seemed amused at his hesitation, as though she was accustomed to her effect on men, and she raised a mocking eyebrow. 'Can you?'

Sharpe nodded and moved to the horse's rear. He pulled the hoof towards him, holding the pastern firmly, and the mare trembled but stayed still. The shoe would have fallen off within a few paces and he pulled it clear with the slightest tug and let the leg go. He held the shoe out to the girl. 'You're lucky.'

Her eyes were huge and dark. 'Why?'

'It can probably be put back on, I don't know.' He felt clumsy and awkward in her presence, aware of her beauty, suddenly tongue-tied because he wanted her very much. She made no move to take the shoe so he pushed it under the strap of a bulging saddlebag. 'Someone will know how to shoe a horse up there.' He nodded up the road. 'There's a Battalion camped up there.'

'The South Essex?' Her English was good, tinged with a Portuguese accent.

'Yes.'

She nodded. 'Good. I was following them when the

shoe came off.' She looked at her servant and smiled. 'Poor Agostino. He's frightened of horses.'

'And you, ma'am?' Sharpe wanted to keep her talking. It was not unusual for women to follow the army; already Sir Arthur Wellesley's troops had collected English, Irish, Spanish and Portuguese wives, mistresses, and whores, but it was unusual to see a beautiful girl, well horsed, attended by a servant, and Sharpe's curiosity was aroused. More than his curiosity. He wanted this girl. It was a reaction to her beauty as much as a reaction to the knowledge that a girl with this kind of looks did not need a shabby Lieutenant without a private fortune. She could take her pick of the rich officers, but that did not stop Sharpe looking at her and desiring her. She seemed to read his thoughts.

'You think I should be afraid?'

Sharpe shrugged, glancing up the road where the Battalion's smoke drifted into the evening. 'Soldiers aren't delicate, ma'am.'

'Thank you for warning me.' She was mocking him. She looked down at his faded red sash. 'Lieutenant?'

'Lieutenant Sharpe, ma'am.'

'Lieutenant Sharpe.' She smiled again, spitting him with her beauty. 'You must know Christian Gibbons?'

He nodded, knowing the unfairness of life. Money could buy anything: a commission, promotion, a sword fashioned to a man's height and strength, even a woman like this. 'I know him.'

'And you don't like him!' She laughed, knowing that her instinct was right. 'But I do.' She clicked her tongue at the horse and gathered up the reins. 'I expect we will meet again. I am going with you to Madrid.'

Sharpe did not want her to go. 'You're a long way from home.'

She turned back, mocking him with a smile. 'So are you, Lieutenant, so are you.'

She led the limping mare, followed by the mute servant, towards the stand of trees and the first drifts of blue smoke where the cooking fires were being blown into life. Sharpe watched her go, let his eyes see her slim figure beneath the man's clothes, and felt the envy and heaviness of his desire. He walked back into the olive grove as if by leaving the road he could wipe her from his memory and regain the peace of the afternoon. Damn Gibbons and his money, damn all the officers who could pay for the beauties who rode their thoroughbred mares behind the army. He encouraged his sour thoughts, swirled them round his head to try to convince himself that he did not want her, but as he walked between the trees he felt the horse-shoe nail still held in his right palm. He looked at it, a short, bent nail, and tucked it carefully into his ammunition pouch. He told himself it would come in useful; he needed a nail to jam the main-spring of the rifle when he stripped the lock for cleaning, but better nails were plentiful and he knew he was keeping it because it had been hers. Angrily he fished among the fat cartridges and threw the nail far away.

From the Battalion there came the sound of musket fire and he knew that two bullocks had been slaughtered for the evening meal. There would be wine with the stew, and Hogan's brandy after it, and stories about old friends and forgotten campaigns. He had been looking forward to the meal, to the evening, but suddenly everything was changed. The girl was in the camp, her laughter would invade the peace, and he thought, as he walked back by the stream, that he did not even know her name.

CHAPTER 5

The Regimiento de la Santa Maria would have conquered the world if words and display had been enough. But punctuality was not among their more obvious military virtues.

The South Essex had marched hard for four days to reach the rendezvous at Plasencia but the town was empty of Spanish troops. Storks flapped lazily from their nests among the steep roofs that climbed to the ancient cathedral which dominated both the town and the circling plain, but of the Santa Maria there was no sign. The Battalion waited. Simmerson had bivouacked outside the walls and the men watched jealously as other units arrived and marched into the tantalising streets with their wine-shops and women. Three men disobeyed the standing order to stay away from the town and were caught, helplessly drunk, by the Provost-Marshal and received a flogging as the Battalion paraded beside the River Jerte.

Finally, two days late, the Spanish Regiment arrived and the South Essex mustered at five in the morning to begin their march south to Valdelacasa. There was a chill in the air which the rising sun would disperse but as five thirty, the hour set for departure, came and went there was still no sign of the Santa Maria and the men stamped their feet and rubbed their hands to ward off the cold. The hour of six chimed from the bells in the town. The children who were waiting with their mothers to see the Battalion depart grew bored and ran through the ranks despite all the shouting that began with Simmerson and worked its way down to the Sergeants and Corporals. The Battalion was paraded beside the Roman bridge that spanned the river and Sharpe followed a grumbling Captain Hogan on to the ancient arches and stared into the water that tumbled round the vast granite boulders which had been left in the river-bed in some long-ago upheaval of the earth. Hogan was impatient. 'Damn them! Why can't we just march and let the beggars catch us up?' He knew well why it was impossible. The answer was called diplomacy and part of the price of cooperation with the touchy Spanish forces was that the native Regiment must march first. Sharpe said nothing. He stared into the water at the long weeds which waved sinuously in the current. He shivered in the dawn breeze. He shared Hogan's impatience and it was alloyed with frustrations that stirred inside him like the slow-moving river weed. He looked up at the cathedral, touched by the rising sun, and tried to pin down his apprehensions about the operation at Valdelacasa. It sounded simple. A day's march to the bridge, a day for Hogan to destroy the already crumbling arches, and a day's march back to Plasencia where Wellesley was gathering his forces for the next stage of the advance into Spain. But there was something, some instinct as difficult to pin down as the grey shadows that receded in the dawn, that told him it would not be that easy. It was not the Spanish that worried him. Like Hogan he knew that their presence was a political imperative and a military farce. If they proved as useless as their reputation suggested that should not matter, the South Essex was strong enough to cope with whatever was needed. And that was the problem. Simmerson had never met the enemy and Sharpe had little faith in the Colonel's ability to do the right thing. If there really were French on the south bank of the Tagus, and if the South Essex had to repel an attack on the bridge while Hogan laid his charges, then Sharpe would have preferred an old soldier to be making the decisions and not this Colonel of Militia whose head was stuffed with theories on battles and tactics learned on the safe fields of Essex.

But it was not just Simmerson. He looked at the road leading to the town where an indistinct group of women stood, the wives of the Battalion, and wondered whether the girl, Josefina Lacosta, was there. He had at least learned her name and seen her, a dozen times, mounted on the delicate black mare with a crowd of Simmerson's Lieutenants laughing and joking with her. He had listened to the rumours about her; that she was the widow of a rich Portuguese officer, that she had run away from the Portuguese officer, no one seemed sure, but what was certain was that she had met Gibbons at a ball in Lisbon's American Hotel and, within hours, had decided to go to the war with him. It was said that they planned to marry once the army reached Madrid and that Gibbons had promised her a house and a life of dancing and gaiety. Whatever the truth of Josefina there was no denying her presence, entrancing the whole Battalion, flirting even with Sir Henry who responded with a heavy gallantry and told the officers that young men would be young men. 'Christian needs his exercise, what?' Simmerson would repeat the joke and laugh each time. The Colonel's indulgence reached to letting his nephew break his standing order and take a suite of rooms in the town where he lived with the girl and entertained friends in the long, warm evenings. Gibbons was the envy of all the officers, Josefina the jewel in his crown, and Sharpe shivered on the bridge and wondered if she would ever go back to the flatlands of Essex and to a big house built on the profits of salted fish.

Seven chimed and there was a stir of excitement as a group of horsemen appeared from the houses and spurred towards the waiting Battalion. The riders turned out to be British and the ranks relaxed again. Hogan and Sharpe walked back to their men paraded next to Lennox's Light Company at the left of the Battalion and watched the newcomers ride to join Simmerson. All the riders but one were in uniform and the exception wore blue trousers under a grey cloak and on his head a plain bicorne hat. Ensign Denny, sixteen years old and full of barely suppressed excitement, was standing near the Riflemen and Sharpe asked him if he knew who the apparent civilian was.

'No, sir.'

'Sergeant Harper! Tell Mr Denny who the gentleman in the grey cloak is.'

'That's the General, Mr Denny. Sir Arthur Wellesley himself. Born in Ireland like all the best soldiers!'

A ripple of laughter went through the ranks but they all straightened up and stared at the man who would lead them towards Madrid. They saw him take out a watch and look towards the town from where the Spanish should be coming but there was still no sign of the Regimienta even though the sun was well over the horizon and the dew fading fast from the grass. One of the staff officers with Wellesley broke away from the group and trotted his horse towards Hogan. Sharpe supposed he wanted to talk to the Engineer and he walked away, back to the bridge, to give Hogan some privacy.

'Sharpe! Richard!'

The voice was familiar, from the past. He turned to see the staff officer, a Lieutenant Colonel, waving to him but the face was hidden beneath the ornate cocked hat.

'Richard! You've forgotten me!'

Lawford! Sharpe's face broke into a smile. 'Sir! I didn't even know you were here!'

Lawford swung easily out of the saddle, took off his hat, and shook his head. 'You look dreadful! You must really buy yourself a uniform one of these days.' He smiled and shook Sharpe's hand. 'It's good to see you, Richard.'

'And to see you, sir. A Lieutenant Colonel? You're doing well!'

'It cost me three thousand, five hundred pounds, Richard, and well you know it. Thank God for money.'

Lawford. Sharpe remembered when the Honourable William Lawford was a frightened Lieutenant and a Sergeant called Sharpe had guided him through the heat of India. Then Lawford had repaid the debt. In a prison cell in Seringapatam the aristocrat had taught the Sergeant to read and write, the exercise had stopped them both going mad in the dank hell of the Sultan Tippoo's dungeons. Sharpe shook his head. 'I haven't seen you for . . .'

'It's been months. Far too long. How are you?'

Sharpe grinned. 'As you see me.'

'Untidy?' Lawford smiled. He was the same age as Sharpe but there the resemblance stopped. Lawford was a dandy, dressed always in the finest cloth and lace, and

Sharpe had seen him pay a Regimental Tailor seven guineas to achieve a tighter fit on an already immaculately tailored jacket. He spread his hands expansively.

'You can stop worrying, Richard, Lawford is here. The French will probably surrender when they hear. God! It's taken me months to get this job! I was stuck in Dublin Castle, changing the bloody guard, and I've pulled a hundred strings to get on to Wellesley's staff. And here I am! Arrived two weeks ago!' The words tumbled out. Sharpe was delighted to see him. Lawford, like Gibbons, summed up all that he hated most about the army; how money and influence could buy promotion while others, like Sharpe, rotted in penury. Yet Sharpe liked Lawford, could feel no resentment, and he supposed that it was because the aristocrat, for all the assurance of his birth, responded to Sharpe in the same way. And Lawford, for all his finery and assumed languor, was a fighting soldier. Sharpe held up a hand to stop the flow of news.

'What's happening, sir? Where are the Spanish?'

Lawford shook his head. 'Still in bed. At least they were, but the bugles have sounded, the warriors have pulled on their trousers and we're told they're coming.' He leaned closer to Sharpe and dropped his voice. 'How do you get on with Simmerson?'

'I don't have to get on with him. I work to Hogan.'

Lawford appeared not to hear the answer. 'He's an extraordinary man. Did you know he paid to raise this Regiment?' Sharpe nodded. 'Do you know what that cost him, Richard? Unimaginable!'

'So he's a rich man. But it doesn't make him a soldier.' Sharpe sounded sour.

Lawford shrugged. 'He wants to be. He wants to be the best. I sailed out on the same boat and all he did, every

day, was sit there reading the Rules and Regulations for
His Majesty's Forces!' He shook his head. 'Perhaps he'll
learn. I don't envy you, though.' He turned to look at
Wellesley. 'Well. I can't stay all day. Listen. You must
dine with me when you get back from this job. Will you
do that?'

'With pleasure.'

'Good!' Lawford swung up into the saddle. 'You've
got a scrap ahead of you. We sent the Light Dragoons
down south and they tell us there's a sizeable bunch of
Frenchies down there with some horse artillery. They've
been trying to flush the Guerilleros out of the hills but
they're moving back east now, like us, so good luck!'
He turned his horse away, then looked back. 'And,
Richard?'

'Sir?'

'Sir Arthur asked to be remembered.'

'He did?'

Lawford looked down on Sharpe. 'You're an idiot.'
He spoke cheerfully. 'Shall I remember you to the
General? It's the done thing, you know.' He grinned,
raised his hat and turned away. Sharpe watched him go,
the apprehension of the cold dawn suddenly dissipated
by the rush of friendship. Hogan joined him.

'Friends in high places?'

'Old friend. We were in India.'

Hogan said nothing. He was staring across the field,
his jaw sagging in astonishment, and Sharpe followed
his gaze. 'My God.'

The Regimienta had arrived. Two trumpeters in pow-
dered wigs led the procession. They were mounted on
glossy black horses, bedecked in uniforms that were a
riot of gold and silver, their trumpets festooned with
ribbons, tassels, and banners.

'Hell's teeth.' The voice came from the ranks. 'The Fairies are on our side.'

The colours came next, two flags covered in armorial bearings, threaded with gold, tasselled, looped, crowned, curlicued, emblazoned, carried by horsemen whose mounts stepped delicately high as though the earth was scarcely fit to carry such splendid creations. The officers came next. They should have delighted the soul of Sir Henry Simmerson for everything that could be polished had been burnished to an eye-hurting intensity; whether of leather, or bronze, silver or gold. Epaulettes of twisted golden strands were encrusted with semi-precious stones; their coats were piped with silver threads, frogged and plumed, sashed and shining. It was a dazzling display.

The men came next, a shambling mess, rattled on to the field by energetic but erratic drummers. Sharpe was appalled. All he had heard of the Spanish army seemed to be true in the Regimienta; their weapons looked dull and uncared for, there was no spirit in their bearing, and Madrid seemed suddenly a long way off if this was the quality of the allies who would help clear the road. There was a renewed energy from the Spanish drummers as the two trumpeters challenged the sky with a resounding fanfare. Then silence.

'Now what?' Hogan muttered.

Speeches. Wellesley, wise in the ways of diplomacy, escaped as the Spanish Colonel came forward to harangue the South Essex. There was no official translator but Hogan, who spoke passable Spanish, told Sharpe the Colonel was offering the British a chance, a small chance, to share in the glorious triumph of the Spanish warriors over their enemy. The glorious Spanish warriors, prompted by their non-commissioned officers, cheered the speech while the South Essex, prompted by Simmerson, did the same. Salutes were exchanged, arms presented, there were more fanfares, more drums, all climaxing in the appearance of a priest who, riding a small grey donkey, blessed the Santa Maria with the help of small, white-surpliced boys. Pointedly the pagan British were not included in the pleas to the Almighty.

Hogan took out his snuff box. 'Do you think they'll fight?'

'God knows.' The year before, Sharpe knew, a Spanish army had forced the surrender of twenty thousand Frenchmen so there was no doubting that the Spaniards could fight if their leadership and organisation were equal to their ambitions. But, to Sharpe, the evidence of the Regimienta suggested that their immediate allies had neither the organisation nor the leaders to do anything except, perhaps, make bombastic speeches.

At half past ten, five hours late, the Battalion finally shrugged on its packs and followed the Santa Maria across the old bridge. Sharpe and Hogan travelled ahead of the South Essex and immediately behind a far from warlike Spanish rearguard. A bunch of mules was being coaxed along, loaded high with luxuries to keep the Spanish officers comfortable in the field, while, in the middle of the beasts, rode the priest who continually turned and smiled nervously with blackened teeth at the heathens on his tail. Strangest of all were three white-dressed young women who rode thoroughbred horses and carried fringed parasols. They giggled constantly, turned and peeped at the Riflemen, and looked incongruously like three brides on horseback. What a way, Sharpe thought, to go to war.

By midday the column had covered a mere five miles and had come to a complete stop. Trumpets sounded at the head of the Regimienta, officers galloped in urgent clouds of dust up and down the ranks, and the soldiers simply dropped their weapons and packs and sat down in the road. Anyone with any kind of rank started to argue, the priest, stuck among the mules, screamed hysterically at a mounted officer, while the three women wilted visibly and fanned themselves with their white-gloved hands. Christian Gibbons walked his horse to the head of the British column and sat staring at the three women. Sharpe looked up at him.

'The middle one is the prettiest.'

'Thank you.' Gibbons spoke with a heavy irony. 'That's civil of you, Sharpe.' He was about to urge his horse forward when Sharpe put a hand on the bridle.

'Spanish officers, I hear, are very fond of duelling.'

'Ah.' Gibbons stared icily down on Sharpe. 'You may have a point.' He wheeled his horse back down the road.

Hogan was shouting at the priest, in Spanish, trying to discover why they had stopped. The priest smiled his blackened smile and raised his eyes to heaven as if to say it was all God's will and there was nothing to be done about it.

'Damn this!' Hogan looked round urgently. 'Damn! Don't they know how much time we've lost? Where's the Colonel?'

Simmerson was not far behind. He and Forrest arrived with a clatter of hooves. 'What the devil's happening?'

'I don't know, sir. Spanish have sat down.'

Simmerson licked his lips. 'Don't they know we're in a hurry?' No one spoke. The Colonel looked round the officers as though one of them might suggest an answer. 'Come on, then. We'll see what it's about. Hogan, will you translate?'

Sharpe fell his men out as the mounted officers rode up the column and the Riflemen sat beside the road with their packs beside them. The Spanish appeared to be asleep. The sun was high and the road surface reflected a searing heat. Sharpe touched the muzzle of his rifle by mistake and flinched from the hot metal. Sweat trickled down his neck and the glare of the sun, reflected from the metal ornaments of the Spanish infantry, was dazzling. There were still fifteen miles to go. The three women rode their horses slowly towards the head of the Regimienta, one of them turned and waved coquettishly to the Riflemen and Harper blew her a kiss, and when they had gone the dust drifted gently on to the thin grass of the verge.

Fifteen minutes of silence passed before Simmerson, Forrest and Hogan pounded back from their meeting with the Spanish Colonel. Sir Henry was not pleased. 'Damn them! They've stopped for the day!'

Sharpe looked questioningly at Hogan. The Engineer nodded. 'It's true. There's an inn up there and the officers have settled in.'

'Damn! Damn! Damn!' Simmerson was pounding the pommel of his saddle. 'What are we to do?'

The mounted officers glanced at each other. Simmerson was the man who had to make the decision and none of them answered his question, but there was only one thing to do. Sharpe looked at Harper.

'Form up, Sergeant.'

Harper bellowed orders. The Spanish muleteers, their rest disturbed, looked curiously as the Riflemen pulled on their packs and formed ranks.

'Bayonets, Sergeant.'

The order was given and the long, brass-handled sword-bayonets rasped from the scabbards. Each blade

65

was twenty-three inches long, each sharp and brilliant in the sun. Simmerson looked nervously at the weapons. 'What the devil are you doing, Sharpe?'

'Only one thing to do, sir.'

Simmerson looked left and right at Forrest and Hogan, but they offered him no help. 'Are you proposing we should simply carry on, Sharpe?'

It's what you should have proposed, thought Sharpe, but instead he nodded. 'Isn't that what you intended, sir?'

Simmerson was not sure. Wellesley had impressed on him the need for speed but there was also the duty not to offend a touchy ally. But what if the bridge should already be occupied by the French? He looked at the Riflemen, grim in their dark uniforms, and then at the Spanish who lolled in the roadway smoking cigarettes. 'Very well.'

'Sir.' Sharpe turned to Harper. 'Four ranks, Sergeant.'

Harper took a deep breath. 'Company! Double files to the right!'

There were times when Sharpe's men, for all their tattered uniforms, knew how to startle a Militia Colonel. With a snap and a precision that would have done credit to the Guards the even numbered files stepped backwards; the whole company, without another word of command, turned to the right and instead of two ranks there were now four facing towards the Spanish. Harper had paused for a second while the movement was carried out. 'Quick march!'

They marched. Their boots crashed on to the road scattering mules and muleteers before them. The priest took one look, kicked his heels, and the donkey bolted into the field.

'Come on, you bastards!' Harper shouted. 'March as if you mean it!'

They did. They pushed their tempo up to the Light Infantry quick march and stamped with their boots so that the dust flew up. Behind them the South Essex were formed and following, before them the Regimienta split apart into the fields, the officers running from the white-walled inn and screaming at the Riflemen. Sharpe ignored them. The Spanish Colonel, a vision of golden lace, appeared at the inn doorway to see his Regiment in tatters. The men had scattered into the fields and the British were on their way to the bridge. The Colonel was without his boots and in his hand he held a glass of wine. As they drew level with the inn Sharpe turned to his men.

'Company! To the right! Salute!'

He drew the long blade, held it in the ceremonial salute, and his men grinned as they presented their arms towards the Colonel. There was little he could do. He wanted to protest but honour was honour and the salute should be returned. The Spaniard was in a quandary. In one hand, the wine, and in the other a long cigar. Sharpe watched the debate on the Spanish Colonel's face as he looked from one hand to the other, trying to decide which to abandon, but in the end the Colonel of the Santa Maria stood to attention in his stockings and held the wine glass and cigar at a dutifully ceremonious angle.

'Eyes front!'

Hogan laughed out loud. 'Well done, Sharpe!' He looked at his watch. 'We'll make the bridge before nightfall. Let's hope the French don't.'

Let's hope the French don't make it at all, thought Sharpe. Defeating an ally was one thing but his doubts about the ability of the South Essex to face the French were as real as ever. He looked at the white, dusty road stretching over the featureless plain and in a fleeting, horrid moment wondered whether he would return. He pushed the thought away and gripped the stock of his rifle. With his other hand he unconsciously felt the lump over his breastbone. Harper saw the gesture. Sharpe thought it was a secret that round his neck he had a leather bag in which he kept his worldly wealth but all his men knew it was there and Sergeant Harper knew that when Sharpe touched the bag with its few gold coins looted from old battlefields then the Lieutenant was worried. And if Sharpe was worried? Harper turned to the Riflemen. 'Come on, you bastards! This isn't a funeral! Faster!'

CHAPTER 6

Valdelacasa did not exist as a place where human beings lived, loved, or traded, it was simply a ruined building and a great stone bridge that had been built to span the river at a time when the Tagus was wider than the flow which now slid darkly between the three central arches of the Roman stonework. And from the bridge, with its attendant building, the land spread outwards in a vast, shallow bowl bisected by the river in one direction and the road which led to and from the bridge in the other. The Battalion had marched down the almost imperceptible incline as the shadows of dusk began to creep across the pale grasslands. There was no farming, no cattle, no sign of life; just the ancient ruin, the bridge, and the water slipping silently towards the far-off sea.

'I don't like it, sir.' Harper's face had been genuinely worried.

'Why not?'

'No birds, sir. Not even a vulture.'

Sharpe had to admit it was true, there was not a bird to be seen or heard. It was like a place forgotten and as they marched towards the building the men in green jackets were unnaturally quiet as if infected by some ancient gloom.

'There's no sign of the French.' Sharpe could see no movement in the darkening landscape.

'It's not the French that worry me.' Harper was really concerned. 'It's this place, sir. It's not good.'

'You're being Irish, Sergeant.'

'That may be, sir. But tell me why there's no village here. The soil is better than the stuff we've marched past, there's a bridge, so why no village?'

Why not? It seemed an obvious place for a village but on the other hand they had passed only one small hamlet in the last ten miles so it was possible that there were simply not enough people on the vast remoteness of the Estramaduran plain to inhabit every likely spot. Sharpe tried to ignore Harper's concern but, coming as it did on top of his own gloomy presentiments, he had begun to feel that Valdelacasa really did have a sinister air about it. Hogan did not help.

'That's the Puente de los Malditos; the Bridge of the Accursed.' Hogan walked his horse beside them and nodded at the building. 'That must have been the convent. The Moors beheaded every single nun. The story goes that they were killed on the bridge, that their heads were thrown into the water but the bodies left to rot. They say no one lives here because the spirits walk the bridge at night looking for their heads.'

The Riflemen heard him in silence. When Hogan had finished Sharpe was surprised to see his huge Sergeant surreptitiously cross himself and he guessed that they would spend a restless night. He was right. The darkness was total, there was no wood on the plain so the men could build no fires, and in the small hours a wind brought clouds that covered the moon. The Riflemen were guarding the southern end of the bridge, the bank on which the French were loose, and it was a nervous

70

night as shadows played tricks and the chill sentries were not certain whether they imagined the noises that could either be headless nuns or patrolling Frenchmen. Just before dawn Sharpe heard the sound of a bird's wings, followed by the call of an owl, and he wondered whether to tell Harper that there were birds after all. He decided not; he remembered that owls were supposed to be harbingers of death and the news might worry the Irishman even more.

But the new day, even if it did not bring the Regimienta who were presumably still at the inn, brought a brilliant blue sky with only a scattering of high, passing clouds that followed the night's belt of light rain. Harsh ringing blows came from the bridge where Hogan's artificers hammered down the parapet at the spot chosen for the explosion and the apprehensions of the night seemed, for the moment, to be like a bad dream. The Riflemen were relieved by Lennox's Light Company and, with nothing else to do, Harper stripped naked and waded into the river.

'That's better. I haven't washed in a month.' He looked up at Sharpe. 'Is anything happening, sir?'

'No sign of them.' Sharpe must have stared at the horizon, a mile to the south, fifty times since dawn but there had been no sign of the French. He watched as Harper came dripping wet out of the river and shook himself like a wolfhound. 'Perhaps they're not here, sir.'

Sharpe shook his head. 'I don't know, Sergeant. I've a feeling they're not far away.' He turned and looked across the river, at the road they had marched the day before. 'Still no sight of the Spanish.'

Harper was drying himself with his shirt. 'Perhaps they'll not turn up, sir.'

It had occurred to Sharpe that possibly the whole job would be done before the Regimienta reached Valdelacasa and he wondered why he still felt the stirrings of concern about the mission. Simmerson had behaved with restraint, the artificers were hard at work, and there were no French in sight. What could go wrong? He walked to the entrance of the bridge and nodded to Lennox. 'Anything?'

The Scotsman shook his head. 'All's quiet. I reckon Sir Henry won't get his battle today.'

'He wanted one?'

Lennox laughed. 'Keen as mustard. I suspect he thinks Napoleon himself is coming.'

Sharpe turned and stared down the road. Nothing moved. 'They're not far away. I can feel it.'

Lennox looked at him seriously. 'You think so? I thought it was us Scots who had the second sight.' He turned and looked with Sharpe at the empty horizon. 'Maybe you're right, Sharpe. But they're too late.'

Sharpe agreed and walked on to the bridge. He chatted with Knowles and Denny and, as he left them to join Hogan, he reflected gloomily on the atmosphere in the officers' mess of the South Essex. Most of the officers were supporters of Simmerson, men who had first earned their commissions with the Militia, and there was bad feeling between them and the men from the regular army. Sharpe liked Lennox, enjoyed his company, but most of the other officers thought the Scotsman was too easy with his company, too much like the Riflemen. Leroy was a decent man, a loyalist American, but he kept his thoughts to himself as did the few others who had little trust in their Colonel's ability. He pitied the younger officers, learning their trade in such a school, and was glad that as soon as this bridge was destroyed his Riflemen would get away from the South Essex into more congenial company.

Hogan was up to his neck in a hole in the bridge. Sharpe peered down and saw, in the rubble, the curving stonework of two arches.

'How much powder will you use?'

'All there is!' Hogan was happy, a man enjoying his work. 'This isn't easy. Those Romans built well. You see those blocks?' He pointed to the exposed stones of the arches. 'They're all shaped and hammered into place. If I put a charge on top of one of those arches I'll probably make the damn bridge stronger! I can't put the powder underneath, more's the pity.'

'Why not?'

'No time, Sharpe, no time. You have to contain an explosion. If I sling those kegs under the arch all I'll do is frighten the fishes. No, I'm going to do this one upside down and inside out.' He was half talking to himself, his mind full of weights of powder and lengths of fuse.

'Upside down and inside out?'

Hogan scratched his dirty face. 'So to speak. I'm going down into the pier and then I'll blow the damn thing out sideways. If it works, Sharpe, it'll bring down two arches and not just one.'

'Will it work?'

Hogan grinned happily. 'It should! It'll be one hell of a bang, I promise you that.'

'How much longer?'

'I'll be finished in a couple of hours. Perhaps sooner.' Hogan heaved himself out of the hole and stood beside Sharpe. 'Let's get the powder up here.' He turned towards the convent, cupped his hands to his mouth, and froze. The Spanish had arrived, their trumpeters in front, their colours flying, the blue-coated infantry straggling behind. 'Glory be,' Hogan said. 'Now I can sleep safe at nights.'

The Regimienta marched to the convent, past the South Essex who were being drilled in the field, and kept on marching. Sharpe waited for the orders which would halt the Spaniards but they were never given. Instead the trumpeters paced their horses on to the bridge, the colours followed, then the gloriously uniformed officers and finally the infantry itself.

'What the hell do they think they're doing?' Hogan stepped to the side of the bridge.

The Regimienta picked its way past the broken section and past the hole Hogan had dug. The Engineer waved his arms at them. 'I'm going to blow it up! Bang! Bang!' They ignored him. Hogan tried it in Spanish but the tide of men flowed on past. Even the priest and the three white-dressed ladies walked their mounts carefully round Hogan's hole and on to the south bank where Captain Lennox had hastily moved the Light Company out of their path. The Regimienta was followed by an apoplectic Simmerson trying to find out what the hell was happening. Hogan shook his head wearily. 'If it had been just you and I, Sharpe, we'd be on our way home by now.' He waved to his men to bring the kegs of powder out to the hole. 'I'm tempted to blow it up with that lot on the wrong side.'

'They're our allies, remember.'

Hogan wiped his forehead. 'So's Simmerson.' He climbed back into the excavation. 'I'll be glad when this lot's over.'

The kegs of powder arrived and Sharpe left Hogan to pack the gunpowder deep in the base of the arches. He walked back to the south bank where his Riflemen waited and watched as the Santa Maria paraded in a

74

long line across the road that led to the distant skyline. Lennox grinned down from his horse.

'What do you think of this, Sharpe?' He waved at the Spaniards who resolutely faced an empty skyline.

'What are they doing?'

'They told the Colonel that it was their duty to cross the bridge! It's something to do with Spanish pride. We got here first so they have to go further.' He touched his hat to Simmerson who was re-crossing the bridge. 'You know what he's thinking of doing?'

'What? Simmerson?' Sharpe looked after the retreating Colonel who had pointedly ignored him.

'Aye. He's thinking of bringing the whole Battalion over.'

'He's what?'

'If they cross, we cross.' Lennox laughed. 'Mad, that's what he is.'

There were shouts from Sharpe's Riflemen and he followed their pointing arms to look at the horizon. 'Do you see anything?'

Lennox stared up the track. 'Not a thing.'

A flash of light. 'There!' Sharpe climbed on to the parapet and dug into his pack for his only possession of value, a telescope made by Matthew Berge of London. He had no idea of its real worth but he suspected it had cost at least thirty guineas. There was a brass plate curved and inset into the walnut tube and engraved on the plate was an inscription. 'In gratitude. AW. September 23rd, 1803.' He recalled the piercing blue eyes looking at him when the telescope had been presented. 'Remember, Mr Sharpe, an officer's eyes are more valuable than his sword!'

He snapped the tube open and slid the brass shutters that protected the lens apart. The image danced in the glass, he held his breath to steady his arms, and panned the tube sideways. There! Damn the tube! It would not stay still.

'Pendleton!'

The young Rifleman came running to the bridge and, on Sharpe's instructions, jumped on to the parapet and crouched so that Sharpe could rest the telescope on his shoulder. The skyline leapt towards him, he moved the glass gently to the right. Nothing but grass and stunted bushes. The heat shimmered the air above the gentle slope as the telescope moved past the innocent horizon.

'Do you see anything, sir?'

'Keep still, damn you!' He moved the glass back, concentrating on the spot where the white, dusty road merged with the sky. Then, with the suddenness of an actor coming through a stage trapdoor, the crest was lined with horsemen. Pendleton gasped, the image wavered, but Sharpe steadied it. Green uniforms, a single white crossbelt. He closed the glass and straightened up.

'Chasseurs.'

There was a murmur from the Regimienta, the men nudged each other and pointed up the hill. Sharpe mentally split the line in half, then in half again, and counted the distant silhouettes in groups of five. Lennox had ridden across.

'Two hundred, Sharpe?'

'That's what I make it.'

Lennox fiddled with his sword hilt. 'They won't bother us.' He sounded resentful.

A second line of horsemen appeared. Sharpe opened the tube again and rested it on Pendleton's shoulder. The French were making a dramatic appearance; two

76

lines of cavalry, two hundred men in each, walking slowly towards the bridge. Through the lens Sharpe could see the carbines slung on their shoulders and on each horse there was an obscene lump behind the stirrup where the rider had strapped a netful of forage for his mount. He straightened up again and told Pendleton he could jump down.

'Are they going to fight, sir?' Like Lennox the young boy was eager for a brush with the French. Sharpe shook his head.

'They won't come near. They're just having a look at us. They've nothing to gain by attacking.'

When Sharpe had been locked in the Tippoo's dungeon with Lawford the Lieutenant had tried to teach him to play chess. It had been a hopeless task. They could never remember which chip of stone was supposed to represent which piece and their jailers had thought the scratched grid on the floor was an attempt at magic. They had been beaten and the chessboard scratched out. But Sharpe remembered the word 'stalemate'. That was the position now. The French could not harm the infantry and the infantry could not harm the French. Simmerson was bringing the rest of the Battalion across the bridge, threading them past an exasperated Hogan and his excavation, but it made no difference how many men the allies had. The cavalry were simply too quick, the foot-soldiers would never get anywhere near them. And if the cavalry chose to attack they would be annihilated by the dreadful close-range volleys and any horse that survived the bullets would swerve away or pull up rather than gallop into the close-packed, steel-tipped ranks. There would be no fight today.

Simmerson thought otherwise. He waved his drawn

sword cheerfully at Lennox. 'We've got them, Lennox! We've got them!'

'Aye, sir.' Lennox sounded gloomy, he would have liked a fight. 'Doesn't the fool realise they won't attack us? Does he think we're going to lumber round this field like a cow chasing a fox? Damn it! We've done the job, Sharpe. We've mined the bridge and it'll take an hour to get this lot back over.'

'Lennox!' Simmerson was in his element. 'Form your company on the left! Mr Sterritt's company will guard the bridge and, if you please, I'll borrow Mr Gibbons from you as my aide-de-camp!'

'Your gain is my loss, sir.' Lennox grinned at Sharpe. 'Aide-de-camp! He thinks he's fighting the Battle of Blenheim! What will you do, Sharpe?'

Sharpe grinned back. 'I'm not invited. I'll watch your gallant efforts. Enjoy yourself!'

The cavalry had stopped half a mile away, lined across the road, their horses' uncropped tails swishing at the summer flies. Sharpe wondered what they made of the scene in front of them; the Spanish advancing clumsily in four ranks, eight hundred men round their colours marching towards four hundred French horsemen while, at the bridge, another eight hundred infantry prepared to advance.

Simmerson assembled his company commanders and Sharpe listened as he gave his orders. The South Essex were to form line, in four ranks like the Spanish, and advance behind them. 'We'll wait and see, gentlemen, what the enemy does and deploy accordingly! Unfurl the colours!'

Lennox winked at Sharpe. It was farcical that two clumsy Regiments of foot thought they could attack four hundred horsemen who would dance out of the way and laugh at the efforts made against them. The French commander probably did not believe what was happening and, at the very least, it would provide him with an amusing story to tell when he rejoined Victor's army. Sharpe wondered what Simmerson would do when it finally dawned on him that the French would not attack. Probably the Colonel would claim that he had scared the enemy away.

The Ensigns pulled the leather covers from the South Essex colours, unfurled them, and hoisted them into their sockets. They made a brave sight even in the middle of this comedy and Sharpe felt the familiar pang of loyalty. The first raised was the King's Colour, a great Union Jack with the Regiment's number in the centre, and next the South Essex's own standard, a yellow flag emblazoned with the crest and with the Union flag stitched in the upper corner. It was impossible to see the flags, the morning sun shining through them, and not be moved. They were the Regiment; should only a handful of men be left on a battlefield, the rest slaughtered, the Regiment still existed if the colours flew and defied the enemy. They were a rallying point in the smoke and chaos of battle, but more than that; there were men who would hardly fight for England's King and Country but they would fight for the colours, for their Regiment's honour, for the gaudy flags that cost a few guineas and were carried in the centre of the line by the youngest Ensigns and guarded by veteran Sergeants armed with long wicked-bladed pikes. Sharpe had known as many as ten men to carry the colours in battle, replacing the dead, picking up the flags even though they knew that then they became the enemy's prime target. Honour was all. The flags of the South Essex were new and gleaming, the Regimental Colour devoid of battle honours, neither was torn by bullet or roundshot, but seeing them filled Sharpe with a sudden emotion and it changed the farce of Simmerson's mad hopes into an affair of honour.

The South Essex followed the Regimienta towards the horsemen. Like the Spanish the British line was a hundred and fifty yards wide, its four ranks tipped with bayonets, the company officers riding or walking with drawn swords. The Spanish had halted, some four hundred yards up the road, and Simmerson had no choice but to stop the Battalion to find out what the Regimienta intended. Hogan joined Sharpe and nodded at the two Regiments.

'Not joining in the battle?'

'I think it's a private party. Captain Sterritt and I are guarding the bridge.'

Sterritt, a mild man, smiled nervously at Sharpe and Hogan. Like his Colonel he was appalled at the appearance of these veteran soldiers and secretly frightened that the enemy might prove to be as tough and carefree as the Rifleman or the Engineer. Hogan was wiping his hands on a piece of rag and Sharpe asked him if the job was finished.

'Aye. It's all done. Ten kegs of powder snuggled down, fuses laid, and the hole filled in. As soon as these gallant soldiers get the hell out of my way I can find out whether it works or not. Now what's happening?'

The Spanish were forming square. A good Battalion could march from line into square in thirty seconds but the Spanish took four times as long. It was the proper formation when faced by attacking cavalry but as the French showed no lunatic inclination to charge four times their own number the Spanish convolutions were hardly necessary. Sharpe watched as the officers and

Sergeants harried and chivvied their men into the rough semblance of a square, a slightly lopsided square, but it would do. Sharpe remembered the three women. He could not see them with the Regimienta and he looked round to see them watch decorously from the river-bank. One of them saw his glance and raised a gloved hand.

'It's a good job the French don't have those guns.'

Hogan raised his eyebrows. 'I'd forgotten that rumour. That would heat things up.'

There was no more fatal combination than cavalry and artillery for men on foot. Infantry in square were totally safe from cavalry; all the horsemen could do was ride round and round the formation hacking uselessly at the bayonets. But if the cavalry were supported by cannons the square became a deathtrap. Grapeshot would blast holes in the ranks, the cavalry would ride into the gaps and slice down with their sabres. Sharpe looked at the skyline. There were no guns.

Simmerson had watched the Regimienta form their square. He was obviously nonplussed. It must have occurred to him that he could not attack the French so the French had to attack him. There was a pause in proceedings. The Spanish had formed their rough square on the right of the track; Simmerson gave his orders and with a marvellous precision the South Essex demonstrated, on the left, how a Battalion should form a square. Even at half a mile Sharpe could see the horsemen clapping ironically.

Now there were two squares, the Spanish nearer the French, and still the horsemen made no move. Time passed. The sun climbed higher in the sky, the grassland shivered in the haze, the French horses lowered their necks and cropped at the thin pasture. Captain

Sterritt, guarding the bridge with his company, became plaintive.

'Why don't they attack?'

'Would you?' Sharpe asked.

Sterritt looked puzzled. Sharpe could understand why. Simmerson was looking increasingly foolish, he had marched to war with drawn sword and unfurled banners and the enemy was refusing to fight. Now he was stranded, like a beached whale, in a defensive square. It was virtually impossible to make an ordered march while in a square formation; it was easy enough for the leading edge, they marched forwards, but the sides had to step sideways, and the rear edge walk backwards, all of them fighting off encircling horsemen. It was not impossible, Sharpe had done it, but when survival depends on doing the impossible then men will find a way. Simmerson wanted to move but he did not want his neat, ordered square to be torn out of alignment as he advanced. He could have resumed the line formation but then he would look even more foolish for having formed a square at all. So he stayed where he was and the French looked on, filled with wonderment at the strange antics of the enemies.

'Someone's got to do something!' Captain Sterritt frowned in bewilderment. War was not supposed to be like this! It was glory and victory, not this humiliation.

'Someone's doing something.' Hogan nodded at the South Essex. A horseman had been released from the square and was galloping towards the bridge.

'It's Lieutenant Gibbons.' Sterritt raised a hand to his Colonel's nephew who pulled his horse to a violent stop. His features were stern, filled with the seriousness of the moment. He looked down on Sharpe.

'You're to report to the Colonel.'

'Why?'

Gibbons looked astonished. 'The Colonel wants you. Now!'

Hogan coughed. 'Lieutenant Sharpe is under my orders. Why does the Colonel want him?'

Gibbons flung an arm towards the immobile French. 'We need a skirmish line, Sharpe, something to sting the French into action.'

Sharpe nodded. 'How far ahead of the square am I supposed to take my men?' He spoke in sweet reasonableness.

Gibbons shrugged. 'Near enough to move the cavalry. Hurry!'

'I'm not moving. It would be madness!'

Gibbons stared down at Sharpe. 'I beg your pardon.'

'I will not kill my men. I go more than fifty yards from that square and the French will ride us down like hares. Don't you know that skirmishers fall back from cavalry?'

'Are you coming, Sharpe?' Gibbons made it sound like an ultimatum.

'No.'

The Lieutenant turned to Hogan. 'Sir? Will you order Lieutenant Sharpe to obey?'

'Listen, laddie.' Sharpe noticed that he had broadened his Irish accent. 'Tell your Colonel from me that the sooner he gets back over the bridge the sooner we can put a hole in it, and the sooner we get home. And, no, I will not instruct Lieutenant Sharpe to commit suicide. Good day, sir.'

Gibbons wrenched his horse round, tearing at its mouth with the bit, and clapped his spurs into its side, shouted something unintelligible at Sharpe or Hogan, and galloped back towards the impotent square in spurts of dust. Sterritt turned to them, appalled.

'You can't refuse an order!'

Hogan's patience snapped. Sharpe had never heard the little Irishman lose his temper but the events had exasperated him. 'Don't you bloody understand? Do you know what a skirmish line is? It's a line of men scattered in front of the enemy. They'll be ridden down like scarecrows! Christ! What does he think he's doing?'

Sterritt blanched in front of Hogan's anger. He tried to placate the Engineer. 'But someone's got to do something.'

'You're quite right. They've got to get back over the bloody bridge and stop wasting our time!'

Some of Sterritt's company began tittering. Sharpe felt his own patience snap. He did not care if it was his job or not.

'Quiet!'

An embarrassed silence settled over the end of the bridge. It was broken by the giggling of the three Spanish women.

'We can start with them.' Hogan turned to them and shouted in Spanish. They looked at him, at each other, but he shouted again, insisting. Reluctantly they walked their horses past the Riflemen, past the officers, and back to the north bank.

'That's three less to get over the bridge anyway.' Hogan looked at the sky. 'It must be midday already.'

The French must have been as bored as anyone else. Sharpe heard the notes of a bugle and watched as they formed into four squadrons. They still faced the bridge; their leading squadron about three hundred yards beyond the Spanish square. Instead of the two long lines they efficiently made ranks of ten men, their commander ironically saluted the squares with his sword, and gave the order to move. The horsemen

84

went into a trot, they circled towards the Spanish, kept on circling, they were turning to ride away, back up the hill and off to the east where they would rejoin Marshal Victor and his army waiting for Wellesley's advance.

The disaster happened when the French were at the closest point where a wide turn would take them to the Regimienta de la Santa Maria. In frustration or in pride, but in complete stupidity, the Spanish Colonel gave the order to fire. Every musket that could be brought to bear exploded in flame and smoke, the balls shot uselessly away. A musket was optimistically effective at fifty yards; at two hundred, the distance between the French and the Spanish, the volley was simply thrown away. Sharpe saw just two horses fall.

'Oh Christ!' He had spoken out loud.

There was a simple mathematics to what happened next. The Spanish had shot their volley and would take at least twenty seconds to reload. A galloping horse could cover two hundred yards in much less time. The French Colonel had no hesitation. His column was sideways to the Spanish, he gave his orders, the bugle sounded, and with a marvellous precision the French turned from a column of forty ranks of ten men each into ten lines of forty men. The first two spurred straight into the gallop, their sabres drawn, the others trotted or walked behind. There was still no reason for them to succeed. An infantry square, even without loaded muskets, was impervious to cavalry. All the men had to do was stay still and keep the bayonets firm and the horses would sheer away, flow down the sides of the square, and be blasted by the loaded muskets at the sides and back of the formation.

Sharpe ran a few paces forward. With a dreadful certainty he knew what would happen. The Spanish soldiers were ill-led, frightened. They had fired a volley terrifying in its noise and smoke but their enemy was suddenly on them, the horses baring their teeth through the veils of musket smoke, the riders tall in their stirrups, shrieking, sabres aloft, and galloping straight for them. Like beads off a burst string the Spanish broke. The French launched another two lines of cavalry as the first crashed into the panicked mass. The sabres fell, rose bloodied, and fell again. The Chasseurs were literally hacking their way into the packed square, the horses unable to move against the crush of screaming men. The third line of Frenchmen swerved away, checked their line, and launched themselves against the Spaniards who had broken clear and were running for their lives. The Spanish dropped their muskets, ran for safety, ran towards the South Essex.

The French were among them, riding along with the running men, hacking down expertly on the heads and shoulders of the fugitives. Behind them more lines of cavalry were trotting knee to knee into the attack. The French sabres came down right and left, more Spaniards broke from the mass, the colours went down, they were sprinting towards the British square, desperate for its safety. The South Essex could not see what was happening, only the Spanish coming towards them and the odd horseman in the swirling dust.

'Fire!' Sharpe repeated the words. 'Fire, you idiot.'

Simmerson had one hope for survival. He had to blast the Spanish out of his way otherwise the fugitives would break into his own square and let the horsemen through after them. He did nothing. With a groan Sharpe watched the Spanish reach the red ranks and beat aside the bayonets as they scrambled to safety. The South Essex gave ground, they split to let the desperate men into the hollow centre, the first Frenchman reached the ranks, cut down with his sabre and was blasted from the saddle by musket fire. Sharpe watched the horse stagger from bullet wounds, it crashed sideways into the face of the square dragging down all four ranks. Another horseman came to the gap, he hacked left and right, then he too was plucked from his horse by a volley. Then it was over. The French came into the gap, the square broke, the men mixed with the Spanish and ran. This time there was only one place to go. The bridge. Sharpe turned to Sterritt.

'Get your company out of the way!'

'What?'

'Move! Come on, man, move!'

If the company stayed at the bridge it would be swamped by fugitives. Sterritt sat on his horse and gaped at Sharpe, stunned and overwhelmed by the tragedy before him. Sharpe turned to the men.

'This way! At the double!'

Harper was there. Dependable Harper. Sharpe led, the men followed, Harper drove them. Off the road and down the bank. Sharpe saw Hogan alongside.

'Get back, sir!'

'I'm coming with you!'

'You're not. Who'll blow the bridge?'

Hogan disappeared. Sharpe ignored the chaos to his right, he ran down the bank, counting his steps. At seventy paces he judged they had gone far enough. Sterritt had disappeared. He whirled on them.

'Halt! Three ranks!'

His Riflemen were there, they had needed no orders. Behind him he could hear screams, the occasional cough of a musket, but above all the sound of hooves and of blades falling. He did not look. The men of the South Essex stared past him.

'Look at me!'

They looked at him. Tall and calm.

'You're in no danger. Just do as I say. Sergeant!'

'Sir!'

'Check the flints.'

Harper grinned at him. The men of Sterritt's company had to be calmed down, their hysteria smoothed by the familiar, and the big Irishman went down the ranks forcing the men to take their eyes off the shambles ahead and look at their muskets instead. One of the men, white with fear, looked up at the huge Sergeant. 'What's going to happen, Sarge?'

'Happen? You're going to earn your money, lad. You're going to fight.' He tugged at the man's flint. 'Loose as a good woman, lad, screw it up!' The Sergeant looked down the ranks and laughed. Sharpe had saved eighty muskets and thirty rifles from the rout and the French, God bless them, were about to have a fight.

CHAPTER 7

It was a shambles. Four minutes ago sixteen hundred infantry had been ranked on the field, officered and organised, now most of them were running for the bridge; they threw away muskets, packs, anything that might slow them down and bring the methodical sabres of the French closer to their heels. The French Colonel was good. He concentrated some of his men on the fugitives, driving them at a trot, cutting left and right as simply as on the practice field, driving the panicked mass to the killing ground at the bridge's entrance. More horsemen had been ordered against the remnants of the British square, a huddle of men fighting desperately round the colours, but Sharpe could see more cavalry, standing motionless in two ranks, the French reserve which could be thrown in to sustain the attack or break any sudden resistance from the infantry.

There was no point in defending the bridge. It was well enough protected from the French by the turbulent mass of men struggling for its dubious safety. Sharpe guessed that perhaps a thousand men were trying to thread themselves on to a roadway just wide enough for an ox-cart. It was an unbelievable sight. Sharpe had seen panic on a battlefield before, but never quite like this. Less than a hundred horsemen were driving ten times their number in horrific flight. The crowd at the bridge could not move forward, the press of bodies was too great, but Spanish and British fought and seethed, clawed and shoved, desperate to escape the Chasseurs who cut at the fringes of the crowd. Even those who succeeded in pushing their way on to the bridge were not safe. Sharpe caught a glimpse of men falling into the water where the bridge was broken and where Hogan had destroyed the parapets. Other men, harried by sabres, joined the back of the crowd. The French had no chance of cutting their way through that immense barrier of bone and flesh; nor were they trying to get to the bridge. Instead the Chasseurs kept the panic boiling so that the men had no chance to reform and turn on their pursuers with loaded muskets and raised bayonets. The horsemen were almost lackadaisical in their sabre cuts. Sharpe saw one man cheerfully urging the fugitives on with the flat of his sword. It took effort to kill a man, especially if he was wearing his pack and had turned his back. Inexperienced horsemen swept their blades in impressive arcs that slammed into a soldier's back; the victim would collapse only to discover, astonished, that his injury was merely a sliced pack and greatcoat. The veteran Chasseurs waited until they were level with their targets and then cut backwards at the unprotected face and Sharpe knew there would be far more wounded than dead, horribly wounded, faces mangled by the blades, heads opened to the bone. He turned to his front.

Here there was proper fighting. The colours of the South Essex were still flying though the men surrounding them had lost all semblance of a proper formation. They had been forced into a crude ring, pressed back by horsemen, and they fought off the sabres and hooves with sword and bayonet. It was a desperate fight. The French had thrown most of their men against the small band; they may have stood no chance of capturing the bridge but inside the terrified ring was a greater prize. The colours. For the French to ride off the field with captured colours was to ride into glory, to become heroes, to know that the tale would be told throughout Europe. The man who captured the colours could name his own reward, whether in money, women, or rank, and the Chasseurs tried to break the British resistance with a savage fury. The South Essex were fighting back, no less desperate, their efforts fired by the fanatical determination that their flags should not fall. To lose the colours was the ultimate disgrace.

It had taken Sharpe only a few seconds to comprehend the utter chaos in front of him; there were no choices to be made, he would go forward towards the colours hoping the ring of survivors could hold out against the horsemen long enough for his company to bring their muskets and bayonets into range. He turned to the men. Harper had done his work well. Riflemen were scattered through the ranks to bolster the frayed nerves of the men from Sterritt's company. The men in green jackets grinned at Sharpe. The men in red stood appalled and nervous. Sharpe noted that Harper had put a file of Riflemen at each end of the company, the vulnerable flanks which would be the weakest points of his force and where only steady nerves and rigid bayonets would deter the swooping horsemen. Two nervous Lieutenants had been pushed into the files and like the other men of Sterritt's company they flicked their eyes at the crowd near the bridge. They wanted to run, they wanted the safety of the other bank, but Sharpe could also see two steady Sergeants who had seen battle before and calmly waited for orders.

'We're going forward. To the colours.' Some of the faces were white with fear. 'There's nothing to be frightened about. As long as you stay in ranks. Understand? You must stay in ranks.' He spoke simply and forcibly. Some of the men still looked towards the fugitives and the bridge. 'If anyone breaks ranks they will be shot.' Now they looked at him. Harper grinned. 'And no one fires without my orders. No one.' They understood. He unslung his rifle, threw it to Pendleton and drew his killing blade. 'Forward!'

He walked a few paces in front listening to Harper call out the dressing and rhythm of the advance. He hurried. There was little time and he guessed that the first two hundred yards would be easy enough. They advanced over the flat, open ground, unencumbered by horsemen. The difficult stretch was the final hundred paces when the company would have to keep in ranks while they stepped over the dead and wounded and when the French would realise the danger and challenge them. He wondered how much time had elapsed since the fatal Spanish volley; it could only be minutes, yet suddenly he was feeling again the sensations of battle. There was a familiar detachment, he knew it would last until the first volley or blow, and he noticed irrelevant details; it seemed as if the ground were moving beneath him rather than he walking on the dusty, cracked soil of early summer. He saw each sparse blade of pale grass, there were ants scurrying round white specks in the dirt. The fight round the colours seemed far away, the sounds tiny, and he wanted to close the gap. There were the beginnings of excitement, elation even, at the nearness of battle. Some men were fulfilled by music, others by trade; there were men who took pleasure in working the soil, but Sharpe's instincts were for this. For the danger of battle. He had been a soldier half his life, he knew the discomforts, the injustices, he knew the half-pitying glances of men whose business let them sleep safe at night but they did not know this. He knew that not all soldiers felt it, he could feel ashamed of it if he gave himself time to think, but this was not the time.

The French were being held. Someone had organised the survivors of the British square and there was a kneeling front rank, its muskets jammed into the turf, bayonets reaching up at the chests of the horses. The sabres cut ineffectively at the angled muskets, there were shouts, screams of men and horses, a veil of powder smoke in which flashes of flame and steel ringed the colours. As he walked, the great sword held low in his hand, he could see riderless horses trotting round the mêlée where Chasseurs had been shot or dragged from the saddles. Some of the French were on foot, scything their blades or even tearing with bare hands at the British ranks. An officer of the South Essex forced his horse out of the ring, the ranks closing instantly behind him. He was hatless, his face unrecognisable under a mask of blood. He wrenched his horse into a charge and lunged his slim, straight sword into the body of a Chasseur. The blade stuck. Sharpe watched him tug at the handle, his crazed fanaticism turning to fear, and in an instant a Frenchman showed how it should be done, his sabre neatly spearing into the Englishman's chest, the blade turned, easily drawn out as the red-coated officer fell with his victim. Another Chasseur, on foot, hacked blindly at the unyielding ranks. A soldier parried the blow, jabbed forward with the bayonet, and the Frenchman was dead. Well done, thought Sharpe, the point always beats the edge.

A bugle call. He looked right and saw the French reserve walk forward. They advanced deliberately towards the carnage round the colours. They held no sabres and Sharpe knew what was in the mind of the French Colonel. The British square, or what was left of it, had held and the light cavalry sabres could not break it. But Chasseurs, unlike most cavalry, carried carbines and they planned to pour a volley from close range into the red-coated ranks that would tear them apart and let the swordsmen into the gap. He increased his pace but knew they could not reach the colours before the fresh cavalry and he watched, sickened, as with meticulous discipline some of the hacking swordsmen wheeled their mounts away from the crude square to give the carbines a field of fire. The horsemen picked their way through the dead and wounded. Sharpe saw the British feverishly loading muskets, skinning their knuckles on the bayonet blades as they rammed the charges into the barrels, but they were too late. The French stopped, fired, wheeled to let a second rank stop and hurl their volley at the South Essex. A few muskets replied, one Chasseur toppled to the ground, a ramrod wheeled wickedly through the air as some terrified soldier shot it from his half-loaded musket. The French volleys tore the front ranks apart; a great wound was opened in the red formation and the enemy poured in their curved blades to hold it apart and claw deeper into the infantry where they could snatch and win the greatest prize a man could win on a battlefield.

Sharpe's men were among the bodies now. He stepped over a British private whose head had been virtually severed by a sabre cut. Behind him someone retched. He remembered that most of the men of the South Essex had never seen a battle, had no idea what weapons did to a man's flesh. The survivors of the square were falling back towards him, retreating from the wounded edge, losing cohesion. He saw the colours dip and rise again, caught a glimpse of an officer screaming at the men, urging them to fight back at the horses that lashed with their hooves and carried the terrible sabres. There was so little time. More Frenchmen were fighting on foot, trying to beat aside the bayonets and force their way to the flag-staffs, to glory. Then he had his own problems. He saw a French officer tugging and hitting at his men; Sharpe's company had been spotted and the Frenchman knew what a hundred loaded muskets could do to the packed horsemen who were concentrated round the flags. He pulled some of the men out of the fight, aligned them hurriedly, and launched them against the new danger. He had only managed to scrape together a dozen men and horses. Sharpe turned.

'Halt!'

He kept his back to the horsemen. In his head he knew how many seconds he had and the frightened men of the South Essex who stared at him desperately needed a demonstration of what well-fought infantry could do to cavalry.

'Rear rank! About turn!' He needed to guard the rear in case any horsemen circled round. Harper was there. 'Front rank, kneel!'

He walked towards them, calmly, and climbed over the kneeling front rank so that he was in the safety of the formation. The horses were fifty yards away.

'Only the middle rank will fire! Only the middle

95

rank! Riflemen, hold your fire! Only the middle rank! Wait for it! Aim low! Aim at the stomach! We're going to let them come close! Wait! Wait! Wait!'

The swords of the French were bloodied to the hilt, their horses were lathered, the riders' faces drawn back in the rictus of men who have fought and killed desperately. Yet their victory over four times their number had been so easily gained that these horsemen thought themselves capable of anything. The dozen Frenchmen rode at Sharpe's company, oblivious of their danger, confident in their ecstasy that these British would collapse as easily as the two squares. Sharpe watched them come at a reckless gallop, saw the clods of turf thrown up by the hooves, the bared teeth and flying manes of the horses. He waited, kept talking in a measured, loud voice.

'Wait for them! Wait! Wait!' Forty yards, thirty. At the last moment the French officer realised what he had done. Sharpe watched him saw at his horse's bit but it was too late.

'Fire!'

The Chasseurs disintegrated. It was a small volley, only a couple of dozen muskets, but he fired it murderously close. The horses fell, a couple skidded almost to the front rank, riders were hurled on to the ground in a maelstrom of hooves, sabres and arms. Not one Chasseur was left.

'On your feet! Forward!'

He stepped in front again and led them past the bloody remains of their attackers. One Frenchman was alive, his leg broken by his falling horse, and he slashed upwards at Sharpe with his sabre. Sharpe did not bother to cut back. He kicked the wounded man's wrist so that the blade fell from his hand. The company stepped round the dead men and horses; they began to hurry, the fight round the colours was being lost, the British being forced back, the French inching forward behind the searing blades. Sharpe saw the long pikes of the Sergeants who guarded the colours being used; one of them swung over the chaos, it crashed on to a horse's head so that it reared up, throwing its rider, blood streaming from its forelock. The discipline of the square had vanished with the French carbine fire. Sharpe could see no officers, they had to be there, but now the French were close to the colours and men from the shattered square were running towards Sharpe and the safety of his levelled bayonets. He beat them aside with his sword, screamed at them to go to the side. He had to halt, unable to make headway against the fugitives, and he swung the flat of his blade at them. Harper joined him and beat at the fugitives with his rifle butt, the Irishman's huge bulk forced the running men to the flanks where they could safely join Sharpe's company. Then it was clear and he went on, the blade still swinging, his blood seething with the joy of it. He had not intended a bayonet charge but there was so little time. The colours were swaying, a Frenchman's hand on a staff was cut down by an officer's sword, and then the colours collapsed.

Sharpe screamed unintelligible words, he was running, the men behind him stumbling on bodies and slipping on the smears of new blood. A dismounted Chasseur came for him, the sabre cutting at him in a great sweep. He put up his blade, the Frenchman's sword shattered, he cut at his neck, felt the man fall and stumbled on. Horses blocked his sight of the colours, there were the cracks of the rifles, a man fell. He caught a glimpse of Harper bodily pulling a Chasseur off his horse, the Sergeant's face was a terrible mask of rage and strength. Another horseman came, heaving on his rein to clear his swing at Sharpe, and disappeared backwards as Sharpe cracked his great sword into the horse's jaw. He saw the horse rear up, screaming, the Chasseur let go of his sabre and Sharpe caught a glimpse of the shining blade hanging from its wrist strap as man and horse fell backwards. There was still a group of red coats by the fallen colours, surrounded by horsemen, and Sharpe saw two Frenchmen dismount to pull at the last defenders with their bare hands.

Then the red jackets seemed to disappear, there were only Chasseurs and French shouts of triumph as the dead were heaved from the staffs and the colours snatched up. Sharpe turned and held the blood-covered blade high over his head.

'Halt! Present!' He was directly in their line of fire and he threw himself flat, pulling Harper down, as he screamed the order to fire. The volley smashed overhead and then they were up and running. The musket balls had plucked the Frenchmen from the colours, the flags had fallen again but this time surrounded by enemy as well as British dead.

There were only a few yards to go but there were more horsemen spurring in towards the place where so many had died for the possession of the colours. Sharpe threw himself over the bodies, scrambled on blood and limbs, reached for a staff and pulled it towards him. It was the Regimental Colour, its bright yellow field torn with fresh holes, and he jammed his sword point downwards into a corpse and swung the staff like a primitive club at the horsemen. The King's Colour was too far away. Harper was going for it but a horse cannoned into the Sergeant and threw him back.

Another horse reared and swerved from the great billow of yellow silk in Sharpe's hand, a sword struck the staff and Sharpe saw splinters fly from the new wood, then he was hit by the net of forage strapped to the saddle and thrown over. He could smell the horses, see the hooves in the air over him, the face of the Frenchman framed by his silver shako chain bending towards him to pluck the colour from his hands. He held on. A hoof came down by his face, the horse twisted away from the flesh it had stepped on, the rider tugged and suddenly let go. Sharpe saw Harper swinging a great sergeant's pike. He had hit the rider in the spine with its blade and the man slid gently on top of Sharpe, his last breath sighing softly in the Rifleman's ear.

Sharpe pulled himself from beneath the body. He left the colour there, it was as safe as in his hands. Harper was swinging the pike, keeping the horsemen at bay. Where was the company? Sharpe looked round and saw them running towards the fight. They were so slow! He looked for his sword, found it, and plucked it from the body where he had thrust it. The horsemen still came, trying desperately to force their unwilling horses on to the mounds of dead. Sharpe screamed again, Harper was bellowing, but there was no enemy within sword's length. He went forward towards the King's Colour. He could see it lying beneath two bodies some five yards away. He slipped on blood, stood again, but there were three dismounted Frenchmen coming for him with drawn sabres. Harper was beside him, one Chasseur went down with the pike blade in his stomach, the other sank beneath Sharpe's blade which had cut through the sabre parry as though the Frenchman's sword was made of fragile ivory. But the third had got the Union Jack, had tugged it from the bodies and was holding it out to the mounted men behind. Sharpe and Harper lunged forward, the pike thunked into the Chasseur's back but he had done his job. A horseman had snatched the fringe of the flag and was spurring away. There were more Frenchmen coming, clawing at the two Riflemen for the second colour, too many!

'Hold them, Patrick! Hold them!'

Harper whirled the pike, screamed at them, was Cuchulain of the Red Hand, the inviolable. He stood with his legs apart, his huge height dominating the fight, begging the green-uniformed Frenchmen to come and be killed. Sharpe scrambled back to the Regimental Colour, pulled it from the body, and threw it like a javelin at the advancing company. He watched it fall into their ranks. It was safe. Harper was still there, growling at the enemy, defying them, but there was no more fight. Sharpe stood beside him, sword in hand, and the Frenchmen turned, found horses, and mounted to ride away. One of them turned and faced the two Riflemen, lifted a bloodied sabre in grave salute, and Sharpe raised his own red sword in reply.

Someone slapped his back, men shouted as though he had won a victory when all he had done was halve the victory of the French. The company was with them, standing with the dead, watching the Chasseurs trot away with their trophy. There was no hope of retrieving the King's Colour, it was already three hundred yards away, surrounded by triumphant horsemen at the beginning of its long journey which would take it over the Pyrenees to be mocked by the Parisian mob before it joined the other colours, Italian, Prussian, Austrian, Russian and Spanish that marked French victories round Europe. Sharpe watched it go and felt sickened and ashamed. The Spanish colours were there too, both of them, but they were not his concern. His own honour was tied up with the captured flag, his reputation as a soldier; it was a question of pride.

He touched Harper on the elbow. 'Are you all right?'

'Yes, sir.' The Sergeant was panting, still holding the pike which was bloodied for half its length. 'Yourself?'

'I'm fine. Well done. And thank you.'

Harper shook the compliment off but grinned at his Lieutenant. 'It was a rare one, sir. At least we got one back.'

Sharpe turned to look at the colour. It hung above the company, tattered and blood-stained, lost and regained. An officer was below it and Sharpe recognised Leroy, morose, solitary Captain Leroy whom Lennox had described as the only other decent soldier in the Battalion. His face was masked in blood and Sharpe pushed through the ranks towards him.

'Sir?'

'Well done, Sharpe. This is a miserable shambles.' The Captain's voice was strange, the accent unusual, and Sharpe remembered he came from America; one of the small band of loyalists who still fought for the Mother country. Sharpe indicated Leroy's head.

'Are you hurt badly?'

'That's just a scratch. I've been cut in the leg though.'

Sharpe looked down. Leroy's thigh was smothered in blood. 'What happened?'

'I was at the colours. Thank God you came, though Simmerson deserves to lose both. The bastard.'

Sharpe looked towards the bridge. Little could be seen of it because the field between was still full of French horsemen. There were puffs of smoke and the crackle of musketry so someone had organised a scratch defence but the Chasseurs were no longer fighting. Bugles called them from the slaughter, back up the road to where they formed ranks round their three trophies. They should feel proud of themselves, thought Sharpe, four hundred light cavalry had broken two Regiments, captured three colours, and all because of the stupidity and pride of Simmerson and the Spanish Colonel. He wondered where Simmerson was. He had not been in the group round the colours unless his dead body lay in one of the heaps. He turned to Leroy.

'Have you seen Simmerson?'

'God knows what happened to him. Forrest was there.'

'Dead?'

Leroy shrugged. 'I don't know.'

'Lennox?'

'I haven't seen him. He was in the square.'

Sharpe looked round the field. It was an appalling sight. The spot where they stood, where the colours had been fought for, was ringed with bodies. There were wounded men, stirring and crying, horses that lay on their sides, coughed blood, and beat the soil in a frantic tattoo. Sharpe found a Sergeant.

'Get those horses shot, Sergeant.'

'Sir?' The man stared dumbly at Sharpe.

'Shoot them! Hurry!'

He could not stand the sight of the wounded animals. Men walked to them and pointed muskets at their heads and Sharpe turned to count his Riflemen.

'They're all safe, sir.' Harper had counted already.

'Thanks.' They had been in little danger as long as they stayed in ranks and kept the bayonets steady. He remembered thinking the same thing as the South

Essex proudly marched up the field, banners waving, and now they were broken. He tried to estimate the butcher's bill. There were no more than thirty or forty dead Frenchmen on the field, a high enough price from four hundred, but they had gained glory for their Regiment and had inflicted appalling losses on the British and Spanish. A hundred dead? He looked at the piles of dead, the broken trail of bodies leading to the bridge, it was impossible to guess the numbers. It would be high, and there would be far more wounded, men whose faces had been laid open by the horsemen, blinded men who would be led to Lisbon, shipped home, and abandoned to the cold charity of a society long inured to maimed beggars. He shivered.

But it was not just the dead and injured. In its first fight Simmerson's Battalion had lost its pride as well. For sixteen years Sharpe had fought for the army, had defended colours in the mêlée of battle and thrust with a bayonet as he tried to reach the enemy's standard, he had seen captured banners paraded through camp and felt the fierce elation of victory, but this was the first time he had seen a British flag taken on the field and he knew how his enemies would celebrate when the trophy reached Marshal Victor's army. Soon Wellesley's army would have to fight a battle, not a skirmish against four squadrons of Chasseurs, but a real battle in which the killing machines of the artillery made survival a game of chance and their enemies would now go into that battle with their spirits raised because they had already humiliated the British. He felt the beginnings of an idea, an idea so outrageous that he smiled and young Pendleton, waiting to return his rifle, grinned back at his officer.

'We did it, sir! We did it!'

'Did what?' Sharpe wanted to savour his idea but there was too much to do.

'Saved the flag, sir. Didn't we?'

Sharpe looked at the teenager's face. After a life of thieving in the streets of Bristol the boy had a pinched, hungry face but his eyes were shining and there was a desperate plea for reassurance in his expression. Sharpe smiled. 'We did it.'

'I know we lost the other one, sir, but that wasn't our fault, was it, sir?'

'No. If it hadn't been for us they'd have lost both flags. Well done!'

The boy beamed. 'And you and Sergeant Harper, sir.' The boy's words tumbled out in his urgent need to share the excitement. 'They were terrified of you, sir!'

Sharpe took his rifle and laughed. 'I don't know about Sergeant Harper, but I was fairly frightened, too.'

Pendleton laughed. 'You're just saying that, sir!'

Sharpe smiled and walked away among the bodies. There was so much to do, the dead to be buried, the wounded to be patched up. He looked towards the bridge. It was empty now, the fugitives had crossed and Sharpe could see them being organised into companies on the far bank. The French were half a mile away, in ordered ranks, and watching a lone horseman who was trotting his horse towards Sharpe. He supposed it was a French officer coming to discuss a truce while they sorted out their wounded. Sharpe felt a great weariness. He looked back at the bridge and wondered why Simmerson was not sending any men across to start the grave-digging, the bandaging, the stripping of the dead. It would take a whole day to clear up this mess. Sharpe slung his rifle and started walking towards the Chasseur officer whose horse was picking a delicate course through the bodies. He raised a hand in salute.

And at that moment the bridge exploded.

CHAPTER 8

The bridge was reluctant to be destroyed. It had stood through two millennia over the waters of the Tagus and the old stonework yielded slowly to the modern explosives. The central pier gave a deep shudder that was felt as far away as Sharpe and his company, they wheeled round to see what had caused it, and dust flew from the crevices of the masonry. For a second it seemed as if the bridge might hold, the stones bulged and then tore themselves apart with an agonising slowness until the black powder finally won and the masonry was blasted outwards in an obscene gout of smoke and flame. The road on the bridge rose into the air, hung suspended for a fraction, and then collapsed into the water. The pier, two arches, the purpose of the bridge, all were destroyed by the thunderous explosion that rolled interminably across the flat grasslands, frightening the horses of the French, making the loose horses whose owners had been unseated in battle whinny and gallop fitfully on the grass as though looking for human reassurance. A huge, dirty plume of smoke, boiling with ancient dust, rose over the ruined spans, the water seethed, far up and down stream the stones fell into the green depths; only slowly did silence follow the thunder, the river rearrange itself to the new pattern of stones on its bed, the black smoke drift slowly westwards like a small, low, malevolent storm cloud. Hogan need not have worried. Forty feet had been ripped from the bridge, Wellesley was safe from marauding cavalry to his south, and Sharpe and his men were now marooned on the wrong side of the Tagus.

Captain Leroy collapsed on the grass. Sharpe wondered if he had been hit by some stray and freakishly driven stone chip from the bridge but the Captain shook his head.

'It's my leg. Don't worry, Sharpe, I'll manage.' Leroy nodded towards the smoking ruins of the bridge. 'Why the hell did they do that?'

Sharpe wished he knew. Had it been a mistake? Hogan surely would have waited for Sharpe and his swollen company of two hundred men to reach the safety of the other bank before lighting the fuses that ran into the base of the pier? He stared across the river but there was no sense to be made of the activity he could see, the men parading in companies, he thought he could see Simmerson on his grey horse surrounded by officers staring at the destruction wrought to the bridge.

'Sir, sir.' Gataker, the Rifleman, was calling him. The French Chasseur officer had arrived, a Captain, with a suntanned face split by a large black moustache. Sharpe walked to him and saluted. The Frenchman returned the salute and looked round at the carnage.

'Congratulations on your fight, Monsieur.' He spoke perfect English; courteously, gravely, with respect. Sharpe acknowledged the compliment.

'You have our congratulations, too. You have won a notable victory, sir.' The words felt stilted and inept. It was extraordinary how men could claw savagely at each other, fight like demented fiends, yet in a few moments become polite, generous even about the damage an enemy had inflicted. The French Captain smiled briefly.

'Thank you, M'sieu.' He paused a moment, looked at the bodies lying near the bridge, and when he turned back to Sharpe his expression had changed; it had become less formal and more curious. 'Why did you come across the river?'

Sharpe shrugged. 'I don't know.'

The Frenchman dismounted and looped his reins on his wrist. 'You were unlucky.' He smiled at Sharpe. 'But you and your men fought well and now this?' He nodded at the bridge.

Sharpe shrugged again. The Chasseur Captain with the big moustache looked at him for a moment. 'I think perhaps you are most unlucky in your Colonel, yes?' He spoke quietly so that the men who were staring curiously at their erstwhile enemy should not hear. Sharpe did not react but the Frenchman spread his hands. 'We have them, too. My regrets, M'sieu.'

It was all getting too polite, too cosy. Sharpe looked at the bodies lying untended in the field. 'You wish to discuss the wounded?'

'I did, M'sieu, I did. Not that I think we have too many but we need your permission to search this piece of the field. As for the rest,' he bowed slightly to Sharpe, 'we are the masters of it.'

It was true. Chasseurs were now riding around the field corralling the stray horses. They were gaining a bonus for there were half a dozen English thoroughbreds, lost by officers of the South Essex, and Sharpe knew they would be better remounts than anything the French could hope to buy in Spain. But there was something curious about the wording the Captain had used.

'You did, sir? Did?' Sharpe looked into the sympathetic brown eyes of the Frenchman who shrugged slightly.

'The situation, M'sieu, has changed.' He waved a hand at the destroyed bridge. 'I think you will have problems on reaching the other side? Yes?' Sharpe nodded, it was undeniable. 'I think, M'sieu, my Colonel will want to renew the fight after a suitable period.'

Sharpe laughed. He pointed at the muskets, the rifles, the long bayonets. 'When you are ready, sir, when you are ready.'

The Frenchman laughed too. 'I will enquire, M'sieu, and inform you in ample time.' He pulled out a watch. 'Shall we say that we have one hour in which to look after our wounded? After that we shall talk again.'

He was giving Sharpe no choice. An hour was not nearly enough for his two hundred men to collect the wounded, carry them despite their agony, bring them to the entrance of the bridge and devise a way of getting them to safety. On the other hand an hour was far more than the French needed and he knew there was no point in asking for more time. The Captain unlooped his reins and prepared to mount.

'My congratulations again. Lieutenant?' Sharpe nodded. 'And my sincere regrets. *Bonne chance!*' He mounted and cantered back towards the skyline.

Sharpe took stock of his new company. The survivors from the square had added some seventy men to his small command. Leroy was the senior officer, of course, but his wound forced him to leave the decisions to Sharpe. There were two more Lieutenants, Knowles from the Light Company, and a man called John Berry.

Berry was overweight with fleshy lips, a young man who petulantly demanded the date of Sharpe's commission, and, on finding Sharpe was his senior, complained sulkily that his horse had been shot. Sharpe suspected that it was the only reason Berry had stayed with the colours.

The working parties took jackets from the dead, threaded the sleeves on to abandoned muskets, and made crude stretchers on which wounded men were carried to the bridge. Half the men worked on the piles round the spot where Sharpe and Harper had clambered across the blood and corpses to rescue the colour, the other half worked among the bodies that formed a fan shape ending at the entrance to the bridge. The French were swiftly finished and started rummaging through the blue-coated bodies of the Spanish. It was not mercy they were showing but a desire to loot the dead and the wounded. The British did the same, there was no stopping them, the spoils of a fight were the one reward of the survivors. The Riflemen, on Sharpe's orders, collected abandoned muskets, dozens of them, and took ammunition pouches from the dead. If the French should attack then Sharpe planned to arm each man with three or four loaded guns and meet the horsemen with a continuous volley that would destroy the attackers. It would not bring back the lost colour. That had gone for ever or until in some unimaginable future the army might march into Paris and take back the trophy. As he moved among the carnage, directing the work, he doubted if the French really meant to attack again. The losses they would incur would hardly be worth the effort; perhaps instead they were hoping for his surrender.

He helped Leroy to the bridge, propped him against

the parapet, and cut away the white breeches. There was a bullet wound in the American's thigh, dark and oozing, but the carbine ball had gone clean through and, despite Leroy's evident disgust, Sharpe summoned Harper to put maggots in the wound before binding it with a strip torn from the shirt of a dead man. Forrest was alive, stunned and bleeding, found where the colours had fallen with his sword still gripped in his hand. Sharpe propped him next to Leroy. It would be minutes before Forrest recovered himself and Sharpe doubted whether the Major, who looked like a vicar, would want to take any more military action that day. He put the colour with the two wounded officers, propped its great yellow flag over the parapet as a symbol of defiance to the French, but what about the British? Twice he had walked gingerly to the edge of the broken roadway and hailed the far bank but it was as if the men there inhabited a different world, went about their business oblivious of the carnage just a few hundred feet away. For the third time Sharpe walked out on to the bridge through the broken stones.

'Hello!' There could only be thirty minutes of the hour left. He cupped his hands again. 'Hello!'

Hogan appeared, waved to him, and came across the other part of the broken bridge. It was reassuring to see the Engineer's blue coat and cocked hat but there was something different about the uniform. Sharpe could not place the oddity but it was there. He waved at the gap between them.

'What happened?'

Hogan spread his hands. 'Not my doing. Simmerson lit the fuse.'

'For God's sake, why?'

'Why do you think? He got frightened. Thought the

French would swarm all over him. I'm sorry. I tried to stop him but I'm under arrest.' That was it! Hogan wore no sword. The Irishman grinned happily at Sharpe. 'So are you, by the way.'

Sharpe swore viciously and at length. Hogan let him finish. 'I know, Sharpe, I know. It's just plain stupid. It's all because we refused to let your Riflemen form a skirmish line, remember?'

'He thinks that would have saved him?'

'He has to blame someone. He won't blame himself so you and I are the scapegoats.' Hogan took off his hat and scratched his balding pate. 'I couldn't give a damn, Richard. It'll just mean enduring the man's spleen till we get back to the army. After that we'll hear no more about it. The General will tear him apart! Don't worry yourself!'

It seemed ridiculous to be discussing their mutual arrest in shouts across the gap where the water broke white on the shattered stonework. Sharpe waved his hand at the wounded.

'What about this lot? We've got dozens of wounded and the French are coming back soon. We need help. What's he doing?'

'Doing?' Hogan shook his head. 'He's like a chicken with its head chopped off. He's drilling the men, that's what he's doing. Any poor sod who doesn't have a musket will be lucky if he only gets three dozen lashes. The bastard doesn't know what to do!'

'But for Christ's sake!'

Hogan held up his hand. 'I know, I know. I've told him he's got to get timber and ropes.' He pointed at the forty-foot gap. 'I can't hope to get timber to bridge this but we can make rafts and float them across. But there's no timber here. He'll have to send back for it!'

'Has he done it?'

'No.' Hogan said no more. Sharpe could imagine the argument he had had with Simmerson and he knew the Engineer would have done his best. For a moment they discussed names, who was dead, who was wounded. Hogan asked after Lennox but Sharpe had no news and he wondered whether the Scotsman was lying dead on the field. Then there was the clatter of hooves and Sharpe saw Lieutenant Christian Gibbons ride on to the bridge behind Hogan. The blond Lieutenant stared down at the Engineer.

'I thought you were under arrest, Captain, and confined?'

Hogan looked up at the arrogant Lieutenant. 'I needed a piss.'

Sharpe laughed. Hogan waved, wished him luck, and turned back to the convent leaving Sharpe facing Gibbons across the water. The Lieutenant's uniform was clean and pristine.

'You're under arrest, Sharpe, and I am ordered to tell you that Sir Henry will request a General Court Martial.'

Sharpe laughed. It was the only possible response and it enraged the Lieutenant. 'It's no laughing matter! You are ordered to surrender your sword to me.'

Sharpe looked at the water. 'Will you fetch it, Gibbons? Or shall I bring it to you?'

Gibbons ignored the comment. He had been given a message to deliver and was determined to reach the end whatever the difficulties. 'And you are ordered to return the Regimental Colour.'

It was unbelievable. Sharpe could scarcely credit his ears. He stood on the shattered bridge in the searing heat while behind him were rows of wounded men whose cries could clearly be heard yet Simmerson had sent his nephew to demand that Sharpe surrender his sword and hand over the colour.

'Why was the bridge blown up?'

'It is not your business, Sharpe.'

'It damn well is, Gibbons, I'm on the wrong bloody side of it.' He looked at the elegant Lieutenant whose uniform was quite unstained by any blood or earth. He suspected Simmerson's uniform would be the same. 'Were you going to abandon the wounded, Gibbons? Was that it?'

The Lieutenant looked at Sharpe with distaste. 'Will you please fetch the colour, Sharpe, and throw it to this side of the bridge?'

'Go away, Gibbons.' Sharpe spoke with an equal disdain. 'Get your precious uncle to talk with me, not his lapdog. As for the colour? It stays here. You deserted it and I fought for it. My men fought for it and it stays with us till you get us back across the river. Do you understand?' His voice was rising with anger. 'So tell that to your fat windbag! He gets his colour with us. And tell him the French are coming back for another attack. They want that colour and that's why I'm keeping my sword, Gibbons, so that I can fight for it!' He drew the thirty-five inches of steel. There had been no time to clean the blade and Gibbons could scarce take his eyes off the crusted blood. 'And Gibbons. If you want this you can bloody well come and get it yourself.' He turned away from the Lieutenant, back to the wounded and dead, back to where Harper was waiting with a distressed face.

'Sergeant?'

'We found Captain Lennox, sir. He's bad.'

Sharpe followed Harper through the rows of wounded

who stared at him dumbly. There was so little he could do! He could bind up wounds but there was no way to dull the pain. He needed brandy, a doctor, help. And now Lennox.

The Scotsman was white, his face drawn with pain, but he nodded and grinned when Sharpe squatted beside him. Sharpe felt a pang of guilt when he remembered the last words he had spoken to the Captain of the Light Company only a few feet from this spot. They had been 'enjoy yourself'. Lennox grinned through the pain.

'I told you he was mad, Richard. Now this. I'm dying.' He spoke matter-of-factly. Sharpe shook his head.

'You're not. You'll be all right. They're making rafts. We'll get you home, to a doctor, you'll be all right.'

It was Lennox's turn to shake his head. It moved with agonising slowness and he bit his lip as a fresh stab of pain shot through him. The lower half of his body was soaked in blood and Sharpe did not dare pull at the soaked and torn uniform for fear of making the wound worse. Lennox breathed a long sigh.

'Don't cheat me, Sharpe. I'm dying and I know it.' His Scottish accent was thicker. He looked up into Sharpe's face. 'The fool tried to make me form a skirmish line.'

'Me too.'

Lennox nodded slowly. He frowned slightly. 'I was caught early on. Bastard laid me open with a sabre, right in the belly. I couldna' do a thing.' He looked up again. 'What happened?'

Sharpe told him. Told how the Spanish had broken the British square by seeking safety inside, how the survivors had rallied and beaten off the French attack, of the carbine fire and the loss of the colour. When he spoke of the King's Colour Lennox flinched in pain.

The disgrace of it hurt more than the ripped open body that was killing him.

'Sir! Sir!' A private was calling Sharpe but he waved him away. Lennox was trying to say something but the private insisted. 'Sir!'

Sharpe turned and saw three Chasseurs trotting towards him. The hour must be up.

'More trouble?' Lennox grinned weakly.

'Yes. But it can wait.'

Lennox's hand gripped Sharpe's. 'No. I can wait. I'll not die yet. Listen. I have something I want to ask you. You and that big Irishman. Will you come back? Promise?' Sharpe nodded. 'Promise?'

'I promise.' He stood up, surprised that he had to wipe his vision clear, and walked between the wounded to where the Chasseurs waited. The Captain who had come before was there and with him two troopers who looked curiously at the charnel house their sabres had created. Sharpe saluted, suddenly realising that he still held the sword with its crusted blade, and the French Captain winced when he saw it.

'M'sieu.'

'Sir.'

'The hour is up.'

'We have still not collected all our wounded.'

The Frenchman nodded gravely. He looked round the field. There was another hour's work and that was before Sharpe could hope to begin dealing with the dead. He turned back to Sharpe and spoke gently.

'I think, M'sieu, you must consider yourselves our prisoners.' He waved down Sharpe's protests. 'No, M'sieu, I understand. You can throw the colour to your compatriots, we are not after that, but your position is hopeless. The wounded outnumber your living. You cannot fight further.'

Sharpe thought of the muskets he had collected, each one loaded, each checked, they would destroy the French if they were foolish enough to attack. He bowed slightly to the Chasseur.

'You are thoughtful, sir, but you will see I am not from the Regiment whose standard you captured. I am a Rifleman. I do not surrender.' A little bravado, he decided, was not out of place. After all, the French Captain had to be bluffing; he was experienced enough to know that his men would not break an infantry formation properly led and he had proof enough that the tall Rifleman with the bloody sword could provide that leadership. The Captain nodded as if he had expected the answer.

'M'sieu. You should have been born a Frenchman. By now you would be a Colonel!'

'I began, sir, as a private.'

The Frenchman showed surprise. It was not uncommon for soldiers from the French ranks to become officers but clearly the Chasseur Captain had thought it impossible in the British army. Gallantly he raised his silver-looped shako.

'I congratulate you. You are a worthy opponent.'

Sharpe decided that the conversation was once again becoming too flowery and polite. He looked pointedly at the rows of wounded. 'I must get on, sir. If you wish to attack again, that is your affair.' He turned away but the Frenchman demanded his attention.

'You do not understand, Lieutenant.'

Sharpe turned back. 'Sir. I understand. Please permit me to continue?'

The Captain shook his head. 'M'sieu. I am not talking about we Chasseurs. We are merely the . . .' he paused, looking for the right word. 'The vanguard? Your position, Lieutenant, is truly hopeless.' He pointed up the hill to the far skyline but there was nothing there. The Captain waited and then turned back to Sharpe with a rueful smile. 'My timing, Lieutenant, is hopeless. I would have been a terrible actor.'

'I'm sorry, sir, I don't understand.'

But then he did. The Captain needed to say nothing more because there was a sudden movement on the crest and Sharpe had no need of his telescope to tell him what he saw. Horses, riderless horses, just a dozen but Sharpe knew what they meant. A gun, the French had brought up a gun, a field gun that could pound his small force into oblivion. He looked back to the Captain who shrugged.

'Now you understand, Lieutenant?'

Sharpe stared at the horizon. Only one gun? It was probably a small four-pounder so why only one? Were there more coming or had the French bent all their effort into getting one gun into action? If they were short of horses then it was possible that the others were miles behind. Presumably the Chasseurs had sent a message back to their main force that they were faced with two Regiments of infantry and the French had sent the gun as fast as they could to help break the squares. There was an idea far back in his head. He looked at the Captain.

'It makes no difference, M'sieu.' He held up his sword. 'Today you are the second person who has demanded my sword. I give you the same answer. You must come and take it for yourself.'

The Frenchman smiled, raised his own sword, and bowed. 'It will be my pleasure, M'sieu. I trust you will survive the encounter and do me the honour of dining with me afterwards. It is poor food.'

'Then I am glad I shall not have the honour of tasting it.'

Sharpe grinned to himself as the Captain rattled orders in French and the three men turned their horses back up the slope. For a bastard risen from the ranks he fancied he had played the diplomatic game like a master. Then the thought of Lennox came to him and he hurried back, all the time trying to pin the thought in his head. There was so much to be done, so many arrangements to make, and so little time but he had promised Lennox. He glanced backwards. The gun, with its limber, was coming slowly down the hill. He had a half hour yet.

Lennox was still alive. He spoke softly and quickly to Sharpe and Harper who looked at each other, back at the Scotsman, but promised him his last request. Sharpe remembered the moment on the battlefield when he had watched the French drag away the King's Colour, he remembered now the nature of that fleeting idea which had eluded him, and he squeezed Lennox's hand.

'I had already promised that to myself.'

Lennox smiled. 'You'll not let me down, I know. And Harper and you can do it, I know you can.'

They had to leave him to die alone, there was no choice, but the Scotsman's only other request was that he should die with a sword in his hand. They walked reluctantly away and the big Sergeant looked at Sharpe.

'Can we do it, sir?'

'We promised, didn't we?'

'Aye, but it's never been done.'

'Then we'll be the first!' Sharpe spoke fiercely. 'Now come on, we've got work to do!' He stared at the gun. It crept closer and closer and he knew now that his idea could work. It had loose ends, there always were unanswered questions, and he put himself in the place of his enemies and tracked the answers down. Harper saw the excitement on his Lieutenant's face, watched his hand grip and re-grip the sword hilt, and waited patiently for the orders.

Sharpe measured distances, angles, lines of fire. He was excited, the elation returning, there was hope despite the field gun. He summoned the Lieutenants, the Sergeants, faced them and slammed a fist into his open palm.

'Listen . . .'

CHAPTER 9

The time for regrets would come later, the time to be saddened by the carnage, to reflect on being alive and unwounded, most of all to regret that he could not have spent more time with the dying Lennox. Sharpe drew the great sword, hefted his rifle in his left hand, turned to the one hundred and seventy men who paraded in three ranks across the road.

'Forward!'

As they marched Sharpe let his thoughts dwell briefly on the conversation with Lennox. Had he convinced the dying man? He thought so. Lennox was a soldier, he understood that Sharpe had so little time, and the Rifleman was convinced he had seen relief in the Scotsman's face. Keeping the promise was another matter; first there was this day's business to complete. Forrest marched beside him, the two of them a few paces in front of the solitary colour that waved over the small formation; the Major was distinctly nervous.

'Will it work, Sharpe?'

The tall Rifleman grinned. 'So far it has, Major. They think we're mad.'

Forrest had insisted on coming along rather than stay with the wounded by the bridge. He was still a little dazed, shaken by the blow on his head, and he had refused Sharpe's offer to command the survivors in the face of the new French onslaught. 'I've never been in battle before today, Sharpe,' Forrest had said. 'Except that I once suppressed a food riot in Chelmsford and I don't think that counts.'

Sharpe could understand the Major's nervousness, was grateful that Forrest had given his blessing to what seemed to be an act of utter folly, yet Sharpe's instincts told him the plan would work. To the watching and waiting Chasseurs it looked as if the small British force was intent on committing suicide by a death or glory charge that stood no hope of success but would at least save them from the attrition of dying piecemeal from the blows of the French gunners. Forrest had asked, almost plaintively, why the enemy were continuing the fight, had they not already won a big enough victory? But the French must know how pitifully small was Wellesley's army, just a little over twenty thousand men. If they could utterly destroy the South Essex the French were taking away a thirtieth of the British infantry and giving themselves that much more certainty of annihilating Wellesley when the real battle came. Besides that, Sharpe was now offering them the chance to capture a second British colour that could be paraded in the French camp to persuade the soldiers of the fragility of the new enemy.

'Is it time, Sharpe?' Forrest was anxious.

'No, sir, no. A minute yet.'

They marched straight up the track towards the gun three hundred yards away. Sharpe's plan had depended on two things, and the enemy had obliged by doing both. First they had brought the small four-pounder as close to the British as safety allowed. They would not want to use solid roundshot against the infantry, instead Sharpe knew they would load the gun with canister, the deadly metal container of musket balls and scrap iron that shattered as soon as it left the barrel and sprayed its lethal mixture like bent nails fired from a coachman's blunderbuss. No doubt the French expected the British to lie down in the broken ground by the waterside, sheltered by the falling river-bank, but the canisters would have sought them out even there and killed them two by two, three by three. Instead the British were marching straight for the gun, like sheep walking into a slaughterhouse, and the French gunners would probably need no more than three rounds to tear them apart and let the cavalry finish the dazed survivors off. Sharpe's second guess was about the cavalry. He had felt an enormous relief when they paraded to the British right. He had expected that, but if they had gone to the left the plan could never have been started and they would have had no option but to die by the bridge. The ground to the right was thinly strewn with bodies, unlike the left which was an obstacle course of dead men and horses, and Sharpe had guessed that the French Colonel, charging obliquely to the fire of his cannon, would want an unobstructed path for the horsemen who now waited for the gun to open fire.

He watched the French gunners. They were unhurried, there was no need for haste, and they glanced constantly at the British force which marched conveniently towards their gun. It was pointing directly at Sharpe. He could see the dirty green-painted carriage, the dulled brass barrel, and the blackened muzzle. He had watched the efficient gun crew lever the three-quarters of a ton until the four and a half feet of barrel pointed straight down the road. Now a blue-coated gunner was putting the serge bag with its one and a half pounds of black powder in the cannon. A second man rammed it down and Sharpe saw a third man lean over the touch-hole and thrust down with a spike so that the serge bag was pierced and the powder could be set off by the fuse. Another gunner was walking forward with the metal canister. It was only seconds now before the gun would be ready to fire. He lifted his rifle into the air and pulled the trigger.

'Now!'

His one hundred and seventy men began to run, a shambling lung-bursting run in their broken shoes. Each soldier carried three loaded muskets, two slung on their shoulders, one carried in their hands. They kept roughly aligned, if the cavalry moved they could close ranks in seconds, form the impenetrable wall of bayonets. The French gunners heard the rifle shot, paused to watch their enemy break into their cumbrous run, and grinned at the futility of the men who thought they could charge a field gun. Then everything changed.

In the twenty minutes after the visit of the Chasseur Captain the British had continued to collect their wounded. Sharpe was certain the French had noticed nothing odd about the stream of men who went to and from the bodies that lay thickly around the spot where he and Harper had saved the Regimental Colour. In those twenty minutes Sharpe had hidden thirty men among the dead, ten Riflemen who lay crumpled in borrowed red jackets, and twenty men of the South Essex. Each Rifleman carried two rifles, one borrowed from a comrade, and every redcoat lay with three loaded muskets. The French had ignored them. They unlimbered the gun and lined it on target and had taken no notice of the scattered bodies that lay thickly just a hundred paces to their right. The time for looting would be later; first the gunners would destroy the presumptuous English who were half running, half walking, towards them.

Harper sweated in his borrowed jacket. It was much too small for him and he had ripped the seams in both armpits but even so he could feel the sweat trickling down to the small of his back. The red jackets were essential. The French had become accustomed to the sight of the dead men and would have been certain to notice if suddenly ten bodies in green uniforms had appeared among the corpses. Harper's biggest fear had been that the French might wander over to loot the bodies, but they had been ignored. He watched Sharpe march towards them, still two hundred and fifty yards away, and heard Lieutenant Knowles sigh with relief as Sharpe lifted his rifle in the air. Knowles was nominally in charge of the thirty men but Harper was satisfied the inexperienced Lieutenant would do nothing without first talking to him and he suspected Sharpe had told Knowles, in no uncertain way, to leave the decisions to Harper.

The sound of the shot came flatly up the field. With relief Harper stretched his muscles and knelt upwards. 'Take your time, lads, make the shots tell.'

To hurry could destroy their purpose. The Riflemen aimed deliberately, let the cramp ease in their arms, the first shots would be the most important. Hagman was first, Harper had expected that, and he watched approvingly as the Cheshire poacher grunted over his backsight and pulled the trigger. The gunner who was on the point of inserting the fuse spun away from the barrel and fell. In the next two seconds another eight bullets slaughtered three more of the French gun crew, the four survivors scrambled desperately for the scanty cover provided by the trail and the spokes of the gun's wheels. The gun could not be fired now. The canister was still not loaded, Harper could see it lying beside a dead gunner who had fallen by the brass muzzle, and any man who dared to try to thrust the projectile into the barrel would be sure to be cut down by the deadly rifles. The French had stopped using rifles on the battlefield, they had abandoned them because they were too slow to load, but these gunners were learning that even the slow rifle had its advantages over the speedy musket which could never hope to be accurate at a hundred paces.

'Cease firing!' The Riflemen looked at Harper. 'Hagman!'

'Sarge?'

'Keep them busy. Gataker, Sims, Harvey!' The three looked at him expectantly. 'You load for Hagman. You others, aim for the cavalry officers.'

Lieutenant Knowles ran and crouched beside the Sergeant. 'Is there anything we can do?'

'Not yet, sir. We'll move in a minute.'

Knowles and the twenty men with muskets were there to protect the Riflemen if the French cavalry charged them, as surely they must. Harper stared at the horsemen. They seemed as surprised as the gunners and sat on their horses staring at the slaughtered artillerymen as if not believing their eyes. They had expected the gun to blow the British infantry into ragged ruin and now it dawned on them that there was no gun, no easy victory. Harper raised his first rifle, snapped the backsight into the upright position, and guessed the horsemen were three hundred yards away. It was a long shot for a rifle, but not impossible, and the French had conveniently bunched their senior officers in a small group forward of their first line. As he pulled the trigger he heard other rifles fire, he saw the group pull apart, a horse went down, two officers fell dead or wounded. The French were temporarily leaderless. The initiative, as Sharpe had planned, had gone totally to the British. Harper stood up.

'Hagman's group! Keep firing. You others! Follow me!'

He ran towards the gun, curving wide so that Hagman had an uninterrupted field of fire, and the men followed him. The plan had been for the Riflemen to destroy the gunners and let Sharpe's company capture the gun but Harper could see his Lieutenant still had a long way to go and neither he nor Sharpe had expected the gun to be placed so conveniently close to the ambush party. Knowles felt astonished at the rush for the gun but the huge Irishman was so infectious that he found himself urging the redcoats on as they dodged the bodies and ran for the gun that loomed larger and larger. The surviving artillerymen took one look at the seeming dead who had come to life, and fled. As Harper sprinted the final few yards he was aware of Hagman's spaced shots ceasing and then he was there, his hands actually on the brass muzzle, the men surrounding him.

'Sir?'

'Sergeant?' Knowles was panting.

'Two ranks between the gun and the cavalry?' Harper made it sound like a request but Knowles nodded as if it had been an order. The young Lieutenant was frantically nervous. He had seen his new Battalion destroyed by cavalry, watched the King's Colour dragged from the field, and fought off the sabres with the sword his father had bought him for fifteen guineas at Kerrigan's in Birmingham. He had watched Sharpe and Sergeant Harper recover the Regimental Colour and had been astonished by their action. Now he wanted to prove to the Riflemen that his men could fight just as effectively and he lined up his small force and stared at the cavalry which was at last moving. It seemed as if a hundred horsemen were advancing towards the gun, the rest were slanting off towards Sharpe, and Knowles remembered the sabres, the smell of fear, and gripped his sword tightly. He was determined not to let Sharpe down. He thought of Sharpe's last words to him, the hands that gripped his shoulders and eyes that bored into him. 'Wait!' Sharpe had said. 'Wait until they're forty paces away, then fire the volley. Wait, wait, wait!' Knowles found it incredible that he was the same rank as Sharpe, he felt sure he would never have the easy manner of command that seemed so natural to the tall Rifleman. Knowles was awed by the French, they were the conquerors of Europe, yet Sharpe saw them as men to be outwitted and outfought and Knowles desperately wanted the same confidence. Instead he felt nervous. He wanted to fire his first volley now, to stop the French horses while they were a hundred paces away, but he controlled the fear and watched the horsemen walk forward, watched as a hundred sabres rasped from their scabbards and caught the afternoon sun in ranks of curved light. Harper came and stood beside him.

'We've got a treat for the bastards, sir.'

He sounded so cheerful! Knowles swallowed, kept his sword low. Wait, he told himself, and was surprised to hear that he had spoken out loud and that his voice had sounded calm. He looked at his men. They were trusting him!

'Well done, sir. May I?' Harper had spoken softly. Knowles nodded, not sure what was happening.

'Platoon!' Harper was in front of the tiny line of men.

He pointed to the ten men on the right. 'Sideways, four paces. March!' Then on the left the same order.

'Platoon! Backwards. March!'

Knowles stepped back with them, watching as the French eased their horses into a trot, and then understood. While he had been standing watching the French the Riflemen had moved the gun! Instead of pointing down the track it was now aimed at the French cavalry; somehow they had loaded it and the canister which should have swept the British off the road like a housewife scattering roaches with a broom was now threatening the cavalry instead. Harper stood at the back of the gun, well clear of the wheel. The gunners had done most of the loading, the Riflemen had thrust the canister into the barrel and found the slow match that burned red at the end of the pole. The fuse was in the touch-hole. It was a reed filled with fine powder and when Harper touched it the fire would flash down the tube and ignite the powder charge in its serge bag.

'Hold your fire!' Harper shouted clearly, he did not want the inexperienced men of the South Essex to fire when the gun went off. 'Hold your fire!'

The cavalry were seventy yards away, just urging their horses into the canter, ten riders in the first rank. Harper guessed that fifty men were aimed at the tiny party round the gun and there were fifty more in reserve. He touched the fuse on to the reed. There was a fizzing, a puff of smoke from the touch-hole, and then the enormous explosion. Grey-white smoke belched from the muzzle; the gun, on its five-foot wheels, lurched back its fifteen hundredweight that dug the trail into the soil and bounced the wheels off the ground. The thin metal canister split apart as it left the muzzle and Harper watched through the smoke as the musket balls and scrap iron snatched the cavalry off the field. The first three ranks were destroyed, the other two were dazed, unable to advance over the bloody corpses and the wounded who staggered upright, bleeding and shocked. Harper heard Knowles shouting.

'Hold your fire! Hold your fire!'

Good lad, thought the Irishman. The cavalry had split either side of the carnage, some of the reserve was galloping forward, but the horsemen seemed dazed by the sudden blow. They came on towards the gun but stayed clear of its line of fire and Knowles watched the two wings of horsemen as they drew nearer. He waited, waited until they put spurs to their horses and tried to gallop the last few paces, and slashed his sword down.

'Fire!'

The muskets coughed out flame and smoke. The leading horses dropped making a barrier to those behind.

'Change muskets!' Knowles felt the stirrings of confidence, the realisation that he could do it!

'Fire!'

A second volley destroyed the horsemen trying to close on the two sides of the gun. More horses fell, more men were pitched from their saddles in a flurry of arms, legs, sabres and scabbards. The horsemen behind went on, lapped round the back of the gun and the rifles started their sharper reports and more horses were shot. Knowles was startled to see no more horsemen in front of the cannon, he turned his men round, changed to the third musket, and blasted a third volley over the heads of the kneeling Riflemen.

'Thank you, sir!'

Harper grinned at the Lieutenant. The cavalry had gone, shattered by the canister, bloodied by the close volleys, prevented from closing with the infantry because of the barriers of dead and wounded horses. Harper watched as Knowles started his men reloading their muskets. He turned back to the gun. There was so much to remember! Sponge out, stop the vent, he summoned the Riflemen to reload their captured cannon.

Sharpe had seen the four-pounder fire, watched the horsemen cut down in a bloody swathe, then he had turned to the Chasseurs attacking his own formation. As the cavalry had come closer he had halted the three ranks, turned them to face the French except for the rear rank that about-turned to deal with the horsemen who would envelop the small formation. The horsemen were in savage mood. An easy victory had been snatched away from them, the gun had been captured, but there was still the insolent colour waving from the small group of infantry. They spurred towards Sharpe, their discipline ragged, their mood simply one of revenge and a determination to crush this tiny force like a boot heel stamping on a scorpion. Sharpe watched them come. Forrest glanced nervously at him and cleared his throat but Sharpe shook his head.

'Wait, Major, always wait.'

He and Forrest stood beneath the defiant colour. It taunted the French. They spurred towards it, the trumpet rang out its curdling charge, the Chasseurs screamed revenge, raised their sabres, and died.

Sharpe had let them come to forty yards and the volley destroyed the first line that opposed the British. The second rank of French horsemen clapped spurs to their mounts. They were confident. Had the British not fired their volley? They jumped over the writhing remains of the first rank and to their horror saw that the red-coated ranks were not busy reloading but were calmly aiming their muskets again. Some pulled desperately at their reins, but it was too late. The volley from Sharpe's second set of muskets piled the horses beside the bodies of the first line.

'Change muskets!'

The rear rank fired, once and twice. Sharpe whirled but the experienced sergeants had done well. His men were ringed with horses, dead and dying, stunned and wounded Chasseurs struggled from the mess and ran into the wide expanse of the field. The French had lost all cohesion, all chance of a further attack.

'Left turn! Forward!'

He ran on. He could see Harper and Knowles. The young Lieutenant looked calm and Sharpe could see the ring of French dead that showed he had learnt to hold his fire. The cannon fired again, shrouding the group in smoke, and Sharpe glanced back to see more horsemen fall where they were reforming ranks off to his right. A few horsemen still galloped round them; once Sharpe stopped and fired a volley of twenty muskets to drive off a group of six Chasseurs who came galloping up on the flank. Then his men reached the gun. Sharpe grabbed Harper, pounded him on the back, grinned up at the huge Irishman, and turned to congratulate Knowles. They had done it! Captured the gun, driven off the cavalry, inflicted terrible damage on men and horses and without a single scratch to themselves.

And that was it. With the gun in his hands Sharpe knew the French dare not attack again. He watched them circle well clear of its range as the British formed square. Forrest was beaming, looking for all the world like a Bishop who had conducted a particularly pleasing confirmation service. 'We did it, Sharpe! We did it!' Sharpe looked up at the colour over the small square. A little honour had been regained, not enough, but a little. A French gun had been captured, the Chasseurs had been mauled, some of the South Essex had learned to fight. But that was not all. Lashed to the trail of the captured gun, festooned on the limber, were ropes. Long, tough, French ropes that could span a broken bridge instead of haul the gun up steep slopes. Ropes and timber, all he needed to start taking the wounded back across the river.

At the bridge Lennox watched as a Chasseur officer walked his horse towards the British square. Negotiating again; but it would be too late for him. He felt cold and numb, the pain had passed and he knew that there was not long. He gripped the sword, some atavistic memory told him it was his pass into a better heaven; perhaps where his wife waited. He felt content, lazy but content. He had watched Sharpe walk suicidally forward, wondered what he was doing, then heard the distinctive crack of rifles, seen the figures running on the gun, and watched as the French cavalry broke themselves on the massed volleys of the infantry. Now it was over. The French would pick up their wounded and go and Sharpe would come back to the bridge. And he would keep the promise, Lennox knew that now; a man who could plan the capture of that gun would have the daring to do what Lennox wanted. That way there could be no shame in this day's work. The image of the colour, far up the smoke-veiled field, dimmed in the Scotsman's eyes. The sun was hot but it was damned cold all the same. He gripped the sword and closed his eyes.

CHAPTER 10

'Damn you, Sharpe! I will break you! I will see you never hold rank again! You will go back to the gutter you came from!' Simmerson's face was contorted with anger; even his jug ears had reddened with fury. He stood with Gibbons and Forrest and the Major tried ineffectually to stem Sir Henry's anger. The Colonel shook Forrest's arm off his elbow. 'I'll have you court-martialled. I'll write to my cousin. Sharpe, you are finished! Done!'

Sharpe stood on the other side of the room, his own face rigid with the effort of controlling his own anger and scorn. He looked out of the window. They were back in Plasencia, in the Mirabel Palace which was Wellesley's temporary headquarters, and he stared down the Sancho Polo street at the huddled rooftops of the poorer quarter of the town which were crammed inside the city's ramparts. Carriages passed below, smart equipages with uniformed drivers, carrying veiled Spanish ladies on mysterious journeys. The Battalion had limped home the night before, its wounded carried in commandeered ox-carts which had solid axles that screeched, Harper said, like the banshees. Mingled with the endless noise was the cries of the wounded. Many had died; many more would die in the slow grip of gangrene in the days ahead. Sharpe had been under arrest, his sword taken from him, marching with his incredulous Riflemen who decided the world had gone mad and swore vengeance for him should Simmerson have his way.

The door opened and Lieutenant Colonel Lawford came into the room. His face had none of the animation Sharpe had seen at their reunion just five days before, he looked coldly on them all, like the rest of the army he felt demeaned and shamed by the loss of the colour. 'Gentlemen.' His voice was icily polite. 'Sir Arthur will see you now. You have ten minutes.'

Simmerson marched through the open door, Gibbons close behind him. Forrest beckoned Sharpe to precede him but Sharpe hung back. The Major smiled at him, a hopeless smile, Forrest was lost in this web of carnage and blame.

The General sat behind a plain oak table piled with papers and hand-drawn maps. There was nowhere for Simmerson to sit so the four officers lined up in front of the table like schoolboys hauled in front of the Headmaster. Lawford went and stood behind the General who ignored all of them, just scratched away with a pen on a piece of paper. Finally the sentence was done. Wellesley's face was unreadable.

'Well, Sir Henry?'

Sir Henry Simmerson's eyes darted round the room as though he might find inspiration written on the walls. The General's tone had been cold. The Colonel licked his lips and cleared his throat.

'We destroyed the bridge, sir.'

'And your Battalion.'

The words were said softly. Sharpe had seen Wellesley like this before, masking a burning anger with an apparent and misleading quietness. Simmerson sniffed and tossed his head.

'The fault was hardly mine, sir.'

'Ah!' The General's eyebrows went up, he laid down his quill and leaned back in the chair. 'Whose then, sir?'

'I regret to say, sir, that Lieutenant Sharpe disobeyed an order even though it was repeated to him. Major Forrest heard me give the order to Lieutenant Gibbons who then carried it to Sharpe. By his action Lieutenant Sharpe exposed the Battalion and betrayed it.' Simmerson had found his rehearsed theme and he warmed to his task. 'I am requesting, sir, that Lieutenant Sharpe be court-martialled . . .'

Wellesley held up a hand and stopped the flow of words. He looked, almost casually, at Sharpe and there was something frightening about those blue eyes over the great, hooked nose that looked, judged, and were quite inscrutable. The eyes flicked to Forrest.

'You heard this order, Major?'

'Yes, sir.'

'You, Lieutenant. What happened?'

Gibbons arched his eyebrows and glanced at Sharpe. His tone was bored, supercilious. 'I ordered Lieutenant Sharpe to deploy his Riflemen, sir. He refused. Captain Hogan joined in his refusal.' Simmerson looked pleased. The General's fingers beat a brief tattoo on the table. 'Ah, Captain Hogan. I saw him an hour ago.' Wellesley drew out a piece of paper and looked at it. Sharpe knew it was all an act. Wellesley knew precisely what was on the paper but he was drawing out the tension. The blue eyes came up to Simmerson again, the tone of voice was still mild. 'I have served with Captain Hogan for many years, Sir Henry. He was in India. I have always found him a most trustworthy man.' He raised his eyebrows in a query as though inviting Simmerson to put him right. Simmerson, inevitably, accepted the invitation.

'Hogan, sir, is an Engineer. He was not in a position to make decisions about the deployment of troops.' He sounded pleased with himself, even anxious to show Wellesley that he bore the General no ill-will despite their political opposition.

Somewhere in the palace a clock whirred loudly and then chimed ten o'clock. Wellesley sat, his fingers drumming the table, and then jerked his gaze up to Simmerson.

'Your request is denied, Sir Henry. I will not court-martial Lieutenant Sharpe.' He paused for a second, looked at the paper and back to Simmerson. 'We have decisions to take about your Battalion, Sir Henry, I think you had better stay.'

Lawford moved to the door. Wellesley's voice had been hard and cold, the tone final, but Simmerson exploded, his voice rising indignantly.

'He lost my colour! He disobeyed!'

Wellesley's fist hit the table with a crash. 'Sir! I know what order he disobeyed! I would have disobeyed it! You proposed sending skirmishers against cavalry! Is that right, sir?'

Simmerson said nothing. He was aghast at the tumult of anger that had overwhelmed him. Wellesley went on.

'First, Sir Henry, you had no business in taking your Battalion over the bridge. It was unnecessary, time wasting, and damned foolish. Secondly.' He was ticking off on his fingers. 'Only a fool, sir, deploys skirmishers against cavalry. Third. You have disgraced this army, which I have spent a year in the making, in the face of our foes and of our allies. Fourthly.' Wellesley's voice was biting hard. 'The only credit gained in this miserable engagement was by Lieutenant Sharpe. I understand, sir, that he regained one of your lost colours and moreover captured a French gun and used it with some effect on your attackers. Is that correct?'

No one spoke. Sharpe stared rigidly ahead at a picture on the wall behind the General. He heard a rustle of paper. Wellesley had picked up the sheet from the desk. His voice was lower.

'You have lost, sir, as well as your colour, two hundred and forty-two men either killed or injured. You lost a Major, three Captains, five Lieutenants, four Ensigns and ten Sergeants. Are my figures correct?' Again no one spoke. Wellesley stood up. 'Your orders, sir, were those of a fool! The next time, Sir Henry, I suggest you fly a white flag and save the French the trouble of unsheathing their swords! The job you had to do, sir, could have been done by a company; I was forced by diplomacy to commit a Battalion and I sent yours, sir, so that your men would have a sight and taste of the French. I was wrong! As a result one of our colours is now on its way to Paris to be paraded in front of the mob. Tell me if I malign you?'

Simmerson had blanched white. Sharpe had never seen Wellesley so angry. He seemed to have forgotten the presence of the others and he directed his words at Simmerson with a vengeful force.

'You no longer have a Battalion, Sir Henry. It ceased to exist when you threw away your men and a colour! The South Essex is a single Battalion Regiment, is that right?' Simmerson nodded and muttered assent. 'So you can hardly make up your numbers from home. I wish, Sir Henry, I could send you home! But I cannot. My hands are tied, sir, by Parliament and the Horse

Guards and by meddling politicians like your cousin. I am declaring your Battalion, Sir Henry, to be a Battalion of Detachments. I will attach new officers myself and draft men into your ranks. You will serve in General Hill's Division.'

'But, sir. Sir?' Simmerson was overwhelmed by the information. To be called a Battalion of Detachments? It was unthinkable! He stammered a protest. Wellesley interrupted him.

'I will furnish you with a list of officers, sir. Are you telling me you have promised promotion already?'

Simmerson nodded. Wellesley looked at the sheet of paper he was holding. 'To whom, Sir Henry, did you give command of the Light Company?'

'To Lieutenant Gibbons, sir.'

'Your nephew?' Wellesley paused to make sure that Simmerson answered. The Colonel nodded bleakly. Wellesley turned to Gibbons.

'You concurred in your uncle's order to advance a skirmish line against cavalry?'

Gibbons was trapped. He licked his lips, shrugged, and finally agreed. Wellesley shook his head.

'Then you are plainly not a fit person to lead a Light Company. No, Sir Henry, I am giving you one of the finest skirmishers in the British army to lead your Light troops. I have gazetted him Captain.'

Simmerson said nothing. Gibbons was pale with anger. Lawford grinned at Sharpe and the Rifleman felt the flutter of hope. The General flicked his gaze to Sharpe and back to Simmerson.

'I can think of few men, Sir Henry, who are better leaders of Light troops in battle than Captain Sharpe.'

He soared, he had done it, he had escaped! It did not matter that it was with Simmerson, he had become a Captain! Captain Sharpe! He could hardly hear the rest of Wellesley's words, the victory was complete, the enemy routed! He was a Captain. What did it matter that the gazette was an artificial promotion, pending the acceptance of the Horse Guards? It would do for a while. A Captain! Captain Richard Sharpe of the Battalion of Detachments.

Wellesley was bringing the interview to a close. Simmerson made one final effort. 'I shall write—' Simmerson was indignant, desperately clinging to whatever shreds of dignity he could rescue from the torrent of Wellesley's disdain— 'I shall write to Whitehall, sir, and they will know the truth of this!'

'You may do what you like, sir, but you will kindly let me get on with waging a war. Good day.'

Lawford opened the door. Simmerson clapped on his cocked hat and the four officers turned to go. Wellesley spoke.

'Captain Sharpe!'

'Sir?' It was the first time he had been called 'Captain'. 'A word with you.'

Lawford closed the door on the other three. Wellesley looked at Sharpe, his expression still grim. 'You disobeyed an order.'

'Yes, sir.'

Wellesley's eyes shut. He looked tired. 'I have no doubt but that you deserve a Captaincy.' He opened his eyes. 'Whether you will keep it, Sharpe, is another matter. I have no power in these things and it is conceivable, likely, that the Horse Guards will cancel all these dispositions. Do you understand?'

'Yes, sir!' Sharpe thought he understood. Wellesley's enemies had succeeded in dragging him before a board of enquiry only last year and those same enemies wished

140

only defeat on him now. Sir Henry was numbered among them and the Colonel would even now be planning the letter that would be sent to London. The letter would blame Sharpe and, because the General had sided with him, would be dangerous for Wellesley too. 'Thank you, sir.'

'Don't thank me. I've probably done you no favour.' He looked up at Sharpe with a kind of wry distaste. 'You have a habit, Sharpe, of deserving gratitude by methods that deserve condemnation. Am I plain?'

'Yes, sir.' Was he being told off? Sharpe kept his face expressionless.

Wellesley's face showed a flash of anger but he controlled it and, quite suddenly, replaced it with a rueful smile. 'I am glad to see you well.' He leaned back in his chair. 'Your career is always interesting to watch, Sharpe, though I constantly fear it will end precipitately. Good day, Captain.' The quill pen was picked up and began to scratch on the paper. There were real problems. The Spanish had delivered none of the food they had promised, the army's pay had not arrived, the cavalry needed horse-shoes and nails, and there was a need for ox-carts, always more ox-carts. On top of that the Spanish hithered and dithered; one day all for charge and glory, the next preaching caution and withdrawal. Sharpe left.

Lawford followed him into the empty ante-room and put out his hand. 'Congratulations.'

'Thank you, sir. A Battalion of Detachments, eh?'

Lawford laughed. 'That won't please Sir Henry.'

That was true. In every campaign there were small units of men, like Sharpe and his Riflemen, who got separated from their units. They were the flotsam and jetsam of the army and the simplest solution, when there

141

were enough of them, was for the General to tie them together as a temporary Battalion of Detachments. It gave the General a chance, as well, to promote men, even temporarily, in the new Battalion but none of that was the reason Simmerson would be displeased. By making the shattered South Essex into a Battalion of Detachments Wellesley was literally wiping the name 'South Essex' from his army list; it was a punishment that was aimed at Simmerson's pride though Sharpe doubted whether a man who appeared to take the loss of his King's Colour with such remarkable equanimity would be for long dismayed by the downgrading of his Battalion. His face betrayed his thoughts and Lawford interrupted.

'You're worried about Simmerson?'

'Yes.' There was no point in denying the fact.

'You need to be. Sir Arthur has done what he can for you, he's given you promotion, you will believe me when I say that he has written home of you in the highest terms.'

Sharpe nodded. 'But.'

Lawford shrugged. He walked across to the window and stared past the heavy velvet curtains at the plain beyond the walls; the whole scene drowsed in the relentless sun. He turned back. 'Yes. There is a but.'

'Go on.'

Lawford looked embarrassed. 'Simmerson is too powerful. He has friends in high places.' He shrugged again. 'Richard, I am afraid that he will damage you. You're a pawn in the battle of politicians. He is a fool, agreed, but his friends in London will not want him to look a fool! They will demand a scapegoat. He's their voice, do you understand that?' Sharpe nodded. 'When he writes from Spain and says the war is being conducted wrongly then people listen to his letter being read in Parliament! It doesn't matter that the man is as mad as a turkey-cock! He's their voice from the war and if they lose him then they lose credibility!'

Sharpe nodded wearily. 'What you're saying is that pressure will be applied for me to be sacrificed so that Simmerson can survive?'

Lawford nodded. 'I'm afraid so. And Sir Arthur's defence of you will be seen as mere party politics.'

'But for God's sake! I was in no way responsible!'

'I know, I know.' Lawford spoke soothingly. 'It makes no difference. He has chosen you as his scapegoat.'

Sharpe knew he spoke the truth. For a few weeks he was safe, safe while Wellesley marched further into Spain and brought the French to battle, but after that a letter would come from the Horse Guards, a short and simple letter that would mean the end of his career in the army. He was sure he would be looked after. Wellesley himself might need an estate manager or would recommend him to someone who did. But he would still eke out his years under a cloud as the man named officially responsible for losing Simmerson's colour. He thought of his last conversation with Lennox. Had the Scotsman foreseen it all?

'There is another way.' He spoke quietly.

Lawford looked at him. 'What?'

'When I saw the colour being lost I made a resolution. I also made a promise to a dying man.' It sounded desperately melodramatic but it was the truth. 'I promised to replace that colour with an Eagle.'

There was a moment of silence. Lawford whistled softly. 'It's never been done.'

'There's no difference between that and them taking a colour.' That was easily said but he knew that the

French would not make the job as easy for him as Simmerson had for them. In the last six years the French had appeared on the battlefield with new standards. In place of the old colours they now carried gilded eagles mounted on poles. It was said that each Eagle was personally presented to the Regiment by the Emperor himself and the standards were therefore more than just a symbol of the Regiment, they were a symbol of all France's pride in their new order. To take an Eagle was to make Bonaparte wince in person. Sharpe felt the anger rise in him.

'I don't mind replacing Simmerson's flag with an Eagle. But I'm bloody angry that I have to carve my way through a company of French Grenadiers just to stay in the army.'

Lawford said nothing. He knew that Sharpe spoke the truth; the only thing that could stop the officials in Whitehall singling out Sharpe for punishment was if the Rifleman performed a deed of such undoubted merit that they would look foolish to make him a scapegoat. Privately Lawford thought Sharpe had done more than enough, he had regained a colour, captured a gun, but the account of his deeds would be muddied in London by Simmerson's telling. No, he had to do more, go further, risk his life in an attempt to keep his job.

Sharpe laughed ironically. He slapped his empty scabbard. 'Someone once said that in this job you're only as good as your last battle.' He paused. 'Unless of course you have money or influence.'

'Yes, Richard, unless you have money or influence.'

Sharpe grinned. 'Thank you, sir. I'll go and join the happy throng. I presume my Riflemen come with me?'

Lawford nodded. 'Good luck.' He watched Sharpe go. If any man could pluck an Eagle from the French he thought that the newly made Captain, Richard Sharpe, was that man. Lawford stood in the window and looked down into the street. He saw Sharpe step into the sunlight and put the battered shako on his head; a huge Sergeant was waiting in the shade, the kind of man Lawford would happily wager a hundred guineas on in a bare-fisted prize fight, and he watched as the Sergeant walked up to Sharpe. The two men talked for a moment and then the big Sergeant clapped the officer's back and uttered a whoop of joy that Lawford could hear two floors above.

'Lawford!'

'Sir?' Lawford crossed to the other room and took the despatch from Wellesley's hand. The General rattled the quill in the ink-pot.

'Did you explain to him?'

'Yes, sir.'

Wellesley shook his head. 'Poor devil. What did he say?'

'He said he'd take his chance, sir.'

Wellesley grunted. 'We all have to do that.' He picked up another piece of paper. 'My God! They've sent us four cases of gum ammoniac, three of Glauber's salts, and two hundred assorted stump-caps! They think I'm running a bloody hospital instead of an army!'

CHAPTER 11

The boots of the Coldstream Guards rang on the flag-
stones, echoing hollowly in the darkness, fading down
the steep street to be replaced by the leading companies
of the 3rd Guards. They were followed by the first
Battalion of the 61st, the second of the 83rd, and
then by four full Battalions of the crack King's German
Legion. Sharpe, standing in a church porch, watched
the Germans march past.

'They're good troops, sir.'

Forrest, shivering despite a greatcoat, peered into the
darkness. 'What are they?'

'King's German Legion.'

Forrest thrust his hands deeper into his pockets. 'I've
not seen them before.'

'You wouldn't have, sir.' The Germans were a foreign
corps of the army and the law said they were allowed
no nearer the British mainland than the Isle of Wight.
Overhead the church clock struck three times. Three
o'clock on the morning of Monday, 17th July, 1809,
and the British army was leaving Plasencia. A company
of the 60th went past, another German unit, with the
incongruous title of the Royal American Rifles. Forrest
saw Sharpe staring ruefully at the marching Riflemen
with their green jackets and black belts.

146

'Homesick, Sharpe?'

Sharpe grinned in the darkness. 'I'd rather it was the other Rifle Regiment, sir.' He yearned for the sanity of the 95th rather than the worsening suspicion and moroseness that was infecting Simmerson's Battalion.

Forrest shook his head. 'I'm sorry, Sharpe.'

'Don't be, sir. I'm a Captain at least.'

Forrest ignored the statement. 'He showed me the letter, you know.' Sharpe knew. Forrest kept apologising and had mentioned the letter twice already. Dereliction of duty, gross disobedience, even the word 'treason' had found its place into Simmerson's scathing account of Sharpe's actions at Valdelacasa; but none of that was surprising. What had disturbed Sharpe was Simmerson's final request; that Sharpe be posted, as a Lieutenant, to a Battalion in the West Indies. No one ever purchased a commission in one of those Battalions even though promotion was quicker there than anywhere else in the army, and Sharpe had even known men resign rather than go to the sun-drenched islands with their lazy garrison duty.

'It may not happen, Sharpe.' Forrest's tone betrayed that he thought Sharpe's fate was sealed.

'No, sir.' Not if I can help it, thought Sharpe, and he imagined an Eagle in his hands. Only an Eagle could save him from the islands where fever reduced a man's life expectancy to less than a year, from the dreadful, sweating disease that made Simmerson's request into a virtual death warrant unless Sharpe resigned his hard won commission.

Almost every unit marched before them. Five Regiments of Dragoons and the Hussars of the King's German Legion, over three thousand cavalry in all, followed by an army of mules carrying fodder for the precious horses. The cumbersome artillery with their guns, limbers, and portable forges added even more mules, more supplies, but mostly it was infantry who disturbed the quiet streets. Twenty-five Battalions of unglamorous infantry, with stained uniforms and worn boots, the men who had to stand and face the world's best artillerymen and cavalry; and with them marched even more mules mixed up with the Battalions' women and children.

The Battalion finally took the road across the river well after sunrise and if the previous days had been hot it now seemed as if nature was intent on baking the landscape into one solid expanse of terracotta. The army crept across the vast, arid plain and stirred up a fine dust that hung in the air and lined the mouths and throats of the parched infantry. There was no trace of wind, just the dust, the heat and glare, the sweat that stung the eyes, and the endless sound of boots hitting the white road. In one village there was a pool that had been trampled into foul sticky mud by the cavalry but even that was welcomed by the men who had long before emptied their canteens and now skimmed the sour water from the surface of the glutinous mud.

There was not much else to be grateful for. The rest of the army shunned the new Battalion of Detachments as if the men were harbouring a repulsive disease. The loss of the colour had stained the reputation of the whole army and when the Battalion bivouacked on the first night they were turned away from a capacious farm by a Colonel of Dragoons who wanted nothing to do with a Regiment which had failed so shamefully. The Battalion's morale was not helped by a shortage of food. The herd of cattle which had left Portugal had long been slaughtered and eaten, the supplies promised by the Spanish had not appeared, and the men were hungry, sullen, and cowed by Simmerson's brutality. He had found his own reasons for the loss of the colour, the behaviour of Sharpe and the actions of his own men, and if he could not punish the first it was well within his practised power to punish the second. Only the Light Company retained some vestiges of pride. The men were proud of their new Captain. Throughout the Battalion Sharpe was now believed to be a magic man, a lucky one, a man whom enemy swords and bullets could not touch. The Light Company believed, in the way of soldiers, that Sharpe would bring them luck in battle, would keep them alive, and pointed to the action at the bridge as proof. Sharpe's Riflemen agreed, they had always known their officer was lucky, and they revelled in his new promotion. Sharpe had been embarrassed by their pleasure, blushed when they offered him drinks from hoarded bottles of Spanish brandy, and covered his confusion by pretending to have duties elsewhere. On the first night of the march from Plasencia he lay in a field, wrapped in his greatcoat, and thought of the boy who had fearfully joined the army sixteen years before. What would that terrified sixteen-year-old, running from justice, have thought if he knew he would one day be a Captain?

On the second night the Battalion was more fortunate. They bivouacked near another nameless village and the woods were filled with soldiers hacking at branches to build the fires on which they could boil the tea-leaves they carried loose in their pockets. Provosts guarded the olive groves, nothing made the army so unpopular as the French habit of cutting down a village's olive trees and denying them harvests for years to come and Wellesley had issued strict orders that the olives were not to be touched. The officers of the South

Essex – the Battalion still thought of itself as that – were billeted in the village inn. It was a large building, evidently a way station between Plasencia and Talavera, and behind it was a courtyard with big cypress trees beneath which were tables and benches. The three-sided yard opened on to a stream and on the far bank the men of the Battalion made fires and beds in a grove of cork trees. There had been pigs in the grove and as Sharpe stripped off his uniform to search the seams for lice he could smell pork cooking on the myriad small fires that showed through the foliage. Such looting was punishable by instant hanging but nothing could stop it. The officers, the provosts, everyone was short of food and the surreptitious offer of some stolen pork would ensure that the provosts would take no action.

The courtyard gradually filled with officers from the dozen Battalions bivouacked in the village. The heat of the day mellowed into a warm, clear evening and the stars came like the camp fires of a limitless army seen far away. From the main room of the inn came the sound of music and cheering as the officers egged on the Spanish dancers to twitch their skirts higher. Sharpe pushed his way through the crowded room and glimpsed Simmerson and his cronies sitting playing cards at a corner table. Gibbons was there, he was now permanently attached to Simmerson's 'staff', and the unpleasant Lieutenant Berry. For a second Sharpe thought about the girl. He had seen her once or twice since the return from the bridge and felt a surge of jealousy. He pushed the thought away; the officers of the Battalion were split enough as it was. There were Simmerson's supporters who toadied to the Colonel and assured him that the loss of the colour had been no fault of his and there were those who had publicly supported Sharpe. It was an uncomfortable situation but there was nothing to be done about it. He passed out of the room into the courtyard and found Forrest, Leroy, and a group of Subalterns beneath one of the cypress trees. Forrest made room for him on the bench.

'Don't you ever take that rifle off?'

'And have it stolen?' Sharpe asked. 'I'd be charged for it.'

Forrest smiled. 'Have you paid for the stocks yet?'

'Not yet.' Sharpe grimaced. 'But now I'm officially on the Battalion's payroll I suppose it will be deducted from my pay, whenever that arrives.'

Forrest pushed a wine bottle towards him. 'Don't let it worry you. Tonight the wine's on me.'

There was an ironic cheer from the officers round the table. Unconsciously Sharpe felt the leather bag round his neck. It was heavier by six gold pieces thanks to the dead on the field at Valdelacasa. He drank some wine. 'It's filthy!'

'There's a rumour,' Leroy said drily. 'I hear that when they tread the grapes they don't bother to get out of the winepress to relieve themselves.'

There was a moment's silence and then a chorus of disgusted voices. Forrest looked dubiously into his cup. 'I don't believe it.'

'In India,' Sharpe said, 'some natives believe it very healthy to drink their own urine.'

Forrest looked owlishly at him. 'That cannot be true.'

Leroy intervened. 'Perfectly true, Major, I've seen them do it. A cupful a day. Cheers!'

Everyone round the table protested but Sharpe and Leroy stuck to their story. The conversation stayed with India, of battles and sieges, of strange animals, of the palaces that contained unimaginable wealth. More wine was ordered and food brought from the kitchens, not the pork that smelt so tantalisingly from the lines but a stew that seemed to consist mainly of vegetables. It felt good to be sitting there. Sharpe stretched his legs under the table and leaned back against the cypress trunk letting the tiredness of the day flow through him. Over the sound of talk and laughter he could hear the thousands of insects that chattered and clicked through the Spanish night. Later he would walk over the stream and visit his company and he let his thoughts wander, not too many miles away, to where he knew a group of French officers would be sitting just like this and where their men would be cooking on fires like the ones across the stream. And somewhere, perhaps propped in the corner of a room in an inn just like this one, would be the Eagle. A hand hit him on the back.

'So they've made you a Captain! This army has no standards!' It was Hogan. Sharpe had not seen him since the day they marched back from the bridge. He stood up and took the Engineer's hand. Hogan beamed at him. 'I'm delighted! Shocked, of course, but delighted. Congratulations!'

Sharpe blushed and shrugged. 'Where have you been?'

'Oh, looking at things.' Sharpe knew that Hogan had been reconnoitring for Wellesley, coming back with news of which bridges could take the weight of heavy artillery, which roads were wide enough for the army to use. The Captain had obviously been forward to Oropesa and perhaps beyond. Forrest invited him to sit and asked for news.

'The French are up the valley. A lot of them.' Hogan poured himself some wine. 'I reckon there'll be a battle within a week.'

'A week!' Forrest sounded surprised.

'Aye, Major. They're swarming all over a place called Talavera.' Hogan pronounced it 'Tally-verra' making it sound like some Irish hamlet. 'But once you join with Cuesta's army you'll far outnumber them.'

'You've seen Cuesta's troops?' Sharpe asked.

'Aye.' The Irishman grinned. 'They're no better than the Santa Maria. The cavalry may be better, but the infantry . . .' Hogan left the sentence unfinished. He turned back to Sharpe and beamed again. 'The last time I saw you, you were under arrest! Now look at you. How's good Sir Henry?' There was a laugh round the table. Hogan did not wait for an answer but dropped his voice. 'I saw Sir Arthur.'

'I know. Thank you.'

'For telling the truth? So what happens now?'

'I don't know.' Sharpe spoke quietly. Only Hogan could hear him. 'Simmerson has written home. I'm told that he has the power to stop the Horse Guards ratifying the gazette so in six weeks I'll be a Lieutenant again, probably for ever, and almost certainly transferred to the Fever Islands, or out of the army altogether.'

Hogan looked intently at him. 'You're serious?'

'Yes. One of Sir Arthur's staff virtually told me as much.'

'Because of Simmerson?' Hogan frowned in disbelief.

Sharpe sighed. 'It has to do with Simmerson keeping his credibility in Parliament with the people who oppose Wellesley. I'm the sacrifice. Don't ask me, it's way over my head. What about you? You were under arrest too.'

Hogan shrugged. 'Sir Henry forgave me. He doesn't take me seriously, I'm just an Engineer. No, it's you he's after. You're an upstart, a Rifleman, you're not a

153

gentleman but you're a better soldier than he'll ever be, so.' He squeezed his thumb and forefinger together. 'He wants rid of you. Listen.' Hogan leaned even nearer. 'There'll be a battle soon, has to be. The idiot will probably make as big a mess as he did before. They can't protect him for ever. It's a terrible thing, God knows, but you should pray he makes as big a mistake again.'

Sharpe smiled. 'I doubt if we need to pray.'

From one of the upper windows that looked on to the balconies that ran round the courtyard there came a woman's scream, terrifying and intense, stopping all conversation beneath the trees. Men froze with their cups half lifted to their mouths and stared at the dark doorways that led to the bedrooms. Sharpe got to his feet and reached instinctively for his rifle. Forrest put a hand on his arm. 'It's not our business, Sharpe.'

In the courtyard there was a moment's silence, some nervous laughter, and then the conversation started again. Sharpe felt uneasy. It could have been anything; one of the women who lived at the inn could be ill, possibly even a difficult childbirth, but he felt certain it was something else. A rape? He felt ashamed that he had done nothing. Forrest tugged at his arm again. 'Sit down. It's probably nothing.'

Before Sharpe could move there came another scream, this time a man's, and it turned into a bellow of rage. A door burst open on the top floor spilling yellow candlelight on to the balcony and a woman ran out of the room and darted towards the stairs. A voice shouted, 'Stop her!'

The girl tore down the stairs as though the fiends of hell were after her. The officers in the courtyard cheered her on and shouted abuse at the two figures who emerged after her, Gibbons and Berry. They stood no chance of catching her; both men looked drunk and as they burst from the room they lurched and blinked round the courtyard.

'It's Josefina,' Forrest said. Sharpe watched the girl half run, half fall down the stairs until she reached the other side of the courtyard from their table. For a second she looked desperately round as though looking for help. She was carrying a bag and Sharpe had a glimpse of what could have been a knife in her hand and then she turned and ran into the darkness, over the stream, towards the lights of the Battalion's fires. Gibbons stopped half way down the stairs, he was dressed in trousers and shirt and one hand was clutching the unbuttoned shirt to his stomach, in the other hand was a pistol. 'Come back, you lousy bitch!'

He jumped the last flight of steps and fumbled with the lock of his pistol.

'What's the matter, Gibbons? Girl took your colours!' The voice came from one of the tables in the courtyard. Gibbons, his face furious, ignored the jibes and laughter and ran with Berry towards the stream.

'There's going to be trouble.' Sharpe climbed from the bench. 'I'm going.'

He threaded his way through the tables, Forrest and Hogan following him. He left the light of the courtyard and splashed through the stream; there was no sight of the girl or her pursuers, just the lights in the cork grove and the occasional silhouette of a man crossing in front of the flames. He paused to let his eyes become accustomed to the dark. Forrest caught up with him.

'Is there going to be trouble, Sharpe?'

'Not if I can help it, sir. But you saw him, he's got a pistol.' There were shouts to the left, a commotion. 'Come on!'

He outpaced the other two; he was running fast, keeping the silver track of the stream to his left, holding the rifle in his right hand.

'What's going on? Who the hell's that?' In the light of a fire he saw an angry private. The man looked surprised when he saw Sharpe and threw a hasty salute. 'You after them two, sir?'

'Was a girl with them?'

'That way, sir.' He pointed downstream, away from the fires of the Battalion, out into the black grassland. Sharpe ran on, Forrest and Hogan now close behind. In front he heard a 'view-halloo', a scream, they had caught the girl. He ran faster, ignoring the rough ground, fearing the sound of a shot, his eyes adjusting to the night. They had not gone far. Suddenly he saw them, Berry standing with a bottle and watching Gibbons who had forced the girl to her knees and was trying to force the bag out of her hands. Sharpe heard Gibbons shouting at Josefina. 'Let go, you bitch!'

Sharpe kept running. Gibbons looked up, startled, and then Sharpe hit him full tilt. The Lieutenant was thrown backwards, the pistol flew from his hand and splashed into the stream, and Sharpe saw the bag fall from Josefina's hand and spill bright gold on to the dark grass. Gibbons tried to struggle to his feet but Sharpe pushed him with the rifle butt. 'Don't move.' There was enough moonlight for the Lieutenant to see the look on Sharpe's face and he sank back on to his elbows. Sharpe turned to Berry. 'What's going on?'

Berry licked his fat lips and grinned foolishly. Sharpe stepped one pace closer and raised his voice. 'What's going on?'

'The girl ran away, sir. Came to get her back.' Berry's natural drawl was accentuated by drink and when he turned to see Forrest and Hogan arrive he staggered slightly.

'Is she all right?' Forrest asked.

Sharpe turned to look at Josefina. He realised, irrelevantly, that it was the first time he had seen her not dressed in riding breeches and his pulse quickened at the sight of her bare shoulders and the shadowed promise of the low cut dress. Her head was down; at first he thought she was sobbing, but then he saw her desperately picking up the scattered gold coins. His mind registered that there was a small fortune on the ground and then Forrest blocked his view as the Major knelt at the girl's side.

'Are you all right?' Forrest's voice was paternal, kindly.

The girl nodded, then shook her head, and Sharpe saw her shoulders heave as she seemed to sob. Her hands still scrabbled at the grass, at the gold pieces.

The Major stood up. 'What's all this about?' He tried, unsuccessfully, to sound authoritative. No one spoke. Sharpe moved his rifle to his left hand and stepped close to Berry, took the bottle from him, and threw it into the stream.

'I say! Steady on!' Berry's voice was slurred.

'What happened?'

'Just an argument. Nothing to worry about.' Berry blinked happily at Sharpe and flapped a hand genially around the small group. The Rifleman hit him, hard in the stomach, and Berry's mouth gaped like a fish. He doubled over and retched on to the grass. Sharpe hauled him upright. 'What happened?'

Berry stared at him, astonished. 'You hit me!'

'I'll bloody crucify you if you don't talk.'

'We were playing cards. I won.'

157

'So?'

'There was an argument.' Sharpe waited. Berry pushed a lank piece of black hair off his forehead as though trying to rescue a shred of dignity. 'She refused to pay her debt.'

Josefina had watched Sharpe hit Berry and, standing silently to one side, Hogan had watched her smile with excitement as the Lieutenant crumpled.

'It's not true!' The girl was angry. 'You cheated! I was winning!' She had stood up, taken two steps towards Berry.

Hogan saw her face and knew that she would scratch the Lieutenant's eyes out, given half a chance. He took her elbow, restrained her. He, at least, knew that the truth of who won, who lost, or who cheated would probably never be known. 'So what happened?' The Irish voice was soft.

Josefina gestured at Berry. 'He wanted to rape me! Christian hit me!'

Sharpe turned towards Gibbons. The blond Lieutenant had scrambled to his feet and watched Sharpe walk towards him. There was a bloodstain on his white shirt, and Sharpe remembered the knife; Josefina had evidently cut at him but done little damage. 'Is it true?' Sharpe asked.

'Is what true?' Gibbons' voice was touched with contempt.

'That you hit her and that Lieutenant Berry tried to rape her?'

Gibbons laughed. 'Trying to rape Josefina Lacosta is like forcing money on to a beggar. If you follow my meaning.'

Hogan knew he should step forward, that the tension was too much, but Sharpe broke the silence that had followed Gibbons' sneering remark. 'Say that again.' Sharpe's voice was soft.

Gibbons looked scornfully at the Rifleman and when he spoke his voice was invested with all the contempt he had for the lower classes. 'Try and understand. We were playing cards. Miss Lacosta lost her money and staked her body instead. She refused to pay up and instead decamped with our money. That is all.'

'It's not true!' Josefina was crying. She left Hogan's side and came up to Sharpe, looked at him with her eyes wet with tears, and clasped the bag between her hands. 'It is not true. We were playing cards. I won. They tried to steal it from me! I thought they were gentlemen!'

Gibbons laughed. Sharpe turned on him. 'You hit her?' He had seen a bruise on her cheek.

'You wouldn't understand.' Gibbons sounded bored.

'What wouldn't I understand?' Sharpe stepped closer to the Lieutenant.

Gibbons negligently brushed a blade of grass from his sleeve. 'How gentlemen behave, Sharpe. You'll believe her, because she's a whore, and you're used to whores. You're not used to gentlemen.'

'Call me "sir".'

Anger flared in Gibbons' face. 'Go to hell.'

Sharpe hit him in the solar plexus and as Gibbons' face came forward Sharpe lowered his own and butted him between the eyes. Gibbons reeled, blood dripping from his nose, and Sharpe dropped the rifle to hit him again. Once, twice, and a final massive punch into the stomach. Like Berry, Gibbons folded up and vomited. He dropped to his knees, clutching his belly, and Sharpe contemptuously pushed him with his boot and the Lieutenant keeled over into the mud.

'Lieutenant Berry?'

159

'Sir?'

'Mr Gibbons is a little the worse for drink. Get him out of here and clean him up.'

'Yes, sir.' Berry was not going to argue with Sharpe. He helped Gibbons uncertainly to his feet. The Colonel's nephew was gasping for breath, heaving from his stomach, and he pushed Berry away and turned to stammer at Forrest, between gasps. 'You saw him. He hit me!'

Hogan stepped forward, his voice crisp and authoritative. 'Nonsense, Lieutenant. You were drunk and fell over. Go home to bed.'

The two Lieutenants stumbled into the darkness. Sharpe watched them go. 'Bastards! You can't play cards over a woman.'

Hogan smiled sadly. 'You know why they made you into an officer, Richard?'

'Why?'

'You're far too much of a gentleman to have stayed in the ranks. Men have been playing cards over women since cards were invented, or women for that matter.' He turned to the girl. 'And what are you going to do now?'

'Do?' She looked at Hogan and then at Sharpe. 'I cannot go back. They tried to rape me!'

'Did they now.' Hogan's voice was flat. The girl nodded, still clutching the bag, and moved closer to Sharpe.

'My clothes,' she said. 'I must get my clothes. All my things! They are in that room.'

Forrest stepped forward, a concerned expression on his face. 'Your clothes?'

'All my things! They'll kill me!'

Hogan's shrewd eyes flicked from the girl to Forrest. 'If you go round the front, Major, and hurry, then you'll

160

be there before those two. It'll take ten minutes for them to throw up all that liquor.'

Forrest looked alarmed but Hogan had taken charge and the Major did not know how to resist. Hogan took Josefina by the elbow and gave her to Forrest. 'Go with Major Forrest and rescue your things. Hurry!'

She stepped to Forrest but turned back to Sharpe. 'But where do I spend the night?'

Sharpe cleared his throat. 'She can use my room. I can double up with Hogan.'

Forrest twitched at her elbow. 'Come on, my dear, we must hurry.' The two of them splashed through the stream and hurried towards the lights of the inn. Hogan watched them go and turned to Sharpe. 'Double up with me?'

'It would be best, wouldn't it?'

'Hypocrite. You mean double up with her.'

Sharpe said nothing. He suspected that Hogan had pushed the girl away with the Major because he wanted to talk to Sharpe alone but the Rifleman had no intention of making his friend's life any easier by bringing up the subject. He leaned down and picked up his rifle and felt the lock to see if any dampness or mud had seeped into the pan. The lights of the Battalion fires smeared the hillside with a dying red glow.

'You know what you're doing, Richard?' Hogan's voice was non-committal.

'What do you mean?'

The Irishman smiled. 'She's beautiful. There aren't many as good-looking as that one; at least, not outside Cork.' The small joke was made to lighten his tone, which was sad. 'Well, you rescued her so she's yours for the moment. Will you be sending her home to Lisbon?' Sharpe started walking beside the stream and said nothing. Hogan caught up with him. 'Are you in love with her?'

'For God's sake!'

'And what's wrong with that?' They walked in silence for a few yards until Hogan took a guinea out of his pocket and held it up. 'I'll bet you this against ten of yours that you'll not double up with me tonight?'

Sharpe smiled in the darkness. 'I don't gamble and I haven't any money.'

'I know. But you'll need it, Richard. Women don't come free.' Hogan still spoke softly. He felt in his pocket and held out a handful of guineas. 'I'll wager you these, Richard, against one rifle bullet that you won't double up with me tonight.'

Sharpe stared down at Hogan's friendly, concerned face. It would be so easy to win the bet. All he had to do was put Josefina in his room and then walk to Hogan's billet and collect the handful of gold. There were six months' wages, there, just for staying clear of the girl. Sharpe pushed the money away. 'I need all my bullets.'

Hogan laughed. 'That's true. But don't tell me I didn't warn you.' He put a hand on Sharpe's belt, opened the ammunition pouch, and poured in the gold. Sharpe protested and pulled away but Hogan forced the money inside. 'You'll need it, Richard. She'll expect a decent room in Oropesa, and in Talavera, and God knows how much it will all cost you. Don't worry. There'll be a battle soon and you'll shoot a rich man and then give me the money back.'

They walked on in silence. Hogan could feel the excitement in Sharpe and knew that if he had offered him ten times ten guineas then he could not have stopped the Rifleman sleeping with the girl that night or, if Josefina said no, then Sharpe would have stayed in the room as her faithful protector, the Baker rifle across his knees. They skirted Berry and Gibbons, one of them doubled over and groaning, and splashed through the stream and back into the lights of the inn's courtyard. Hogan looked up at Sharpe, at the eyes that were alive with anticipation, and cuffed him gently on the arm. 'Sleep well, Richard.'

Sharpe grinned back. 'Don't worry.' He took the stairs three at a time, his boots squelching on the wooden steps, and Hogan watched him go. ''Tis brief, my Lord.' He was speaking to himself. 'As woman's love.'

'What's that, sir?' Lieutenant Knowles was standing beside him.

'Do you never read Shakespeare, lad?'

'Shakespeare, sir?'

'A famous Irish poet,' Hogan said.

Knowles laughed. 'And what play was that from, sir?'

'Hamlet.'

'Oh him.' Knowles grinned. 'The famous Irish Prince?'

Hogan grinned at him. 'Oh no. Hamlet was no Irishman. He was a fool. Good night, Lieutenant. Time for bed.'

Hogan looked up at Sharpe's room. He would trust Sharpe with his life, trust the Rifleman against almost any odds, but with a woman? He would be disarmed, defeated; one girl could do what a Battalion of French could never hope to achieve. Hogan muttered under his breath as he walked away, his voice quiet in the empty courtyard, repeating the line over and over as though, perhaps, repetition would rob it of truth. 'Beauty provoketh fools sooner than gold.'

CHAPTER 12

'Officer of the day?'

Sharpe nodded. 'Come on in.'

The Commissary officer, a plump Lieutenant, grinned cheerfully and closed the door behind him. 'Good afternoon, sir. Your signature?'

'For what?'

The Lieutenant pretended to be surprised. He looked at the piece of paper he had been holding out to Sharpe. '3rd Battalion of Detachments? Right?' Sharpe nodded. 'Your rations, sir.' He held the list out again. 'Will you sign, sir?'

'Wait.' Sharpe looked down the list. 'Seven hundred and fifty pounds of beef? That's generous, isn't it?'

The Lieutenant put on his professional smile. 'I'm afraid that's not just for today, sir. That's the next three days' ration altogether.'

'What! Three days? That's half bloody rations!'

The Lieutenant spread his hands. 'I know, sir, I know, but it really is the best we can do. Will you sign?'

Sharpe took his hat and weapons from the table. 'Where are they?'

The Lieutenant sighed. 'I'm sure you don't want to . . .'

'Where are they?' Sharpe's voice boomed in the

small room. The Lieutenant smiled, opened the door, and beckoned Sharpe into the courtyard where the Lieutenant's working party was standing by a string of pack mules. The Lieutenant pulled the cover off a keg of freshly killed beef. 'Sir?'

Sharpe picked up the top piece and dangled it in front of the plump Commissary officer. 'Put laces in it and you could march on it.' The Lieutenant smiled, he had heard it all before. Sharpe took another piece of gristle from the keg. 'It's uneatable! How many kegs?'

The Lieutenant waved at the mules. 'All this, sir.'

Sharpe looked out of the courtyard into the bright street. Another mule stood patiently in the late afternoon sunlight. 'What's that?'

'A mule, sir.' The Lieutenant smiled brightly. He saw Sharpe's face. 'Sorry, sir. My little joke.' He became serious. 'That's the supplies for the castle, sir. Sir Arthur's. You understand.'

'I do?' Sharpe walked under the arch towards the mule, the Lieutenant alongside, and waved the muleteer away. 'I happened to see the supplies delivered to the castle this morning, Lieutenant, and nothing went missing.'

The Lieutenant smiled helplessly. Sharpe was lying, they both knew that, but then so was the Lieutenant, and they both knew that, too. Sharpe pulled the cover off the nearest keg. 'Now that, Lieutenant, is beef. I'll have both these kegs instead of two of the others.'

'But, sir! This is for . . .'

'Your dinner, Lieutenant? And you and your fellow officers will sell the rest. Right? I'll take it.'

The Lieutenant recovered the keg. 'Why don't you let me give you a fine chicken we just happened to find, Captain, as a gift, of course.'

Sharpe put his hand on the mule. 'You want me to sign, Lieutenant? I think I'll weigh the beef first.'

The Lieutenant was beaten. He smiled brightly and gave Sharpe the list. 'I wouldn't want you to go to the trouble, sir. Let's just say you'll take all the kegs, these included?'

Sharpe nodded. The day's bargaining was over and his own working party unloaded the mules and took the beef down to the outskirts of Oropesa where the men of the Battalion were quartered. The supply situation was hopeless and getting worse. The Spanish army had been waiting at Oropesa and they had long eaten any spare food from the surrounding countryside. The town's steep streets were filled with troops, Spanish, British and Germans from the Legion, and there was already friction between the allies. British and German patrols had ambushed Spanish supply wagons, even killing their guards, to get hold of the food Cuesta had promised to Wellesley but never delivered. The army's hopes of reaching Madrid by the middle of August had faded when they saw the waiting Spanish troops. The Regimienta de la Santa Maria was at Oropesa parading beneath two huge new colours and Sharpe wondered whether General Cuesta kept a limitless supply to replace the trophies that ended up in Paris. As he walked down the steep street he watched two officers with their long swords tucked, in the strange Spanish fashion, under their armpits and nothing about them, from their splendid uniforms to their thin cigars, gave the Rifleman any comfort about the army of Spain.

He felt his own hunger as he walked down the street. Josefina's servant had found food, at a price, and at least tonight he would eat and every mouthful was almost a day's pay. The two rooms she had found were costing a fortnight's pay every night but, he thought, the hell with it. If the worst came to pass and he was forced to choose between a West Indies commission and civilian life then damn the money and enjoy it. Rent the rooms, pay through the nose for a scrawny chicken that would boil into grey scraps, and carry into the fever ward the remembrance of Josefina's body and the extraordinary luxury of a wide, shared bed. So far there was only the memory of the one night at the inn and then she had ridden ahead, grudgingly escorted by Hogan, while Sharpe spent two days marching through the dust and heat with the Battalion. He had seen her briefly at midday, been dazzled by a smile of welcome, and now there was a whole evening, a long night, and no march tomorrow.

'Sir!'

Sharpe turned. Sergeant Harper was running towards him; another man, one of the South Essex's Light Company, with him. 'Sir!'

'What is it?' Sharpe noticed that Harper was looking agitated and worried, an unusual sight, but he felt a twinge of impatience as he returned their salutes. Damn them! He wanted to be with Josefina. 'Well?'

'It's the deserters, sir.' Harper was almost wriggling in embarrassment.

'Deserters?'

'You know, sir. The ones who escaped at Castelo?'

The day they had met up with the South Essex. Sharpe remembered the men being flogged because four deserters had slipped past the guard in the night. He looked hard at Harper. 'How do you know?'

'Kirby's a mate of theirs, sir.' He pointed to the man standing next to him. Sharpe looked at him. He was a small man who had lost most of his teeth. 'Well, Kirby?'

'Dunno, sir.'

'You want to be flogged, Kirby?'

The man's eyes jerked up to his, astonished. 'What, sir?'

'If you don't tell me I'll have to presume you are helping them to escape.'

Harper and Kirby were silent. Finally the Sergeant looked at Sharpe. 'Kirby saw one of them in the street, sir. He went back with him. Two of them are wounded, sir. Kirby came to see me.'

'And in turn you came to see me.' Sharpe kept his voice harsh. 'And what do you expect me to do?'

Again they said nothing. Sharpe knew that they hoped he could work a miracle; that somehow lucky Captain Sharpe could find a way to save the four men from the savage punishment the army gave to deserters. He felt an unreasonable anger mount inside him, alloyed with impatience. What did they think he was? 'Fetch six men, Sergeant. Three Riflemen and three others. Meet me here in five minutes. Kirby, stay here.'

Harper stood to attention. 'But, sir . . .'

'Go!'

There was a translucent quality to the air, that quality of light just before dusk when the sun seems suspended in coloured liquid. A gnat buzzed irritatingly round Sharpe's face and he slapped at it. The church bells rang the Angelus, a woman hurrying down the street crossed herself, and Sharpe cursed inside because he had promised Josefina to join her just after six o'clock. Damn the deserters! Damn Harper for expecting a miracle! Did the Sergeant really think that Sharpe would condone desertion? Behind him, frightened and nervous, Kirby fidgeted in the roadway and Sharpe thought gloomily of what this could mean to the Battalion. The whole army was frustrated but at least they could look forward with a mixture of fear and eagerness to the inevitable battle that gave their present discomforts some purpose. The South Essex did not share the anticipation. It had been disgraced at Valdelacasa, its colour shamefully lost, and the men of the Battalion had no stomach for another fight. The South Essex was sullen and bitter. Every man in it would wish the deserters well.

Harper reappeared with his men, all of them armed, all of them looking apprehensively at Sharpe. One of them asked nervously if the deserters would be shot.

'I don't know,' Sharpe snapped. 'Lead on, Kirby.'

They walked down the hill into the poorest section of the town, into a tangle of alleyways where half-dressed children played in the filth that was hurled from the night-buckets into the roadway. Washing hung between the high balconies, obscuring the light, and the closeness of the walls seemed to heighten the stench. It was a smell the men had first encountered in Lisbon and they had become accustomed to it even though its source made walking through the streets after dark a risky and nauseating business. The men were silent and resentful, following Sharpe reluctantly to a duty they had no wish to perform.

'Here, sir.' Kirby pointed to a building that was little more than a hovel. It had partly collapsed and the rest looked as if it could fall at any moment. Sharpe turned to the men. 'You wait here. Sergeant, Peters, come with me.'

Peters was from the South Essex. Sharpe had noted him as a sensible man, older than most, and he needed someone from the deserters' own Battalion so that no one could think that the green-jacketed Riflemen had ganged up on the South Essex.

He pushed open the door. He had half expected someone to be waiting with a gun but instead he found himself looking at a room of unimaginable squalor. The four men were on the floor, two of them lying, the others sitting by the dead embers of a fire. Light filtered thickly through holes that had once been windows and through the broken roof and upper floors. The men were dressed in rags.

Sharpe crossed to the two sick men. He crouched and looked at their faces; they were white and shivering, the pulse beat almost gone. He turned to the others.

'Who are you?'

'Corporal Moss, sir.' The man had a fortnight's growth of beard and his cheeks were sunken. They had obviously not been eating. 'This is Private Ibbotson,' he pointed to his companion. 'And those are Privates Campbell and Trapper, sir.' Moss was being punctilious and polite as though it could save him from his fate. Dust lay heavy in the air, the room was filled with the stench of illness and ordure.

'Why are you in Oropesa?'

'Came to rejoin the Regiment, sir,' Moss said, but it was said too quickly. There was silence. Ibbotson sat by the dead fire and stared at the ground between his knees. He was the only one with a weapon, a bayonet held in his left hand, and Sharpe guessed that he did not approve of what was happening.

'Where are your weapons?'

'Lost 'em, sir. And the uniforms.' Moss was eager to please.

'You mean you sold them.'

Moss shrugged. 'Yes, sir.'

'And you drank away the money?'

'Yes, sir.'

There was a sudden noise in the next room and Sharpe whirled to face the doorway. There was nothing there. Moss shook his head. 'Rats, sir. Bloody armies of them.'

Sharpe looked back to the deserters. Ibbotson was now staring at him, the frightening stare of a crazed fanatic. For a moment Sharpe wondered if he was planning to use the bayonet.

'What are you doing here, Ibbotson? You don't want to rejoin the Regiment.'

The man said nothing. Instead he lifted his right arm that had been hidden behind his body. There was no hand, just a stump wrapped in blood-soaked rags.

''Ibbs got in a fight, sir,' Moss said. 'Lost 'is 'and. He's no use to anyone no more, sir. 'E's right-handed, you see,' he added lamely.

'You mean he's no use to the French.'

There was silence. The dust hung thick in the air. 'That's right.' Ibbotson had spoken. He had an edu-cated voice. Moss tried to quieten him but Ibbotson ignored the Corporal. 'We would have been with the French a week ago but these fools decided to drink.'

Sharpe stared at him. It was strange to hear a cultured voice coming from the rags, stubble and blood-soaked bandages. The man was ill, he probably had gangrene, but it hardly mattered now. By admitting they were running towards the enemy Ibbotson had condemned all four. If they had been caught trying to get to a neutral country they might have been sent, as Sharpe might be, to the garrison in the West Indies where the fever would kill them anyway, but there was only one punishment for men who deserted to the enemy. Corporal Moss knew it. He looked up at Sharpe and pleaded. 'Honest, sir, we didn't know what we was doing. We waited 'ere, sir . . .'

'Shut your teeth, Moss!' Ibbotson glared at him then turned to Sharpe, his hand moved the bayonet higher but it was only to emphasise his remarks. 'We're going to lose this war. Any fool can see that! There are more French armies than Britain could raise in a hundred years. Look at you!' His voice was filled with scorn. 'You might beat one General, then another, but they'll keep coming! And they'll win! And do you know why? Because they have an idea. It's called freedom, and justice, and equality!' He stopped abruptly, his eyes blazing.

'What are you, Ibbotson?' Sharpe asked.

'A man.'

Sharpe smiled at the dramatic challenge in the answer. The argument wasn't new, Rifleman Tongue could be relied on to trot it out most nights, but Sharpe was curious why an educated man like Ibbotson should be in the ranks of the army and preaching the French shibboleths of freedom.

'You're educated, Ibbotson. Where are you from?'

Ibbotson did not answer. He stared at Sharpe, clutching his bayonet. There was silence. Behind him Sharpe heard Harper and Peters shuffle their feet on the hard earth floor. Moss cleared his throat and beckoned at Ibbotson. ''E's a vicar's son, sir.' He said it as if it explained everything.

Sharpe looked at Ibbotson. The son of a vicarage? Perhaps the father had died or the family was too large and penury could lie at the end of both those roads. But what fate had driven Ibbotson to join the army? To pit his puny strength against the drunks and hardened criminals who were the usual scrapings gathered by the recruiting parties? Ibbotson stared back at him and then, to Sharpe's disgust, began to cry. He let go of the bayonet and buried his face in the crook of his left elbow and Sharpe wondered if he were suddenly thinking of a vicarage garden beside a church and a long-lost mother baking bread in the ripeness of an English summer. He turned to Harper.

'They're under arrest, Sergeant. You'll have to carry those two.'

He stepped outside the hovel into the foetid alleyway. 'Kirby?'

'Sir?'

'You can go.' The man ran off. Sharpe did not want him to face the four deserters whose arrest he had caused. 'You others. Inside.'

He stared up between the narrowing walls at the patch of sky. Swallows flashed across the opening, the colours were deepening into night, and tomorrow there would be executions. But first there was Josefina. Harper came to the door. 'We're ready, sir.'

'Then let's go.'

CHAPTER 13

Sharpe woke with a start, sat up, instinctively reached for a weapon and then, realising where he was, sank back on the pillow. He was covered with sweat though the night was cool and a small breeze stirred the edges of the curtains either side of the open window through which he could see a full moon. Josefina sat beside the bed, watching him, a glass of wine in her hand. 'You were dreaming.'

'Yes.'

'What about?'

'My first battle.' He did not say any more but in his dream he had been unable to load the Brown Bess, the bayonet would not fit the muzzle, and the French kept coming and laughing at the frightened boy on the wet plains of Flanders. Boxtel, it had been called, and he rarely thought of the messy fight in the damp field. He looked at the girl. 'What about you?' He patted the bed. 'Why are you up?'

She shrugged. 'I couldn't sleep.' She had put on some kind of dark robe and only her face and the hand holding the glass were visible in the unlit room.

'Why couldn't you sleep?'

'I was thinking. About what you said.'

'It may not happen.'

She smiled at him. 'No.'

Somewhere in the town a dog barked but there were no other sounds. Sharpe thought of the prisoners and wondered if they were spending their last night awake and listening to the same dog. He thought back to the evening after he had come back from the guardroom and the long conversation with Josefina. She wanted to reach Madrid, was desperate to reach Madrid, and Sharpe had told her he thought it unlikely that the allies would get as far as Spain's capital. Sharpe thought that Josefina had little idea why she wanted to reach Madrid, it was the dream city for her, the pot of gold at the end of a fading rainbow, and he was jealous of her desire to get there. 'Why not go back to Lisbon?'

'My husband's family won't welcome me, not now.'

'Ah, Edward.'

'Duarte.' Her correction was automatic.

'Then go home.' They had had this conversation before. He tried to force her to reject every option but staying near him as though he thought he could afford to keep her.

'Home? You don't understand. They will force me to wait for him just like his parents do. In a convent or in a dark room, it doesn't matter.' Her voice was edged with despair. She had been brought up in Oporto, the daughter of a merchant who was rich enough to mix with the important English families in the town who dominated the Port trade. She had learned English as a child because that language was the tongue of the wealthy and powerful in her home town. Then she had married Duarte, ten years her senior, and Keeper of the King's Falcons in Lisbon. It was a courtier's job, far from any falcons, and she had loved the glitter of the palace, the balls, the fashionable life. Then, two years before,

175

when the Royal Family had fled to Brazil, Duarte had taken a mistress instead of his wife and she had been left in the big house with his parents and sisters. 'They wanted me to go into a convent. Can you believe that? That I should wait for him in a convent, a dutiful wife, while he fathers bastards on that woman?'

Sharpe rolled off the bed and walked to the window. He leaned on the black ironwork, oblivious of his nakedness, and stared towards the east as if, in the night sky, he might see the reflection of the French fires. They were there, a long day's march away, but there was nothing to be seen except the moonlight on the countryside and the falling roofs of the town. Josefina came and stood beside him and ran her fingers down the scars on his back. 'What happens tomorrow?'

Sharpe turned and looked down on her. 'They get shot.'

'It's quick?'

'Yes.' There was no point in telling her of the times when the bullets missed and the officers had to walk up and blow the heads apart with a pistol. He put an arm round her and drew her to him, smelling her hair. She rested her head on his chest, her fingers still exploring the scars. 'I'm frightened.' Her voice was very small.

'Of them?'

'Yes.'

Gibbons and Berry had been in the guardroom when the deserters had been brought in. Sir Henry was there, rubbing his hands, and in his delight at the capture of the fugitives had effusively thanked Sharpe, all enmity suddenly put aside. The court-martial was a formality, a matter of moments, and then the paper had gone to be signed by the General and the fate of the four men sealed. Sharpe, for a few moments, had been left in the room with the two Lieutenants but nothing had been said to him. They had talked quietly, occasionally laughing, looking at him as if to provoke his anger, but it was the wrong time and place. It would come. He tilted her face towards him. 'Would you need me if they were not here?'

She nodded. 'You still don't understand. I'm a married woman and I've run away. Oh, I know he's done worse, but that does not count against him. The day I left Duarte's parents I became alone. Do you see? I can't go back there, my parents will not forgive me. I thought in Madrid . . .' She tailed away.

'And Christian Gibbons said he would look after you in Madrid?'

She nodded again. 'Other girls went, you know that. There are so many officers. But now.' She stopped again. He knew what she was thinking.

'Now you're worried. No Madrid and you're with someone who has no money and you're thinking of all those nights in the fields or flea-ridden cottages?'

She smiled up at him and Sharpe felt the pang of her beauty. 'One day, Richard, you'll be a Colonel with a big horse, and lots of money, and you'll be horrible to all the Captains and Lieutenants.'

He laughed. 'But not quickly enough for you?' He had spoken the truth, he knew, but it did not help her. There were other girls, girls of good family like Josefina, who had risked everything and run to the soldiers. But they had been unmarried and had found refuge in a fast wedding and their families had been forced to make the best of it. But Josefina? Sharpe knew she would find a man richer than he, a cavalry officer with money to spare and an eye for a woman, and her affection for Sharpe would be over-ridden by the need for comfort and security. He pulled her very tight to his chest, feeling the night air chill on his skin. 'I'll look after you.'

'Promise?' Her voice was muffled.

'I promise.'

'Then I won't be frightened.' She pulled slightly away. 'You're cold?'

'It doesn't matter.'

'Come on.' She led him back into the dark room. He knew that she was his for a short time, and only a short time, and he was saddened by it. Outside the dog barked on at the empty sky.

CHAPTER 14

The Battalion paraded in companies forming three sides of a hollow square. The fourth side, instead of the accustomed flogging triangle, was made up of two leaning poplar trees that grew beside a shallow pool. The fringes of the pond had been trampled by cavalry and the mud had dried into ochre lumps streaked with green scum. Between the trees lay the Battalion's bass drum and on its grey stretched skin there rested an open bible and prayer book. There was no wind to stir the pages, just the sun continuing its relentless assault on the plain and on the men who sweated at attention in full uniform.

Sharpe stood before the Light Company at the left of the line and stared over the heads of the Grenadier Company opposite at the castle of Oropesa. It dominated the plain for miles, its curtain walls rising like stone slabs above the roofs of the town and Sharpe wondered idly what it must have been like to ride in full knightly armour in the days when the castle was a real obstacle. Today's modern siege artillery would punch through the seemingly solid walls and bring the stones tumbling into the steep streets in devastating avalanches. Sweat stung his eyes, dripped on to his green jacket, trickled down his spine. He felt curiously light-hearted, not at all a fit state to watch deserters blown into eternity, and as he stared at the castle he thought of Josefina and somehow, in the morning light, the bargain did not seem such a bad one. She was his for as long as she needed him but, in return, she offered him her happiness and vivacity. And when the arrangement ends? A good soldier, he knew, always planned for the battle after the one ahead but he could make no plans for the moment when Josefina would take herself away.

He looked at Gibbons who paraded on his horse with the Light Company. Simmerson was mounted in the centre of the square next to General 'Daddy' Hill who, with his staff, had come to fulfil his duty of watching execution done. Gibbons sat, stony faced, and stared straight ahead. As soon as this parade was done Sharpe knew he would return to the safety of his uncle's side and the Lieutenant had spoken no word to Sharpe, just ridden his horse over to the company, turned it, and sat still. There was no need for words. Sharpe could feel the hatred almost radiating from the man, the determination for revenge, for Sharpe had not only gained the promotion Gibbons wanted but worse than that the Rifleman had the girl too. Sharpe knew the matter was unresolved.

Fourteen men, all guilty of minor crimes, marched into the square and were stood facing the trees. Their punishment was to act as the firing squad and as the men stood there, their muskets grounded, they stared with fascination at the two newly dug graves and the crude wooden coffins that waited for Ibbotson and Moss. The other two prisoners had died in the night. Sharpe half wondered whether Parton, the Battalion's doctor, had helped them on their way rather than force the Battalion to watch two desperately sick men lashed to the trees and shot to pieces. Sharpe had seen many executions. As a child he had watched a public hanging and listened to the excitement of the crowd as the victims jerked and twitched on the gallows. He had seen men blown from the muzzles of decorated brass cannon, their bodies shredded into the Indian landscape, he had watched comrades tortured by the Tippoo's women, fed to wild beasts, he had hung men by a casual roadside himself, yet most often he had seen men shot in the full panoply of ritual execution. He had never enjoyed the spectacle; he supposed no sensible man did, but he knew it was necessary. Somehow this execution was subtly different. It was not that Moss and Ibbotson did not deserve to die, they had deserted, planned to join the enemy, and there could be no end for them other than the firing squad. Yet coming on top of the fight at the bridge, coming on top of Simmerson's floggings, his repeated condemnation of his men for losing the colour, the execution was seen by the Battalion as summing up Simmerson's contempt and hatred for them. Sharpe had rarely felt such sullen resentment from any troops.

In the distance, threading its way through the crowds of British and Spanish spectators, the Provost-Marshal's party appeared, prisoners and guard. Forrest walked his horse forward of Simmerson.

''Talion! Fix bayonets!'

Blades scraped out of scabbards and steel rippled round the ranks of the companies. The men must die with due ceremony. Sharpe watched Gibbons bend down to talk to the sixteen-year-old Ensign Denny.

'Your first execution, Mr Denny?'

The youngster nodded. He was pale and apprehensive like the younger soldiers in the ranks. Gibbons chuckled. 'Best target practice the men can have!'

'Quiet!' Sharpe glared at them. Gibbons smiled secretly.

''Talion!' Forrest's horse edged sideways. The Major calmed it. 'Shoulder arms!'

The lines of men became tipped with bayonets. There was silence. The prisoners wore trousers and shirts, no jackets, and Sharpe supposed them to be half full of rough brandy or rum. A Chaplain walked with them, the mumble of his words just carrying to Sharpe, but the prisoners seemed to take no notice of him as they were marched to the trees. The drama moved inexorably forward. Moss and Ibbotson were tied to the trunks, blindfolded, and Forrest stood the firing squad to attention. Ibbotson, the son of the vicarage, was nearest to Sharpe and he could see the man's lips moving frenetically. Was he praying? Sharpe could not hear the words.

Forrest gave no commands. The firing party had been rehearsed to obey signals rather than orders and they presented and aimed to jerks of the Major's sword. Suddenly Ibbotson's voice came clear and loud, the educated tones filled with desperation, and Sharpe recognised the words. 'We have erred and strayed from thy ways like lost sheep . . .' Forrest dropped the sword, the muskets banged, the bodies jerked maniacally, and a flock of birds burst screeching from the branches. Two Lieutenants ran forward with drawn pistols but the musket balls had done their work and the bodies hung with crushed and bloodied chests in front of the lingering white musket smoke.

A murmur, barely audible, went through the ranks of the Battalion. Sharpe turned on his men.

'Quiet!'

The Light Company stood silent. The smoke from the firing party smelt pungent in the air. The murmur became louder. Officers and Sergeants screamed orders but the men of the South Essex had found their protest and the humming became more insistent. Sharpe kept his own company quiet by sheer force, by standing glaring at them with drawn sword, but he could do nothing about the contempt that they showed on their faces. It was not aimed at him, it was for Simmerson, and the Colonel twitched his reins in the centre of the square and bellowed for silence. The noise increased. Sergeants ran into the ranks and struck at men they suspected of making any sound, officers screamed at companies, adding to the din, and from beyond the Battalion came the jeers of the British soldiers from other units who had drifted out of the town to watch the execution.

Gradually the moaning and humming died away, as slowly as the executioners' smoke thinned into the air, and the Battalion stood silent and motionless. 'Daddy' Hill had not moved or spoken but now he motioned to his aides-de-camp and the small group trotted delicately away, past the firing squad who now lifted the bodies into the coffins, and off towards Oropesa. Hill's face was expressionless. Sharpe had never met 'Daddy' Hill but he knew, as did the rest of the army, that the General had a reputation as a kind and considerate officer and Sharpe wondered what he thought of Simmerson and his methods. Rowland Hill commanded six Battalions but Sharpe was certain none would offer him as many problems as the South Essex.

Simmerson rode his horse to the graves, wrenched the beast round, and stood in his stirrups. His face was suffused with blood, his rage obvious and throbbing, his voice shrill in the silence. 'There will be a parade for punishment at six o'clock this evening. Full equipment! You will pay for that display!' The men stood silent. Simmerson lowered his rump on to the saddle. 'Major Forrest! Carry on!'

The Battalion marched past, company by company, the open coffins and the men were made to stare at the mangled bodies waiting by their graves. There, said the army, is what will happen to you if you run away; and more than that because the names of the dead men would be sent home to be posted on their parish notice boards so that shame could descend on their families as well. The companies marched past in silence.

When the Battalion was gone and the other spectators had gawped at the remains a working party lowered the coffins into the graves. Earth was shovelled into the holes, the grass turves carefully replaced so that to a casual eye there were no visible signs of the burials. They were deliberately left unmarked, the final insult, but when all the soldiers had gone Spanish peasants found the graves and hammered wooden crosses into the turf. It was no measure of respect, just the precaution of sensible men. The dead were Protestants, buried in unhallowed ground, and the crude crosses were there to keep the unquiet spirits firmly underground. The people of Spain had enough problems with the war; the armies of France, Spain, and now Britain crossed and recrossed their land. There was little a peasant could do about that, or about the men who fought the Guerilla, the little war. But the ghosts of heathen Englishmen were another matter. Who needed them to scare the cattle and stalk the fields by night? They hammered the crosses deep and slept easy.

CHAPTER 15

One man in ten was to be flogged. Sixty men from the Battalion, six from each company, the Captain of each company to deliver his six men, stripped to the waist, ready to be tied to the flogging triangles that Simmerson was having made by local carpenters. The Colonel had made his announcement and then he glared with his small red eyes round the assembled officers. Were there any comments?

Sharpe took a breath. To say anything was useless, to say nothing was cowardly.

'I think it a bad idea, sir.'

'Captain Sharpe thinks it a bad idea.' Simmerson dripped acid with every word. 'Captain Sharpe, gentlemen, can tell us how to command men. Why is it a bad idea, Captain Sharpe?'

'To shoot two men in the morning and flog sixty in the afternoon seems to me to be doing the work of the French for them, sir.'

'You do. Well, damn you, Sharpe, and damn your ideas. If the discipline in this Battalion was as strictly enforced by the Captains as I demand then this punishment would not be necessary. I will have them flogged! And that includes your precious Riflemen, Sharpe! I expect three of them in your six! There'll be no favouritism.'

There was nothing to be said or done. The Captains told their companies and, like Sharpe, cut straws and drew lots to determine who should be Simmerson's victims. Three dozen strokes each for sixty men. By two o'clock the victims were scrounging for spirits that might dull their flesh and their sullen companions began the long afternoon of cleaning and polishing their kit for Simmerson's inspection. Sharpe left them to their work and went back to the house that served as the Battalion's headquarters. There was trouble in the air, a mood reminiscent of the heaviness before a thunderstorm, Sharpe's happiness of the morning was replaced by apprehension and he found himself wondering what might happen before he went back to the house where Josefina waited for him and dreamed of Madrid.

He spent the afternoon laboriously filling in the company books. Each month the Day Book had to be copied into the Ledger and the Ledger was due for Simmerson's inspection in a week. He found ink, sharpened a quill, and with his tongue between his teeth began writing the details. He could have delegated the job to the Sergeant who looked after the books but he preferred to do the job himself and then no one could accuse the Sergeant of favouritism. To Thomas Cresacre, Private, was debited the cost of one new shoebrush. Fivepence. Sharpe sighed; the entry in the columns hid some small tragedy. Cresacre had hurled the brush at his wife and the wooden back had split against a stone wall. Sergeant McGivern had seen it happen and reported the man and so on top of his marital troubles Thomas Cresacre would now lose fivepence from a day's pay of twelvepence. The next entry in the small Day Book that lived in Sharpe's pocket was for a pair of shoes for Jedediah Horrell. Sharpe hesitated.

Horrell claimed the shoes had been stolen and Sharpe was inclined to believe him. Horrell was a good man, a sturdy labourer from the Midlands, and Sharpe always found his musket cared for and his equipment orderly. And Horrell had already been punished. For two days he had marched in borrowed boots and his feet were blistered and burst. Sharpe crossed the entry from his Day Book and wrote in the Ledger 'Lost in Action'. He had saved Private Horrell six shillings and sixpence. He drew the Accoutrement Book towards him and laboriously copied the information from the Ledger into the book. He was amused to see that Lennox had already described every man in the company as having lost a stock 'in Action' so officially the stocks, like Horrell's boots, were now a charge on the government rather than on the individual who had lost them. For an hour he kept copying from Day Book to Ledger to Accoutrement Book, the small change of daily soldiering. When he had finished he drew the Mess Book towards him. This was easier. Sergeant Read, who kept the books, had already crossed out the names of the men who had died at Valdelacasa and written in the new names, Sharpe's Riflemen and the six men who had been drafted into the Light Company when Wellesley made them the new Battalion of Detachments. Against each of the names Sharpe wrote the figure three shillings and sixpence, the sum that was debited each week for the cost of their food. It was unfair, he knew, because the men were already on half rations and the word was that the supply situation was worsening. The Commissary officers were scouring the Tagus valley, there were frequent clashes between British and French patrols to decide which side could search a village for hidden food. There were even battles between the

British and their Spanish allies who had failed to deliver a hundredth part of the supplies they had promised yet they daily drove in herds of pigs, sheep, cattle or goats for their own men. But it was not in Sharpe's power to reduce the amount the men paid even if the rations were not delivered in full. Instead he noted at the bottom of the page that the sum was double the food delivered and hoped that he would be ordered to redress the balance later. In the next column he wrote fourpence in each line, the cost of having the men's clothes washed by the wives on the strength. A man's washing cost him seventeen shillings and fourpence a year, his rations over eight pounds. Each private earned a shilling a day, seventeen pounds and sixteen shillings a year, but by the time he had been deducted for food, for washing, for pipeclay and blackball, for soling and heeling, and the one day's pay each year that went to the Military hospitals at Chelsea and Kilmainham each man was left with the three sevens. Seven pounds, seven shillings and seven pence and Sharpe knew from bitter experience that they were lucky if they got even that. Most men lost further sums to replace missing equipment and the truth was that each private was paid about fourpence halfpenny a day to fight the French.

As a Captain Sharpe received ten shillings and six-pence a day. It seemed like a fortune but more than half was deducted for his food and then the officers' mess demanded a further levy of two shillings and eightpence a day to pay for wine, luxury foods, and the mess servants. He paid more for cleaning, for the hospitals, and he knew the sums backwards. They simply did not add up. And now Josefina was looking to him for money. Hogan had lent him money and, added to the contents of his leather bag, he had enough for the next fortnight, but after that? His only hope was to find a rich corpse on the battlefield. A very rich corpse.

Sharpe finished with the books, shut them, laid the quill on the table and yawned as a clock in the town struck four. He opened the Weekly Mess Book again and looked down at the names, wondering morbidly how many would still be there in a week's time and how many would have the word 'deceased' entered against them. Would his name be crossed out? Would some other officer look at the Ledger and wonder who had written 'Fivepence, one shoe-brush', against the name Thomas Cresacre? He shut the books again. It was all academic. The army had not been paid for a month and even then they had not been paid up to date. He would give the books to Sergeant Read who would store them on the company mule and when, and if, the pay arrived Read would make the deductions from the books and pay the men their handfuls of coins. There was a knock on the door.

'Who is it?'

'Me, sir.' It was Harper's voice.

'Come in.'

Harper's face was bleak, his manner formal. 'Well, Sergeant?'

'Trouble, sir. Bad. The men are refusing to parade.'

Sharpe remembered his apprehension. 'Which men?'

'Whole bloody Battalion, sir. Even our lads have joined in.' When Patrick Harper spoke of 'our lads' he meant the Riflemen. Sharpe stood up and slung on the big sword. 'Who knows about this?'

'Colonel does, sir. Men sent him a letter.'

Sharpe swore under his breath. 'They sent him a letter? Who signed it?'

Harper shook his head. 'No one signed it, sir. It just

tells him that they won't parade and if he comes near they'll blow his bloody head off.'

Sharpe picked up the rifle. There was a word for what was happening and the word was 'mutiny'. Simmerson's flogging of one man in ten could easily change into decimation and instead of being flogged the men would be stood against the trees and shot. He looked at Harper. 'What's happening?'

'Lot of talk, sir. They're barricading themselves in the timber yard.'

'All of them?'

Harper shook his head. 'No, sir. There's a couple of hundred still in the orchard. Your company's there, sir, but the lads in the yard are trying to persuade them to join in.'

Sharpe nodded. The Battalion had been bivouacked in an olive grove which the men called an orchard simply because the trees were laid out in neat rows. The grove was behind a timber yard, a walled yard with just one entrance. 'Who delivered the letter?'

'Don't know, sir. It was pushed under the door of Simmerson's house.'

Sharpe hurried out of the door. The courtyard of the house was shadowed and silent, most officers were taking the chance of looking at the town before they marched the next day to meet the French. 'Are there any officers at the timber yard?'

'No, sir.'

'What about the Sergeants?'

Harper's face was expressionless. Sharpe guessed that many of the Sergeants were sympathetic to the protest but, like the big Irishman, knew better than the men what the result would be if the Battalion refused to parade. 'Wait here.'

Sharpe ran back into the house. The rooms lay cool and empty. A woman looked at him from the kitchen, a string of peppers held in her hand, and quickly shut the door when she saw his face. Sharpe took the stairs two at a time and threw open the door of the room where the Light Company's junior officers were quartered. Ensign Denny was the only occupant and the sixteen-year-old was lying fast asleep on a straw mattress.

'Denny!'

The boy came awake, frightened. 'Sir!'

'Where's Knowles?'

'Don't know, sir. In town, I think.'

Sharpe thought for a second. The boy stared wide-eyed from the mattress. Sharpe's hand gripped and re-gripped the sword hilt. 'Join me in the courtyard as soon as you're dressed. Hurry.'

Harper was waiting in the street where the heat of the sun had seared the stones so that Sharpe could feel the burning even through the soles of his boots. 'Sergeant, I want the Light Company on parade in five minutes in the track behind the orchard. Full kit.'

The Sergeant opened his mouth to ask a question, saw the look on Sharpe's face, and threw a salute instead. He strode off. Denny came out of the courtyard buckling on his sword which trailed on the stones beside him. He looked apprehensive as Sharpe turned to him. 'Listen carefully. You are to find out for me where Colonel Simmerson is and what he is doing. Understand?' The boy nodded. 'And you're not to let him know that's what you're doing. Try the castle. Then come and find me. I'll either be on the track beside the orchard or on the square in front of the timber yard. If I'm not in either place then find Sergeant Harper and wait with him. Understand?' Denny nodded again. 'Repeat it to me.'

The boy went through his instructions. He desperately wanted to ask Sharpe what the excitement was about but dared not. Sharpe nodded when he finished. 'One more thing, Christopher.' He deliberately used Denny's Christian name to give the lad reassurance. 'You are not, in any circumstance, to go in the timber yard. Now, be off. If you see Lieutenant Knowles, or Major Forrest, or Captain Leroy, ask them if they'll join me. Hurry!'

Denny clutched his sword and ran off. Sharpe liked him. One day he would make a good officer if he was not first spitted on the bayonet of a French Grenadier. Sharpe turned down the hill towards the timber yard and the billets of the men. There was only one chance of averting a disaster and that was to get the Battalion on parade as soon as possible before Simmerson had time to react to the threat of mutiny. There was a clatter of hooves behind him and he turned to see a rider waving at him. It was Captain Sterritt, the officer of the day, and he looked understandably nervous.

'Sharpe!'

'Sterritt?'

Sterritt pulled up his horse. 'There's an officers' call at the castle. Now. Everyone.'

'What's happening?'

Sterritt looked frantically round the deserted street as though someone might overhear the further disaster that had overtaken Simmerson's Battalion. Sharpe had hardly seen Sterritt since the fight at the bridge. The man was patently frightened of Simmerson, of the men, of Sharpe, of everyone and deliberately made himself insignificant so as to escape notice. He sketched in the events at the timber yard. Sharpe interrupted him. 'I know about that. What's happening at the castle?'

'The Colonel's asked to see General Hill.'

There was still time. He looked up at the frightened Captain. 'Listen. You haven't seen me. Understand, Sterritt? You have not seen me.'

'But . . .'

'No buts. Do you want to see those sixty men shot?'

Sterritt's mouth dropped open. He looked round the street again and back to Sharpe. 'The Colonel's orders are that no one is to go near the timber yard.'

'You haven't seen me so how could I have heard the order?'

'Oh.' Sterritt did not know how to react. He watched Sharpe go on down the street and wished again that he had been born four years earlier; then he would have been the eldest and would now be a gentleman farmer. As it was he felt like a rag doll swept away in a flood. He turned sadly away towards the castle and wondered what would become of it all.

In front of the timber yard was a huge open space like an English village green except that the grass here was bleached yellow and grew thinly on the shallow soil. The space was used for a weekly market but today it was a football ground for soldiers from a dozen Battalions. Sharpe could see troops from the 48th, the 29th, and a company of Royal American Rifles whose green jackets reminded him of happier days. The men cheered and jeered the players; soon, thought Sharpe, they would have a more interesting spectacle to watch.

He turned left, beside a wall of the timber yard, and down towards the orchard. No one was on the track as he had expected but as he drew nearer he shouted for Harper and was rewarded by hearing a flurry of commands as the Light Company Sergeants ordered the men on to the track. He assumed the men would be reluctant to parade but doubted if they would dare oppose him, and he stopped and watched as Harper paraded the company in four ranks.

'Company on parade. Sir!'

'Thank you, Sergeant.'

Sharpe walked to the front of the company, his back to the trees and to the crowd of spectators drawn from the Battalion's women mixed with men from the other companies who had come over the wall from the yard.

'We're going on parade early.' They didn't move. Their eyes stared rigidly in front of them. 'The six men detailed for punishment one step forward.'

There was a fractional hesitation. The six men, three Riflemen and three from the original Light Company, looked left and right but took the pace. There was a murmur in the ranks.

'Quiet!'

The men went silent but from behind, from the orchard, a group of women began shouting insults and telling their men not to be cowards. Sharpe spun round.

'Hold your tongues! Women can be flogged too!'

He marched the company to the market square and moved the footballers reluctantly from the thin turf. The six men to be flogged stood in the front rank wearing only their trousers and shirts. They went easily enough. Sharpe could tell from their faces that they were relieved that he had taken them over and forced them on to parade. Whatever hot words had been spoken in the burning Spanish afternoon Sharpe knew that no man really wanted to go through the hopeless business of taking on the full authority of the army. That sounded simple, he thought, and now he had to persuade nine other companies. He walked close to the six men in the front rank and looked hard at them.

'I know it's unfair.' He spoke quietly. 'You didn't make the noise this morning.' He stopped. He was not sure what he wanted to say and to go further would be to sound too sympathetic to their protest. Gataker, one of the unlucky Riflemen, grinned cheerfully.

'It's all right, sir. It's not your fault. And we've bribed the drummer boys.'

Sharpe smiled back. The bribe would be of little use, Simmerson would make sure of that, but he was grateful for Gataker's words. He stepped back five paces and raised his voice.

'Wait here! If any man moves he'll replace one of these six men!'

He walked over the turf towards the double gates of the timber yard. He had never really worried about his own men, knew that they would follow him, but as he paced towards the shut gates he wondered what trouble was brewing inside. And, more importantly, what trouble was being brewed behind the slab-like walls of the castle. He felt for his sword hilt and walked on.

CHAPTER 16

'Sir! Captain! Sir!'

Ensign Denny was running towards him, sword trailing, his face streaming with sweat. 'Sir?'

'What did you find out?'

'Colonel's at the castle, sir. I think he's with the General. I met Captain Leroy and Major Forrest. Captain Leroy asked you to wait for him.'

Over Denny's shoulder Sharpe saw Leroy, on his horse, coming from the steep streets that led to the castle. The American, thank God, was not hurrying. He walked his horse as though there were no emergency; if the men in the timber yard saw panic and worry among the officers they would think they were winning and merely become more obstinate.

Leroy's horse almost sauntered the last few yards. The American nodded at Sharpe, took his hands off the reins, and lit a long black cheroot. 'Sharpe.'

Sharpe grinned. 'Leroy.'

Leroy slid off the horse and looked at Denny. 'You ride a horse, young man?'

'Oh yes, sir!'

'Well climb up on that one and keep her quiet for me. Here you are.' Leroy cupped his hands and heaved the Ensign into the saddle.

'Wait for us at the company,' Sharpe said.

Denny rode away. Leroy turned to Sharpe. 'There's bloody panic upstairs. Simmerson's turned green and is shrieking for the artillery, Daddy Hill's telling him to calm down.'

'You were up there?'

Leroy nodded. 'Met Sterritt. He's giving birth to kittens, thinks it's all his fault because he's officer of the day. Simmerson's screaming mutiny. What's happening?'

They walked on towards the timber yard. Sharpe refused the offer of a cheroot. 'They've said they won't go on parade. But no one's actually ordered them to yet. My lads went easy enough. As I see it we've got to get the rest out of there fast.'

Leroy blew a thin stream of smoke into the air. 'Simmerson's getting the cavalry.'

'What?'

'Daddy didn't have much choice, did he? Colonel comes to him and says the troops are mutineers. So the General's ordered the KGL down here. They'll be some time, though; they weren't even saddled up.'

The King's German Legion. They were the best cavalry in Wellesley's army; fast, efficient, brave, and a good choice to break up a mutiny. Sharpe dreaded the thought of the German horsemen clearing out the timber yard with their sabres.

'Where's Forrest?'

Leroy gestured at the castle. 'He's coming down here. He went to look for the Sergeant Major. I don't think he'll wait for Sir Henry and his heavies.' Leroy grinned. They were at the gates which were ajar. Harper had spoken of barricades but Sharpe could see none. Leroy gestured to him. 'Go ahead, Sharpe. I'll let you do the talking. They think you're some kind of a bloody miracle worker.'

His first impression was of a yard full of men lying, standing, sitting, their weapons piled, their jackets and equipment discarded. There was a fire burning in the centre of the yard which struck him as odd because of the heat of the day and then he remembered the extra triangles which Simmerson had ordered for the mass flogging. The Colonel must have ordered the work done at this yard and the men had burned the timber which had been crudely nailed together ready for the punishments. There was a momentary hush as the two officers came through the gate followed by a buzz of excited talk. Leroy leaned against the entrance, Sharpe walked slowly through the groups of men, heading for the fire which seemed to be the focus of the yard. The men were drinking, some already drunk, and as Sharpe walked slowly through the muttered comments and hostile looks a man ironically offered him a bottle. Sharpe ignored it, knocked the man's arm with his knee as he walked past, and heard the bottle break on the ground. He came to the space in front of the fire and as he turned to face the bulk of the men the muttering died down. He guessed there was not much fight in them, no ringleader had protested, there had only been sullen muttering.

'Sergeants!'

No one moved. There had to be Sergeants in the yard. He shouted again.

'Sergeants! On the double! Here!'

Still no one moved but in the corner of his eye he had the impression of a group of men, in shirts and trousers, stir uneasily. He pointed at them.

'Come on. Hurry! Put your equipment on!'

They hesitated. For a moment he wondered if the Sergeants were the ringleaders but then realised that they were probably afraid of the men. But they picked up jackets and belts. There was some shouting at them but no one made a move to stop them. Sharpe began to relax.

'No!' A man stood up to the left. There was a hush, all movement stopped, the Sergeants looked at the man who had spoken. He was a big man with an intelligent face. He turned to the men in the yard and spoke in a reasonable voice.

'We're not going. We decided that and we must keep to it!' His voice, like the dead Ibbotson's, was educated. He turned to Sharpe. 'The Sergeants can go, sir, but we're not. It isn't fair.'

Sharpe ignored him. This was not the time to discuss whether Simmerson's discipline was fair or unfair. Discipline, at moments like this, was not open to discussion. It existed and that was that. He turned back to the Sergeants.

'Come on! Move yourselves!'

The Sergeants, a dozen of them, came sheepishly to the fire. Sharpe was suddenly aware of the scorching heat of the blaze, added to the sun it was breaking his back into a prickly sweat. The Sergeants shuffled to a halt. Sharpe spoke loudly. 'You've got two minutes. I want everyone on parade, in this yard, properly dressed. The men to be flogged wearing shirts and trousers only. Grenadier Company by the gate, the rest formed on them. Move!'

They hesitated. Sharpe took a step towards them and they suddenly snapped into action. He turned and walked into the crowded men. 'On your feet! You're on parade! Hurry up!'

The burly man tried one last protest and Sharpe whipped round on him. 'You want more bloody executions? Move!'

It was all over. Some of the drunker men needed kicking

on to their feet but the little fight had gone out of them. Leroy joined Sharpe and, with the Sergeants, they dressed the companies. The men looked a mess. Their uniforms were unbrushed, spotted with sawdust, their belts stained and muskets dirty. Some of the men were pale with drink. Sharpe had rarely seen a Battalion in worse parade order but that was better than a mutinous rabble being chased by the efficient German cavalry.

Leroy swung open the gates, Sharpe gave the order, and the Battalion marched out in formation to line up on the Light Company. Forrest was outside. His mouth dropped as the first company emerged. He had a handful of officers and other Sergeants with him and they ran to their companies and shouted orders. The Battalion began to march crisply, the Sergeant Major hammered them into place, stood them at ease, stood the ranks easy. Sharpe marched up to Forrest's horse, snapped to attention, and saluted.

'Battalion on parade, sir!'

Forrest looked down on him. 'What happened?'

'Happened, sir? Nothing.'

'But I was told they refused to parade.'

Sharpe pointed at the Battalion. The men were pulling their uniforms into shape, brushing the worst dirt off their jackets, punching their shakoes into shape. Forrest stared at them and back to Sharpe. 'He's not going to like this.'

'The Colonel, sir?'

Forrest grinned. 'He's coming here with the cavalry, Sharpe. And General Hill.' Forrest checked his grin, it was unseemly, but Sharpe understood his amusement. Simmerson would be furious; he had disturbed a General, roused a Regiment of cavalry, and all for a mutiny that had not happened. The thought pleased Sharpe.

The Battalion stood in the heat, the bells in the town marked five o'clock and quarter past, they dusted their uniforms as well as they could. Perhaps half the officers were present, they dribbled in from the town, but the rest were with Simmerson. As the clock struck the half hour there was the thunder of hooves, a cloud of dust, and in a display of force calculated to demoralise the supposedly mutinying troops the blue-uniformed Dragoons of the King's German Legion galloped on to the market square. They were splendidly turned out in their blue jackets, fur-trimmed pelisses and, on their heads, brown fur colbacks. Their sabres were drawn and they rode straight for the timber yard. Slowly it dawned on them that it was empty and that the heads they had been sent to break were on parade. Orders were shouted, horses turned, the cavalry subsided into an embarrassed silence and watched the gaggle of red-coated horsemen follow them on to the market place; Colonel Sir Henry Simmerson with Major General Rowland Hill, aides-de-camp, officers of the Battalion like Gibbons and Berry, and behind them a gaggle of other mounted officers who had come to see the excitement. They all stopped and stared. Simmerson peered into the timber yard, looked back at the parade, and then once more into the yard. The Sergeant Major took his cue from Forrest.

''Talion! 'Shun!'

The Battalion of Detachments snapped to attention. The Sergeant Major filled his chest.

''Talion! Shoulder arms!'

The three movements were perfectly timed. There was only the sound of six hundred palms slapping six hundred muskets in unison.

''Talion will make the General Salute!' There was a General present. 'Present arms!'

Sharpe swept his sword into the salute. Behind him the companies slammed the ground with their right feet, the muskets dipped in glorious precision, the parade quivered with pride. 'Daddy' Hill saluted back. The Sergeant Major shouldered the Battalion's arms, ordered them, and stood the men at ease. Sharpe watched Forrest ride his horse to Simmerson and salute. He could see gesticulations but could hear nothing. Hill seemed to be asking the questions and Sharpe saw Forrest turn in his saddle and point in the direction of the Light Company. The pointed arm turned into a beckoning one. 'Captain Sharpe!'

Sharpe marched across the parade ground as though he were the Regimental Sergeant Major on a Royal parade. Damn Simmerson. He might as well have his face rubbed in the dirt. He cracked to a halt, saluted, and waited. Hill looked down on him, his round face shadowed by his large cocked hat.

'Captain Sharpe?'

'Sir!'

'You paraded the Battalion? Is that correct?'

'Sir!' Sharpe had learned as a Sergeant that repeating the word 'sir' with enough force and precision could get a man through most meetings with senior officers. Hill realised it too. He looked at his watch and then back at Sharpe. 'The parade is thirty minutes early. Why?'

'The men seemed bored, sir. I thought some drill would do them good so Captain Leroy and myself brought them out.'

Hill smiled, he liked the answer. He looked at the ranks standing immobile in the sunlight. 'Tell me, Captain, did anyone refuse to parade?'

'Refuse, sir?' Sharpe sounded surprised. 'No, sir.'

Hill looked at him keenly. 'Not one man, Captain?'

'No, sir. Not one man.' Sharpe dared not look at Simmerson. Once more the Colonel was looking foolish. He had cried 'mutiny' to a General of Division only to find that a junior Captain had paraded the men. Sharpe sensed Simmerson shifting uneasily on his saddle as Hill looked down shrewdly. 'You surprise me, Captain.'

'Surprise, sir?'

Hill smiled. He had dealt with enough Sergeants in his life to know the game Sharpe was playing. 'Yes, Captain. You see your Colonel received a letter saying that the men were refusing to parade. That's called mutiny.'

Sharpe turned innocent eyes on Simmerson. 'A letter, sir? Refusing to parade?' Simmerson glared at him, he would have killed Sharpe on the spot if he had dared. Sharpe looked back to Hill and let his expression change from innocent surprise to slow dawning of awareness. 'I think that must be a prank, sir. You know how playful the lads get when they're ready for battle.'

Hill laughed. He'd been beaten by enough Sergeants to know when to stop playing the game. 'Good! Well, what a to-do about nothing! Today seems to be the South Essex's day! This is the second parade I've attended in twelve hours. I think it's time I inspected your men, Sir Henry.' Simmerson said nothing. Hill turned back to Sharpe. 'Thank you, Captain. 95th, eh?'

'Yes, sir.'

'I've heard of you, haven't I? Sharpe. Let me think.' He peered down at the Rifleman then snapped his fingers. 'Of course! I'm honoured to make your acquaintance, Sharpe! Did you know the Rifles are on their way back?'

Sharpe felt his heart leap in excitement. 'Here, sir?'

'They might even be in Lisbon by now. Can't manage

without the Rifles, eh, Simmerson?' There was no reply. 'Which Battalion are you, Sharpe?'

'Second, sir.'

'You'll be disappointed, then. The first are coming. Still, it'll be good to see old friends again, eh?'

'Yes, sir.'

Hill seemed genuinely happy to be chatting away. Over the General's shoulder Sharpe caught a glimpse of Gibbons sitting disconsolate on his horse. The General slapped away a fly. 'What do they say about the Rifles, eh, Captain?'

'First on the field and last off it, sir.'

Hill nodded. 'That's the spirit! So you're attached to the South Essex, are you?'

'Yes, sir.'

'Well I'm glad you're in my division, Sharpe, very glad. Carry on!'

'Thank you, sir.' He saluted, about turned, and marched back towards the Light Company. As he went he heard Hill call out to the cavalry's commanding officer. 'You can go home! No business today!'

The General walked his horse down the ranks of the Battalion and talked affably with the men. Sharpe had heard much about 'Daddy' Hill and understood now why he had been given the nickname. The General had the knack of making every man think that he was cared for, seemed genuinely concerned about them, wanted them to be happy. There was no way in which he could not have seen the state of the Battalion. Even allowing for three weeks' marching and the fight at the bridge the men looked hastily turned out and sloppily dressed but Hill turned a blind eye. When he reached the Light Company he nodded familiarly to Sharpe, joked about Harper's height, made the men laugh. He left the company grinning and rode with Simmerson and his entourage to the centre of the parade ground.

'You've been bad lads! I was disappointed in you this morning!' He spoke slowly and distinctly so that the flank companies, like Sharpe's, could hear him clearly. 'You deserve the punishment that Sir Henry ordered!' He paused. 'But really you've done very well this afternoon! Early on parade!' There was a rustle of laughter in the ranks. 'You seem very keen to get your punishment!' The laughter died. 'Well, you're going to be disappointed. Because of your behaviour this afternoon Sir Henry has asked me to cancel the punishment parade. I don't think I agree with him but I'm going to let him have his way. So there will be no floggings.' There was a sigh of relief. Hill took another deep breath. 'Tomorrow we march with our Spanish allies towards the French! We're going to Talavera and there's going to be a battle! I'm proud to have you in my division. Together we're going to show the French just what being a soldier means!' He waved a benign hand at them. 'Good luck, lads, good luck!'

They cheered him till they were hoarse, took off their shakoes and waved them at the General who beamed back at them like an indulgent parent. When the noise died down he turned to Simmerson.

'Dismiss them, Colonel, dismiss them. They've done well!'

Simmerson had no alternative but to obey. The parade was dismissed, the men streamed off the field in a buzz of talk and laughter. Hill trotted back towards the castle and Sharpe watched Simmerson and his group of officers ride after him. The man had been made to look foolish and he, Sharpe, would be blamed. The tall Rifleman walked slowly back towards the town, head down to discourage conversation. It was true that he had enjoyed discomfiting Simmerson but the Colonel had asked for the treatment; he had not even bothered to check whether the men would refuse an order, he had simply screamed for the cavalry. Sharpe knew he had heaped too many insults on the Colonel and his nephew. Sharpe doubted now that Simmerson would be content with the letter that would be in Lisbon by now, waiting for a ship and a fair wind to carry the mail to London. The letter would blight Sharpe's career and unless he could perform a miracle in the battle that was coming nearer by the hour then Simmerson would have the satisfaction of seeing Sharpe broken. But there was more to it now. There was honour and pride and a woman. He doubted if Gibbons would seek an honourable solution, he doubted if the Lieutenant would be satisfied by the letter his uncle had written, and he felt a shiver of apprehension at what might happen. The girl would be Gibbons' target.

A man ran up behind him. 'Sir?'

Sharpe turned. It was the burly man who had tried to stop the Battalion parading in the timber yard. 'Yes?'

'I wanted to thank you, sir.'

'Thank me? For what?' Sharpe spoke harshly. The man was embarrassed. 'We would have been shot, sir.'

'I would happily have given the order myself.'

'Then thank you, sir.'

Sharpe was impressed. The man could have kept silent. 'What's your name?'

'Huckfield, sir.' He was educated and Sharpe was curious.

'Where did you get your education, Huckfield?'

'I was a clerk, sir, in a foundry.'

'A foundry?'

'Yes, sir. In Shropshire. We made iron, sir, all day and night. It was a valley of fire and smoke. I thought this might be more interesting.'

'You volunteered!' Sharpe's astonishment showed in his voice.

Huckfield grinned. 'Yes, sir.'

'Disappointed?'

'The air's cleaner, sir.' Sharpe stared at him. He had heard men talk of the new 'industry' that was springing up in Britain. They had described, like Huckfield, whole landscapes that were bricked over and dotted with the giant furnaces producing iron and steel. He had heard stories of bridges thrown over rivers, bridges made entirely of metal, of boats and engines that worked from steam, but he had seen none of these things. One night, round a camp fire, someone had said that it was the future and that the days of men on foot and on horseback were numbered. That was fantasy, of course, but here was Huckfield who had seen these things and the image of a country given over to great black machines with bellies of fire made Sharpe feel uncertain. He nodded to the man.

'Forget this afternoon, Huckfield. Nothing happened.'

He ignored the man's thanks. Being uncertain of the future was the price a soldier paid. Sharpe could not imagine being in an army that was not at war; he could not imagine what he might do if there was suddenly a peace and he had no job. But before then there was a battle to fight and an Eagle to win and a girl to fight for. He climbed up into the streets of Oropesa.

CHAPTER 17

In sixteen years' soldiering Sharpe had rarely felt such certainty that battle was about to be joined. The Spanish and British armies had combined at Oropesa and marched on to Talavera, twenty-one thousand British and thirty-four thousand Spanish, a vast army swollen by mules, servants, wives, children, priests, pouring eastwards to where the mountains almost met the River Tagus and the vast arid plain ended at the town of Talavera. The wheels of the hundred and ten field guns ground the white roads to fine dust, the hooves of over six thousand cavalry stirred the powder into the air where it clung to the infantry who trudged through the heat and listened to the far-off crackle as the leading Spanish skirmishers pushed aside the light screen of French Voltigeurs. To left and right Sharpe could see other plumes of dust where cavalry patrols rode parallel to the line of march; closer by, in the fields, the Battalion saw small groups of Spanish soldiers who had fallen out of the march and now lay, apparently unconcerned, chatting with their women, smoking, watching the long columns of British infantry file past.

The men were hungry. Hard as Wellesley tried, thorough as the Commissary could be, nevertheless there was simply not enough food for the whole army. The area between Oropesa and Talavera had already been scoured by the French, now it was searched by Spanish and British, and the Battalion had only eaten 'Tommies', pancakes made from flour and water, since they left Oropesa the day before. It was a time for tightening belts but the prospect of action had raised men's spirits and when the Battalion marched past the bodies of three French skirmishers they forgot their hunger at their first sight of French infantry. Sharpe told his Light Company that the dead men with their fringed epaulettes were the famous French Voltigeurs, the skirmishers, the men with whom the Light Company would fight their own private battle between the lines before the big Battalions clashed. The men of the South Essex, who had not seen enemy infantry before, stared curiously at the blue-jacketed bodies that had been thrown down beside a church wall. Dark stains marked the uniforms, their heads were bent back in the strange attitude of the dead, one man had a finger missing where Sharpe supposed it had been hacked off to get at a valuable ring. Ensign Denny stared at them with fascination, these were the famous French infantry that had marched the length and breadth of Europe, he looked at the moustached faces and wondered how he would feel when he saw similar faces, but animated, staring at him over the browned barrel of the French musket.

The French made no resistance to the west of Talavera or in the town itself. The armies marched through or past the town and on a mile until they stopped at dusk on the banks of a small river that flowed into the Tagus. The Battalion marched to the north of the town and Sharpe wondered how Josefina would find a room there. Hogan had promised to look after her and Sharpe stared at the crowds pressing into the narrow streets as though he might catch a glimpse of her. The men grumbled. They were tired and hungry and they resented being denied the pleasures of the town. They could see officers on horseback riding towards the old walls, their wives and children walked there, but the troops went on to the Alberche and camped in the cork groves that sloped down to the shallow river. Tomorrow they must fight. If they survived tomorrow then would come the time to buy drink in Talavera but first they must cross the River Alberche and defeat the army of Marshal Victor. Fires were lit throughout the trees, the Battalions swiftly settling in for the night, glancing apprehensively at the far river-bank where hundreds of smoke plumes mingled and shivered over the French camp. The armies had finally been brought together, British, Spanish and French, and tomorrow they must fight and Sharpe's company squatted by their fires and wondered about the men just across the river who sat by similar fires and made the same jokes in a different language.

Sharpe and Harper strolled to the river's edge where the Battalion's leading picquets were settling for a night's guard duty. Two men of the Light Company, dressed in greatcoats, nodded at Sharpe and jerked their thumbs across the river. A French picquet stood watching them, three men smoking pipes, while another Frenchman filled his canteen at the water's edge. The man looked up, saw the Riflemen, and raised a hand. He shouted something but they did not understand him. Sharpe shivered slightly. The sun had lost its heat, was reddening in the west, and the chill of the night was already making itself felt. He waved back at the Frenchman and turned back towards the cork grove.

Now was the time for the rituals before battle. Sharpe walked through the trees and chatted with men who prepared themselves with the obsessions for detail that all men thought might protect them in the chaos of the fight. The Riflemen had stripped their locks, pinned the massive rifle main springs with nails, and brushed every scrap of dirt from the machinery. Men put new flints in their muskets or rifles, unscrewed them and put them in again, looking for the perfect fit that would never come loose, turn sideways, or shatter in the pan. Pots of boiling water were carried carefully from the fires and poured into the barrels of the guns to flush out every last powder deposit because tomorrow a man's life might depend on how fast he could reload his musket. Joining the noise of the insects were the sounds of hundreds of stones rubbing endlessly on bayonets, the countrymen sharpening the blades as they used to sharpen reaping hooks or wide-bladed scythes. Men repaired uniforms, sewed on buttons, made new laces, as though to be comfortable was to be safer. Sharpe had been through the ritual a hundred times; he would go through it again tonight the way that a knight in times far past must have strapped every piece of armour, tightened each piece, delayed the next until the first was secure. Some Riflemen emptied all the fine powder from their horns and spread the black grains on clean white cloth to ensure there were no damp lumps that could clog the measuring spout in battle. There were the same jokes; 'Don't wear your hat tomorrow, Sarge, the French might see your face and die laughing.' That one always worked as long as the Sergeant did not see which man had shouted from the shadows; other men were asked to go and sleep with the French so their snoring would keep the enemy awake, the stale jokes were as much a part of the battle as the bullets which would begin to fly at first light.

Sharpe walked past the fires, swapping jokes, accepting tots of hoarded spirits, feeling the edges of bayonets, telling the men that the next day would not be bad. Nor should it be. The combined British and Spanish far outnumbered the French; the allies had the initiative, the battle should be short, swift, and victory almost a certainty. He listened to men boasting of the deeds they would perform next day and knew that the words covered their fear; it was right that they should. Other men, more quietly, asked him what it would be like. He smiled and told them they would see in the morning, but it would not be as bad as they feared, and shrugged away his knowledge of the chaos they would all have to control when the attacking infantry walked into the storm of canister and musket shot. He left the fires behind, skirted the bigger blaze where the officers' servants prepared the thin stew of salt beef that was the last of the hoarded supplies, and out of the trees altogether. In the last light of dusk he could see a farmhouse five hundred yards away where earlier he had seen the 16th Light Dragoons go with their horses. He crossed the fields and went into the yard. A line of troopers in blue and scarlet uniforms waited by the armourer. Sharpe waited for them to finish and then unsheathed the huge sword and carried it to the wheel. This was part of his ritual, to have the sword sharpened by a cavalry armourer because they made a finer edge, and the armourer looked at his Rifleman's uniform and grinned. He was an old soldier, too old to ride into battle, but he had seen it all, done it all himself. He took the blade from Sharpe, tested it with a broad thumb, and then pressed it on to the pedalled stone. The sparks flowed off the wheel, the blade sang, the man swept it lovingly up and down the edge and then sharpened the top six inches of the back blade. He wiped the sword with an oily piece of leather.

'Get yourself a German one, Captain.' It was an old argument, whether the Kligenthal blades were better than the British. Sharpe shook his head. 'I've eaten German swords with this one.'

The armourer cackled a toothless laugh and peered down the edge. 'There you are, Captain. Take care of it.'

Sharpe put some coins on the wheel frame and held the sword up to the last light of the western sky. There was a new sheen on the edge, he felt it with his thumb and smiled at the armourer. 'You'll never get a Kligenthal as sharp as that.'

The armourer said nothing but from behind him he took out a sabre and handed it to Sharpe. Sharpe sheathed his sword and took the curved blade. It felt as if it had been made for him, its balance was a miracle, as if the steel were not there even though it flashed in the red light. He touched the blade. It would have sliced through silk as cleanly as it must cut through the breast-plate of the French cavalry. 'German?' Sharpe asked.

'Yes, Captain. Belongs to our Colonel.' The armourer took the blade back. 'And I haven't begun to sharpen it yet!'

Sharpe laughed. The sabre must have cost two hundred guineas. One day, he promised himself, one day he would own such a sword, not taken from the dead, but a sword that was inscribed with his name, forged to his height, balanced for his grip. He went back to the trees and in the sky over the river he could see the glow of the enemy fires where twenty-two thousand Frenchmen were sharpening their own blades and wondering about the morning. Not many would sleep. Most would doze through the night, their wakefulness laced with apprehension, searching the eastern sky for a dawn that might be the last one they would ever see. Sharpe lay awake for part of the night and rehearsed the next day in his head. The plan was simple enough. The Alberche ran in a curve to join the River Tagus and the French were on the inside of the bend. In the morning the Spanish trumpets would sound, their thirty guns be unleashed, and the infantry would splash across the shallow river to attack the outnumbered French. And as the French retreated, as assuredly they must, so Wellesley would throw the British on to their flank. And Marshal Victor would be destroyed, his army broken between the hammer of the Spanish and the anvil of the British, and as the blue infantry withdrew the cavalry would come through the water and turn retreat into carnage. And once that was done, all perhaps before the citizens of Talavera went to their Sunday morning mass, there would only be King Joseph Bonaparte's twenty thousand men between the allies and Madrid. It was all so simple. Sharpe slept in his greatcoat, curled by the embers of a fire, a bronze eagle threading his sleep.

There were no bugles to wake them in the morning, nothing that might alert the French to the dawn attack instead of the more civilised hour of mid-morning when most men could be expected to fight. Sergeants and corporals shook the men awake, soldiers cursed the dew and the cold air that rasped in their throats. Every man glanced towards the river but the far bank was shrouded in mist and darkness, there was nothing to be seen, no sound to be heard. They had been forbidden to relight the fires in case the sudden lights should warn the French but somehow they managed to heat water and threw in the loose tea-leaves and Sharpe gratefully accepted a tin mug of the scalding liquid from his Sergeants. Harper was kicking dirt on to the fire, the men had risked a small blaze rather than go without tea and he looked up at Sharpe and grinned. 'Permission to go to church, sir?'

Sharpe grinned back. It was Sunday. He tried to work out the date. They had left Plasencia on the seventeenth and that had been a Monday and he counted the days forward on his fingers. Sunday, 23 July, 1809. There was still no light in the eastern sky, the stars shone brightly, the dawn still two hours away. Behind them, on a track that ran between the cork grove and the fields, there was a rumbling and clanking and cursing as a battery of artillery unlimbered. Sharpe turned, the tea cradled in his hands, and watched the dim shapes as the horses were led away and the field guns pointed across the river. They would herald the attack, hurling their roundshot at the French lines, tearing holes in the French Battalions as Sharpe led his skirmishers into the river. It was cold, too cold to feel any excitement, that would come later. Now were the hours to feel apprehensive, to tighten belts and buckles, to feel hungry. Sharpe shivered slightly in his greatcoat, nodded his thanks to Harper, and made his way down the grove between the lines of his men who stamped their feet and swung their arms and resurrected the more successful jokes of the previous evening. Somehow they were not as funny in the small hours before dawn.

He left the trees and walked on to the patch of grass that lay beside the river. His boots swished through the dew and warned the sentries of his coming. He was challenged, gave the password, and greeted as he jumped down on to the shingle at the water's edge.

'Anything happening?'

'No, sir.'

The water slid blackly beneath the tendrils of mist. There was an occasional slap and swirl from the river as a fish twisted and disturbed the surface. Sharpe peered over his cupped hands and blew on his fingers, there was the faintest dot of red light on the far bank that suddenly glowed brighter. The French sentry was smoking a cigar or a pipe. Sharpe looked to his left. The eastern sky at last had a suspicion of colour, a flat silver grey that silhouetted the hills, the first sign of dawn. He clapped one of the sentries on the shoulder. 'Not long now.'

He climbed the brief bank between the shingle and the grass and walked back to the trees. From the French lines he could hear a dog barking, the whinny of a horse, and then the sound of bugles. They would start lighting their fires, start cooking a breakfast and hopefully they would be still eating it when the Spanish bayonets came at them from the west. He suddenly felt a longing for devilled kidneys and coffee, for any food other than the thin stew and the Tommies and the old ship's biscuits that the Battalion had lived on for a week. He remembered that garlic sausage they had collected from the enemy dead at Rolica and hoped he would find some that morning on the bodies of the men who were grumbling round their fires just across the river.

Back in the grove he took off his greatcoat, rolled it tight, and strapped it to his pack. He shivered. He took the rag off the lock of his rifle that had protected it from the dew and tested the tension of the spring with his thumb. He slung it on his shoulder, slapped his sword, and started moving the Light Company down to the treeline. The skirmishers would go first, the thin line of Riflemen and redcoats wading the Alberche to drive off the sentries and lock up the French Voltigeurs so that they could not blunt the attack of the massed British Battalions which would follow on to the French flank. He made the men lie down a few feet inside the grove where they merged into the shadows of the trees while behind he could see the other nine companies of the Battalion forming up for the assault that could not be far away.

Dawn crept over the mountains, flooding the valley with a silver-grey light, shrinking the pools of shadow and revealing the shapes of trees and bushes on the far bank. It would still be a few moments, Sharpe decided, before the Spanish would break the silence and start the attack. He walked along the treeline, nodded to the Captain of the Light Company of the 29th who was on his right flank, made the polite small talk, wishing each other luck, and then strolled back to stand beside Harper. They did not speak but Sharpe knew the big Irishman was thinking of the promise Lennox had extracted from them by the bridge. But for Sharpe the Eagle had more urgency. If he could not pluck it from its perch today there might not be another chance for months and that meant no chance at all. In a few weeks, unless he could blunt Simmerson's letter, he might be on a ship for the West Indies and the inevitable fever that made the posting a virtual death warrant. He thought of Josefina, asleep in the town, her black hair spread on a pillow and wondered why suddenly his life had been enmeshed in a series of problems that one month ago he had not even suspected existed.

Muskets banged erratically in the distance. The men

cocked their ears, murmured to each other, listened to the sporadic firing that rattled up and down the French lines. Lieutenant Knowles came up to Sharpe and raised his eyebrows in a question. Sharpe shook his head. 'They're clearing their muskets, that's all.' The French sentries had been changed and the men going off duty were getting rid of their charges that might have become damp in the night air. Musket fire would not herald the attack. Sharpe was waiting for the red flashes that would illumine the western sky like summer lightning and show that the Spanish artillery was opening the battle. It could not be far off.

There were shouts from the river. Again the men pricked their ears, strained forward, but again it was a false alarm. A group of the enemy appeared, chasing and shouting at each other in horseplay, carrying buckets to the water's edge. One of them held up his bucket and shouted something to the British bank, his companions all laughed, but Sharpe had no idea what the joke was.

'Watering horses?' Knowles asked.

'No.' Sharpe stifled a yawn. 'Artillery buckets. There must be guns to our front.' That was bad news. A dozen men were carrying buckets in which the sponges that damped out the sparks in discharged guns were dipped. The water in the pails would be black as ink after a few shots and if the guns were directly ahead Sharpe knew that the South Essex might be marching into a storm of canister fragments. He felt tired, achingly tired, he wanted to begin the fight, he wanted the Eagle out of his dreams.

Simmerson and Forrest appeared, both on foot, and stared at the artillerymen filling their buckets. Sharpe said good morning and Simmerson, his antagonism blunted by nervousness, nodded back. 'Those musket shots?'

'Just clearing their charges, sir. Nothing else.'

Simmerson grunted. He was doing his best to be civil as if he realised at this moment that he needed Sharpe's skill on his side. He pulled out a vast watch, opened the lid, and shook his head. 'Spanish are late.'

The light began to lose its greyness. There was a sparkle on the far bank and behind them Sharpe could see the smoke of the hundreds of French cooking fires. 'Permission to relieve the picquets, sir?'

'Yes, Sharpe, yes.' Simmerson was making a huge effort to sound normal and Sharpe wondered if suddenly the Colonel was regretting the letter he had written. Sometimes the imminence of battle made seemingly intractable quarrels seem like things of no importance. Simmerson looked as if he would say more but instead he shook his head again and led Forrest further down the line.

The sentries were changed, the minutes passed, the sun climbed over the mist and the last vestiges of night disappeared like fading cannon smoke in the western sky. Damn the Spanish, thought Sharpe, as he listened to the bugles calling the French Regiments to parade. A group of horsemen appeared on the far bank and inspected the British side through telescopes. There would be no surprise now. The French officers would be able to see the batteries of guns, the saddled cavalry horses, the rows of infantry lined in the trees. All surprise had gone, vanished with the shadows and the cold, for the first time the French would know how many men opposed them, where the attack was planned, and how they should meet it.

The sound of church bells came from the town and

Sharpe wondered what Josefina was doing; had the bells wakened her? He imagined her body stretching between warm sheets, a body that would not be his till after battle. The sound of the bells reminded him of England and he thought of all the village churches that would be filling with people. Would they be thinking of their army in Spain? He doubted it. The British were not fond of their army. They celebrated its victories, of course, but there had been no such celebrations for a long time. The navy was fêted, Nelson's captains had been household names, but Trafalgar was a memory and Nelson was in his tomb and the British went their way oblivious of the war. The morning became warm, the men somnolent, they leaned against the cork trees and slept with their muskets propped on their knees. From somewhere in the French camp was the harsh sound of a muleteer's bell reminding Sharpe of normality.

'Sir!' A Sergeant was calling him from one of the companies higher in the grove. 'Company officers, sir. To the Colonel!'

Sharpe waved his reply, picked up the rifle, left Knowles in charge and walked up the grove. He was late. The Captains stood in a bunch listening to a Lieutenant from Hill's staff. Sharpe caught snatches of his words.

'Fast asleep . . . no battle . . . usual routine.'

There was a buzz of questions. The Lieutenant, glorious in the silvered Dragoon uniform, sounded bored. 'The General requests that we keep posted, sir. But we're not expecting the French to do anything.'

He rode away leaving the officers puzzled. Sharpe made his way towards Forrest to find out what he had missed when he saw a familiar figure riding hard down the track. He walked into the road and held up a hand.

It was Lieutenant Colonel Lawford and he was furious. He saw Sharpe, reined in, and swore.

'Bloody hell, Richard! Bloody, bloody, bloody hell! Bloody Spanish!'

'What's happened?'

Lawford could barely contain his anger. 'The bloody Spanish refused to wake up! Can you believe it?'

Other officers drew round. Lawford took off his hat and wiped his forehead, he had deep circles under his eyes. 'We get up at two o'clock in the bloody morning to save their bloody country and they can't be bothered to get out of bed!' Lawford looked round as though hoping to see a Spaniard on whom to vent his seething fury. 'We rode over there at six. Cuesta's in his bloody coach lying on bloody cushions and says his army is too tired to fight! Can you believe it? We had them. Like that!' He pinched a finger and thumb together. 'We would have murdered them this morning! We could have wiped Victor off the map. But no. It's *manana, manana,* tomorrow and tomorrow! There won't be a bloody tomorrow! Victor's no fool, he'll march today. Damn, damn, damn.' The Honourable William Lawford stared down at Sharpe. 'You know what happens now?'

'No.'

Lawford pointed towards the east. 'Jourdan's over there, with Joseph Bonaparte. They'll join up with Victor then we'll have twice as many to fight. Twice as many! And there are rumours that Soult has scraped an army together and is coming from the north. God! The chance we lost today! You know what I think?' Sharpe shook his head. 'I think the bastard wouldn't fight because it's Sunday. He's got priests mumbling prayers round his bloody bed on wheels. Bloody Catholics! And there's still no bloody food!'

Sharpe felt the tiredness course through him. 'What do we do now?'

'Now? We bloody wait. Cuesta says we'll attack tomorrow. We won't because the French won't be there.' Lawford dropped his shoulders and let out a sigh. 'Do you know where Hill is?'

Sharpe pointed along the track and Lawford rode on. Damn the Spanish, thought Sharpe, damn everything. He was officer of the day and he would have to organise the picquets, inspect the lines, scrape together some supplies from the Commissary who would have none. He would not be able to see Josefina. There would be no battle, no Eagle, not even a taste of garlic sausage. Damn.

CHAPTER 18

'I saw a man today . . .'

'Yes?' Sharpe looked over at Josefina. She was sitting naked on the bed with her knees drawn up and trying to file her toe-nails on the edge of his sword. She was laughing at her attempts and then she dropped the blade and looked at him. 'He was lovely. A blue coat with white bits here.' She brushed her breasts with her hands. 'And lots of gold lace.'

'On a horse?'

She nodded. 'And there was a bag hanging down . . .'

'His sabretache. And a curved sword?' She nodded again and Sharpe grinned at her. 'Sounds like the Prince of Wales Dragoons. Very rich.'

'How do you know?'

'All cavalrymen are rich. Unintelligent, but rich.'

She cocked her head in her characteristic gesture and frowned slightly. 'Unintelligent?'

'All cavalry officers are. The horse has all the brains and they have all the money.'

'Ah, well,' She shrugged her bare shoulders. 'It doesn't matter. I have enough brains for two.' She looked at him and grinned. 'You're jealous.'

'Yes.' He had picked up her penchant for honesty. She nodded seriously.

'I'm bored, Richard.'

'I know.'

'Not with you.' She looked up from her toe-nails and stared at him gravely. 'You're good for me. But we've been here a week and nothing is happening.'

Sharpe leaned forward and tugged his boots up over the overalls. 'Don't worry. Something will happen tomorrow.'

'Are you sure?'

'Tomorrow we fight.' This time though, he thought, we will be outnumbered.

She pulled her knees tight into her body, clasped them, and rested her chin on them. 'Are you frightened?'

'Yes.'

She raised her eyebrows. 'Who'll win?'

'I don't know.'

'Will you get your Eagle?'

'I don't know.'

She smiled at him. 'I'll have a present for you after the battle.'

'I don't want a present. I want you.'

'You have me already.' She knew what he meant but she deliberately misunderstood him. She watched him stand up. 'You want your sword?'

'Yes.' Sharpe buckled the belt tight, pulling the scabbard into place.

She grinned at him. 'Come and get it.' She lay the great blade on the bed and, rolling over, laid her naked belly on its chill steel.

Sharpe crossed to her. 'Give it to me.'

'Get it yourself.'

Her body was warm and strong, the muscles hardened by exercise, and she clung to him. Sharpe pushed her face away and stared into her eyes. 'What will happen?' he asked.

'You will get your Eagle. You always get what you want.'

'I want you.'

She shut her eyes and kissed him hard, then pulled away and smiled at him. 'We're just stragglers, Richard. We drifted together, but we're both on a journey.'

'I don't understand.'

'You do. We're going two different ways. You want a home. You want someone to love you and want you, someone to take the burden away from you.'

'And you?'

She smiled. 'I want silk dresses and music. Candles in the dawn.' He began to say something, but she put a finger on his lips. 'I know what you think. That's just silliness, but it's what I want. Perhaps one day I'll want something sensible.'

'Am I sensible?'

'There are times, my love, when you take things a little too seriously.'

'Are you saying goodbye?'

She laughed. 'There! You see? You are taking things too seriously.' She kissed him swiftly, on the tip of his nose. 'Come after the battle. Get your present.'

He reached down for the handle of his sword. 'Move over, I don't want to cut you.'

She moved to one side and touched the blade with her finger. 'How many men have you killed with it?'

'I don't know.' It slid into the scabbard, the weight congenial on his hip. He crouched by the bed and took her naked waist in his hands. He stared at her body as if trying to commit it to memory: the fullness of it, the beauty of it, the mystery that made it seem unattainable. She touched his face with a finger.

'Go and fight.'

'I'll be back.'

'I know.'

Everything seemed unreal to Sharpe. The soldiers in Talavera's streets, the people who avoided his passage, the afternoon itself. Tomorrow there would be a battle. Hundreds would die, mangled by roundshot, sliced by cavalry sabres, pierced by musket shot, yet still the town was busy. People were in love, out of love, bought their food, made jokes, yet tomorrow there would be a battle. He wanted Josefina. He could hardly think of the battle, of the Eagle – only of her teasing face. She was going from him, he knew that, yet he could not accept it. The battle was almost an irrelevance to the overwhelming need to entrap her, to make her his, and he knew it could not happen.

He walked to the town gate that overlooked the plain to the west. The Light Company was mounting a guard on the gate, and Sharpe nodded at Harper and then climbed the steep steps to the parapet, where Hogan stared down into the olive groves and woods that were full of Spanish soldiers filing into the positions Wellesley had carefully prepared for them. Cuesta, after refusing to attack last Sunday, had impetuously marched after the retreating French. Now, four days later, his army was scuttling back, their tails between their legs, and bringing after them a French army that had more than doubled its size. Tomorrow, Sharpe reflected, the Spanish would have to fight, the French would wake them up, the allied army that could have taken its victory last Sunday must now fight a defensive battle against the united forces of Victor, Jourdan and Joseph Bonaparte.

Not, Sharpe thought bitterly, that the Spanish would

have to do too much of the actual killing. Wellesley had drawn his army back to create a defensive line next to Talavera itself. The right-hand end of the line was made up of the town walls, olive groves, tangled fields and woods, all made impregnable by Hogan's hard work. He had felled trees, thrown up earthworks, strengthened walls, and in the tangle of barricades and obstacles the Spanish troops took up their positions. No French infantryman could hope to fight his way across Hogan's breastworks as long as the defenders stayed at their posts; instead the French army would swing north to the left side of Wellesley's line where the British would wait for the attack. Sharpe looked at the northern plain. There were no obstacles there that an Engineer could make more formidable, there was just the Portina stream that a man could cross without the water coming over his boot-tops, and rolling grassland that was an invitation for the massed French Battalions and their long lines of splendid cavalry. In the distance was the Medellin, the hill which dominated the plain, and Sharpe had walked the grass often enough to know what would happen tomorrow. The French columns would cross the stream and attack the gentle slopes of the Medellin. That was the killing place. The Spanish troops, thirty thousand of them, could stay safely behind their breastworks and watch as the Eagles stormed the British in the open northern plain and the smoke covered Medellin.

'How are you?' Hogan asked.

'I'm fine.' Sharpe grinned.

The Irishman turned to watch the Spanish filling up the positions he had prepared. On the plain beyond, hidden by the trees where the Alberche River emptied itself into the Tagus, came the crackle of musketry. It had gone on all afternoon like a distant forest fire and

Sharpe had seen dozens of British wounded carried through the gate into town. The British had covered the last mile of the Spanish retreat and the wounded men said that the French skirmishers had won the day. Two British Battalions had been mauled badly, there was even a rumour that Wellesley himself had just escaped capture, the Spanish looked nervous, and Sharpe wondered what kind of troops the French had found to hurl against the allied army. He looked down at Harper. The Sergeant, with a dozen men, was guarding the gate of the town, not against the enemy, but to stop any British or Spanish soldiers who might be tempted to lose themselves in Talavera's dark alleyways and avoid the fight that was inevitable. The Battalion itself was on the Medellin and Sharpe waited for the orders that would send his company up the shallow Portina stream to find the patch of grass they would defend in the morning.

'And how's the girl?' Hogan was sitting on the powdery stone.

'She's happy. Bored.'

'That's the way of women. Never content. Will you be needing more money?'

Sharpe looked at the middle-aged Engineer and saw the concern in his eyes. Already Hogan had lent Sharpe more than twenty guineas, a sum that was impossible for him to repay unless he was lucky on the battlefield. 'No. I'm all right for the moment.'

Hogan smiled. 'You're lucky.' He shrugged. 'God knows, Richard, she's a beautiful creature. Are you in love?'

Sharpe looked over the parapet where the Spanish had filled Hogan's makeshift fortresses. 'She won't let me be.'

'Then she's more sensible than I thought.'

The afternoon passed slowly. Sharpe thought of the girl, bored in her room, and watched the Spanish soldiers chop at the beeches and oaks to build their evening fires. Then, with a suddenness that Sharpe had been waiting for, there were flashes of light far away in the hazy trees and bushes that edged the plain to the east. It was the sun, he knew, reflecting from muskets and breastplates. Sharpe nudged Hogan and pointed. 'The French.'

Hogan stood up and stared at them. 'My God.' He spoke quietly. 'There's a good few of them.'

The infantry marched on to the far plain like a spreading dark stain on the grass. Sharpe and Hogan watched Battalion after Battalion march into the pale fields, squadron after squadron of cavalry, the small squat shapes of guns scattered in the formations, the largest army Sharpe had ever seen in the field. The galloping figures of staff officers could be seen as they directed the columns to their places ready for the next morning's advance and battle. Sharpe looked left to the British lines that waited beside the Portina. The smoke from hundreds of camp fires wound into the early evening air, crowds of men clustered by the stream and on the Medellin for a far glimpse of their enemy, but the British force looked woefully small beside the massive tide of men, horses and guns that filled the plain to the east and grew by the minute. Napoleon's brother was there, King Joseph, and with him two full Marshals of France, Victor and Jourdan. They were leading sixty-five Battalions of infantry, a massive force of the men who had made Europe into Napoleon's property, and they had come to swat this small British army and send it reeling to the sea. They planned to break it for ever to

ensure that Britain never again dared to challenge the
Eagles on land.

Hogan whistled softly. 'Will they attack this evening?'

'No.' Sharpe scanned the far lines. 'They'll wait for
their artillery.'

Hogan pointed into the darkening east. 'They've got
guns. Look, you can see them.'

Sharpe shook his head. 'Those are just the small
ones they attach to each infantry Battalion. No, the big
bastards will be back on the road somewhere. They'll
come in the night.'

And in the morning, he thought, the French will open
with one of their favourite cannonades, the massed
artillery hurling its iron shot at the enemy lines before
the dense, drummed columns follow the Eagles across
the stream. French tactics were hardly subtle. Not for
them the clever manoeuvrings of turning an enemy's
flank. Instead, again and again, they massed the guns
and the men and they hurled a terrifying hammer blow
at the enemy line and, again and again, it worked. He
shrugged to himself. Who needed to be subtle? The
guns and men of France had broken every army sent
against them.

There were shouts from behind him and he crossed
the battlement and peered down at the gate where
Harper and his men were on guard. Lieutenant Gibbons
was there with Berry, both mounted, both shouting at
Harper. Sharpe leaned over the parapet.

'What's the problem?'

Gibbons turned round slowly. It dawned on Sharpe
that the Lieutenant was slightly drunk and was having
some difficulty in staying on his horse. Gibbons saluted
Sharpe with his usual irony.

'I didn't see you there, sir. So sorry.' He bowed.

Lieutenant Berry giggled. Gibbons straightened up. 'I was just telling your Sergeant here that you can go back now, all right?'

'But you stopped on the way for refreshment?'

Berry giggled loudly. Gibbons looked at him and burst into a laugh himself. He bowed again. 'You could say so, sir.'

The two Lieutenants urged their horses under the gateway and started up the road to the British lines to the north. Sharpe watched them go.

'Bastards.'

'Do they give you problems?' Hogan was sitting on the parapet again.

Sharpe shook his head. 'No. Just insolence, remarks in the mess, you know.' He wondered about Josefina. Hogan seemed to read his thoughts. 'You're thinking about the girl?'

Sharpe nodded. 'Yes. But she should be all right.' He was thinking out loud. 'She keeps the door locked. We're on the top floor and I can't see how they'd find us.' He turned to Hogan and grinned. 'Stop worrying about it. They've done nothing so far; they're cowards. They've given up!'

Hogan shook his head. 'They would kill you, Richard, with as little regret as putting down a lame horse. Less regret. And as for the girl? They'll try to hurt her, too.'

Sharpe turned back to the spectacle on the plain. He knew Hogan was right, knew that too much was unsettled, but the game was not in his hands; everything must wait for the battle. The French troops had flooded the end of the plain, they flowed round woods, trees, farms, coming ever forward towards the stream and the Medellin Hill. They darkened the plain, filled it with a tide of men flecked with steel, and still they came;

Hussars, Dragoons, Lancers, Chasseurs, Grenadiers and Voltigeurs, the followers of the Eagles, the men who had made an Empire, the old enemy.

'Hot work tomorrow.' Hogan shook his head as he watched the French.

'It will be.' Sharpe turned and called to Harper. 'Come here!' The big Irish Sergeant scrambled up the broken wall and stood beside the two officers. The first of thousands of fires sparkled in the French lines. Harper shook his massive head.

'Perhaps they'll forget to wake up tomorrow.'

Sharpe laughed. 'It's the next morning they have to worry about.'

Hogan shaded his eyes. 'I wonder how many more armies like that we'll have to meet before it's done.'

The two Riflemen said nothing. They had been with Wellesley the year before when he defeated the French at Rolica and Vimeiro yet this army was ten times bigger than the French force at Rolica, three times larger than Junot's army at Vimeiro, and twice the size of the force they had thrown out of Portugal in the spring. It was as if for every Frenchman killed another two or three marched from the depots, and when you killed them then a dozen more came, and so it went on. Harper grinned. 'There's no point in worrying ourselves by looking at them. The man knows what he's doing.'

Sharpe nodded. Wellesley would not be waiting behind the Portina stream if he thought the next day could bring defeat. Of all the British Generals he was the only one trusted by the men who carried the guns, they knew he understood how to fight the French and, most important, when not to fight them. Hogan pointed.

'What's that?'

Three-quarters of a mile away French horsemen were

firing their carbines. Sharpe could see no target. He watched the puffs of smoke and listened to the faint crackle.

'Dragoons.'

'I know that,' Hogan said. 'But what are they firing at?'

'Snakes?' During his walks up the Portina Sharpe had noticed small black snakes that wriggled mysteriously in the dank grass by the stream. He had avoided them but he supposed it was possible they lived out on the plain as well and the horsemen were merely amusing themselves with target practice. It was evening and the flames from the carbine muzzles sparkled brightly in the dusk. It was strange, Sharpe thought, how often war could look pretty.

'Hello.' Harper pointed down. 'They've woken up our brave allies. Looks like a bloody ants' nest.'

Below the wall the Spanish infantry had become excited. Men left the fires and lined themselves behind the earth and stone walls and laid muskets over the felled and piled trunks Hogan had placed in the gateways. Officers stood on the wall, their swords drawn, there was shouting and jostling, men pointing at the distant Dragoons and their twinkling muskets.

Hogan laughed. 'It's so good to have allies.'

The Dragoons, too far away to be seen clearly, went on firing at their unseen targets. Sharpe guessed it was just horseplay. The French were oblivious of the panic they were causing in the Spanish ranks. Every Spanish infantryman had crowded to the breastworks, their backsides illuminated by the fires, and their muskets bristled towards the empty field. The officers barked out commands and to Sharpe's horror he watched as the hundreds of muskets were loaded.

'What the hell are they doing?' He listened to the rattle of ramrods being thrust down barrels, watched as officers raised their swords. 'Watch this,' Hogan said. 'You might learn a thing or two.'

No order was given. Instead a single musket fired, its ball thrumming uselessly into the grass, and it was followed by the biggest volley Sharpe had ever heard. Thousands of muskets fired, gouted flame and smoke, a rolling thunder assailed them, the sound seemed to last for ever and mingled with it came the yells of the Spaniards. The fire and lead poured into the empty field. The Dragoons looked up, startled, but no musket ball would carry even a third of the distance towards them so they sat their horses and watched the fringe of musket smoke drift into the air.

For a second Sharpe thought the Spanish were cheering their own victory over the innocent grass but suddenly he realised the shouts were not of triumph, but of alarm. They had been scared witless by their own volley, by the thunder of ten thousand muskets, and now they ran for safety. Thousands streamed into the olive trees, throwing away muskets, trampling the fires in their panic, screaming for help, heads up, arms pumping, running from their own noise. Sharpe shouted down to his men on the gate.

'Let them through!'

There was no point in trying to stop the panic. Sharpe's dozen men would have been swamped by the hundreds of Spanish who crowded into the gate and streamed into the town. Others circled north towards the roads that led eastwards away from the French. They would loot the baggage parks, raid the houses in town, spread alarm and confusion but there was nothing to be done. Sharpe watched Spanish cavalry use

234

their swords on the fugitive infantry. They would stop some of them, perhaps by morning they might collect most of them, but the bulk of the Spanish infantry had evaporated, scared, defeated by a handful of Dragoons three-quarters of a mile away. Sharpe began laughing. It was too funny, too idiotic, somehow exactly fitting for this campaign. He saw the Spanish cavalry slash furiously at the infantry, forcing groups of them back to the line, and far away he heard the bugles call more Spanish horse into the hunt. On the plain the French fires formed lines of light, thousands and thousands of flames marking the enemy lines, and not one of the men round those fires would know they had just routed several thousand Spanish infantry. Sharpe collapsed on the wall and looked at Harper.

'What is it you say, Sergeant?'

'Sir?'

'God save Ireland? Not a chance. He's got his hands full coping with Spain.'

The noise and panic subsided. There were a handful of men left in the grove, others were being driven back by the Spanish cavalry, but Sharpe guessed it would take the horsemen all night to round up the fugitives and force them back to the breastworks, and even then thousands would escape to spread rumours of a great French victory outside Talavera. Sharpe stood up. 'Come on, Sergeant, time we were getting back to the Battalion.'

A voice called up from the street. 'Captain Sharpe! Sir!'

One of the Riflemen was gesticulating and, next to him, stood Agostino, Josefina's servant. Sharpe felt his carefree mood disappear to be replaced with an awful dread. He scrambled down the broken stonework,

Harper and Hogan behind him, and strode across to the two men. 'What is it?'

Agostino burst into Portuguese. He was a tiny man who normally said little but watched all from his wide, brown eyes. Sharpe held up his hand for quiet. 'What's he saying?'

Hogan knew enough Portuguese. The Engineer licked his lips. 'It's Josefina.'

'What about her?' Sharpe had the inklings of disaster, a cold feeling of evil. He let Hogan take his elbow and walk him, with Agostino, away from the listening Riflemen. Hogan asked more questions, let the small servant talk, and finally turned to Sharpe. His voice was low. 'She's been attacked. They locked Agostino in a cupboard.'

'They?' He already knew the answer. Gibbons and Berry.

Sergeant Harper crossed to them, his manner formal and correct. 'Sir!'

'Sergeant?' Sharpe forced the hundreds of jostling fears down so that he could listen to Harper.

'I'll take the man back, sir.'

Sharpe nodded. It occurred to him that Patrick Harper knew more of what was going on than Sharpe had assumed. Behind the careful words there was a concern that made Sharpe regret that he had not taken Harper more into his confidence. There was also a controlled anger in the Irishman. Your enemies, he was saying, are mine.

'Carry on, Sergeant.'

'Yessir. And sir?' Harper's face was bleak. 'You will let me know what happens?'

'Yes, Sergeant.'

Sharpe and Hogan ran into the dark streets, slipping

on the filth, pushing their way through the fugitives who were forcing the doors of wine-shops and private houses. Hogan panted to keep up with the Rifleman. It would be a bad night in Talavera, a night of looting, destruction, and rape. Tomorrow a hundred thousand men would march into a maelstrom of fire and Hogan, catching a glimpse of Sharpe's snarling face as he hurled two Spanish infantrymen out of his way, feared for the evil that seemed to be welling up in preparation for the morrow. Then they were in the quiet street where Josefina was living and Hogan peered up at the quiet windows, the closed shutters, and prayed that Richard Sharpe would not destroy himself with his huge anger.

CHAPTER 19

Sharpe's boots crunched on broken plaster, he listened to the voices murmuring in the room on the other side of the splintered door, and stared unseeing through a small window at the high ragged clouds which raced past the moon. Hogan sat on the top step of the steep stairs next to the sheets they had taken from Josefina's bed. In the half light of the candles seeping through the doorway the sheets seemed to be patterned in red and white. There was a cry from the room. Sharpe spun round in irritation.

'What are they doing to her?'

Hogan hushed him. 'The doctor's bleeding her, Sharpe. He knows what he's doing.'

'As if she hasn't lost enough blood already!'

'I know, I know.' Hogan spoke soothingly. There was nothing he could say that would ease the turmoil in Sharpe's head, to soften the blow or deflect the revenge which Hogan knew was being minutely plotted as the Rifleman paced up and down the tiny landing. The Engineer sighed and picked up a tiny plaster head. The house belonged to a seller of religious statues and the stairs and corridors were stacked with his wares. When Gibbons and Berry had forced their way into the girl's room they had trampled on twenty or thirty images of Christ, each with a bleeding heart, and the scraps of statues still littered the landing. Hogan was a peaceful man. He enjoyed his job, he liked the fresh challenges of each day, he was happy with his head full of angles and re-entries, yardages and imperial weights; he liked company that laughed easily, drank generously, and would pass the time with stories of happiness past. He was no fighter. His war was fought with picks, shovels and powder yet when he had burst with Sharpe into the attic room he had felt in himself a searing anger and lust for revenge. The mood had passed. Now he sat, saddened and quiet, but as he watched the tall Rifleman he knew that in Sharpe the mood was being refined and fed. For the twentieth time Sharpe stopped.

'Why?'

Hogan shrugged. 'They were drunk, Richard.'

'That's no answer!'

'No.' Hogan carefully replaced the broken head on the floor, out of reach of Sharpe's pacing. 'There isn't an answer. They wanted revenge on you. Neither you nor the girl are important. It's their pride more ...' He tailed away. There was nothing to say, just the enormous sadness to feel and the fear of what Sharpe would do. Hogan regretted his first reaction to the girl, he had thought her calculating and cold, but as he escorted her from Plasencia to Oropesa, and from there to Talavera, he had been captivated by the charm, the easy laughter, and the honesty with which she planned a future away from a cloying past and a fugitive husband.

Sharpe was staring through the window at the clouds patterning the moon. 'Do they think I'll do nothing?'

'They're terrified.' Hogan spoke flatly; he was afraid of what Sharpe might do. He thought of the line of

Shakespeare; 'beauty provoketh fools'. Sharpe turned on him again.

'Why?'

'You know why. They were drunk. Good God, man, they were so drunk they couldn't even do that properly. So they beat her. It was all on the spur of the moment, and now? They're terrified, Richard. Terrified. What will you do?'

'Do? I don't know.' Sharpe spoke irritably and Hogan knew he was lying.

'What can you do, Richard? Call them out to a duel? That will ruin your career, you know that. Will you charge them with rape? For God's sake, Richard, who'd believe you? The town's full of bloody Spanish tonight, raping anything that moves! And everyone knows the girl was with Gibbons before you. No, Richard, you must think. You must think before you do anything.'

Sharpe turned on him and Hogan knew there could be no argument with that implacable face. 'I'll bloody murder them.'

Hogan sighed and rubbed his face with both hands. 'I didn't hear that. So you get hung? Shot? Beat the bones out of them if you must but no more, Richard, no more.'

Sharpe did not answer and Hogan knew he was seeing in his mind the body they had found with the blood-soaked sheets. She had been raped and beaten and when they arrived the landlady was screaming at the girl. It had taken more money to silence the woman, find a doctor, and now they waited. Agostino peered up the stairs, saw Sharpe's face, and went back to the front door where he had been told to wait. New sheets had been carried into the room, water, and Sharpe had listened to the landlady tidy up the floor and he remembered the girl, bruised and bleeding, crawling among the broken saints and stained sheets.

The door opened, scrunching on the shards, and the landlady beckoned to them. The doctor was kneeling beside the bed and his eyes flicked warily at the two officers. Josefina lay on the bed, her black hair fanned on the pillow, but her eyes were tight shut. Sharpe sat beside her, saw the spreading yellow bruise on her unnaturally pale skin, and he took one of her hands that clutched at the fresh linen. She pulled away but he held on and her eyes opened.

'Richard?'

'Josefina. How are you?' It seemed a stupid thing to say but he could think of nothing else. She closed her eyes and the faintest smile came and went.

She opened her eyes again. 'I'll be all right.' There was a flash of the old Josefina but as she spoke a tear ran from her eye and she sobbed and turned away from him. Sharpe turned to the doctor. 'How is she?'

The doctor shrugged and looked hopelessly towards the landlady. Hogan intervened and rattled in his Spanish at the doctor. Sharpe listened to the voices and as he did he stroked the girl's averted face. All he could think of was that he had failed her. He had promised to protect her and now this had happened, the worst, the unthinkable. Hogan sat beside him. 'She'll be all right. She lost some blood.'

'How?'

Hogan closed his eyes and took a deep breath before opening them. 'She was beaten, Richard. They were not gentle. But she'll mend.'

Sharpe nodded. There was silence in the room but from the street outside Sharpe could hear the screams and shouts generated by the drunken Spanish soldiers.

The girl turned back to him. She had stopped crying. Her voice was very low. 'Richard?'

'Yes?'

'Kill them.' She spoke flatly. Hogan half shook his head but Sharpe bent down and kissed her by the ear. 'I will.'

As he straightened up he saw another half smile on the face and then she forced it into a proper smile that went oddly with the tears. She squeezed his hand. 'Will there be a battle tomorrow?'

'Yes.' Sharpe spoke as if the subject could be brushed away, as if it was not of importance.

'Be lucky.'

'I'll come and see you afterwards.' He smiled at her.

'Yes.' But there was no conviction in her voice. Sharpe turned to Hogan.

'You'll stay?'

'Till daybreak. I'm not needed till then. But you should go.'

Sharpe nodded. 'I know.' He kissed her again, stood up, and put on his rifle and pack. Hogan thought his face was as cruel as a face could be. The Engineer walked with him to the stairs.

'Be careful, Richard.'

'I will.'

Hogan put a hand on his shoulder to stop him moving. 'Remember what you have to lose.'

Sharpe nodded again. 'Bring me news when you can.'

Sharpe pushed his way into the street, ignoring the Spaniards, and as he walked towards the north he did not see the tall man in the blue coat with the white facings who watched from a doorway opposite Josefina's lodgings. The man looked at Sharpe sympathetically, then up at the windows, and settled back into the doorway where he tried to make himself comfortable despite the broken arm with its splints and sling that would keep him from the battle tomorrow. He wondered what was happening on the second floor but he would soon know; Agostino would tell him all in exchange for a piece of gold.

Sharpe hurried up the track that led away from the town between the Portina stream and the Spanish lines. The frightened infantry were being forced back into their positions but even as he hurried through the trees he could hear the occasional musket shot from the town, the shouting, the coinage of Talavera's night of fear and rape. The moon had disappeared behind a bank of clouds but the lights of the Spanish fires showed the path and he half ran as he headed north towards the Medellin Hill. To his right the sky was glowing a deep red where the thousands of French fires were reflected in the air. He should have been concerned for the morning; he knew it would be the greatest battle he had ever fought, yet his mind was dominated by the need to find Berry and Gibbons. He came to the Pajar, the tiny hill that marked the end of the Spanish lines and the place where the Portina bent to his right and, from running behind the Spanish troops, the stream now flowed in front of the British position. He saw the shapes of the field guns Wellesley had placed on the small hill and part of his mind registered how the fire of those guns would sweep protectively in front of the Spanish lines and deflect the massive French attack on to the British lines. But tomorrow was another battle.

The track melted away into the grass. He could see the scattered fires of the British but he had no idea which was the South Essex. They were positioned at the

Medellin Hill, he knew that, so he ran by the stream, tripping over tussocks of grass, splashing through patches of marsh, keeping the silvered Portina as his guide to the Medellin. He was alone in the darkness. The British fires were far off to his left, the French even further to the right, the two armies still and quiet. Something was wrong. The old instinct prickled him and he stopped, sank to one knee and searched the darkness ahead. In the night the Medellin Hill looked like a long, low ridge pointing at the French army. It was the key to Wellesley's left flank, if the French assaulted the hill they could turn and crush the British between the Medellin and Talavera. Yet there were no fires on the ridge. He could see a bright smear of flames at the western end, furthest from the enemy, but on the side facing the town, and on the half of the flat summit nearest the enemy there were no lights. He had thought the South Essex to be bivouacking on the gentle slope that faced him but it was black and empty. He listened. There were the sounds of night, the noises from the town that had faded to a dull murmur, the wind in the grass, insects, the splashing of the stream, and the far-off sounds of a hundred thousand men crouching by fires waiting for morning. Behind him the small Pajar hill was bright with fires, the guns silhouetted against the white wall of the farmhouse on its crest, but in front it was dark and quiet. He stood up and walked softly on, his instincts alive to a danger he could not define, his mind searching for clues in the darkness and from the murmured sounds of the night. Why had he not been challenged? There should be picquets on the line of the Portina, sentries huddled against the chill wind looking towards the enemy, but no one had stopped him and asked his business. He kept by the stream until the black loom of the Medellin was above him, then turned left and began to climb the slope. By daylight it looked a gentle slope but as he climbed with his pack and rifle the ground felt steep and each step made the muscles at the back of his legs ache. Tomorrow, he thought, this is precisely where the French columns will come. They will march up this slope, heads down, while the guns crack iron shot into their ranks and the muskets wait in silence at the crest.

Half way up the slope he stopped and turned round. On the far side of the stream was another hill, similar in shape to the Medellin but lower and smaller. On its level top Sharpe could see the fires of the French, the flitting shadows of his enemy, and he turned and hurried on up the hill. His mind was still alerted to danger, to a threat he did not understand, but continually he thought of the girl's black hair fanned on the pillow, of her hand gripping the sheet, of the blood stains, her terror in the attic when the two men had burst in. He had no idea what he could do. Gibbons and Berry were probably safe in the company of Simmerson and his cronies. Somehow he must flush them out, get them into the darkness, and he pushed himself to go faster.

The slope levelled out on to the plateau. Far off he could see the fires of the British and he ran slowly towards them, the pack bumping awkwardly, the rifle flapping at his side. He had still not been challenged. He was approaching the army from the direction of the enemy and there were no sentries, no line of picquets in the darkness, as if the army had forgotten about the French just the other side of the Portina. Two hundred yards from the line of fires he stopped and crouched low on the grass. He had found the South Essex. They were on the edge of the hill and he could see the bright yellow facings of their uniforms glowing in the light of the flames. He searched the fires, saw the green uniforms of his Riflemen, and went on looking as though, from this distance, he might see the figures of his enemies. His anger was turning into frustration. He had walked and run more than a mile to find the Battalion yet he knew that there was nothing he could do. Gibbons and Berry would be safe with the Colonel and his cronies, sitting round a fire with the officers, secure from his revenge. Hogan was right. He would throw his career away if he fought them, yet he had made a promise to Josefina, and he did not know how to keep the promise. And tomorrow he must try to keep the earlier promise to Lennox. He tugged the great sword from its scabbard and laid its tip on the grass in front of him. The blade shone dully in the light of the fires, he stared at the length of steel and felt the sting of tears in his eyes as he remembered the girl's body lying teasingly and naked along its flat blade. That had been only this afternoon. Now he cursed the fate that had led to this night, to the promises he could not keep. He thought of the girl, of the men clawing at her and he looked up at the fires and felt his helplessness. It was better, he knew, to give it all up, to walk into the light of the fires and concentrate on tomorrow but how was he to face Gibbons or Berry and see the triumph on their faces without swinging the blade at them?

He turned round and stared at the far horizon and the red glow of the French fires that lined the edge of the hill with a faint light. There were rabbits moving on the crest of the hill he had climbed, he could see their small shapes bobbing and suddenly he froze. Had there been sentries there he had missed? They were not rabbits. He could see the silhouettes of men, he had mistaken their heads for rabbits, but as they climbed over the crest he could see a dozen men, carrying guns, heading towards him. He lay flat on the grass, gripping the sword, and stared at the dim glow of the skyline. He put his ear to the ground and heard what he had feared to hear, the faint thump of marching feet, and he raised his head and kept looking as the dozen men turned into a misshapen mass. He remembered telling Hogan that the French would not attack at night, yet he suspected he was seeing just that; a night attack on the Medellin. The dozen men would be some of the skirmishers, the French Voltigeurs, and the solid mass was a French column climbing the hill in the silence of night. But how to be sure? It could as easily be a British Battalion moving in the dark, finding a new place to camp, but this late at night? He wriggled forward on knees and elbows, keeping his body close to the earth so that whoever was coming in the dark would not see him silhouetted in the fires. The sword rustled on the grass, he seemed to be making a deafening sound, but the men walked on towards him. He stopped when they stopped and he watched them kneel. He was almost sure they were Voltigeurs, the skirmish line that had been sent ahead to flush out the sentries, and now that they were in sight of their targets they were waiting for the column so that the attack should crash home in unison. Sharpe held his breath. The kneeling men were calling softly to each other and he wanted to hear the language.

French. He turned his head and stared at the fires marking the British line. No one moved there, the men were sitting staring at the flames, waiting for the morning and completely unaware that their enemy had found the plateau of the Medellin undefended and were about to attack. Sharpe had to warn the British, but how?

A single rifle shot would be put down to a nervous sentry, seeing shadows in the night; he could not shout that far, and if he turned and ran then he would not reach the British fires much before the French. There was only one way. That was to provoke the French into firing a volley, a rattle of musketry that would startle the British, warn them of danger and make them form a crude line. He gripped the sword, noted the nearest shadow of a kneeling Voltigeur, then scrambled to his feet and sprinted towards the enemy. The man looked up as Sharpe neared him and put a finger to his lips. Sharpe screamed, a curdling yell of anger and challenge, and chopped sideways with the sword. He did not wait to see if he had caused any damage but ran on, wrenching the blade free, screaming at the next man. This one stood up, shouted a question, and died with the blade in his belly. Sharpe went on shouting. He tugged the sword free, whirled it in the air so that it sang, spotted movement to his left and ran at yet another Voltigeur. The suddenness of his attack had startled them, they had no idea how many men were among them, or where they came from. Sharpe saw two skirmishers together, their bayonets levelled at him, but he screamed, they faltered, and he cut at one man as he swerved past and disappeared in the night.

He dropped flat in the grass. No one had fired. He heard the French running through the grass, the moans of a wounded man, but no one had fired at him. He lay still, stared at the skyline, and waited until his eyes could see the dim shapes of the approaching column. Questions were shouted forward, he could hear the Voltigeurs hissing back their answers, but still they were undetected, the British sat at their fires and waited for a

248

dawn that might never happen. Sharpe had to provoke that volley.

He laid the sword flat on the grass and pulled the Baker off his shoulder. He slid it forward, opened the pan and felt that the powder was still in place, then eased the flint back until he felt it click into place. The French were quiet again, their attacker had disappeared as quickly as he had come.

''Talion! 'Talion will fire by companies! Present!'

He shouted meaningless orders at the French. He could see the shape of the column just fifty yards away. The skirmishers had pulled back to join in the final march when this mass of men would crash into the unsuspecting British.

''Talion!' He drew the word out. 'Fire!'

The Baker spat its bullet towards the French and he heard a sharp cry. They would have seen the muzzle flash but Sharpe rolled to his right and snatched up the sword.

'Tirez!' He shouted the order at the column. A dozen nervous soldiers pulled their triggers and he heard the bullets whirring over the grass. At last! The British must have woken up and he turned round to see men standing by the fires, signs of movement, even panic.

'Tirez! Tirez! Tirez!' He screamed at the column and more muskets banged in the night. Officers shouted at their men to stop firing but the damage was done. The British had heard the firing, seen the musket flashes, and Sharpe could see men grabbing weapons, fixing bayonets, waiting for whatever crouched in the dark. It was time to be going. The French were moving again and Sharpe sprinted towards the British lines. His running body was silhouetted against the fires and

249

he heard a crackle of musketry and felt the bullets go past him. He shouted as he ran.

'The French! Form line! The French!'

He saw Harper and the Riflemen running down the line, away from the centre where the French would strike home, and out to the dimly lit edge of the plateau. That was sensible. Rifles were not for close work and the Sergeant was hiding his men in the shadows where they could snipe at the enemy. Sharpe's breath echoed in his ears, he was panting, the run had become a struggle against tiredness and the weight of his pack. He watched the South Essex form small nervous groups that kept splitting up and reforming. No one knew what was happening. To their right another Battalion was in equal disarray and behind Sharpe could hear the steady sound of the French advancing at a trot.

'The French!' He had no more breath. Harper had disappeared. Sharpe hurdled a fire and ran full tilt into a Sergeant who held on to him and supported him as he gasped for breath.

'What's happening, sir?'

'French column. Coming this way.'

The Sergeant was bewildered. 'Why didn't the first line stop them?'

Sharpe looked at him, astonished. 'You are the first line!'

'No one told us!'

Sharpe looked round him. Men ran to and fro looking for their Sergeants or officers, a mounted officer rode forward through the fires. Sharpe could not see who it was, and disappeared towards the column. Sharpe heard a shout, the scream of the horse as muskets fired, and the thump of the beast falling. The musket flashes showed where the French were and Sharpe, with a pang of satisfaction, heard the crisp sound of the Bakers at the hill's edge.

Then the column was visible, their white trousers showing in the firelight, angling across their front and aiming at the centre of the British line. Sharpe screamed the orders. 'Present. Fire!' A few muskets banged, the white smoke swallowed immediately in the darkness, and Sharpe was alone. The men had fled at the sight of the massive column. Sharpe ran after them, beating at men with his sword. 'You're safe here! Stand still!' But it was no good. The South Essex, like the Battalion next to them, had broken and panicked and were streaming back towards the fires in their rear where Sharpe could see men forming in companies, the ranks tipped with bayonets.

It was chaos. Sharpe cut across the fugitives, making for the edge of the hill and the darkness where his Riflemen lay hidden. He found Knowles, with a group of the company, and pushed them ahead to join Harper but most of the Battalion was running back. The French fired their first volley, a massive rolling thunder of shots that cracked the night with smoke and flame, and cut a swathe in the troops ahead of them. The Battalion ran blindly back towards the safety of the next line of fires, Sharpe crashed into fugitives, shook them off, struggled towards the comparative peace of the edge of the hill. A voice shouted, 'What's happening?' Sharpe turned. Berry was there, his jacket undone, his sword drawn, his black hair falling over his fleshy face. Sharpe stopped, crouched, and growled. He remembered the girl, her terror, her pain, and he rose to his feet, walked the few paces, and grabbed Berry's collar. Frightened eyes turned on him.

'What's happening?'

He pulled the Lieutenant with him, over the crest, down into the darkness of the slope. He could hear Berry babbling, asking what was happening, but he pulled him down until they were both well below the crest and hidden from the fires. Sharpe heard the last fugitives pound past on the summit, the crackle of musketry, the shouts diminishing as the men ran back. He let go of Berry's collar. He saw the white face turn to him in the darkness, there was a gasp.

'My God. Captain Sharpe? Is that you?'

'Weren't you expecting me?' Sharpe's voice was as cold as a blade in winter. 'I was looking for you.'

CHAPTER 20

A spent musket ball whirred over Sharpe's head, the sounds of the battle were fainter now that he was below the crest and the only light came from the eerie reflections of the deserted fires on the undersides of the battle-smoke that drifted from the plateau of the Medellin.

'Sharpe!' Berry was still babbling. He lay on his back and tried to wriggle his way uphill away from the tall, dark shape of the Rifleman. 'Shouldn't we go, Sharpe, the French? They're on the hill!'

'I know. I've killed at least two of them.' Sharpe held his blade at Berry's breast and stopped the wriggling. 'I'm going back to kill a few more soon.'

The talk of killing silenced Berry. Sharpe could see the face staring up at him but it was too dark to read the expression. Sharpe had to imagine the wet lips, the fleshy face, the look of fear.

'What did you do to the girl, Berry?'

The Lieutenant remained silent. Sharpe could see the slim sword lying forgotten on the grass; there was no fight in the man, no will to resist, just a pathetic hope that Sharpe could be placated.

'What did you do, Berry?' Sharpe stepped closer and the blade flickered at Berry's throat. Sharpe saw the face twist to and fro, heard the breath gulping in the Lieutenant's throat.

'Nothing, Sharpe, I swear it. Nothing.'

Sharpe flicked his wrist so that the blade nicked Berry's chin. It was razor sharp and he heard the gasp.

'Let me go. Please! Let me go.'

'What did you do?' Sharpe heard the distinctive sound of the rifles firing to his right. The rolling crackle of musketry was to the left and he guessed that the French column had thrown its skirmishers out to the flanks to clear away the scattered groups that still offered resistance. He had not much time; he wanted to be with his men and to see what was happening on the hilltop but first he wanted Berry to suffer as the girl had suffered, to fear as she had feared.

'Did Josefina plead with you?' The voice was like a night wind off the North Sea. 'Did she ask you to let her go?'

Berry stayed silent. Sharpe twitched the blade again. 'Did she?'

'Yes.' It was a mere whisper.

'Was she frightened?' He moved the point on to the flesh of Berry's neck.

'Yes, yes, yes.'

'But you raped her just the same?'

Berry was too terrified to speak. He made incoherent noises, rolled his head, stared at the blade which ran up to the dim, avenging shape above him. Sharpe could smell the pungent smoke of the musketry on the hill. He had to be quick.

'Can you hear me, Berry?'

'Yes, Sharpe. I can hear you.' There was the faintest hint of hope in Berry's voice. Sharpe dashed it.

'I'm going to kill you. I want you to know that

so you are as frightened as she was. Do you under-stand?'

The man babbled again, pleaded, shook his head and held his hands together as if in prayer to Sharpe. The Rifleman stared down. He remembered a strange phrase he had once heard at a Church Parade in far-off India. A Chaplain had appeared and stood in his white surplice on the parade ground and out of the meaningless mumbles a phrase had somehow lodged in Sharpe's mind, a phrase from the Prayer Book that came back to him now as he wondered whether he really could kill a man for raping his woman. 'Deliver my soul from the sword, my darling from the power of the dog.' Sharpe had thought to let the man stand up, pick up his sword, and fight for his life. But he thought of the girl's terror, let the picture of her blood on the sheets feed his anger once more, saw the babbling fleshy face beneath him and as if he were tired and simply wanted to rest, he leaned forward with both hands on the hilt of the sword.

The babbling almost became a scream, the body thrashed once, the blade went through skin and muscle and fat and into Berry's throat and the Lieutenant died. Sharpe stayed bent on the sword. It was murder, he knew that, a capital offence but somehow he did not feel guilty. What troubled him was the knowledge that he ought to be guilty yet he was not. He had avenged his darling on the dog. His hands were wet and he knew, as he tugged the blade free, that he had severed Berry's jugular. He would look like someone from a slaughterhouse but he felt better and grinned in the darkness as he dropped to one knee and ran his hands swiftly across Berry's pockets and pouches. Revenge, he decided, felt good and he pulled coins from the dead man's tunic and thrust them into his own pockets. He walked away from the body towards the sounds of the rifles, walked slowly uphill to where the flashes spat bullets towards the French, and sank down beside Harper. The Sergeant looked at him and then turned back to face the hilltop and pulled his trigger. Smoke puffed from the pan, belched from the barrel, and Sharpe saw a Voltigeur fall backwards into a fire. Harper grinned with satisfaction.

'He's been annoying me, that one, so he has. Been jumping around like a regular little Napoleon.'

Sharpe stared at the hilltop. It was like the paintings of hell he had seen in Portuguese and Spanish churches. Smoke rolled redly in weird patches across the hilltop, thickly where the column was pushing deeper through the fires that marked the British lines, and thinly where small groups fought the skirmishers who tried to clear the hilltop. Hundreds of small fires lit the battle, muskets pumped smoke and flame into the night, the whole accompanied by the shouts of the French and the cries of the wounded. The French skirmishers had suffered badly from the Riflemen. Harper had lined them in the shadows on the hill's edge and they picked off the blue figures who ran through the fires long before the French were close enough to use their muskets with any accuracy. Sharpe pulled his own rifle forward and reached down for a cartridge.

'Any problems?'

Harper shook his head and grinned. 'Target practice.'

'The rest of the company?'

The Sergeant jerked his head backwards. 'Most of them are down below with Mr Knowles, sir. I told him they weren't needed here.'

For an instant Sharpe wondered whether anyone had seen him murder Berry but he dismissed the thought. He trusted his instinct, an instinct that warned him of the enemy and on this night every man had been his enemy until Berry had died. No one had seen him. Harper grunted as he rammed another bullet into his rifle.

'What happened, sir?'

Sharpe grinned wolfishly and said nothing. He was reliving the instant of Berry's death, feeling the satisfaction, the relief of the pain of Josefina's ordeal. Who had said revenge was stale and unprofitable? They were wrong. He primed the rifle, cocked it, and slid it forward but no Voltigeurs were in sight. The battle had passed off to the left where it flashed and thundered in the darkness.

'Sir?'

He turned and looked at the Sergeant. He told him, flatly and simply, what had happened and watched the broad Irish face turn bleak with anger.

'How is she?'

Sharpe shook his head. 'She lost a lot of blood. They beat her.'

The Sergeant searched the ground in front of him, sifting through the firelight and the humped shadows, the far musket flashes that could be French or English. When he spoke his voice was soft.

'And the two of them? What will you do?'

'Lieutenant Berry died in tonight's battle.'

Harper turned and looked at his Captain, at the blade which lay red beside him, and smiled slowly. 'The other one?'

'Tomorrow.'

Harper nodded and turned back to the battle. The

French had been held, judging by the position of the musket flashes, as if in pushing ever deeper into the lines they had marched into a thickening opposition they at last could not break. Sharpe searched the darkness to his right. The French must have sent more troops but there was no sign of them. The ground in front was bare of movement. He turned round.

'Lieutenant Knowles!'

'Sir!' The voice came from the darkness but was followed by Knowles' anxious face coming up the slope. 'Sir? You're all right, sir?'

'Like a dog with a bone, Lieutenant.' Knowles could not understand Sharpe's seeming content. Rumours had run through the company since Harper and the Riflemen had returned without the Captain. 'Tell the men to fix bayonets and come up here. It's time we joined in.'

Knowles grinned. 'Yes, sir.'

'How many men do we have?'

'Twenty, sir, not counting the Rifles.'

'Good! To work then.'

Sharpe stood up and walked on to the hilltop. He waved the Riflemen forward and waited for Knowles and his group to climb into the light. Sharpe waved left and right with the sword.

'Skirmish order! Then slowly forward. We're not trying to take on the column but let's flush out their skirmishers.'

The bayonets gleamed red in the firelight, the line walked steadily forward, but the enemy skirmishers had disappeared. Sharpe took them to a hundred yards from the enemy column and waved the men down. There was nothing they could do except watch a demonstration of British infantry at its best. The French had ploughed their way almost to the end of the hill but had been checked by a Battalion that Sharpe guessed must have marched from the foot of the hill and now stretched itself ahead of the French like an impassable barrier. The Battalion was in line and firing in controlled platoon volleys. It was superb. No infantry could stand against Britain's best and the Battalion was shredding the column with musketry that rolled up and down the Battalion's line, the ramrods flashing in unison, the platoons firing in sequence, an irresistible hammering of close-range musket fire that poured into the tight French ranks. The enemy wavered. Each volley decimated the column's leading ranks. Their commander tried to deploy into line but he was too late. The men at the back of the column would not go forward into that hail of lead that rippled methodically and murderously from the British muskets. Groups of blue-coated French began to melt into the dark, a mounted British officer saw it and raised his sword, the red ranks cheered and went forward with levelled bayonets and, as suddenly as it had begun, the battle was done. The French went backwards, stepping over the dead, retreating ever faster from the reaching blades. The enemy had done well. A single column had so nearly captured the hill, even without the other two columns that had never arrived, but now the French Colonel had to go back, had to take his men from the musket fire that overwhelmed them. As they drew level with the skirmish line some of Sharpe's Riflemen lifted their weapons but Sharpe shouted to let them go. There would be killing enough tomorrow.

Sharpe crouched by a fire and wiped the blade free of the sticky blood with a dead Frenchman's jacket. It was the time for collecting the dead and counting the living.

He wanted Gibbons to worry about Berry, to feel fear in the night, and he felt the elation again of the killing stroke. From the town came the bells of midnight and he thought briefly of the girl lying in the candlelight and he wondered if she thought of him. Harper squatted beside him, his face black with powder smoke, and held out a bottle of spirits.

'Get some sleep, sir. You need it.' Harper grinned briefly. 'We have a promise to keep tomorrow.'

Sharpe lifted the bottle towards the Sergeant as if in a toast. 'A promise and a half, Sergeant. A promise and a half.'

CHAPTER 21

It was a short, bad night. After the repulse of the French the army rescued the wounded and, in the thin firelight, searched and piled the dead that could be found. Battalions that had thought themselves safe in an imaginary second line now posted sentries and the brief night was broken by frequent rattles of musketry as the nervous picquets imagined fresh enemy columns in the dark. The bugles sounded at two in the morning, the fires were restored to life, and hungry men shivered round the flames and listened to the distant French bugles rousing the enemy. At half past three, when a silvery grey light touched the flanks of the Medellin, Berry's body was found and carried to the fire where Simmerson and his officers sipped scalding tea. Gibbons, appalled at the great wound disfiguring his friend's throat, looked at Sharpe with pale and suspicious eyes. Sharpe looked back and smiled, saw the suspicion, and then Gibbons turned abruptly away and shouted for his servant to clear up the blankets. Simmerson flicked a glance round the officers. 'He died a brave death, gentlemen, a brave death.'

They all muttered the right words, more concerned with hunger and what was to come than with the death of a fat Lieutenant, and watched bleakly as the body was stripped of its valuables before being piled with the scores of dead that would be buried before the sun rose high and made them offensive. No one thought it odd that Berry's body had been found so far from the other dead. The events of the night had been muddled, there were stories that the Germans below the Medellin had fought a running skirmish with another column and groups of French fugitives had become lost in the darkness and wandered in the British lines and it was assumed Berry had met such a group.

By four o'clock the army was in position. Hill's Brigades were on the Medellin and the Brigade Majors lined the Battalions back from the hill crest so that they would be invisible to the French gunners. The South Essex were on the flank of the hill overlooking the Germans and the Guards who would defend the flat plain between the Medellin and the Pajar. Sharpe stared at the town, half hidden in mist, and wondered what was happening to Josefina. He was impatient for the battle to start, to take his Light Company away from Simmerson and up to the skirmish line that would form in the mist-shrouded Portina valley. He was surprised that Simmerson had said nothing to the Battalion. Instead the Colonel sat his grey horse and stared moodily at the myriad smoke trails from the French camp that rose and mingled in front of the rising sun. He ignored Sharpe, he always did, as though the Rifleman was a small nuisance that would be brushed from his life when his letter was received in London. Gibbons sat beside Simmerson and it suddenly occurred to Sharpe that the two men were frightened. In front of them the solitary colour drooped from its staff, beaded with morning moisture, a lonely reminder of the Battalion's disgrace. Simmerson did not know war and he was staring at the mist along the Portina wondering what would emerge from the whiteness to challenge his

Battalion. It was not just Sharpe's future that depended on this battle. If the Battalion did badly then it would stay a Battalion of Detachments and dwindle away under the onslaught of disease and death until it would simply disappear from the army list; the Battalion that never was. Simmerson would survive. He would sail home to his country estate, take his seat in Parliament, become an armchair expert on the war but wherever soldiers met the names of Simmerson and the South Essex would be scorned. Sharpe grinned to himself; ironically, on this day, Simmerson needed the Riflemen far more than Sharpe needed the Colonel.

At last the signal came and the Light Companies went forward, spreading themselves into a thin screen of skirmishers to become the first men to meet the attack. As he walked down the slope towards the mist Sharpe stared at the Cascajal Hill that was topped with French guns, almost wheel to wheel, the barrels pointing at the Medellin. Somewhere behind the guns the French Battalions would be parading into the huge columns that would be thrown at the British line, behind them there would be cavalry waiting to pour through the opening; more than fifty thousand Frenchmen preparing to punish the British for their temerity in sending Wellesley's small army into their Empire. The Light Company walked into the mist, into the private world where skirmisher would fight Voltigeur, and Sharpe thrust away the thoughts of defeat. It was unthinkable that Wellesley could lose, that the army might be shattered and sent reeling back to the sea, that Sharpe's problems, Simmerson's problems, the fate of the South Essex, all would become drowned in the disastrous flood of defeat. Harper ran up to him and nodded cheerfully as he pulled the muzzle stopper from his rifle.

'The weather's hot for us, sir.'

Sharpe grimaced. 'It will clear in an hour or so.' The mist hid everything beyond a hundred paces and took away the advantage of the long-range rifles. Sharpe saw the stream ahead.

'Far enough. See if Mr Denny is all right.'

Harper went off to the right to where Denny should be joining up with the German skirmishers. Sharpe walked upstream where he suspected the attack would be and found Knowles at the end of the line. Beyond in the mist he could see the redcoats of the 66th and some Riflemen from the Royal Americans.

'Lieutenant?'

'Sir?' Knowles was nervously alert; half dreading, half enjoying his first day of real battle. Sharpe grinned cheerfully at him.

'Any problems?'

'No, sir. Will it be long?' Knowles glanced constantly at the empty far bank of the Portina as though he expected to see the whole French army suddenly materialise.

'You'll hear the guns first.' Sharpe stamped his feet against the cold. 'What's the time?'

Knowles took out his watch, inscribed from his father, and opened the case. 'Nearly five, sir.' He went on looking at the ornate watch face with its filigree hand. 'Sir?' He sounded embarrassed.

'Yes?'

'If I die, sir, would you have this?' He held the watch out.

Sharpe pushed the watch back. He wanted to laugh but he shook his head gravely. 'You're not going to die. Who'd take over if I went?'

Knowles looked at him fearfully and Sharpe nodded.

'Think about it, Lieutenant. Promotion can be rapid in battle.' He grinned, attempting to dispel Knowles' gloom. 'Who knows? If it's a good enough day we may all end up Generals.'

A gun banged on the Cascajal. Knowles' eyes widened as he heard, for the first time, the rumbling thunder of iron shot in the air. Unseen by the skirmishers the eight-pound ball struck the crest of the Medellin, bounced over the troops in a spray of dirt and stones, and rolled harmlessly to rest four hundred yards down the plateau. The sound of the shot echoed flatly from the hills, was muffled by the mist, and died into silence. A hundred thousand men heard it, some crossed themselves, some prayed, and some just thought fitfully of the storm that was about to break across the Portina. Knowles waited for another gun but there was silence.

'What was that, sir?'

'A signal to the other French batteries. They'll be reloading the gun.' Sharpe imagined the sponge hissing as it was thrust into the gun, the steam rising from the vent, and then the new charge and shot being rammed home. 'About now, I'd think.'

The silence was over. From now Sharpe would tell the story of the battle by the sounds and he listened as the iron shot from seventy or eighty French guns screamed and thundered in the air. He could hear the crash of the guns, imagined them throwing their massive weights back on to the trails, bucking in the air and slamming back on to the wheels as the rammer was dipped in water and the men prepared the next shot. Behind was a different noise, the muted sound of the roundshot gouging the Medellin, the thud of iron on earth. He turned back to Knowles. 'This is my unlucky day.'

Knowles turned a worried face on him. The Captain

265

was supposed to be 'lucky'. Sharpe and the company depended on the superstition. 'Why, sir?'

Sharpe grinned. 'They're firing to our left.' He was shouting over the sound of the massed cannons. 'They'll attack there. I thought I might be the proud owner of a watch otherwise!' He slapped a relieved Knowles on the shoulder and pointed across the stream. 'Expect them in about twenty minutes, over to the left a bit. I'll be back!'

He walked down the line of men, checking flints, making the old jokes and looking for Harper. He felt desperately tired, not just the tiredness of disturbed and little sleep, but the weariness of problems that seemed to have no end. Berry's death was like a half-forgotten dream and solved nothing except half a promise and he had little idea how to solve the other half or the promise about the Eagle. The promises were like barriers he had erected in his own life and honour demanded that they were overcome but his sense told him the task was impossible. He waved at Harper and as the Sergeant walked towards him the noise of the battle changed. There was a whining quality to the roar of the shot overhead and Harper looked up into the mist.

'Shells?'

Sharpe nodded as the first one exploded on the Medellin. The sound rose in intensity, the crash of the shells echoing the thunder of the guns, and added to the din was the sharper sound of the long British six-pounders firing back. Harper jerked a thumb at the unseen Medellin. 'That's a rare hammering, sir.'

Sharpe listened. 'The bands are still playing.'

'I'd rather be down here.'

Distantly, through the incessant crashes that merged into one long rumble, Sharpe could hear the sound of Regimental bands. As long as the bandsmen were playing then the British Battalions were not suffering overmuch from the French bombardment. If Wellesley had not pulled the British line behind the crest the French gunners would be slaughtering the Battalions file by file and the bandsmen would be doing their other job of picking up the wounded and taking them to the rear. Sharpe knew Harper, like himself, was thinking of the promise to Lennox, of the Eagle. He stared across the stream at the empty grass, listened to the cannonade as though it were someone else's battle, and turned to the Sergeant.

'There will be other days, you know. Other battles.'

Harper smiled slowly, crouched, and flicked a pebble into the clear water. 'We'll see what happens, sir.' He stayed still, listening, then pointed ahead. 'Hear that?'

It was the noise Sharpe had been waiting for, faint but unmistakable, the sound he had not heard since Vimeiro, the sound of the French attack. The enemy columns were not in sight, would not be visible for minutes, but through the mist he could hear the serried drummers beating the hypnotic rhythm of the charge. Boom-boom, boom-boom, boomaboom, boomaboom, boom-boom. On and on it would go until the attack was won or lost, the drummer boys thrashing the skins despite the volleys, the endless rhythm that had carried the French to victory after victory. There was a relentless menace about the drumbeats, each repeated phrase brought the French nearer by ten paces, on and on, on and on.

Sharpe smiled at Harper. 'Look after the boy. Is he all right?'

'Denny, sir? Tripped over his sword three times but

otherwise he's fine.' Harper laughed. 'Look after yourself, sir.'

Sharpe walked back up the stream, the drumbeats nearer, the skirmish line peering apprehensively into the empty mist. Their job was about to begin. The French guns had failed to break the British Battalions and in front of the drums, spread in a vast cloud, the Voltigeurs were coming. Their aim was to get as close to the British Battalions as they could and snipe at the line with their muskets, to thin the ranks, weaken the line, so that when the drummed column arrived the British would be rotten and give way. Sharpe's skirmishers with the other Light Companies had to stop the Voltigeurs and their private battle, fought in the mist, was about to begin. He found Knowles standing by the stream.

'See anything?'

'No, sir.'

The drumming was louder, competing with the crash of the shells, and at the end of each drummed phrase Sharpe could hear a new sound as the drummers paused to let thousands of voices chant 'Vive L'Empereur'. It was the victory noise that had terrified the armies of Europe, the sound of Marengo, of Austerlitz, of Jena, the voices and drums of French victory. Then, upstream and out of sight, the Light troops met and Sharpe heard the first crackle of musketry; not the rolling volleys of massed ranks but the spaced, deliberate cracks of aimed shots. Knowles looked at Sharpe with raised eyebrows, the Rifleman shook his head. 'That's only one column. There'll be at least another one, probably two, and nearer. Wait.'

And there they were, dim figures running in the mist, dozens of men in blue jackets with red epaulettes who angled across their front. The men raised their muskets.

'Hold your fire!' Sharpe pushed a musket down. The Voltigeurs ran into the fire of the 66th and the Royal Americans, they were a hundred paces upstream and Sharpe waited to see if the French skirmish line would reach the South Essex. 'Wait!'

He watched the first Frenchmen crumple on the turf, others knelt and took careful aim but it was not his fight. He guessed the French attack, aimed at the Medellin, was going to pass by the South Essex but he was glad enough to let his raw troops see real skirmishing before they had to do it themselves. The French, like the British, fought in pairs. Each man had to protect his partner, firing in turn and calling out warnings, constantly watching the enemy to see if the guns were aimed at him or his partner. Sharpe could hear the shouts, the whistles that passed on commands, and in the background, insistent as a tocsin, the drumming and shouting. Knowles was like a leashed hound wanting to go up the bank to the fight but Sharpe held him back. 'They don't need us. Our turn will come. Wait.'

The British line was holding. The Frenchmen tried to rush the stream but fell as they reached the water. The British pairs moved in short rushes, changing position, confusing their enemy, waiting for the Voltigeurs to come in range and then letting off their shots. The green-jacketed Riflemen of the Royal Americans looked for the enemy officers and Sergeants and Sharpe could hear the crack of the rifles as they destroyed the enemy leaders. The sound was rising to its first crescendo, the roar of the cannon, the melding crashes of shells, the drums and voices of the column, and the sound of bugles mixing with the musketry. The mist was thickening with the smoke of the French batteries that drifted westward towards the British line but soon,

Sharpe knew, the mist would be burned off. He felt the faintest breeze and saw a great swirl of whiteness shiver and move and heard Knowles draw breath with amazement before the mist closed down. In the gap was a mass of men, tight-packed marching ranks tipped with steel, one of the columns aiming for the stream. It was time to retreat and, sure enough, Sharpe heard the whistles and bugles and saw the skirmishers to the left start to go backwards towards the Medellin. They left bodies, red and green, behind them.

He blew his own whistle, waved an arm, and listened for the Sergeants to repeat the signal. His men would be disappointed. They had not fired a shot but Sharpe suspected that they would have their opportunities soon enough. The drumming and the chanting went on, the shot crashed overhead, but as the company climbed the hill the mist cut them off from the battle. No one was shooting at them, no shells landed with spluttering fuses on their piece of the hillside, and Sharpe continued to have the strange sensation of listening to a battle that had nothing to do with him. The illusion vanished as the line climbed out of the mist on to a hillside bright with the early sun. Sharpe checked the line, turned, and heard his men gasp and swear at the view they suddenly encountered.

The crest of the Medellin was empty of soldiers. Only the French shells continued to tear up the earth in great gouts of soil and flame. The skirmishers in front of the French attack scrambled up the slope, ever nearer to the bursting shells, and turned to shoot at the columns that crawled out of the mist like great, strange animals emerging from the sea. The nearest column was two hundred yards to the left and to Sharpe's raw troops it must have seemed overwhelming. The Voltigeurs were joining its ranks, swelling it, the drummers beat it along with their relentless, hypnotic beating and the deep shouts of 'Vive L'Empereur' punctuated the grinding advance. There were three columns climbing the slope; each, Sharpe guessed, had close to two thousand men and over each there hung, glittering in the new sun, three gilded Eagles reaching for the crest.

Sharpe turned his skirmish line to face the column and then waved the men down. There was little they could do at this range. He decided not to rejoin the Battalion, the company would suffer less by staying on the hillside and watching the attack than if they tried to run through the barrage of shells, and as they knelt, watching the huge formation march up the slope, Sharpe saw the men of the King's German Legion join his crude line. They would be privileged spectators on the edge of the French attack. Ensign Denny came and knelt beside Sharpe and his face betrayed the worry and fear that the drumming, chanting mass engendered. Sharpe looked at him. 'What do you think?'

'Sir?'

'Frightening?' Denny nodded. Sharpe laughed. 'Did you ever learn mathematics?'

'Yes, sir.'

'So add up how many Frenchmen can actually use their muskets.'

Denny stared at the column and Sharpe saw realisation dawn on his face. The French column was a tried and tested battle winner but against good troops it was a death trap. Only the front rank and the two flank files could actually use their guns and of the hundreds of men in the nearest column only the sixty in the front rank and the men on the ends of the thirty or so other ranks could actually fire at their enemies. The mass of men in the middle were there merely to add weight, to look impressive, cheer, and fill up the gaps left by the dead.

The sound of the battle changed abruptly. The shelling stopped. The great marching squares were close to the crest of the Medellin and the French gunners were afraid of hitting their own men. For a moment there was just the drumming, the sound of thousands of boots hitting the hillside in unison, and suddenly a great cheer as the French infantry thought they had won. It was easy to see why they thought victory was in their grasp. There was no enemy in front of them, just the empty skyline, and the skirmish line had scrambled back over the crest to join their Battalions. They had done their job. They had kept the Voltigeurs from the British line and the French cheer died away as the British orders rang out and suddenly the hilltop was lined two deep with waiting men. It still looked ridiculous. Three great fists, enormous masses, aimed at a tenuous two deep line but the look was deceptive; mathematics in this situation was all.

The column nearest Sharpe was headed for the 66th and the 3rd. The two British Battalions were outnumbered two to one but every redcoat on the crest could fire his musket. Of the hundreds of Frenchmen who climbed in the column only a few more than a hundred could actually fire back and Sharpe had seen it happen too often to have any doubts about the outcome. He watched the order given, saw the British line appear to take a quarter turn to the right as they brought their muskets to their shoulders, and watched as the French column instinctively checked in the face of so many guns. The drums rattled, the French officers shouted, a kind of low growl came from the columns, swelled to a roar, to a cheer, and the French charged towards the summit.

And stopped. The slim steel blades of the British officers swept down and the relentless volleys began. Nothing could stand in the way of that musket fire. From right to left along the Battalions the platoon volleys flamed and flickered, a rolling fire that never stopped, the machine-like regularity of trained troops pouring four shots a minute into the dense mass of Frenchmen. The noise rose to the real crescendo of battle, the awesome sound of the ordered volleys and mixed with it the curious ringing as the bullets struck French bayonets. Sharpe looked to his left and saw the South Essex watching. They were too far away for their muskets to be of any use but he was glad that Simmerson's raw troops could see a demonstration of how practised firepower won battles.

The drumming went on, the boys banging their instruments frenetically to force the column up the slope and, incredibly, the French tried. The instinct of victory was too strong, too ingrained, and as the front ranks were destroyed by the murderous fire the men behind struggled over the bodies to be thrown backwards in turn by the relentless bullets. They faced an impossible task. The column was stuck, hunched against the storm, soaking up an incredible punishment but refusing to give in; to accept defeat. Sharpe was amazed, as he had been at Vimeiro, that troops could take such punishment but they did and he watched as the officers tried to organise a new attack. The French, too late, tried to form into line and he could see the officers waving their swords to lead the rear ranks into the open flanks. Sharpe held his rifle up.

'Come on!'

His men cheered and followed him across the hillside. There was little danger that the French could form line but the appearance of a couple of hundred skirmishers on the flank would deter them. The Germans of the Legion went with Sharpe's company and they all stopped a hundred paces from the struggling mass of Frenchmen and began their own volleys, more ragged than the ordered fire from the crest, but effective enough to repel the Frenchmen who were bravely trying to form a line. The Germans began fixing bayonets, they knew the column could not stand the fire much longer, and Sharpe yelled at his own men to fix blades. The sound of drums faded. One boy gave a further determined rattle with his sticks but the distinctive rhythm of the charge faded away and the attack was done. The crest of the hill rippled with light as the 66th fixed bayonets, the volleys died, the British cheered and the French were finished. Broken and smashed by musket fire they did not wait for the bayonet charge. The mass split into small groups of fugitives, the Eagles dropped, the blue ranks broke and ran for the stream.

'Forward!' Sharpe, the German officers, and from the ridge the company officers of the 66th shouted as they led the red-steel-tipped line down the slope. Sharpe looked for the Eagles but they were far ahead, being carried to safety, and he forgot them and led his men diagonally down the hill to cut off the fleeing groups of Frenchmen. It was a time for prisoners and as the skirmishers cut into the blue mass the Frenchmen threw down their guns and held their hands high. One officer refused to surrender and flickered his blade towards Sharpe but the huge cavalry sword beat it aside and the man dropped to his knees and held clasped hands towards the Rifleman. Sharpe ignored him. He wanted to get to the stream and stop his men pursuing the French on to the far bank where reserve Battalions waited to punish the British victors. The mist had almost cleared.

Some Frenchmen stopped at the stream and turned their muskets on the British. A ball plucked at Sharpe's sleeve, another scorched past his face, but the small group broke and fled as he swept the sword towards them. His boots splashed in the stream, he could hear shots behind him and saw bullets strike the water, but he turned and screamed at his men to stop. He drove them back from the stream, herded them with the prisoners, away from the French reserve troops who waited with loaded muskets on the far bank.

It was done. The first attack beaten and the slope of the Medellin was smothered in bodies that lay in a blue smear from the stream almost to the crest they had failed to reach. There would be another attack but first each side must count the living and collect the dead. Sharpe looked for Harper and saw, thankfully, that the Sergeant was alive, Lieutenant Knowles was there, grinning broadly, and with his sword still unbloodied.

'What's the time, Lieutenant?'

Knowles tucked the blade under his arm and opened his watch. 'Five minutes after six, sir. Wasn't that incredible?'

Sharpe laughed. 'Just wait. That was nothing.'

Harper ran down the slope towards them and held out a bundle in his hands. 'Breakfast, sir?'

'Not garlic sausage?'

Harper grinned. 'Just for you.'

Sharpe broke off a length and bit into the pungent, tasty meat. He stretched his arms, felt the tenseness ease in his muscles, and began to feel better. The first round was over and he looked up the littered slope to the single colour of the Battalion. Beneath it was Gibbons, mounted beside his uncle, and Sharpe hoped the Lieutenant had watched the skirmishers and was feeling the fear. Harper saw where he was looking and he saw the expression on his Captain's face. The Sergeant turned to the men of the company, guarding their prisoners and boasting of their exploits. 'All right, this isn't a harvest bloody festival! Reload your guns. They'll be back.'

CHAPTER 22

The battle had flared briefly then died into silence and, as the sun climbed higher and the smoke drifted into nothingness, the Portina valley filled with men, British and French, who came to rescue the wounded and bury the dead. Men who an hour before had struggled desperately to kill each other now chatted and exchanged tobacco for food, and wine for brandy. Sharpe took a dozen men down to the stream to find four men of the Light Company who were missing. They had not died in the skirmish; all had been killed as they climbed back up the slope with their prisoners. The French guns had opened fire but this time with their barrels depressed and the shells blew apart in the loose ranks of the British trudging up the hill. The men began to run, the French prisoners turned and sprinted for their own lines, but there was no cover from the shelling. Sharpe had watched one iron ball strike a rabbit hole and bounce into the air with smoke spiralling crazily from its fuse. The shell, small enough to pick up with one hand, landed by Gataker. The Rifleman had bent down to pinch out the fuse but he was too late, it exploded, spitting him with its fractured casing and belching smoke and flame as it hurled his corpse backwards. Sharpe had knelt beside him but Gataker was dead;

the first of Sharpe's Riflemen to die since the fighting in the northern mountains of the last winter.

When the guns stopped they were ordered back to bury the dead quickly and the men scraped shallow holes in the soft earth beside the stream. The French came as well. For a few minutes the troops avoided each other but soon someone made a joke, held out a hand, and within minutes the enemies shook hands, tried on each other's shakoes, shared the meagre scraps of food and treated each other like long lost friends rather than sworn enemies. The valley was littered with the remains of battle; unexploded shells, weapons, looted packs, the usual garbage of defeat.

'Sharpe! Captain!' Sharpe turned to see Hogan picking his way through the dead and the wounded. 'I've been looking for you!' The Engineer slid from his horse and looked round. 'Are you all right?'

'I'm all right.' Sharpe accepted Hogan's offered water bottle. 'How's Josefina?'

Hogan smiled. 'She slept.'

Sharpe looked at the dark rings under the Irishman's eyes. 'But you didn't?'

Hogan shook his head and then indicated the bodies. 'One sleepless night isn't much to complain about.'

'And Josefina?'

'I think she's all right. Really, Richard.' Hogan shook his head. 'She's subdued; unhappy. But what would you expect after last night?'

Last night, thought Sharpe. Good God, it was only last night. He turned away and looked at the bloodied water of the Portina stream and at the Frenchmen on the far bank who were excavating a wide shallow hole into which their stripped dead were being thrown. He turned back to Hogan. 'What's happening in town?'

'In the town? Oh, you're worried about her safety?' Sharpe nodded. Hogan took out his snuff box. 'Everything's quiet. They rounded up most of the Spanish and they're back in their lines. There's a guard in the town to stop any more looting.'

'So she's safe?'

Hogan looked at Sharpe's red-rimmed eyes, at the deep shadows on the face, and nodded. 'She's safe, Richard.' Hogan said no more. Sharpe's face scared him; a grim face, he thought, like the face of a desperate adventurer who would risk everything on the single fall of a pair of dice. The two men began walking beside the stream, between the bodies, and Hogan thought of the Prince of Wales Dragoon, a Captain with a broken arm, who had called at the house early in the morning. Josefina had been surprised to see him, but pleased, and told Hogan that she had met the cavalry officer in the town the day before. The Dragoon had taken over Hogan's vigil but this, the Engineer thought, was no time to tell Sharpe about Captain Claud Hardy. Hogan had liked the man, had taken immediately to Hardy's laughing description of how he had fallen from his horse and the Irishman could see how relieved Josefina was to have someone sitting beside her who told her jokes, talked blithely of balls and banquets, hunting and horses, but who shrewdly understood whatever horrors still lurked in her memories of the night before. Hardy was good for Josefina, Hogan knew, but this was not the time to tell that to Sharpe. 'Richard?'

'Yes?'

'Have you done anything about . . . ?' Hogan broke off.

'Gibbons and Berry?'

'Yes.' Hogan stepped aside and led his horse away

from a Frenchman dragging a naked corpse over the grass. Sharpe waited until the man had gone.

'Why?'

Hogan shrugged. 'I was thinking.' He spoke hesitantly. 'I was hoping that after a night to think about it you would be careful. It could destroy your career. A duel, a fight. Be careful.' Hogan was virtually pleading. Sharpe stopped and turned to him.

'I promise you one thing. I will do nothing to Lieutenant Berry.'

Hogan thought for a moment. Sharpe's face was unreadable but finally the Irishman nodded slowly. 'I suppose that's a good thing. But you're still determined about Gibbons?'

Sharpe smiled. 'Lieutenant Gibbons will soon join Lieutenant Berry.' He turned away and began walking up the slope. Hogan ran after him.

'You mean?'

'Yes. Berry's dead. Tell Josefina that, will you?'

Hogan felt an immense sadness, not for Berry, who had probably deserved whatever Sharpe had done to him, but for Sharpe who saw all of life as one immense battle and had equipped himself to fight it with an unparalleled ferocity. 'Be careful, Richard.'

'I will. I promise.'

'When will we see you?' Hogan dreaded that Sharpe would walk into Josefina's room and find Hardy there.

'I don't know.' Sharpe indicated the waiting French army. 'There's a hell of a fight still to come and I suspect we'll all have to stay on the field till one side goes home. Maybe tonight. Probably tomorrow. I don't know.'

Bugles split the valley, calling the troops back to their positions, and Hogan gathered his reins in his hand. The two men watched as British and French soldiers shook hands and slapped each other's backs before the killing restarted. Hogan heaved himself into the saddle. 'I'll tell her about Berry, Richard. Be careful, we don't want to lose you.' He put spurs to his horse and cantered beside the stream, back towards Talavera.

Sharpe walked up the slope of the Medellin with his men as they counted the spoils they had collected from the dead. He himself had found nothing but as he walked up the hill he knew that there would be richer pickings on the field before the sun fell; there was an Eagle to be plucked.

The morning crept on. The two armies faced each other, the cavalry chafing that there were no broken infantry to slaughter, the artillery piling their ammunition to break the infantry, while the infantry sat on the grass and made up their ammunition and cleaned the locks of their muskets. No one seemed to be in a hurry. The first attack had been repulsed and now the French were doubly determined to break the small British army in front of them. Through his telescope Sharpe watched the blue Battalions moving sluggishly into place, Regiment after Regiment, Brigade after Brigade, until between the Pajar and the Cascajal he could see more than thirty Eagles gathering for the attack. Forrest joined him and smiled nervously as he took the proffered telescope.

'Are they getting ready, Sharpe?'

Forrest scanned the French line. It was obvious what was about to happen. On the Cascajal the gunners were levering the pieces round so that they could fire at the troops to the right of the South Essex, at the Legion and at the Guards. Opposite those Regiments was gathering a vast horde of enemy Battalions. The French had failed to take the Medellin, by night or day, so now they were planning a hammer blow of such weight that no troops in the world could withstand the fury and intensity of their attack. Behind the French infantry Sharpe could see impatient cavalry waiting to pour through the gap and slaughter the defeated British. The day was gathering its strength, pausing before the carnage, readying itself for the emphatic demonstration of French superiority that would destroy Britain's army, swat it contemptuously aside, and to that end, at one o'clock, the French guns opened fire again.

CHAPTER 23

Sir Henry Simmerson had hardly moved all morning. He had watched the repulse of the first attack but, apart from the Light Company, the South Essex had not been needed; now, Sir Henry knew, things would be very different. The eastern side of the Portina was filled with French troops, Battalion after Battalion, preparing to come forward in the inevitable columns and Sir Henry had silently inspected them with his telescope. Fifteen thousand men were about to launch themselves against the centre of the British position and, beyond them, another fifteen thousand were already beginning to approach the Pajar and the network of obstacles that sheltered the Spanish. To Sir Henry's right the four Battalions of the King's German Legion, the Coldstream and the 3rd Guards waited for the attack but Sir Henry knew that the battle was lost. No troops, not even the vaunted Legion and the Guards, could stand up to the overwhelming numbers that waited for the signal to begin their massive approach.

Sir Henry grunted and shifted in his saddle. He had been right all along. It had been madness to let Wellesley have an army, it was madness to fight in this God-forsaken, heathen country when the British should more properly be fighting behind the walls of Flemish towns. He looked again at the French. Any fool could see what was about to happen; that the huge columns would punch through the thin British line like an angry bull going through a matchwood fence. Talavera would be cut off, the Spanish hunted like rats through the streets, but the troops on the Medellin, like his own Battalion, were in a worse position. At least the troops near Talavera stood a chance of reaching the bridge and beginning the long retreat to ignominy, but for the South Essex and for the other Battalions the only fate was to be cut off and the inevitable surrender.

'We will not surrender.'

Lieutenant Gibbons edged his horse closer to his uncle. It had not occurred to him that they might surrender but he had long known that the easiest way to stay in Sir Henry's favour was to offer agreement. 'Quite right, sir.'

Simmerson pushed his telescope shut. 'It will be a disaster, Christian, a disaster. The army is about to be destroyed.'

His nephew agreed and Simmerson reflected, for the thousandth time, what a waste of talent it was that Gibbons was only a Lieutenant. He had never heard anything but military sense from his nephew, the boy understood all his problems, agreed with his solutions, and if Sir Henry had found it temporarily impossible to give his nephew a deserved Captaincy then at least he could keep him away from that damned Sharpe and use him as a trusted adviser and confidant. A new Battalion appeared in the French line, almost opposite the South Essex, and Simmerson opened the telescope and looked at them.

'That's strange.'

'Sir?' Simmerson handed the telescope to his nephew.

The fresh Battalion marching from behind the Cascajal was dressed in white jackets with red turnbacks and collars. Simmerson had never seen troops like them.

'Major Forrest!'

'Sir?'

Simmerson pointed to the new troops who were forming a column. 'Do you know who they are?'

'No, sir.'

'Find out.'

The Colonel watched Forrest spur his horse down the line. 'Going to see Sharpe. Thinks he knows it all.' But not for long, thought Simmerson, this battle would see the end of military adventurers like Sharpe and Wellesley and return the army to prudent men, officers of sense, men like Sir Henry Simmerson. He turned and watched the shells exploding among the KGL and the Guards. The Battalions were lying flat and most of the French shots exploded harmlessly or bounced over their heads. Every now and then, though, there was a puff of smoke in the centre of the ranks and Simmerson could see the Sergeants pulling the mangled dead from the line and closing up the gaps. The skirmish line was forward, lying in the long grass by the stream, a futile gesture in the face of the imminent French attack. Forrest came back. 'Major?'

'Captain Sharpe tells me they're from the German Division, sir. Thinks they're probably the Dutch Battalions.'

Simmerson laughed. 'Germans fighting Germans, eh? Let 'em kill each other!' Forrest did not laugh.

'Captain Sharpe asks that the Light Company go forward, sir. He thinks the Dutchmen will attack part of the line.'

Simmerson said nothing. He watched the French

and certainly the Dutch, if that was who they were, were very nearly opposite the South Essex. A second Battalion formed a separate column behind the first but Simmerson had no intention of letting his Battalion get involved in the death struggle of Wellesley's army. The King's German Legion could fight the Dutchmen of the German Division while Simmerson would at least save one Battalion from disaster.

'Sir?' Forrest prompted him.

Simmerson waved down the interruption. There was an idea in his head and it was exciting, an idea that stretched into the future and depended on what he did at this moment, and he watched the beauty of it grow in his mind. The army was doomed. That was certain and in an hour or so Wellesley's force would be dead or prisoners but there was no need for the South Essex to be part of that disaster. If he were to march them now, march them away from the Medellin to a position in the rear, then they would not be encircled by the French. More than that, they would be the rallying point for what fugitives managed to escape the fury of the French, and then he could lead them, the only unit to escape unscathed from the destruction of an army, back to Lisbon and England. Such an action would have to be rewarded and Simmerson imagined himself in the lavish gold lace and cocked hat of a General. He gripped the pommel of his saddle in excitement. It was so obvious! He was not such a fool that he did not realise that the loss of the colour at Valdelacasa was a black mark against him, even though he was satisfied that in his letter he had plausibly and firmly fixed the blame on Sharpe, but if he could salvage even a small part of this army then Valdelacasa would be forgotten and the Horse Guards in Whitehall would be forced to recognise his ability and reward his initiative. His confidence soared. For a time he had been unsettled by the hard men who fought this war but now they had marched the army into a terrible position and only he, Simmerson, had the vision to see what was needed. He straightened in the saddle.

'Major! Battalion will about turn and form column of march on the left!' Forrest did not move. The Colonel wheeled his horse. 'Come on, Forrest, we haven't much time!'

Forrest was appalled. If he did as Simmerson ordered then the South Essex would hinge back like a swinging gate and leave a gap in the British line through which the French could pour their troops. And the French columns had started their advance! Their Voltigeurs were swarming towards the stream, the drums had begun their war rhythm, the shells were falling ever more thickly among the German Legion below them. Simmerson slapped the rump of Forrest's horse. 'Hurry, man! It's our only hope!'

The orders were given and the South Essex began the clumsy wheeling movement that left the flank of the Medellin an open slope to the enemy. Sharpe's company was the pivot of the movement and the ranks shuffled awkwardly and stared behind them, aghast, as the enemy columns began their advance. The skirmish line was already fighting, Sharpe could hear the muskets and rifles, but three hundred yards beyond the stream the Eagles were coming. This attack was not only vaster than the first but this time the French were sending their field artillery with the columns and Sharpe could see the horses and guns waiting to begin their journey to the stream. And the South Essex were retreating! Sharpe ran clumsily along the swinging line.

'Sir!'

Simmerson looked down on him. 'Captain Sharpe?'

'For God's sake, sir! There's a column aimed for us . . .' He was interrupted by a Dragoon Lieutenant, one of Hill's staff, who slid his horse to a stop in a spray of earth. Simmerson looked at the newcomer. 'Lieutenant?'

'General Hill's compliments, sir, and would you stay in position and deploy skirmishers.'

Simmerson nodded benignly. 'My compliments to General Hill but he will find out I am doing the right thing. Carry on!'

Sharpe thought of arguing but knew it was hopeless. He ran back to the company. Harper stood behind it, keeping the dressing, and he looked woefully at his Captain.

'What's happening, sir?'

'We're going forward, that's what's happening.' Sharpe pushed through the ranks. 'Light Company! Skirmish order. Follow me!'

He ran down the hill, his men following. Damn Simmerson! The Voltigeurs from the white-jacketed Battalion were already over the stream and outflanking the King's Germans and Sharpe could see too many men lying dead or injured where the Legion was fighting against twice their number. It was a lung-bursting run, hampered by packs, pouches, haversacks and weapons, but the men forced themselves on towards the Dutchmen who had crossed the stream. Shells burst among the Light Company and Harper, driving them from the back, watched two men fall but there was no time to look after them. He watched Sharpe drag his sword clumsily from the scabbard and realised the Captain planned to charge right into the Voltigeurs and push them back across the stream. Harper took a deep breath. 'Bayonets! Bayonets!'

The men with muskets had little chance of fixing their bayonets in time but the Riflemen had no need to try. The Baker's bayonet was long and equipped with a handle and Sharpe's Riflemen held them like swords; the French saw them coming, turned, and fumbled with their ammunition. A first bullet passed Sharpe, singing in his ear, a second struck the ground and ricocheted up to hit his canteen and then he was swinging the sword at the nearest man, the rest of the company were stabbing and shouting, and the white-coated Voltigeurs were scrambling back to the far side of the Portina.

'Down! Down! Down!' Sharpe screamed at his men and pushed two of them to the ground. The skirmish line had been restored but that was a small victory. He ran among his men. 'Aim low! Kill the bastards!'

The Dutch skirmishers reformed and started sniping across the stream. Sharpe ignored them and kept running until he found a Captain of the King's German Legion whose company had suffered because Simmerson refused to send out his Light Company.

'I'm sorry!'

The Captain waved down Sharpe's apology. 'You are welcome! Ve are fighting the German Division, no?' The Captain laughed. 'They are good soldiers but ve are better. Enjoy yourself!'

Sharpe went back to his company. The enemy were fifty yards away, across the stream, and Sharpe's Riflemen were asserting their superiority thanks to the seven spiralling grooves in the barrels of their weapons. The Voltigeurs were edging backwards and Sharpe's redcoats of the South Essex crept nearer to the stream to improve their aim; he watched them proudly, helping each other, pointing out targets, firing coolly and remembering the lessons he had pounded into them during the advance to Talavera. Ensign Denny was standing up, shouting shrill encouragement, and Sharpe pushed him to the ground. 'Don't make yourself a target, Mr Denny, they like to kill promising young officers!'

Denny beamed from ear to ear at the compliment. 'What about you, sir? Why don't you get down?'

'I will. Remember to keep moving!'

Harper was kneeling by Hagman, loading for him, and picking out ripe targets for the old poacher. Sharpe gave them his own rifle and left them to pick off the enemy officers. Knowles was sensibly watching the open end of the line, directing the fire of half a dozen men to stop the whitecoats outflanking the South Essex, and Sharpe was not needed there. He grinned. The company was doing well, it was fighting like a veteran unit, and already there were a dozen bodies on the far side of the stream. There were two, dressed in red, on their own side but the South Essex, perhaps due to the ferocity of their charge, held the initiative and the Dutchmen did not want to risk coming too close to the British skirmish line.

But beyond the Voltigeurs, coming steadily, was the first column, the right-hand column of a series that filled the plain between the Cascajal and the town. The attack was only minutes away and when it came, Sharpe knew, the skirmish line would be thrown back. The whole horizon was hidden by the clouds of dust thrown up by the thousands of French infantry, their drumming and cheering rivalled the sound of the guns and exploding shells, and in the background was the sinister noise of the jangling chains which were part of the artillery harness. Sharpe had never seen an attack on this scale, the columns covered half a mile in the width of their attack and behind them, hardly seen in the dust and smoke, was a second line, equally strong, that the French would throw in if the British checked the first Battalions. Sharpe looked behind. Simmerson had swung the Battalion and it was marching away from the great gap he had created in the line, Sharpe could see a horseman riding recklessly towards the single colour and he guessed that Hill or even Wellesley was dealing furiously with Simmerson, but for the moment the gap existed and the white-coated Dutchmen were marching straight for it.

He joined Harper. There were only seconds before the column would force them back and he stared at its slow advance and at the Eagle which flashed tantalisingly from its centre. Beside it rode a horseman with a fringed and cockaded hat and Sharpe tapped Hagman on the shoulder.

'Sir?' The Cheshire man gave a toothless grin. Sharpe shouted over the drumbeats and the crackle of musketry. 'See the man with the fancy hat?'

Hagman looked. 'Two hundred yards?' He took his own rifle and aimed carefully, ignoring the buzzing of the enemy bullets around them, let his breath out half way and squeezed the trigger. The rifle slammed back into his shoulder, there was a billow of smoke, but Sharpe leapt to one side and saw the enemy Colonel fall into the mass of the column. He slapped Hagman on the back. 'Well done!' He walked to the other Riflemen. 'Aim at the artillery! The guns!' He was frightened of the horse artillery that the French were bringing with the columns; if the gunners were allowed to get close enough and load with canister or grape-shot they would blast great holes in the British line and give to the French columns the fire-power that was normally denied to them by their packed formation. He watched his

Riflemen as they aimed at the horses and at the gunners riding on the French four-pounders; if anything could stop the artillery it would be the long-range accuracy of the Baker rifle but there was so little time before the column would force them back and the skirmish would become an affair of running and firing, running and firing, and all the time getting closer and closer to the huge space that Simmerson had created in the British defence.

He ran back to Harper, at the centre of the line, and retrieved his rifle. As the column was drummed closer the enemy Voltigeurs were plucking up courage and making short dashes towards the stream in an attempt to force the British skirmish line back. Sharpe could see half a dozen of his men lying dead or badly wounded, one of them in a green jacket, and he pointed at the man and raised his eyebrows to Harper.

'Pendleton, sir. Dead.'

Poor Pendleton, only seventeen, and so many pockets left to pick. The Voltigeurs were firing faster, not bothering to aim, just concentrating on saturating their enemy with musket fire and Sharpe saw another man go down; Jedediah Horrell, whose new boots had given him blisters. It was time to retreat and Sharpe blew his whistle twice and watched as his men squeezed off a last shot before running a few paces back, kneeling, and loading again. He rammed a bullet into his rifle and slid the steel ramrod back into the slit stock. He looked for a target and found him in a man wearing the single stripe of a French Sergeant who was counting off Voltigeurs for the rush that would take them over the stream. Sharpe put the rifle to his shoulder, felt the satisfying click as the flat, ring-neck cock rode back on the mainspring, and pulled the trigger. The Sergeant spun round, hit in the shoulder, and turned to see who had fired. Harper grabbed Sharpe's arm.

'That was a terrible shot. Now let's get the hell out of here! They'll want revenge for that!'

Sharpe grinned and sprinted back with the Sergeant towards the new skirmish line that was seventy paces behind the stream. The air was full of the 'boom-boom, boom-boom, boomaboom boomaboom, boom-boom, Vive L'Empereur, and the columns were splashing through the stream, the whole plain smothered in French infantry marching beneath countless Eagles towards the thin defensive line that was still being shelled by the guns on the Cascajal. The British guns had a target they could not miss and Sharpe watched as, time and time again, the solid shot lanced into the columns, crushing men by the dozen, but there were too many men and the files closed, the ranks stepped over the dead, and the columns came on. There was a cheer from the British skirmishers when a spherical case shot, Britain's secret weapon developed by Colonel Shrapnel, successfully detonated right over one of the columns and the musket balls, packed in the spherical case, splattered down on to the French and shredded half the ranks, but there were not enough guns to check the attack and the French took the punishment and kept coming.

Then, for ten minutes, there was no time to watch anything but the Voltigeurs to the front, to do anything but run and fire, run and fire, to try and keep the French skirmishers pinned back against their column. The enemy seemed more numerous, the drumming louder, and the smoke from the muskets and rifles silted the air with an opaque curtain that surrounded Sharpe's company and the white-coated Voltigeurs with their strange, guttural cries. Sharpe was taking the Light Company back towards the spot where the South Essex should have been, widening the gap between his company and the German skirmishers. His company was down to less than sixty men and, at the moment, they were the only troops between the column and the empty plain at the rear of the British line. He had no chance of stopping the column but as long as he could slow down the advance then there was a hope that the gap might be filled and the sacrifice of his men justified. Sharpe fought with the rifle until it was so fouled he could hardly push the ramrod into the barrel; the Riflemen had long stopped using the greased patch that surrounded the bullet and gripped the rifling instead; like Sharpe, they were ramming charge and naked ball into their guns as fast as they could to discourage the enemy. Some men were running back, urinating into their guns, and rejoining the battle. It was crude but the fastest method of cleaning the caked powder out of a fouled barrel on the battlefield.

Then, at last, the blessed sound of raking volleys, of the platoon fire, as the troops of the Legion and the Guards tore apart the heads of the French columns and shattered them, drove the ranks back, destroyed the leading troops, hammering the volleys into the out-gunned columns. Sharpe could see nothing. The Dutch Battalion had marched into the gap on to the flank of the 7th Battalion of the King's German Legion and stopped. The Germans were fighting on two fronts, ahead of them, and to the side where the South Essex should have been and Sharpe could give them little help. The Voltigeurs had disappeared, back into the column to swell its numbers, and Sharpe and his company, black-faced and exhausted, were left in the centre of the gap watching the rear of the enemy column as it tried to roll up the flank of the Germans.

'Why don't they march on?' Lieutenant Knowles was beside him, bleeding from the scalp, and with the face, suddenly, of a veteran.

'Because the other columns are being defeated. They don't want to be left on their own.' He accepted a drink from Knowles' canteen, his own was shattered, and the water was wonderfully cool in his parched throat. He wished he could see what was happening but the sound, as ever, told its own story. The drumming from the twelve French columns faltered and stopped, the cheers of the British rose into the air, the volleys paused while bayonets scraped from scabbards and clicked on to muskets. The cheers became vengeful screams and from the top of the Medellin the General Officers watched as the first line of the French attack disintegrated and the line of Germans and Guardsmen chased them backwards, pursuing the shattered columns at bayonet point across the stream, past the horse artillery which had simply been abandoned by the enemy without firing a shot.

'Oh God,' Sharpe groaned in disbelief.

'What?' Knowles looked towards the stream, behind the backs of the Dutch Battalion who were marooned in the middle of the field, to where the victorious Germans were in trouble. The first French columns had fled, broken and defeated, but at the stream was a second line of columns, as large as the first, and the shattered Frenchmen found shelter behind the waiting guns of their reserve. The German and British troops, their blood roused, bayonets wet but muskets unloaded, ran straight into the fire of the reserve French troops and it was the turn of the British to be shattered by musket volleys. They turned and fled, in total disorder, and behind them the second line of columns, reinforced with the survivors of the first, struck up the drumbeats and started to march into a plain where Simmerson's gap had been widened to half a mile and where the only British troops were running in disorder.

Sir Henry, safe with the South Essex at the back of the Medellin, saw the second French advance and breathed a sigh of relief. For a moment he had been terrified. He had watched the French columns creep over the plain, the dust rising behind them, the Voltigeurs pushing ahead of them. He had seen the sun flash silver off thousands of bayonets and burn gold off thousands of badges as the trumpets and drums drove the Eagles of twelve columns right up to the stretched British line. And stop. The musketry had gone up and down the British line like a running flame, its thunder drowning all other sounds, and from his vantage point on the hillside Simmerson watched as the columns shook like standing corn struck by a sudden wind as the volleys smashed into them. Then the columns had crumbled, broken, and run and he could hardly believe that such a thin line could throw back such an attack. He watched, dumbfounded, as the British cheered, as the Union flags went forward, as the bayonets reached for the blue enemy and came back red. He had expected defeat, and in its place saw victory, he had expected the French to carve their way through the British line as though it did not exist and instead the British were driving twice their number in bloody chaos before them and with them went his dreams and hopes.

Except the British went too far. The new French columns opened their fire, the Germans and the Guards were split apart and broken, and a new French attack, even bigger than the first, was driving its way forward from the stream. The cheers of the British had gone, the drums were back, and the Union flags were falling back in chaos before the triumphant Eagles. He had been right after all. He turned to point out his perspicacity to Christian Gibbons but instead of his nephew he found himself looking into the eyes of a strange Lieutenant Colonel; or not so strange? He had an idea that he had seen the man before but could not place him. He was about to ask the man what he wanted but the strange, elegant Lieutenant Colonel spoke first.

'You are relieved, Sir Henry. The Battalion is mine.'

'What . . .' The man did not wait to argue. He turned to a smiling Forrest and rapped out a stream of orders. The Battalion was halting, turning, heading back for the battle. Simmerson rode up behind the man and shouted a protest but the Lieutenant Colonel wheeled on him with a drawn sword and bared teeth and Sir Henry decided that this was no place for an argument and reined in his horse instead. The new man then looked at Gibbons.

'Who are you, Lieutenant?'

'Gibbons, sir.'

'Ah yes. I remember. Of the Light Company?'

'Yes, sir.' Gibbons flashed a frantic look at his uncle but Simmerson was staring at the advancing French. The new Colonel hit Gibbons' horse with the flat of his sword.

'Then join the Light Company, Mr Gibbons! Hurry! They need help, even yours!'

The French advanced across a plain that was dotted with bodies, hung about by smoke, but tantalisingly empty of troops. Sir Henry sat his horse and watched the South Essex march towards the battle, saw another Battalion, the 48th, hurrying into the path of the enemy and from the far side of the gaping hole other British Battalions marched desperately to make a thin screen in front of the massing Eagles. Staff officers kicked up dust as they galloped down the slope, the long six-pounders reared back on their trails as they pounded the enemy, British cavalry hovered menacingly to stop the enemy's horsemen trying to exploit the shattered British Battalions. The battle was still not lost. Sir Henry looked round the hilltop and felt terribly alone.

CHAPTER 24

Sharpe's view of the battle was blocked by the Battalion of Dutch troops and by the smoke which drifted like strange fog patches in the burning Spanish heat. With the retreat of the first line of French columns the Dutchmen had become a target for the British guns and, sensibly enough, the white-coated troops had deployed from column into line. They now stood like a dirty white wall at right angles to the stream and faced the fleeing remnants of the King's German Legion who ran across their front. Sharpe could see the Dutchmen ramming and firing their muskets at the broken Battalions but they made no move to advance and finish off the survivors and Sharpe guessed that, with their Colonel shot by Hagman, the Battalion was uncertain what to do and was waiting for the second French attack to catch up with them.

'Sir! Sir!' Ensign Denny tugged Sharpe's jacket and pointed. Through the hanging smoke from the Medellin guns Sharpe saw a British Battalion marching down the hill. 'It's ours, sir! Ours!' Denny was excited, jumping up and down, as the single standard cleaved the smoke and came into full sight on the hillside. They were still a quarter of a mile away and behind them, dimly glimpsed through the smoke, Sharpe could see another Battalion marching for the gap to put itself in front of this second, larger French attack. He could hear the drums again, as persistent as ever, and he sensed that the crisis of the battle was coming and, as if in confirmation, the French guns started again and from their searing hot barrels threw shell after shell into the British Battalions that were racing to form a new line to meet the next attack. Victory was so close for the French, they had only to break through the scratch defence that was scrappily forming and the day was theirs.

Sharpe's men were forgotten. They were a small band in the bottom of a shallow valley on the edge of a great fight. Battalions had been broken on both sides, there were hundreds of dead, the brook was running with blood and now, in the smoke and noise, thousands of Frenchmen marched at the splintered British line. At any moment the attack would strike stunningly home and the British reserves would crumble or hold and Sharpe stood, sword in hand, uncertain what to do. Harper tapped his arm and pointed to a horseman who was coming slowly towards them from the Medellin. 'Lieutenant Gibbons, sir!'

Sharpe turned back to the fight. Presumably Gibbons was coming with orders from Simmerson but Sharpe had no confidence in the Colonel and was not particularly interested in whatever message Gibbons was bringing. The South Essex was still some moments away from opening fire on the white-coated Battalion in front and when they did Sharpe knew the Dutchmen would turn on their attackers and he had no trust in Simmerson's ability to fight the Battalion. It was best to ignore the South Essex.

The Dutchmen were covered in smoke. As the fighting grew to a new intensity the powder smoke thickened into a dirty white cloud that hid everything and the far sounds of cavalry trumpets took on a sinister threat. Sharpe relaxed. There were no decisions to make, the battle was being decided by thousands of men beyond the Dutch musket smoke and the South Essex Light Company had done its duty. He turned to Harper and smiled.

'Can you see what I see?'

Harper grinned, his white teeth brilliant against his powder-blackened face. 'It's very tempting, sir. I was thinking of it myself.'

Two hundred yards away, in the centre of the Dutch line, was an Eagle. It flashed gold in the light, its outstretched wings shadowing the pole on which it was mounted. Harper stared at the backs of the Dutch infantry who fired at an unseen target in the smoke beyond. 'It would make a great story, so it would.'

Sharpe plucked a blade of grass and chewed it, then spat it out. 'I can't order you to come.'

The Sergeant smiled again, a big, happy smile on a craggy face. 'I've nothing better to do. It will take more than the two of us.'

Sharpe nodded and grinned. 'Perhaps Lieutenant Gibbons might lend a hand?'

Harper turned and stared at Gibbons who now hovered fifty yards behind the company. 'What does he want?'

'God knows. Forget him.' Sharpe walked in front of his men and looked at them. They squatted on the grass, their faces filthy, their eyes red and sunken from the powder smoke and the strain of battle. They had done more than well. They looked at him expectantly.

'You've done well. You were good and I'm proud of you.' They grinned, embarrassed at the praise, pleased by it. 'I'm not asking a thing more of you. The Battalion's on its way here and in a minute Mr Denny will take you back and form you up on the left as usual.' They were puzzled, their grins gone. 'Sergeant Harper and I are not coming. We think it's bad that our Battalion only has one colour so we're going to fetch another one. That one.' He pointed at the Eagle and saw the men look past him. One or two grinned, most looked appalled. 'We're going now. Anyone who wants to come is a fool but they'll be welcome. The rest of you, all of you if you like, will go back with Mr Denny and the Sergeant and I will join you when we can.'

Denny protested. 'I want to come, sir!'

Sharpe shook his head. 'Whoever else comes, Mr Denny, you are not. I'd like you to have a seventeenth birthday.'

The men grinned, Denny blushed, and Sharpe turned away from them. He heard Harper unsheath his bayonet and then came the sound of other blades clicking into place. He began to walk towards the enemy, sword held low, and heard the steps behind him. Harper was beside him and they walked on towards the unsuspecting Battalion.

'They've all come, sir. All.'

Sharpe looked at him. 'All?' He turned. 'Mr Denny? Go back to the Battalion! That is an order!'

'But, sir . . .'

'No, Mr Denny. Back!'

He watched as the boy turned and took a few steps. Gibbons was still sitting on his horse and watching them and Sharpe wondered again what the Lieutenant was doing, but it was immaterial; the Eagle was all. He turned back and went on, praying that the enemy would not notice them, praying to whatever was beyond the blue sky skeined in smoke that they would be successful. He had set his heart on an Eagle.

The enemy still faced away from them, still fired into the smoke, and the noise of battle became louder. At last Sharpe could hear the regular platoon volleys and knew that the second French attack had met the new British line and the dreadful monotony of the British volleys once again wrestled with the hypnotic drumming. The six-pound roundshot of the British thundered overhead and cut vicious paths in the unseen French columns but the drumming increased, the shouts of 'Vive L'Empereur' were unabated, and suddenly they were within a hundred yards of the Eagle and Sharpe twisted the sword in his hand and hurried the pace. Surely the enemy would see them!

A drummer boy, rattling his sticks at the rear of the enemy line, turned to be sick and saw the small group coming silently through the smoke. He shouted a warning, but no one heard, he shouted again and Sharpe saw an officer turn. There was movement in the ranks, men were swivelling to face them but they had ramrods half down their barrels and were still loading. Sharpe raised his sword. 'On! On!'

He began to run, oblivious of everything except the Eagle and the frightened faces of the enemy who were desperately hurrying to load their muskets. Around the standard-bearer Sharpe could see Grenadiers wearing the tall bearskins, some of them armed with axes, the protectors of French honour. A musket banged and a ramrod cartwheeled over his head; Harper was beside him, the sword-bayonet in his hand, and the two men screamed their challenge as the drummer boys fled to either side and the two huge Riflemen ploughed into the centre of the enemy line. Muskets exploded with a terrible crash, Sharpe had an impression of men in green uniforms being thrown backwards, and then he could see nothing except a tall Grenadier who was lunging in short and professional jabs with a bayonet. Sharpe twisted to one side, let the blade slide past him, grabbed the muzzle of the musket with his left hand and pulled the Grenadier on to his levelled sword blade. Someone cut at him from the left, a swinging down-stroke with a clubbed musket, and he turned so that it thudded viciously into his pack to throw him forward onto the body of the Grenadier whose hands were clutching the blade embedded in his stomach. A gun deafened him, one of his own rifles, and suddenly he was clear and dragging the blade from the heavy corpse and screaming murder at the men who guarded the Eagle. Harper had cut his way, like Sharpe, through the first rank but his sword-bayonet was too short and the Irishman was being driven back by two men with bayonets and Sharpe crushed them to one side with his sword, slicing a vast splinter from the nearest musket, and Harper leapt into the gap, cutting left and right, as Sharpe struggled alongside.

More muskets, more screams, the white-jackets were clawing at them, surrounding them, reloading to blast the tiny band with musket fire that would crush them unmercifully. The Eagle was retreating, away from them, but there was nowhere for the standard-bearer to go except towards the musket fire of an unseen British Battalion that was somewhere in the smoke that poured from the crash of column on to line. An axeman came at Sharpe; he was a huge man, as big as Harper, and he smiled as he hefted the huge blade and then swung it powerfully down in a blow that would have severed the head of an ox. Sharpe wrenched himself out of the way, felt the wind of the blade, and saw the axe thud into the blood-wet ground. He stabbed the sword down into the man's neck, knew he had killed him, and watched as Harper plucked the axe from the earth and threw away his bayonet. The Irishman was screaming in the language of his ancestors, his wild blood surging, the axe searing in a circle so wildly that even Sharpe had to duck out of the way as Patrick Harper went on; lips wrenched back in the blackened face, his shako gone, his long hair matted with powder, the great silver blade singing in his hands and the old language carving a path through the enemy.

The standard-bearer jumped out of the ranks to carry the precious Eagle down the Battalion to safety but there was a crack, the man fell, and Sharpe heard Hagman's customary 'got him'. Then there was a new sound, more volleys, and the Dutch Battalion shook like a wounded animal as the South Essex arrived on their flank and began to pour in their volleys. Sharpe was faced by a crazed officer who swung at him with a sword, missed, and screamed in panic as Sharpe lunged with the point. A man in white ran out of the ranks to pick up the fallen Eagle but Sharpe was through the line as well and he kicked the man in the ribs, bent, and plucked the staff from the ground. There was a formless scream from the enemy, men lunged at him with bayonets and he felt a blow on the thigh, but Harper was there with the axe and so was Denny with his ridiculously slim sword.

Denny! Sharpe pushed the boy down, swung the sword to protect him but a bayonet was in the Ensign's chest and even as Sharpe smashed the sword down on the man's head he felt Denny shudder and collapse. Sharpe screamed, swung the gilded copper Eagle at the enemy, watched the gold scar the air and force them back, screamed again and jumped the bodies with his bloodied sword reaching for more. The Dutchmen fell back, appalled, the Eagle was coming at them and they retreated in the face of the two huge Riflemen who snarled at them, swung at them, who bled from a dozen cuts yet still came on. They were unkillable! And now there were volleys coming from the right, from the front, and the Dutchmen, who had fought so well for their French masters, had had enough. They ran, as the other French Battalions were running, and in the smoke of the Portina valley the scratch Battalions like the 48th and the men of the Legion and the Guards who had reformed and come forward to fight again marched forward on ground made slippery with blood and thrust with their bayonets and forced the massive French columns backwards. The enemy went, away from the dripping steel, backwards in a scene that was like the most lurid imaginings of hell. Sharpe had never seen so many bodies, so much blood spilt on a field; even at Assaye which he had thought unrivalled in horror there had not been this much blood.

From the Medellin, through the smoke, Sir Henry watched the whole French army go backwards, blasted once more by British muskets, shattered and bleeding, a quarter of their number gone; defeated, broken by the line, by the musket that could be fired five times a minute on a good day, and by men who were not frightened by drums. And in his head Sir Henry composed a letter that would explain how his withdrawing the South Essex from the line was the key move that brought victory. Had not he always said that the British would win?

CHAPTER 25

It was still not over, but very nearly so. As the British troops in the centre of the field sank in exhausted lines by the edge of the discoloured Portina stream they heard flurries of firing and the shrill tones of cavalry trumpets from the ground north of the Medellin. But nothing much happened; the 23rd Light Dragoons made a suicidal charge, the British six-pounders ground twelve French Battalion squares into horror and then the French gave up. Silence fell on the field. The French were done, defeated, and the British had the victory and the field.

And with it the dead and wounded. There were more than thirteen thousand casualties but no one knew that yet. They did not know that the French would not attack again, that King Joseph Bonaparte and the two French Marshals would ride away eastward through the night, so the exhausted and blackened victors stayed in the field. The wounded cried for water, for their mothers, for a bullet, for anything other than the pain and helplessness in the heat. And the horror was not done with them. The sun had burned relentlessly for days, the grass on the Medellin and in the valley was tinder dry, and from somewhere a flame began that rippled and spread and flared through the grass and burned wounded and dead alike. The smell of roasting flesh spread and hung like the lingering palls of smoke. The victors tried to move the wounded but it was too much, too soon, and the flames spread and the rescuers cursed and dropped beside the fouled Portina stream and slaked their thirst in its bloodied water.

Vultures circled the northern hills. The sun dropped red and slanted shadows on the burning field, on the men who struggled to escape the flames, and on the blackened troops who stirred themselves to loot the dead and move the wounded. Sharpe and Harper wandered their own course, two men in the curtains of smoke and burning grass, both bleeding but with their faces creased in private mirth. Sharpe held the Eagle. It was not much to look at; a light blue pole eight feet long and on its top the gilded bird with wings outspread and in its left raised claw a thunderbolt it was about to launch at the enemies of France. There was no flag attached; like so many other French Battalions the previous owners had left their colour at the depot and just carried Napoleon's gift to the war. It was less than two hands' breadth across, and the same in height, but it was an Eagle and it was theirs.

The Light Company had watched them go. Only Sharpe, Harper and Denny had gone through the ranks of the enemy Battalion and when the French attack crumbled the rest of the Light Company had been pushed to one side by the panicked rush of the survivors fleeing from the clockwork volleys. Lieutenant Knowles, a bullet in his shoulder, watched as the men went on firing at the retreating French and then led them back to meet the Battalion. He knew Sharpe and Harper were somewhere in the smoke and they would turn up, with or without the Eagle.

Lieutenant Colonel the Honourable William Lawford sat his horse and stared at the bodies on the field. He had led the South Essex down the slope and watched as they fired their muskets, slowly but calmly, into the white-jacketed enemy. He had seen the fight for the Eagle but the spreading smoke of the Battalion's volleys had blotted out the scene and the survivors of the Light Company told him little more. A Lieutenant brought in forty-three bleeding and stained men, grinning like monkeys, who talked of the Eagle but where was it? He wanted to see Sharpe, wanted to see his friend's face when he discovered that his companion of the Seringapatam jail was now his Colonel, but the field was shrouded in flames and smoke so he gave up looking and started the Battalion on the grisly task of stripping the dead and piling the naked bodies like cordwood for the fire. There were too many to bury.

Sir Henry Simmerson was done. Wellesley had sworn, briefly and fluently, and sent Lawford to take over the Battalion. Lawford hoped to keep it, it was time he commanded a Battalion, and there was much to be done with it. Major Forrest rode up to him and saluted.

'Major?'

'Except for the Light Company, sir, we've lost very few.'

'How many?' Lawford watched as Forrest fetched a piece of paper from his pouch.

'A dozen dead, sir, perhaps twice as many wounded.'

Lawford nodded. 'We've got off lightly, Major. And the Light Company?'

'Lieutenant Knowles brought in forty-three, sir, and most of them are wounded. Sergeant Read stayed with the baggage with two others, that's forty-six. There were five men too sick to fight who are in the town.' Forrest paused. 'That's fifty-one, sir, out of a complement of eighty-nine.'

Lawford said nothing. He leaned forward on his saddle and peered into the shifting smoke. Forrest cleared his throat nervously. 'You don't think, sir . . .' He tailed the question away.

'No, Major, I don't.' Lawford sat upright and turned his charm on to the Major. 'I've known Richard Sharpe since I was a Lieutenant and he was a Sergeant. He should have died a dozen times, Major, at least a dozen, but he crawls through somehow.' Lawford grinned. 'Don't worry about Sharpe, Major. It's much better to let him worry about you. Who else is missing?'

'There's Sergeant Harper, sir . . .'

'Ah!' Lawford interrupted. 'The legendary Irishman.'

'And Lieutenant Gibbons, sir.'

'Lieutenant Gibbons?' Lawford remembered the meeting in Wellesley's headquarters at Plasencia and the petulant expression on the blond Lieutenant's face. 'I wonder how he'll get on without his uncle?' The Lieutenant Colonel smiled briefly; Gibbons was his least concern. There was still so much to do, so many men to be rescued before the townspeople spread into the carnage to loot the bodies. 'Thank you, Major. We'll just have to wait for Captain Sharpe. In the meantime would you arrange a party to get water for the men? And let's hope these French dead have got food in their packs, otherwise we're in for a lean night.'

The French did carry food, and gold, and Sharpe, as he always did, split his finds with Harper. The Sergeant was carrying the Eagle and he peered at the bird thoughtfully.

'Is it worth money, sir?'

'I don't know.' Out of habit Sharpe was reloading his

rifle and he grunted as he forced the ramrod into the fouled barrel.

'But they'll reward us, sir, surely?'

Sharpe grinned at the Sergeant. 'I'd think so. The Patriotic fund ought to be good for a hundred guineas, who knows?' He slid the ramrod back into place. 'Perhaps they'll just say "thank you".' He bowed ironically to the Irishman. 'Thank you, Sergeant Harper.'

Harper bowed clumsily back. 'It was a pleasure, Captain Sharpe.' He paused. 'The bastards had better pay something. I can't wait to see Simmerson's face when you give him this.'

Sharpe laughed, he was looking forward to that moment. He took the Eagle from Harper. 'Come on. We'd better find them.'

Harper touched Sharpe's shoulder and froze, staring into the smoke above the stream. Sharpe could see nothing. 'What is it?'

'Don't you see it, sir?' Harper's voice was hushed, excited. 'There! Damn! It's gone.'

'What, for God's sake, what?'

Harper turned to him. 'Would you wait, sir? Two minutes?'

Sharpe grinned. 'A bird?'

'Aye. The magpie with the blue tail. It went over the stream and it can't be far.' Harper's face was lit up, the battle suddenly forgotten, the capture of the Eagle a small thing against the spotting of the rare bird he had yearned so long to see.

Sharpe laughed. 'Go on. I'll wait here.'

The Sergeant went silently towards the stream, leaving Sharpe in the drifting smoke among the bodies. Once a horse trotted past, intent on its own business, its flank a sheet of blood, and far off, behind the flames, Sharpe could hear bugles calling the living into ranks. He stared at the Eagle, at the thunderbolt gripped in the claw, the wreath round the bird's neck, and felt a fresh surge of elation at its capture. They could not send him to the West Indies now! Simmerson could do his worst, but the man who brought back the first captured French Eagle was safe from Sir Henry. He smiled, held the bird up so its wings caught the light, and heard the hoof beats behind him.

His rifle was on the ground and he had to leave it as he rolled desperately to avoid Gibbons' charge. The Lieutenant, curved sabre drawn, was wild-eyed and leaning from the saddle; the blade hissed over Sharpe's head, he fell, kept rolling, and knelt up to see Gibbons reining in the horse, turning it with one hand, and urging it forward. The Lieutenant was giving Sharpe no time, even to draw his sword, instead he pointed the sabre like a lance and spurred forward so that the blade would spear into Sharpe's stomach. Sharpe dropped and the horse went thundering beside him, turned on its back legs, and Gibbons was high over him with the sabre stabbing downwards. Neither man spoke. The horse whinnied, reared and lashed with its feet, and Sharpe twisted away as the sabre jabbed down.

Sharpe swung with the Eagle aiming for the horse's head but Gibbons was too good a horseman and he smiled as he easily avoided the wild blow. The Lieutenant hefted the sabre in his hand. 'Give me the Eagle, Sharpe.'

Sharpe looked round. The loaded rifle was five yards away and he ran towards it, knowing it was too far, hearing the hooves behind him, and then the sabre cut into his pack and threw him flat on the ground. He fell on the Eagle, twisted to his right, and the horse was pirouetting above him, the hooves like hammers above his face, and the sabre blade was a curve of light behind the glinting horse-shoes. He rolled again, felt a numbing blow as one of the hooves struck his shoulder, but he kept rolling away from Gibbons' sabre. It was hopeless. The grass smelt in his nostrils, the air was full of the flying hooves, the horse staying above him, treading beside him, he waited for the blade to spike into him, and pin him to the dry ground. He was angry with himself, for being caught, for forgetting about Gibbons and he wondered how long the Lieutenant had stalked him through the smoke.

He could hardly move his right arm, the whole of it seemed paralysed by the blow from the hoof, but he lunged up with the Eagle as if it was a quarterstaff, trying to force the hooves away from his body. Damn that magpie! Couldn't Harper hear the fight? Then the sabre was over his stomach and Gibbons' smiling face was above him, and the Lieutenant paused. 'She felt good, Sharpe. And I'll take that Eagle as well.'

Gibbons seemed to laugh at him, the Lieutenant's mouth stretching and stretching, and still he did not stab downwards. His eyes widened and Sharpe began to move, away from the sabre, climbing to his feet and he saw the blood coming from Gibbons' throat and falling, slowly and thickly, on the sabre. Sharpe was still moving, the Eagle swinging, and the wing of the French trophy smashed into Gibbons' mouth, breaking the teeth, forcing back the head, but the Lieutenant was dead. The Eagle had forced him back, but the body toppled towards Sharpe and in its back, through the ribs, was a bayonet on a French musket. Sergeant Harper stood on the far side of the horse and grinned at Sharpe.

Gibbons' body slumped beside the horse and Sharpe stared at it, at the bayonet and strange French musket that had been driven clean into the lungs and was stuck there, swaying above the body. He looked at Harper.

'Thank you.'

'My pleasure.' The Sergeant was grinning broadly as if he had been pleased to see Sharpe scrambling for his life. 'It was worth being in this army just to do that.'

Sharpe leaned on the Eagle's staff, catching his breath, appalled at the closeness of death. He shook his head at Harper. 'The bastard nearly got me!' He sounded astonished as if it had been unthinkable for Gibbons to prove the better fighter.

'He would have had to finish me off first, sir.' It was said lightly enough, but Sharpe knew the Sergeant had spoken the truth and he smiled in acknowledgement and then went to pick up his rifle. He turned again. 'Patrick?'

'Sir?'

'Thank you.'

Harper brushed it off. 'Just make sure they give us more than a hundred guineas. It's not every day we capture a bloody Eagle.'

Gibbons was not carrying much; a handful of guineas, a watch broken by his fall, and the expensive sabre that they would be forced to leave behind. Sharpe joined Harper and, kneeling by the crumpled body, he thrust his hand into Gibbons' collar and found what he had half expected; a gold chain. Most soldiers carried something valuable round their necks and Sharpe knew that, should he die, some enemy would find the bag of coins round his own neck. Harper glanced up. 'I missed that.'

It was a locket and inside, a girl's picture. She was

314

blonde, like Gibbons, but her lips were full where his were thin. Her eyes, despite the smallness of the miniature, seemed to look out of the gold case with amusement and life. Harper leaned over. 'What does it say, sir?'

Sharpe read the words inscribed inside the open lid. 'God keep you. Love, Jane.'

Harper whistled very softly. 'She's a pretty one, sir.'

Sharpe took the locket and pushed it into his cartridge pouch and then glanced once more at the dead man with the blood glistening on his thin face. Did she know what kind of man her brother was?

'Come on, Sergeant.'

They walked over the grass, stamping through the flames, until they saw the solitary yellow colour of the South Essex. Lieutenant Knowles saw them first, shouted, and suddenly the Light Company were round them, slapping their backs, speaking words they could not hear and pushing them towards the group of horsemen by the colour. Sharpe looked past a beaming Forrest to see Lawford. 'Sir?'

Lawford laughed at Sharpe's surprise. 'I understand you have the honour to command my Light Company?'

'Yours?'

Lawford raised his eyebrows. He was exquisite with silver lace. 'Do you disapprove, Captain Sharpe?'

Sharpe grinned and shook his head. 'Sir Henry?'

Lawford shrugged his elegant shoulders. 'Shall we just say that Sir Henry suddenly felt a burning desire to return to the good Burghers of Paglesham.'

Sharpe wanted to laugh. He had kept the promise to Lennox but he knew the real reason he had hacked his way to the French Eagle was to save his own career, and had it all been unnecessary? Denny's death, the killing

315

of so many others, just so he would not go to the West Indies? The trophy was low at his side, hidden in the press of men, but he dragged it clear so that the gilded statuette suddenly flashed in the light. He handed it up to Lawford. 'The Battalion's missing colour, sir. It was the best Sergeant Harper and I could do.'

Lawford stared at the two men, at the tiredness beneath the powder stains, at the lines on their faces grooved with blood from scalp wounds, and at the black patches where bayonets had sprung blood into their green jackets. He took the Eagle, disbelieving, knowing it was the one thing that would restore the Battalion's pride, and hoisted it high into the air. The South Essex, so long scorned by the army, saw it and cheered, slapped each other's backs, hoisted their muskets triumphantly into the air, and cheered until other Battalions stopped to see what the noise was about.

Above them, on the Medellin, General Hill heard the excitement and trained a telescope on to the Battalion that had so nearly lost the battle. He caught the Eagle in the lens and his mouth dropped open. 'I'll be damned! Bless my soul! The strangest thing. The South Essex have captured an Eagle!'

There was a dry laugh beside him and Hill turned to see Sir Arthur Wellesley. 'Sir?'

'I'll be damned too, Hill. That's only the third time I've ever heard you swear.' He took the glass from Hill and looked down the slope. 'God damn it! You're right! Let's go and see this strange bird.'

EPILOGUE

The wine was dark red in the crystal glasses, the deep polished table shone from a score of candles in their silver holders, the paintings whose ancient varnish reflected the circle of light showed grave and eminent ancestors of the Spanish family in whose Talavera mansion Sir Arthur Wellesley was host to a dinner party. Even the food was fairly equal to the occasion. In the week since the battle the supply situation had worsened, the Spanish promises unfulfilled, and the troops were on meagre half-rations. Wellesley, as befitted a General, had done better than most and Sharpe had sipped a slightly watered down chicken soup, enjoyed jugged hare, eaten amply of Wellesley's favourite mutton, and listened to his fellow guests grumble about the diet as they drank unending bottles of wine. 'Daddy' Hill was there, rubicund and happy, continually smiling at Sharpe, shaking his head and saying 'Bless me, Sharpe, an Eagle.' Robert Crauford sat opposite Sharpe; Black Bob, whom Sharpe had not seen since the retreat to Corunna. Crauford had missed the Battle of Talavera by one day even though he had marched his crack Light Division forty-two miles in twenty-six hours to catch up with Wellesley. Among the troops he had brought from England were the First Battalion of the 95th Rifles and Sharpe had already been generously entertained by their mess in celebration of his feat. They had done more than that. They had presented him with a new uniform and he sat at Wellesley's table resplendent in smart green cloth, black leather, and silver trappings. He had kept his old uniform. Tomorrow, when the army marched again, he would prefer to wear the bloodstained cavalry overalls and the comfortable French boots rather than this immaculate uniform and fragile shoes.

Black Bob Crauford was in good form. He was the sternest disciplinarian in the army, a tyrant of excessive rages, loved and hated by his troops. Few Generals asked more of their men, or received it, and if his demands were backed up by savage punishments then at least the men knew Crauford's justice was even-handed and impartial. Sharpe remembered seeing Crauford catch a company officer being carried piggy-back across an ice cold stream in the northern mountains.

'Drop him, sir! Drop him!' The General shouted from the dry safety of his horse to the astonished private and, to the delight of the suffering troops, the officer was dumped unceremoniously into the waist high water. Now Crauford fixed Sharpe with a cynical eye and thumped the table, rattling the silverware. 'You were lucky, Sharpe, lucky!'

'Yes, sir.'

'Don't you "yes sir" me.' Sharpe saw Wellesley watching him with an amused eye. Crauford pushed a bottle of red wine towards Sharpe. 'You lost damn near half your company! If you hadn't come back with the Eagle you would have deserved to have been broken right back to private again. Aren't I right?'

Sharpe inclined his head. 'You are, sir.'

Crauford leaned back, satisfied, and raised his glass to the Rifleman. 'But it was damn well done, all the same.'

There was laughter round the table. Lawford, a confection of silver and lace and confirmed, at least temporarily, as Commanding Officer of the South Essex, leaned back and put two more opened bottles on the table. 'How's the excellent Sergeant Harper?'

Sharpe smiled. 'Recovering, sir.'

'Was he wounded badly?' Hill leaned forward into the candlelight, his round, farmer's face suffused with concern. Sharpe shook his head. 'No, sir. The Sergeants' mess of the First Battalion were kind enough to celebrate with him. I believe he proposed the theory that one man from Donegal could drink as much as any three Englishmen.'

Hogan slapped the table. The Irish Engineer was cheerfully drunk and he raised his glass to Wellesley. 'We Irishmen are never beaten. Isn't that so, sir?'

Wellesley raised his eyebrows. He had drunk less than Sharpe. 'I never count myself an Irishman, Captain Hogan, though perhaps I share that characteristic with them.'

'Damn that, sir,' Crauford growled. 'I've heard you say that just because a man is born in a stable it doesn't make him into a horse!'

There was more laughter. Sharpe leaned back and listened to the talk round the table and let the meal rest heavy in his stomach. The servants were bringing in brandy and cigars which meant that the evening would soon be over but he had enjoyed it. He was never comfortable at formal dinners; he had not been born to them, had been to few of them, but these men had made him feel at home and pretended not to notice when he waited for them to pick up their cutlery so that he would know which was the correct pair to use for each course. He had told once more the story of how he and Patrick Harper had hacked their way through the enemy line, of the death of Denny, and how they had been swept along with the fugitives before hacking their way clear with sword and axe.

He sipped his wine, wriggled his toes in the new shoes, and reflected again on his fortune. He remembered his despondency before the battle, of feeling that the promises could not be kept, yet it had all happened. Perhaps he really was lucky, as his men said, but he wished he knew how to preserve that luck. He remembered Gibbons' falling body, the bayonet deep in his back, and the sight of Harper back from his bird-watching just in time to stop the sabre stabbing down into Sharpe. The next day all traces of the crime had been burned away. The dead, Gibbons among them, had been stacked in naked piles and the living had thrust wooden faggots deep into the corpses and set fire to them. There had been far too many for burial and for two days the fires were fed with more wood and the stench hung over the town until the ashes were scattered across the Portina valley and the only signs of the battle were the discarded equipment no one could be bothered to retrieve and the scorched grass where the flames had roasted the wounded.

'Sharpe?'

He started. Someone had spoken his name and he had missed what was said. 'Sir? I'm sorry.'

Wellesley was smiling at him. 'Captain Hogan was saying that you've been improving Anglo-Portuguese relations?'

Sharpe glanced at Hogan who raised his eyebrows impishly. All week the Irishman had been determinedly cheerful about Josefina, and Sharpe, with three Generals watching him, had no option but to smile and give a modest shrug.

'Fortune favours the brave, eh, Sharpe?' Hill grinned.

'Yes, sir.'

He leaned back and let the conversation flow on. He missed her. It was only just over two weeks since the night he had followed her from the inn courtyard into the darkness by the stream and since then he had spent only five nights with her. And now there would be no more. He had known as soon as he had reached Talavera, on the morning after the battle, and she had kissed him and smiled at him while in the background Agostino packed the leather saddlebags and folded up the dresses he had not had time to see her wear. She had walked with him through the town, clinging on to his elbow, looking up into his face as though she were a child. 'It would never have lasted, Richard.'

'I know.' He believed otherwise.

'Do you?'

She wanted him to say goodbye gracefully and it was the least he could do. He told her about Gibbons; about the final look before the bayonet took its revenge. She held his arm tight. 'I'm sorry, Richard.'

'For Gibbons?'

'No. That you had to do it. It was my fault, I was a fool.'

'No.' It was strange, he thought, how when lovers say goodbye they take all the blame. 'It wasn't your fault. I promised to protect you. I didn't.'

They walked into a small, sunlit square and stared at a convent which formed one side of the plaza. Fifteen hundred British wounded were in the building and the army surgeons were working on the first floor. Screams came clearly from the windows and, with them, a grisly flow of severed limbs that piled up beside a tree; an ever growing heap of arms and legs that was guarded by two bored privates whose job was to chase away the

hungry dogs from the mangled flesh. Sharpe shivered at
the sight and prayed the soldiers' prayer; that he would
be delivered from the surgeons with their serrated blades
and blood-stiff aprons.

Josefina had plucked his elbow and they turned away
from the convent. 'I have a present for you.'

He looked down at her. 'I have nothing for you.'

She seemed embarrassed. 'You owe Mr Hogan twenty
guineas?'

'You're not giving me money!' He let his anger
show.

Josefina shook her head. 'I've already paid him. Don't
be angry!' He had tried to pull away but she clung on.
'There's nothing you can do about it, Richard. I paid him.
You kept pretending you had enough money but I knew
you were borrowing.' She gave him a tiny paper packet
and did not look at him because she knew he was upset.

Inside the paper was a ring, made of silver, and on
the boss was engraved an eagle. Not a French eagle,
holding a thunderbolt, but an eagle all the same. She
looked up at him, pleased at his expression. 'I bought
it in Oropesa. For you.'

Sharpe had not known what to say. He had stammered
his thanks and now, sitting with the Generals, he let his
fingers feel the silver ring. They had walked back to the
house and, waiting outside, there had been a cavalry
officer with two spare horses. 'Is that him?'

'Yes.'

'And he's rich?'

She had smiled. 'Very. He's a good man, Richard.
You'd like him.'

Sharpe had laughed. 'I doubt it.' He wanted to tell
her how much he would not like Claud Hardy, with
his stupid sounding name and his rich uniform and his

thoroughbred horses. The Dragoon had watched them as she looked up at Sharpe.

'I can't stay with the army, Richard.'

'So you're going back to Lisbon?'

She nodded. 'We're not going to Madrid, are we?' He shook his head. 'Well, it has to be Lisbon.' She smiled at him. 'He has a house in Belem; a big one. I'm sorry.'

'Don't be.'

'I can't follow an army, Richard.' She was pleading for understanding.

'I know. But armies follow you, yes?' It was a clumsy attempt at gallantry and it had pleased her but now it was time to part and he wanted her to stay. He did not know what to say. 'Josefina? I'm sorry.'

She touched his arm and there was the gleam of tears in her eyes. She blinked them away and forced herself to sound happy. 'One day, Richard, you will fall in love with the right girl? You promise?'

He had not watched her walk to the Dragoon but instead turned away to rejoin the company in the stench of the dead on the battlefield.

'Captains shouldn't marry.' Crauford thumped the table and Sharpe jumped. 'Isn't that true?'

Sharpe did not reply. He suspected Crauford was right and he determined, again, to thrust away the memory of Josefina. She was on her way to Lisbon, to the big house, to live with a man who was to join the Lisbon garrison and live a life of dancing and diplomacy. Damn all of it. He drank his wine, reached for the bottle, and forced himself to listen to the conversation which was now as gloomy as his thoughts. They were talking of the fifteen hundred wounded men in the convent who would have to be abandoned to the care of the Spanish. Hill was peering worriedly at Wellesley. 'Will Cuesta look after them?'

'I wish I could say "yes".' Wellesley sipped his wine. 'The Spanish have failed us in every promise. It was not easy to leave our wounded to their care but we have no choice, gentlemen, no choice.'

Hill shook his head. 'The retreat will not be received well in England.'

'Damn England!' Wellesley spoke with asperity, his eyes suddenly alive with anger. 'I know what England will say; that once again we have been driven from Spain, and so we have, gentlemen, so we have!' He leaned back in his chair and Sharpe could see the tiredness on his face. The other officers were still, listening intently, and like Sharpe they could see in Wellesley's face the difficulty of the decision he had taken. 'But this time—' the General ran his finger round the wine glass so that it rang— 'this time we have been driven out, not by the French, but by our allies.' He let the sarcasm come through on the word. 'A starving army, gentlemen, is worse than no army. If our allies cannot feed us then we must go where we can feed ourselves and we will come back, I promise you that, but we will come back on our terms and not on the Spanish terms.' There were murmurs of agreement round the table. Wellesley sipped his wine. 'The Spanish have failed us everywhere. They promised us food and delivered none. They promised to shield us from Soult's northern army and now I find that they did not. Soult, gentlemen, is behind us and unless we move now we will find ourselves a surrounded and starving army simply because we believed General Cuesta and his promises. Now he has promised to look after our wounded.' Wellesley shook his head. 'I know what will happen. He will insist on advancing to meet the French, he will be thrashed, and the town will be abandoned to the enemy.' He shrugged. 'I am convinced, gentlemen, that they will treat our wounded better than our allies.'

There was silence round the table. The candles flickered and shimmered their reflections on the polished wood. From somewhere, far away, there came the sound of music but it faded with the breeze beyond the heavy curtains. And what happens to Josefina now? Sharpe filled his glass with wine and passed the bottle to Hill. If Wellesley was right, and he was, then in a matter of days the French would be masters of Talavera and the British army would be well on its way back to Portugal and probably to Lisbon. Sharpe knew that he wanted her still and wondered what would happen if the swirling currents of war brought them together again.

A knock on the door interrupted his thoughts and he watched as a Staff Captain entered and gave Wellesley a sealed paper. The officers talked, inventing topics of conversation so that Wellesley could open the paper and talk to the Captain in some privacy. Hill was telling Sharpe about the Drury Lane Theatre. Did he know it had been burned down in February? Sharpe nodded and smiled, made the right noises, but he looked round the table, at the three Generals, at the aristocrats, and he thought of the foundling home and prisons he had known as a child. He remembered the foetid barracks where two men shared a cot, the vicious beatings, the unprincipled struggle just to stay alive. And now this? The candles danced in the draught, the red wine was rich and deep, and he wondered where the road they must take in tomorrow's cold dawn would lead. If Bonaparte was to be defeated then tomorrow's march could last for years before it ended at the gates of Paris.

The Captain left and Wellesley tapped the table. The

conversation tailed away and they looked at their hook-nosed General who lifted the paper into the air. 'The Austrians have made peace with Bonaparte.' He waited for the exclamations to die down. 'Effectively, gentlemen, we are on our own. We can expect more French troops, maybe even Napoleon himself, and even more enemies at home.' Sharpe thought of Simmerson, already on the way home, planning to conspire in Parliament and in the smoking rooms of London against Wellesley and the British army in the Peninsula. 'But, gentlemen, we have beaten three Marshals this year so let the rest come on!'

The officers pounded the table and raised their glasses. In the town a clock struck eight o'clock and, abruptly, Sir Arthur Wellesley got to his feet and held up his wine-glass. 'I see the cigars are here and the evening is getting on. We leave early so, gentlemen, I give you the King.'

Sharpe scraped his chair back, took the glass, and joined in the murmuring. 'The King, God bless him.'

He was sitting down again, looking forward to the brandy and one of the General's cigars, when he noticed that Wellesley was still standing. He straightened up, cursing his lack of social manners and hoping that the others would not see his blushing. Wellesley waited for him. 'I remember one other battle, gentlemen, which almost matched our recent victory in carnage. After Assaye I had to thank a young Sergeant, today we salute the same man, a Captain.' He raised his glass to Sharpe who was convulsed with embarrassment. He watched the officers smile at him, raise their glasses to him, and he looked down at the silver eagle. He wished Josefina could see him at this moment, that she could hear Wellesley's toast. He only half heard it himself.

'Gentlemen. I give you Sharpe's Eagle.'

HISTORICAL
NOTE

Sir Arthur Wellesley (who was soon to become, thanks to the events of July 27th and 28th, 1809, Viscount Wellington of Talavera) lost 5365 dead and wounded in the battle. About 15 per cent of those casualties were killed outright. French casualties numbered 7268 and there were also about 600 Spanish to add to the 'butcher's bill'. The French also lost seventeen guns but, alas, no Eagle. The first Eagle to be captured by the British in the Peninsular War was won by Ensign Keogh and Sergeant Masterman of the 87th, an Irish Regiment, at the Battle of Barossa on March 5th, 1811. Keogh died of his wounds but Masterman survived and was rewarded with a commission thus joining the small number of officers in the Peninsular Army, perhaps 5 per cent of the total, who had risen from the ranks. I hope that the ghosts of Keogh and Masterman, as well as the modern successors of the 87th, The Royal Irish Rangers, will forgive me for pre-empting their achievement.

There is no such place as Valdelacasa, nor was there ever a South Essex Regiment, but beyond those inventions the campaign of Talavera happened much as described in the novel. In the account of the battle only the adventures of the South Essex and the capture of the Eagle are fictitious; there was a Dutch Battalion fighting with the French and I took the liberty of moving them from their position opposite the Spanish fortifications and offered them as a sacrifice to Sharpe and Harper instead. The account of the Spanish army, sadly, is not fabricated; they did run away on the eve of the battle, frightened by their own volley, and within days General Cuesta was to lead them on to total defeat. Talavera was abandoned to the French who, as Wellesley predicts in the novel, treated the British wounded with kindness and consideration. The ineffectiveness of the Spanish army was more than compensated for by the bravery of the Guerilleros who caused Napoleon to liken Spain to a 'running sore' on his armies.

Much of the detail in the book is taken from contemporary letters and diaries. Scenes like the growing pile of arms and legs outside the convent in Talavera defy imagination and can only come from the accounts of eyewitnesses. In addition to those accounts I drew heavily on the scholarship of Michael Glover's *The Peninsular War*, Jac Weller's *Wellington in the Peninsula*, and Lady Elizabeth Longford's *Wellington: The Years of the Sword*. To those three authors I acknowledge a special debt.

Richard Sharpe and Patrick Harper are, sadly, inventions. I hope that today's Royal Green Jackets, who once marched as the 95th Rifles, will not be ashamed of them or of their picaresque adventures on the long road that will, eventually, take them to Waterloo.

Sharpe's Battle
Bernard Cornwell

In the spring of 1811, while quartered in the crumbling Portuguese fort of San Isidro, Richard Sharpe and his men are attacked by an elite French unit commanded by the formidable Brigadier Guy Loup, and suffer heavy losses. Sharpe has already clashed once with Loup, and the Frenchman has sworn to have his revenge.

After the attack, Sharpe faces the ruin of his career and reputation, as the army's high command tries to blame him for the disaster. With thousands of French troops massing at a tiny village nearby, Sharpe's only hope is to redeem himself on the battlefield. To save his honour, Sharpe must lead his men to glory in the narrow streets of Fuentes de Oñoro.

'What makes these books such a successful formula is the blend of action, well-researched historical setting, colourful characterization and a juicy sub-plot'   *The Times*

ISBN 0 00 647324 5

Sharpe's Rifles

Bernard Cornwell

In the bitter winter of 1809 the French are winning the war in Spain and Britain's forces are retreating towards Corunna, with Napoleon's victorious armies in pursuit. Lieutenant Richard Sharpe and a detachment of Riflemen are cut off from the British army and surrounded by enemy troops. Their only hope of escape is to accept the help of an unlikely ally, a Spanish cavalry officer, Major Blas Vivar.

Unknown to Sharpe, the Spaniard harbours a desperate and quixotic ambition which will lead to a suicidal assault on the holy city of Santiago de Compostela and a savage fight against overwhelming French numbers. Sharpe's determination must be tested to its limit if victory is to be snatched from disaster.

'Consistently exciting . . . these are wonderful novels'

STEPHEN KING

ISBN 0 00 617697 6

Sharpe's Enemy

Bernard Cornwell

Newly promoted, Major Richard Sharpe leads his small force into the biting cold of the winter mountains. His task is to rescue a group of well-born women held hostage by a rabble of deserters. And one of the renegades is Sergeant Hakeswill, Sharpe's most implacable enemy.

But the rescue is the least of Sharpe's problems. He must face a far greater threat. With only the support of his own company and the new Rocket Troop – the last word in military incompetence – to back his gamble, Sharpe cannot afford even to recognize the prospect of defeat. For to surrender – or to fail – would mean the end of the war for the Allied armies . . .

'Stirring . . . imaginative . . . inventive' *Evening Standard*

ISBN 0 00 617013 7

Sharpe's Honour

Bernard Cornwell

Major Richard Sharpe awaits the opening shots of the army's campaign with grim expectancy. For victory depends on the increasingly fragile alliance between Britain and Spain – an alliance that must be maintained at any cost.

Pierre Ducos, the wily French Intelligence officer, sees a chance both to destroy the alliance and to achieve a personal revenge on Richard Sharpe. And when the lovely spy, La Marquesa, takes a hand in the game, Sharpe finds himself enmeshed in a web of political intrigue for which his military expertise has left him fatally unprepared. Soon, he is a fugitive – a man hunted by enemy and ally alike . . .

'The best thing to happen to military heroes since Hornblower'   *Daily Express*

ISBN 0 00 617198 2

The Bloody Ground
Bernard Cornwell

'The best so far in Cornwell's American Civil War series . . . The cacophony of the cornfield slaughter is stunningly conveyed'   *Daily Mail*

It is late summer 1862 and the Confederacy is at last invading the United States of America. Nathaniel Starbuck, the northern preacher's son who fights for the rebel South, is given command of a punishment battalion, a despised unit of shirkers and cowards. His enemies expect the appointment to be his downfall. To prove them wrong, Starbuck must lead the ramshackle unit against the northern garrison at Harper's Ferry and then across the frontier to the bank of the Antietam Creek. There he will fight in what will prove to be the bloodiest battle of the Civil War.

A superbly exciting novel which vividly captures the horror of the battlefield, *The Bloody Ground* is the fourth volume in the Starbuck Chronicles.

'Cornwell is as masterly as ever at conjuring up the grisly nature of nineteenth-century campaigning and the terrifying adrenaline surge experienced on a battlefield reeking of black powder and blood'   *The Times*

'A very fine novel indeed; Bernard Cornwell at his distinctive best . . . builds to a gripping climax . . . stirring stuff'   *Sunday Telegraph*

'Cornwell is a natural storyteller with a vivid sense of history'   *Mail on Sunday*

ISBN 0 00 649666 0

Sharpe's Eagle
Bernard Cornwell

The newly raised South Essex Regiment has just arrived in Portugal and Sharpe is ordered to accompany the inexperienced unit. He quickly comes into conflict with its arrogant colonel, Sir Henry Simmerson, whose incompetence leads to the loss of many of his men in the regiment's disastrous first operation.

When Wellesley promotes Sharpe to captain, Simmerson's resentment deepens, and Sharpe discovers just how dangerous an enemy he has made. As he leads his men into battle at Talavera, Sharpe knows that only through courage and outstanding bravery can he save his career and the honour of the regiment.

'Richard Sharpe . . . will become as popular as Hornblower'
Financial Times

ISBN 0 00 617313 6

Sharpe's Sword
Bernard Cornwell

Richard Sharpe is once again at war. But this time his enemy is a single man – the ruthless, sadistic Colonel Leroux. Sharpe's mission is to safeguard El Mirador, the spy whose network of agents is vital to the British victory.

So Sharpe must enter a new world of political and military intrigue. And in the unfamiliar surroundings of aristocratic Spanish society, his only guide is the beautiful Marquesa – a woman with her own secrets to conceal . . .

'The best thing to happen to military heroes since Hornblower'   *Daily Express*

ISBN 0 00 616834 5

Sharpe's Trafalgar
Bernard Cornwell

It is 1805 and Ensign Richard Sharpe, having secured a reputation as a fighting soldier in India, is on his way home to join the newly formed Green Jackets. The voyage should be a period of rest but his ship is riven with treachery and threatened by a formidable French warship, the *Revenant*, which is terrorizing British shipping in the Indian Ocean. An old opponent of Sharpe's is aboard his ship, and the voyage is further disturbed by the Lady Grace Hale, apparently as unreachable as she is beautiful.

Sharpe also has friends, notably a captain of the Royal Navy who is hunting the *Revenant* and who rescues Sharpe when all seems lost. The hunt turns into a stern chase as the French warship races home, carrying a treaty that could ignite India into a new war against the British. Yet when the *Revenant* encounters the combined French and Spanish fleets off Cadiz it seems that Sharpe's enemies have found safety, even as his enemies on board appear to have him trapped.

Yet over the horizon is another fleet, led by Nelson, and Sharpe's revenge will come in a savage climax when the two armadas meet on a calm October day off Cape Trafalgar.

Sharpe's Trafalgar introduces Richard Sharpe to the horrors of a battle at sea, and finds him at his most ruthless as he struggles not just for revenge, but for a woman he loves.

Sharpe's Company

Bernard Cornwell

It was a hard winter. For Richard Sharpe it was the worst he could remember. He had lost his command to a wealthy man – a man with money to buy the promotion Sharpe coveted. And from England came his oldest enemy – the ruthless, indestructible Hakeswill – utterly intent on ruining Sharpe.

But Sharpe is determined to change his luck. And the surest way is to lead the bloody attack on the impregnable fortress town of Badajoz, a road to almost certain death – or unimagined glory . . .

'Brilliant . . . Sharpe is a great creation'   *Daily Mirror*

ISBN 0 00 616573 7

Battle Flag
Bernard Cornwell

'Cornwell unerringly hits his form . . . battle-scenes of exceptional grandeur pictured in brisk, pungent prose'
DAVID HUGHES, *Mail on Sunday*

Captain Nathaniel Starbuck has survived the early battles of the Civil War, but his northern breeding still makes him an object of suspicion to many of his southern comrades, and his enmity with his regiment's founder, General Washington Faulconer, makes his position even harder.

When Faulconer attempts to discipline his opponents, he sets in train events that will culminate in a savage battle – and Starbuck, his friends and his enemies will find themselves once more staring death in the face.

A superb story of courage, friendship and betrayal, *Battle Flag* is the third volume in Bernard Cornwell's Starbuck Chronicles.

'Admirably catches the chaotic and bloody nature of the action . . . it's a state-of-the-art swashbuckler'
Sunday Times

'A humdinger of a blood-and-guts battle'   *Daily Mail*

'Cornwell's descriptions . . . have a narrative verve and excitement which sweep the reader along behind Jackson and Lee'   T J BINYON, *Standard*

ISBN 0 00 647902 2

Sharpe's Gold
Bernard Cornwell

It is August 1810 and, after long months spent patrolling the bleak southern border between Spain and Portugal, Sharpe and the South Essex Regiment have finally been summoned north by Wellington. There Sharpe embarks on a desperate mission. He must recover the treasure, vital to the success of the war, now hidden behind enemy lines. The gold is in the possession of a powerful guerrilla leader, feared by ally and enemy alike. And he has no love for Sharpe, the man who has stolen his woman.

But Sharpe's fiercest battles lie with the British officers, ignorant of his deadly secret and mistrustful of his ruthless methods.

'Exciting, exuberant . . . leaves the reader waiting for the next'   *Irish Times*

ISBN 0 00 617314 4

Sharpe's Triumph
Bernard Cornwell

India, 1803. Sergeant Richard Sharpe witnesses a murderous act of treachery by an English officer who has defected from the East India Company to join the Mahratta Confederation. In the hunt for the renegade Englishman, Sharpe penetrates deep into the enemy's territory where he faces temptations more subtle than he has ever dreamed of. And behind him, relentlessly stalking him, comes his worst enemy, the baleful, twitching Sergeant Obadiah Hakeswill who is determined to break Sharpe once and for all.

The paths of treachery all lead to the small village of Assaye where Sir Arthur Wellesley, with a tiny British army, faces the Mahratta horde. Outnumbered and outgunned, Wellesley decides to fight, and Sharpe is plunged into the white heat of a battle that will make Wellesley's reputation. It will make Sharpe's name too, but only if he can survive the carnage and killing frenzy, for it is at Assaye that he at last realizes his ambition and has a chance to seize it.

'A gripping tale with swashbuckling action and colourful characters. Guaranteed to be yet another bestseller'

Sunday Telegraph

ISBN 0 00 651030 2

Sharpe's Tiger
Bernard Cornwell

Sharpe's Tiger describes the adventures of the raw young private soldier Richard Sharpe in India, before the Peninsular War.

Sharpe and the rest of his battalion, along with the rising star of the general staff Arthur Wellesley, are about to embark upon the siege of Seringapatam, island citadel of the Tippoo of Mysore.

When a senior British officer is captured by the Tippoo's forces Sharpe is offered a chance to attempt a rescue, a chance he snatches in order to escape from the tyrannical Sergeant Obadiah Hakeswill. But in fleeing Hakeswill he enters the confusing, exotic and dangerous world of the Tippoo, and Sharpe will need all his wits just to stay alive, let alone save the British army from catastrophe.

'Cornwell's combination of breakneck action and pig-headed men behaving badly – but with dazzling brio – is still unbeatable'   *Daily Telegraph*

ISBN 0 00 649035 2

Sharpe's Fortress
Bernard Cornwell

It is December 1803, and Richard Sharpe is now an officer in Sir Arthur Wellesley's army which is seeking to end the Mahratta War. Relegated to a tedious job in the baggage train, Sharpe discovers a treason conjured up by his old enemy, Sergeant Obadiah Hakeswill, but in uncovering this Sharpe finds himself alone and under dreadful threat. He falls back on his fighting ability to regain his confidence and his treasure, the jewels of the Tippoo Sultan, which have been stolen from him.

The search for revenge on the men who robbed him takes him to Gawilghur, a seemingly impregnable fortress poised high above the Deccan Plain. Bolstering its defences is the renegade Englishman, William Dodd, who has escaped from Sharpe before. Dodd is confident that no redcoat can reach him, but Sharpe is desperate and so he joins Wellesley's troops as they surge across the neck of land that leads to the breaches. There, in the horror of Gawilghur's ravine, dominated by walls and guns, he will fight as he has never fought before.

'The battle scenes spring from the page like a puff of musket smoke'   *Sunday Times*

ISBN 0 00 651031 0

'Sharpe' now has its own fan club which encompasses the books and TV series. If you would like further details on membership, please write to the following address:

Sharpe Appreciation Society
PO Box 14
Lowdham
Notts
NG14 7HU